Praise for *Dark Obsession*

"The solid writing, riveting opening, and clever plot twists recommend this worthy debut."
—*Library Journal* (starred review)

"Following in the footsteps of Daphne du Maurier, Victoria Holt, and Phyllis Whitney, Chase delivers a classic Gothic, complete with a haunted house, an intrepid heroine, dark secrets, and grand passion that will enthrall readers."   —*Romantic Times*

"Allison Chase's *Dark Obsession* dishes up a wonderful story in a charming, romantic tradition, complete with a handsome and tortured hero, real conflict, and a touch of mystery! Anyone who loves . . . a well-written historical romance will relish this tale."
—Heather Graham, *New York Times* bestselling author

"A compelling and exquisitely written love story that raises such dark questions along the way, you've no choice but to keep turning the pages to its stunning conclusion. Allison Chase is a master at touching your heart."—Jennifer St. Giles, author of *Silken Shadows*

"Intriguing! A beguiling tale. Moody and atmospheric."   —Eve Silver, author of *Dark Prince*

"A haunted hero and a determined heroine create sparks in *Dark Obsession*. With a nod to Daphne du Maurier, this sexy story weaves together irresistible romance and ghostly warnings that lead to the truth hidden in a wounded heart. Filled with adventure and danger, deception and desire, this is a book you won't forget."   —Jocelyn Kelley, author of *Kindred Spirits*

Dark Temptation

ALLISON CHASE

A NOVEL OF BLACKHEATH MOOR

A SIGNET ECLIPSE BOOK

SIGNET ECLIPSE
Published by New American Library, a division of
Penguin Group (USA) Inc., 375 Hudson Street,
New York, New York 10014, USA
Penguin Group (Canada), 90 Eglinton Avenue East, Suite 700, Toronto,
Ontario M4P 2Y3, Canada (a division of Pearson Penguin Canada Inc.)
Penguin Books Ltd., 80 Strand, London WC2R 0RL, England
Penguin Ireland, 25 St. Stephen's Green, Dublin 2,
Ireland (a division of Penguin Books Ltd.)
Penguin Group (Australia), 250 Camberwell Road, Camberwell, Victoria 3124,
Australia (a division of Pearson Australia Group Pty. Ltd.)
Penguin Books India Pvt. Ltd., 11 Community Centre, Panchsheel Park,
New Delhi - 110 017, India
Penguin Group (NZ), 67 Apollo Drive, Rosedale, North Shore 0632,
New Zealand (a division of Pearson New Zealand Ltd.)
Penguin Books (South Africa) (Pty.) Ltd., 24 Sturdee Avenue,
Rosebank, Johannesburg 2196, South Africa

Penguin Books Ltd., Registered Offices:
80 Strand, London WC2R 0RL, England

First published by Signet Eclipse, an imprint of New American Library,
a division of Penguin Group (USA) Inc.

First Printing, November 2008
10 9 8 7 6 5 4 3 2 1

This book is dedicated to my parents, who just happen to think I'm one heck of a writer. Thanks, Mom and Dad, for being my biggest fans!

ACKNOWLEDGMENTS

A huge thank-you to everyone at NAL for the incredible launch you've given me, and special thanks to my editor, Ellen Edwards, and her assistant, Rebecca Vinter, for all the time and energy you've been willing to spend on my behalf. You are my dream team! Without you, well, I just don't know . . .

Prologue

Cornwall 1829

In the dark of the new moon, the *Druid's Lady* veered hard to starboard, sailing at a good ten knots toward a cove ringed with towering cliffs. Though blackness spanned the coast in either direction, some half dozen torches lit a narrow beach and tossed flickering light onto the inlet's sheer rock walls. Where the waves lapped the shore, three silhouettes hovered, waiting amid the dancing shadows.

Watching from the quarterdeck, the midshipman felt his apprehensions leap with each lick of the flames. When he'd asked the first mate about this sudden detour from their journey home from the French coast to Penzance, he'd been told curtly, "Captain's orders. Cargo to unload."

The brigantine dropped anchor about fifty yards out. Hemp ropes creaked as the pulleys were used to hoist brandy casks and crates containing china, silks and a quarter ton of tobacco from the cargo hold. Men began transferring the goods onto a flat-bottomed lighter, while others waited to lower the ship-to-shore craft into the water. In the midshipman's estimate, they would need to make three runs ashore before resuming their course. He wouldn't breathe easily until a brisk wind filled the *Lady*'s sails.

With a grin, the quartermaster approached him and

clapped his shoulder. "Relax, mate. The devil himself couldn't find this cove. The nearest coast-guard cutter is two-score leagues away, at least."

A shout from above tore through the quartermaster's assurances. Balanced on the crow's nest of the mainsail, the watchman held a spyglass to his eye and gestured wildly to the port side. The midshipman followed his line of sight. At first he saw nothing, only black waves and midnight sky. Then, nearly all at once, the beams of countless lanterns speared the water.

From bow to stern, havoc exploded on the *Druid's Lady*. Scurrying deckhands collided in their haste to man their positions. A sudden blast knocked men off their feet. The midshipman hit the deck hard, bruising his hip, his shoulder. When he sat up he found himself enveloped in a noxious cloud of sulfur that propelled the crew into blind, choking chaos.

A second explosion racked the ship. Blinking the stinging smoke from his eyes, the midshipman spied the sleek hull of a clipper as she glided alongside the brigantine. Brusque demands were shouted across that the *Lady* should prepare to be boarded.

In a desperate maneuver, the brigantine thrust to starboard. Another blast followed. The screams of men clashed with the shrieks of firearms as bullets zinged back and forth. The *Druid's Lady* tilted drunkenly in the water. Pulse pounding, the midshipman raised his gaze to the top of the clipper's mainmast— where a small, square topsail, emblazoned with a black rose on a field of crimson, raked the night sky.

Not the coast guard. The *Ebony Rose*.

Hope abandoned him in a violent surge that slammed his heart against his chest. A thunderous shot reverberated overhead, sending down a cascade of splintered wood. Pain exploded at the back of his head, and all went black.

Chapter 1

Cornwall
September 1830

Where the stark expanse of Blackheath Moor met the rocky thrust of the Cornish coast, Sophie St. Clair hurried along a dusty road to the one place in the windswept countryside that was expressly forbidden to her.

The air today shivered with an intense, startling light she had never experienced before coming to Cornwall, as crisp and sharp as springwater on a winter's day, brightening colors, deepening outlines and rendering futile any attempt to be inconspicuous.

Sophie knew she presented an all-too-apparent blotch on the nearly treeless landscape, a small, dark figure scrambling along a pitted road bordered by a patchwork of autumn-darkened heather and faded gorse, miles and miles of it, beneath a sky so thoroughly unblemished as to rival the brilliant blues of her mother's most prized Sèvres porcelain.

Only minutes ago, after calling out a quick reassurance that she was only going for a walk along the beach, she had put as much distance as quickly as possible between her and Aunt Louisa's house. One hand gripped her bonnet brim to fight the tug of the wind; the other steadied the satchel slung over her shoulder.

As she topped a rise, the sight of the gray slashes of four stone chimneys and a bit of peaked roof sped her steps. She was almost to Edgecombe, a sprawling property perched between the moors and the sea, abandoned these two years since the death of its previous owner. The fourth Earl of Wycliffe had tragically succumbed to a fire that had broken out in one of the rooms, and apparently his heir, having no desire to spend time here, had shut the place down.

Sophie's interest in the estate lay not in its recent history, but in the legends that connected Edgecombe to a married pirate couple who used the place for their headquarters three centuries ago. The tales of the Keatings had long since captured her fascination, and as a child she'd spent many a happy hour poring over the details of their exploits. Oh, but never had she thought she'd have a chance to see the rambling estate firsthand. Not until the incident last month that altered the course of her life.

Her first glimpse of the place had been little more than a jagged shadow thrust across the evening landscape, framed by the window of her grandfather's barouche, whose driver had conveyed her from London and summarily dumped her at Aunt Louisa's front gate. But from that first glance, she had felt the somber stone gables beckoning with an invitation that could not be ignored.

"Stay away from there, girl," her aunt had warned when Sophie broached the subject yesterday. "Don't you so much as point your toes in the direction of that old wreckage of a house. The place is abandoned, falling apart."

"It appears solid enough from the road. And so dark and brooding, poised so precariously at the edge of the land. And the history . . ."

"Is one of violence, whether deliberate or no. An ill fortune hangs about the place. Some say . . ." Aunt Louisa had leaned closer and whispered, "Some say that sort of bedevilment never entirely leaves a place, even when its occupants have long since gone to their graves."

"Are you speaking of curses, Aunt Louisa? Or ghosts? I know it's said the Keatings haunt Edgecombe, but surely you don't believe—"

"What I believe is that the place is best avoided. You'd do well to put it out of your mind at once."

Sophie had tried questioning her cousins about the estate, but eighteen-year-old Rachel had echoed her mother's admonishments, while Dominic, two years older, had merely scowled, grumbled something unintelligible and stalked away.

The admonitions had only strengthened Sophie's desire to see the house firsthand. Reaching the drive, she halted before a pair of wrought-iron gates—closed, locked, doubly secured by a boat chain coiled several times around and held by a padlock twice the width of her palm.

KEEP OUT. The gate's message echoed Aunt Louisa's words of warning. The two flanking stone pillars and the high granite walls that marched away in either direction issued the same command: STAY AWAY.

"I hardly think so," Sophie whispered.

The house itself stood but a stone's throw beyond a short drive that opened onto a cobbled forecourt. An imposing pair of gargoyles guarded either side of an elaborate portico topped by a Gothic arch. The windows were shuttered, emphasizing the air of abandonment permeating the property.

A property likely to have more than one entrance. Sophie set off to search.

Past the carriage house along the south boundary wall she discovered another, smaller gate half-hidden behind a tangle of hawthorn. She shoved the spiky branches aside and found the latch. No chains barred her way. With a fluttering breath of excitement, of refusing to take no for an answer, she slipped inside.

A slate path took her through a narrow gap in a box hedge, past a gardener's shed and onto the slopes of a tiered garden. A hothouse stood not far away, an octagonal structure that resembled a giant gazebo, much of its paint peeled away to reveal the wood beneath. At the apex of its steep roof, a weather vane in the shape of two crossed swords topped by a sail whimpered on its rusty pin.

The path led her past a dry fountain and across a wooden footbridge. Bushy fern and tall, bristly spikes of bulrush choked the narrow brook below. From there she made her way beneath a stand of fruit trees and up the garden slopes. A set of steps mounted a grassy surge to a terrace, onto which several sets of French doors opened from the house. Sophie climbed the steps and enjoyed a private laugh at Aunt Louisa's superstitions. Edgecombe was only a house, after all. Filled with history and misty legend, yes. But ghosts?

She perched on the top step, removed the satchel from her shoulder and reached inside for her quill, pot of ink and leather-bound writing tablet. Tucking a windblown lock of hair beneath her bonnet, she flipped to a blank page.

A house crouched at the edge of the world, she wrote, *defying the elements—wind, storms and sea—to attempt their worst and be damned.*

Well. She'd need to modify that last word, of course. Grandfather St. Clair, owner and editor in chief of the *Beacon,* one of London's most popular weekly newspapers, would never set it to print. Just as he never published any of Sophie's feature pieces under her true, decidedly feminine name. No, if she wished to continue writing occasional articles for the *Beacon,* she must do so under the pen name of Silas Sinclair and, furthermore, must stick to such topics as her family deemed appropriate for a lady.

Sophie St. Clair, nice girls do not ask bothersome questions. . . . Nice girls leave news reporting to men. . . . Nice girls spend their time in appropriate endeavors, such as needlework, sketching and playing the pianoforte. . . .

Sophie, can you not, for once, behave like a proper young lady?

How she loathed *proper.* Despised *appropriate.* Detested *nice.* Despite a lifetime of trying to emulate all three concepts and more, she had always fallen a lengthy stride short of success. If curiosity killed the cat, as her mother always warned, then Sophie had flirted with death all her life.

Besides, she was no lady, certainly not in the strictest sense. The St. Clairs could boast no titles, and owned no land other than what had been purchased in recent years with the fortune Grandfather had amassed through his newspaper and business investments. The St. Clairs were working people, hawks in peacock feathers, and Sophie saw no shame in that.

Pen hovering above the page, she studied the house. A quick count of the shuttered windows suggested fifteen or so rooms, laid out on either side of a square tower that had, three centuries earlier, served as the seaside fortress of Sir Jack and Lady Margaret Keating.

According to the legends Sophie had read as a child, the pair had ruled the seas for ten years, from Cornwall to northern France to Ireland and back, dispersing goods among people who could not afford the excise taxes. In reality, their methods had not always been benevolent. The Keatings brutally attacked any who opposed them, naval vessels included, employing the horrific practice of tying wounded victims together and throwing them overboard to drown.

Finally Sir Jack's luck ran out. After his death just off the coast here at the hands of the Royal Navy, Lady Meg snapped. In a ship of her own she embarked on an indiscriminate, high-seas rampage of murder and pillage until she was caught, tried and hanged.

Be a nice girl, Sophie.

Oh, very well. Today she would try to think architecture, not violent pirate history. She set her pen to paper.

A gaunt sentinel whose granite walls seemed quarried from an ancient haze, with mysteries and memories trapped within each chiseled block . . .

The whirling breezes abruptly dropped, replaced by an utter stillness that immediately felt . . . unnatural. A weighty silence fell over the trees, while the birds roosting in their boughs seemed caught in a state of hushed expectancy.

Uneasy. Apprehensive. She glanced up at the house.

A cloud covered the sun, plunging the stones and timbers into gloom and raising prickles down her spine. A sense of nervous expectancy quivered in her stomach. Had the shutters on the bay window in the far corner been open all along?

She sat quite still, watching. Waiting . . . for the wind to pick up; for the sprawling rowans and dogwoods and unkempt fruit trees to resume their creaking; for the house to remain as dark, empty and unchanging as ever.

The house did not comply. As Sophie watched, a curtain in the exposed window flicked to one side and then fell back into place.

In an instant she was on her feet, hand flying to her mouth as her writing tablet slapped the terrace. Her quill fluttered down the steps. Her pulse leaping, she backed away until her foot met with insubstantial air. She nearly tumbled down the stairs but for a quick maneuver that restored her balance.

Quickly she retrieved her notebook and ink. Hooking the satchel over her shoulder, she straightened and found herself staring directly into a male face on the other side of the window. Through the mullioned panes she could make out a tumble of fair hair, darker brows knotted over piercing eyes and a full mouth bracketed in lines of displeasure.

He stood in shirtsleeves and a waistcoat, one hand

fisted against the buttons. He glowered long and hard at her, rendering her immobile, locked in a silent battle of scrutiny. Good heavens, she was caught!

A whisper of logic brought a measure of reassurance. She was a neighbor, after all, or at least a guest of this man's neighbor. There was nothing for it but to offer a friendly apology for trespassing and hope the man, be he servant or nobleman, possessed a forgiving nature. Or a sense of humor.

She raised her hand to wave, but he had vanished. The sun burst from the clouds and the wind picked up, plucking at her skirts and whipping loose hair in her eyes. She shoved it back under her bonnet and waited, expecting the man to come walking out of a terrace door. A minute passed, and another, with no sound or sign of movement issuing from the house.

Confused, Sophie descended the steps, was about to turn and leave when an impulse sent her back up to the nearest set of doors. Rapping several times on the glass, she called out, "Good morning. Is anyone here? I'm dreadfully sorry to be trespassing. I believed the place to be empty. My name is Miss Sophie St. Clair, and I'm a guest of the Gordons down the road. Perhaps you know them?" She knocked again. "I say, won't you come out and become properly acquainted?"

Nothing.

She crossed the terrace to where the bay window jutted and peeked into a room, the walls of which were lined from floor to ceiling with books. She spied a settee, a roomy wingback chair, a large desk upon which several books lay open. But no man.

"How insufferably rude." She turned to go.

At the bottom of the stairs a realization brought her up short. Only moments ago clouds had blocked the sun, but as she scanned the sky now she detected not the faintest trace of a cloud, not in any direction. She shielded her eyes with her hand and peered out at the horizon. Nothing but unending blue stretched above the sea.

She made it as far as the footbridge when a rustling sifted through the bulrush along the banks of the brook. The sound brought her to a halt. It was more than the wind stirring the plants, more . . . solid. The rub of fabric, the catch of a thread.

Sophie stood motionless, listening, searching her surroundings. "Is . . . is anyone there?" she asked in a small voice. Her knuckles whitened where she gripped the rail. Leaning out over the stream, she scrutinized the bank. At the thud of a footfall on the wooden planking beside her, she pulled back with a gasp. Seeing nothing, panting for breath, she braced to run.

And then she felt, quite plainly, a graze against the back of her hand. Not the wind, not a falling leaf, but fingertips—cool, slightly rough as if from an old callus, and then . . . the sound of her name tingling in her ear.

Sophie . . .

"You have been found guilty of the crimes of theft, piracy and murder. It is the decision of this court that in two days' time, you shall be hanged within the precincts of the Truro jailhouse. May God have mercy upon your soul."

Chad Rutherford, Earl of Wycliffe, watched in a horrified daze as the condemned man was led out of the courtroom, the chains clapped to his ankles clanking in protest on the floorboards.

Giles Watling himself said nothing, hadn't so much as flinched as the judge handed down the sentence. But Chad had. His insides had pulled into impossible knots because he knew the penalty could have been his. *Should* have been his.

"It's child's play, gov'nor," Watling had said the day he first approached Chad, nearly two years ago. "Like those gents that do business at the Royal Exchange. We procure the goods, and you provide the means to hide 'em, divert 'em, and sell 'em on the black market. See, it's your connections we want, your resources.

You'll leave the rest to us. Nice and easy-like, and you not ruffling a single hair outta place."

Easy, Watling said. A warning had immediately whispered its way along Chad's spine. "Where will these goods come from?"

"Now, don't be concerning yourself with that, gov'nor. We know you need the blunt. And we need you."

Yes, he had needed money. Badly. Months earlier he had inherited a title and estates swimming in debt, thanks to the excesses of the past several generations of Rutherfords. But again, wariness had tingled across his shoulders. "Who's 'we'?"

"Never you mind." The man's grin had released the stench of decaying teeth to waft in Chad's face. "I'm talking about a bit o' fair trading here—nothing to get worked up about. Our fellow Cornishmen'll be grateful for the chance to purchase goods they can afford. Nobody loses out but the revenue collectors. And they're a scurvy lot, they are. So, gov'nor, are you in or out . . . ?"

Yes, fair trading, they called it here. The running of foreign goods—French brandy; Irish whiskey; American tobacco, sugar and cotton—past the excise men to avoid the import taxes. The merchandise would then be smuggled into villages throughout Cornwall, where otherwise such luxuries would have been financially out of reach.

As with all dealings that appeared too easy, too pat, there'd been a heavy price. The guilt that woke him in the dead of night with a racing heart and a brow bathed in sweat. The disappointment burning in the eyes of his best friend, Grayson Lowell, who was the first to discover the evidence of Chad's involvement, and the first to insist he come clean and turn his life around.

Only Chad's status as a peer and the information he'd been willing to provide the authorities had saved

his neck from the hangman's noose. Even his name
had been kept quiet, with much of the evidence presented by the prosecutor ascribed to an anonymous
witness. The Wycliffe name would remain untar-
nished, but he could still lose everything to the fines
levied against his estates . . . unless he managed to
help deliver the leader of the smuggling ring to the
authorities.

A leader who could be anyone, anywhere. Chad
simply didn't know. He'd never had any direct contact
with the man.

Now, as the judge, jury and gaggle of curious onlookers made their way out of the courtroom, Chad
stood immobile, staring up at the empty witness box
where Watling had sat two days in a row and almost
happily, proudly spewed the particulars of their business dealings. Particulars Chad hadn't known. Hadn't
ever imagined or wished to know.

Details now branded indelibly on his soul.

Ships scuttled. Crews murdered. Passengers left
aboard to drown. Oh, yes, he now knew where the
larger portion of their booty had originated. Fair trading? As if the innocent moniker could make a gentleman's sport of the devil's work.

Two days later, a pounding shook Chad's bedroom
door at the inn where he was staying. Stumbling out
of bed, bleary-eyed, he opened the door to a messen-
ger who delivered Watling's last request. He wished
to speak to Chad.

As the first cold, comfortless light glazed the eastern
horizon, Chad stepped into the stinking jail cell, wary
curiosity and pure dread churning his gut to a relentless froth. Holding his breath against the fetidness of
the man's rotting mouth, he listened to what Giles
Watling had to say.

"Got a message for you, gov'nor. You're to go to
Penhollow, to that estate of yours, Edgecombe, and
wait for instructions."

The pulse in Chad's temple sent shooting pain into

his eye. "From whom? For what? I'm not in it any-more. Even if I were, it was part of the deal that Edgecombe would never be used as a stronghold."

That was the one stipulation he'd insisted upon when entering into the smuggling business. His fa-ther's favorite estate, the property where Franklin had spent his final days, would not be touched; his father's memory would not be so dishonored. Instead, the smugglers had agreed to use a secluded beach farther up the coast, on Grayson Lowell's family estate.

"The time for bargains is past, gov'nor. Ended the instant you testified. Best do as ye're told now."

"So whoever sent this summons can kill me?"

"Naw. 'E don't want you dead. Not yet. More useful to have you alive. And you'd best cooperate, or your family'll suffer. Your sister, her husband . . ." The man's cracked lips stretched grotesquely, the sneering grin of a moldering jack-o'-lantern. "Let us not forget your dearest friends. Grayson Lowell stood by you. His pretty wife too—"

Chad grabbed fistfuls of the bastard's shirt and pinned him, manacles and all, to the slimy wall behind him. "Who sent this message? Tell me, damn you. What bloody loyalty can you possibly owe anyone now?"

But the whoreson only grinned his nasty grin, even later, as they led him up the scaffold steps.

Go to Edgecombe and wait. . . .

By nightfall of the following day, Chad reached the seaside village of Penhollow beneath a blue-black sky dusted with stars. Set at the southernmost reaches of Blackheath Moor on Cornwall's Lizard Peninsula, the tiny hamlet lay exposed to the whim of the Atlantic gales, which battered the coast almost continually throughout the year.

Those gales were oddly quiet tonight. An eerie calm gripped Penhollow as Chad passed through on horse-back. Cooking aromas poured from squat, uneven chimneys to vie with the pungent odors of the incoming tide. He trotted his chestnut Thoroughbred, Prince, down the main thoroughfare, a narrow, weather-gouged lane lined with a few shops and cottages.

Penhollow had never been prosperous, but thanks to his father's generosity it had never been destitute, either, at least not in the years Franklin had spent here. Chad had seen the records kept by the family solicitor. To his right sat a relatively new church and schoolhouse, built, he had learned, with Wycliffe funds. The snug enclosure, encircled by a low stone wall, appeared well maintained, but as Chad surveyed his surroundings he discovered little other evidence of his father's largesse.

The village was constructed almost entirely of granite, and the whitewash, typically reapplied yearly, had long since been stripped from the stones by wind and weather. Even in the gathering darkness, other signs of neglect stood out. Splintered timbers. Broken and missing roof tiles. Ragged holes where thatch should have been. More than one creaking door drew his attention to the fact that some of the establishments stood empty and abandoned.

The tavern, however, appeared open for business, the lights inside tossing golden squares onto the roadway. He hunched in the saddle to peer through the windows at the men sitting at the tables or ranged along the bar. A rough crowd, by the looks of it, and a noisy one too. Penhollow, at least, seemed not to lack for whiskey or ale.

Turning about and resuming his course along the coastal road, Chad experienced a stab of guilt. When he had inherited Edgecombe, he should have taken a personal interest in the village. Penhollow's reversal of fortune reflected his utter failure to do so.

A sliver of moon lit the way. Here and there rutted lanes and cart paths veered off from the side of the road and twisted away to the farms scattered across Blackheath Moor. A few minutes past the village a fine mist crept across the landscape, pooling between the hillocks and spilling over onto the road to swallow Prince's gait from the fetlocks down.

Low and faint, an odd sound drifted off the moors. Not like the other night noises, not crickets or bats or burrowing animals. This was a moaning, like the wind hissing through trees. But there were no trees on the barren landscape, only the night-blackened heather clinging to the hillsides. A tendril of unease curled around Chad's spine. He brought Prince to a halt and listened.

Weeping. Soft sobs. The baleful notes of a woman's voice. She could not be far off, perhaps a few dozen yards. He strained his eyes to search the obscurity beyond the road. Rising from the mist, a stony peak reflected the pale moonlight. A cry surged from behind, and Chad spurred his horse onto the fog-choked moor.

Chapter 2

Sophie rolled, slapped her pillow and pulled the bed-clothes higher over her shoulder. She'd lain in bed for over an hour, but her eyes refused to remain closed. Something didn't feel right. Her skin prickled; the very air sizzled as if charged with lightning.

Beside her, her cousin Rachel slept soundly, the younger girl's black hair streaming like spilled ink across the pillow. Rachel always sank deep into slumber within moments of her head hitting the pillow; even the other night's storm had failed to disturb her.

Flipping back the coverlet, Sophie reached for her dressing gown. Shivers raised gooseflesh down her arms. In her week here she hadn't experienced a night as cold as this. Even through her slippers the floorboards chilled the soles of her feet.

She went to the window. Beyond the barnyard and outbuildings the coastline wriggled like a glowing snake against the moon-tipped waves. Something was different—what?

The harbor lights. Penhollow's quay lay to the north, but tonight that direction lay in darkness, while a golden glow emanated to the south of her relatives' farm. Was she mistaken? She shut her eyes and tried to picture the coastline. The village, the beach behind her aunt's property, the cliffs, Edgecombe. *Good heavens.* If that ship put in between this house and Edgecombe, it would run aground against a treacherous, jutting headland.

She opened her eyes to see ship lights appear on the horizon. As she watched, they grew steadily larger, closer. Sophie's heart hit her throat. Someone had made a mistake—how, she could not fathom—and lit the beacons in altogether the wrong place.

She spun about. "Rachel! Rachel, wake up!"

The girl let out a murmur and turned her face into the pillow. Sophie realized the futility of rousing her. What could her eighteen-year-old cousin do to remedy the situation?

Hugging her robe around her trembling body, Sophie scurried from the room. Across the small landing she pounded on another bedroom door. Without waiting for permission to enter, she threw the door open so hard it thwacked the wall.

"Uncle Barnaby. Aunt Louisa. You must wake up. Something dreadful is about to happen."

"W-what on earth . . . ?" Her aunt's sleep-slurred query drifted softly through the darkness, in contrast to her uncle's gravelly baritone.

"What in bloody hell's going on?"

"Uncle Barnaby." Sophie approached the bed, caught the hairy wrist extending from his nightshirt and tugged. "Please wake up. There is about to be a shipwreck and we must do something."

"Let go of me, girl." He yanked his arm free. "You've had a bad dream is all. Stop raising a ruckus and go back to bed."

"But you don't understand. You must listen to me. There's a ship putting in, and the shore lights are all wrong. I saw it out my window."

"God's teeth, lass. Your eyes were playing tricks on ye. Now go away and leave us in peace." Uncle Barnaby turned on his side, his back to Sophie.

"Aunt Louisa, you believe me, don't you? Someone has made a horrible mistake with the harbor lights."

The woman sat up, holding the covers to her chin with one hand and pushing her drooping mobcap off her brow. "Listen to your uncle, child. Cornwall is like that—moonlight on the water, reflections in the mist." Her pupils were ringed white in the darkness, and glistening with fear, Sophie thought—with urgency. "Folk are always imagining things that aren't there. Go back to bed and never mind silly night phantoms."

"Oh, but—"

"There's no cause for concern. In the morning all will be well." Aunt Louisa lay back down and turned her face to the wall, but the slight tremor in her voice belied her words. "Now go back to bed; there's a good lamb."

Sophie stood a moment longer, immobilized by indignation and sheer incredulity. How could they simply roll over and go back to sleep? Especially when Aunt Louisa's reassurances had sounded far more like warnings?

Someone *had* to do something, and quickly. Should she try her other cousin, Dominic? Oh, he'd only scowl at her, as he had done repeatedly since her arrival here.

She might not be able to stop a ship in midstream, but she could run to the village, rouse someone and see that the proper beacons were lit. Scampering down to the kitchen, she blew an ember to life in the hearth, retrieved a flaming piece of kindling and lit a lantern. Then, snatching a cloak hanging from the hooks beside the garden door, she flung it across her shoulders and hurried out to the road.

The echoing sobs drew Chad on, sending him beyond the next rise, around the next outcropping, but never any closer. Farther and farther he wandered from the road.

Just as he decided perhaps the wind *was* deceiving him, that he should make his way back to the road, the mist closed like a fist around him, sealing him in a void that lacked direction, points of reference, even dimension.

The stars were gone, the moonlight doused, the hillsides absorbed into swirling nothingness. The air grew icy sharp, penetrating his clothing and chilling him to the bone. The keening voice surged from all around. Prince bucked, stumbled and reared.

Only skilled horsemanship prevented Chad from falling. He tightened the reins and clung with his knees, leaning to speak reassuring words to calm the animal. The horse lurched again as a face, thin and wan and framed by lank wisps of hair, appeared from the churning fog. The small figure stood barely a breath away, practically beneath Prince's kicking hooves. Alarm shuddered through Chad, nearly jolting him from the saddle.

"Good Christ, my horse might have trampled you." His heart rate slowed as the shock of the narrowly avoided accident receded. He worked the reins to bring the distraught animal under control. "You could have been killed."

The face tipped to peer up at him, and he recoiled at the sight of blue lips, sunken eyes, a jagged gash across the forehead. Soaked rags that had once been a dress encased an emaciated figure and raised a bitter reek of ocean brine. And more. Some indescribable odor that hinted of decay. Of death.

"Sweet Jesus," he whispered. Revulsion sucked the remaining heat from his body. A single conviction pounded through his skull: *This creature can't be alive. Nothing that lives could cast such a fearsome spectacle.*

The figure moved closer, its lifeless eyes holding him in a vacant stare. Soundless words formed on the fissured lips. Despite the sickening fear rocking his gut, he leaned down, straining to hear the croak of a whisper that spiraled on the mist.

So many dead. Killed for the cargo.

He whipped upright in the saddle as fresh shock ricocheted through him. He couldn't pretend he didn't understand what those words meant.

Boats scuttled. Innocent lives lost. All in the name of profit.

Profits he had reaped.

"Are you . . . Did you . . . die . . . because of . . ." He clenched his teeth and tried to steady his shaking limbs. "What do you want of me?"

She cannot see me. Cannot hear me.

"Who can't?"

She is alone. Distraught. Grieving.

A gust of wind tore through the haze, shredding the vapors like tattered linen. Riding the air currents, an owl swooped low, its forlorn hoot echoing across the moor. Chad flinched, and when he looked back to the spot where the girl had stood, she was gone.

He gave himself a shake. A hard one.

Cargo. People dying. His throat closed until he choked on his own breath. No, he couldn't pretend he didn't understand. Couldn't dismiss the guilt evoked by those words. Had he truly seen a ghost, or had his own conscience risen up to goad him?

The truth writhed inside him. *So many dead.* Dead if not by his hand, then through his complicity, and through the arrogance that had assured him, all his life, that he could get away with anything.

He swung Prince about, intending to find his way back to the road.

You must help her. She cannot see me.

Prince heaved, staggered in tight, panicked circles. Fighting for control, Chad searched the darkness. Once more the stench of salty decay filled his nose. A shriek rang in his ears. With a terrified whinny his horse reared.

He slid backward, falling, tumbling over Prince's hindquarters. The descent seemed to take an eternity, and then his back slammed against the ground. The blow reverberated through him, rattled his bones.

His heart threatening to burst through his chest, he rolled to his feet and grabbed for the bridle. "Easy, Prince. It's all right, boy."

He thrust a foot into the stirrup. As he tried to swing up, a shove at his chest pushed him down. He tried again, but a second blow toppled him. He smacked the ground, the impact shooting pain through his back and shoulders.

Winded, bruised, he sat up and rubbed his throbbing arm. With his good one he reached up, caught the dangling stirrup and used it to haul himself to his feet. In the whorls of mist before him, her face took shape again, her vacant gaze an indictment all the more terrifying for its utter lack of expression. As if he'd already been tried, convicted, condemned.

He forced his trembling lips open. "Tell me what you wish me to do."

Instead of an answer, a spinning blackness engulfed him, swallowing every thought, every hope. A crushing pressure filled his chest. The pain and cold became unbearable. He opened his mouth, gasping for air, but none came. He was dying. Wishing he would die. Praying for an end.

Can you understand what torment is?

He opened his eyes to discover that he was on his knees, hands cradling his head. The pain receded, reduced to a dull throb inside him. He lowered his hands to his sides and stumbled to his feet. "By God, is that what it is to die?"

The little drowned ghost hovered a few feet away, surrounded by a host of ghastly faces, each one telling the story of a brutal, watery death.

For some. For me. For her as well.

"Then whoever she is, she too has died?" He pointed into the faces swirling with the mist. "Is she among them?"

No. Her soul is dying.

"I don't understand. Please . . ."

Come.

Turning, she drifted off into the wisps of fog. With the accusing stares of the other apparitions burning into his back, he gathered the reins and placed his foot in the stirrup. As before, a buffeting force prevented him from climbing into the saddle.

On foot, he trailed the little ghost and her swarm of grisly companions across the unfamiliar landscape. He resisted the urge to recoil as specters flitted like shadows across his path, as wasted fingers reached out from the darkness to poke at his conscience. As whispers grazed his ears: *All dead . . . killed for the cargo.*

Where were they leading him him? Into a bog, over a cliff? Blindfolded by the night and the mist and his roiling apprehensions, he had no way of knowing. Had no choice but to do the very thing he'd always found hardest in life: submit to a will other than his own.

Gray against the darker gloom, the rectangular dimensions of a small chapel gathered shape. A waist-high forest of gravestones, leaning hither-thither and cloaked in moss, crowded one side of the churchyard. Chad moved to a gap in the encircling wall where a gate used to be and, leading Prince behind him, stepped into the yard. "What is this place?"

No answer came but the sifting of the wind through the heather. He had no idea where he was, how far from the road or in what direction it lay. With little choice but to spend the remainder of the night here, he walked Prince to the stoop and tied the reins to the railing.

"You'll be safe here on hallowed ground, I should think, and I shan't be far away." He ran his palm down the horse's nose. Then, feeling like the sole inhabitant of a lifeless world, abandoned, ironically, by the spirits that had led him here, Chad tugged open the heavy oak door.

Somewhere between Aunt Louisa's house and the village, Sophie found herself wandering in a sea of mist, her sense of direction hopelessly lost. She ground to a halt as the fog surrounded her. Sharp pebbles dug into the soles of her slippers, making her dearly regret the haste that had prevented her from changing into a pair of boots. Standing still, she prayed for a glimpse of the road. The peal of a buoy bell. Anything to help her find her bearings.

There was nothing. No sights. No sounds but the distant pull and tug of the sea, which, muted by the haze, seemed to come from no direction in particular. She didn't know this area at all well, but in the past week she had learned enough to be aware of its dangers. A step in the wrong direction could lead her over a cliff, into the muck of a swamp, or so deep into the moors she'd never find her way back.

The night blew its clammy breath against her skin. She couldn't stand here on this spot, unmoving, until morning. She toed the ground through her slipper. It felt packed and solid, as a road should feel. Perhaps if she made her way carefully . . .

In the next instant she gasped in both surprise and relief. From up ahead beams of light pierced the fog. She started toward them, trying not to break into a run however much she wished to race to safety. Stone walls rose up against the mist, framing narrow, peaked windows bathed in beckoning light.

To her surprise, a horse stood dozing just outside the door, its muzzle grazing the stair rail. The animal stirred at her approach and let out a snort, but seemed all too content to slip back into slumber. She gazed up at the stonework of the building, damp and gleaming where the lamplight touched it. A church by the looks of it. Who would be inside at such a late hour? Surely not the rector. Someone lost, as she was?

Or perhaps the very sort of person she would wish to avoid on a night like tonight. But what alternative did she have? She couldn't go back the way she had come; she had no idea which way that was. Even when the dawn sun burned off all this confounded mist, she might still find herself utterly lost.

She had no choice, then, but to cast her lot with the mysterious person inside.

*   *   *

Chad lurched upright. The wooden pew creaked beneath his weight, the sound echoing in the empty chapel. He hadn't meant to fall asleep, and oh, God, how he wished he hadn't. The dreams, the visions . . .

What woke him? Tense and alert, he listened.

A damp breeze rushed the length of the nave. Footsteps thrust him to his feet. Whirling, he peered up the aisle. Illuminated by lantern light, a shapeless figure stood silhouetted in the open doorway.

"I'm lost," a woman's voice reverberated off the stone walls. "Will you help me, please?"

His heart hit his throat as the entreaty for help brought back the night's horrors. He gripped the back of a pew. "Be gone. How dare you trespass on hallowed ground?"

"I . . . I'm sorry, sir." The voice shrank to a murmur. He heard a little cough and then, stronger, clearer, "Are you the rector? If you'll allow me to stay till the mist clears, sir, I promise not to be any trouble."

From within the hood of a cloak that swallowed her figure, her eyes stood out, large and shimmering in the lamplight. His gaze traced the lines of her plump lips and high cheekbones, the tousled waves of glossy hair. Good God, she was real. Human. Alive.

Relief sent him dashing up the aisle, only to halt when she let out a cry. She drew back, nearly tripping over the cloak's hem in her haste to put distance between them.

You must help her. She cannot see me. Could this be the woman the little ghost had spoken of? The one who was alone and grieving? Had he been led to this chapel in order to help her?

He held up his hands. "I won't hurt you; I swear it. I'm just so vastly relieved to no longer be alone on so strange a night as this."

For a moment he felt foolish, pathetic to have admitted to such vulnerability, but she gave him no cause to regret his confession. Relief filled her face as a quiet sob escaped her. As if by silent agreement, they closed the remaining space between them.

She handed him her lantern. He set it on the floor and opened his arms to her. Shivering violently, she stepped into them as if it were the most natural place in the world for her to be. She laid her cheek against his chest, and her quivering breath traveled through his shirt to nestle against his skin with a warmth that tugged at his heart.

"I thought I'd never find my way . . . shouldn't have left as I did . . . such foolishness . . ."

"Hush now." Tugging back her hood, he swept the dark hair from her face. It sifted like cool silk through his fingers, and he drew its sweet fragrance deep into his lungs. Whoever she was, wherever she had come from, she would never know how welcome she was at this moment. "You're safe. No harm will come to you here."

He loosened his arms, tipped her chin and felt his breath catch in his throat. Even with her disheveled clothing and her hair all askew, she was beautiful, lovely and delicate, with lips full and pink, nose small and upturned, cheeks high and round and faintly flushed.

"I'm sorry I spoke sharply when you came in," he said. "I'd thought . . . Well, never mind."

Despite the chill clinging to the folds of her cloak, she felt deliciously warm against him. Awareness stirred. He couldn't resist holding her another moment before sliding his hands the length of her arms to lightly encircle her wrists. "Are you hurt? Have you been wandering long? What on earth brought you out on such a night?"

She blinked up at him. Sable lashes veiled her eyes, but somehow not the ingenuous nature within. Desire tugged at his loins.

"I'm not hurt," she said. "I can't say how long I wandered. This fog confuses everything, and I . . ."

With a sigh, she swayed. He caught her, holding

her tightly against him until steadiness returned to her limbs. It took only moments before he felt renewed resolve shore her up. Slight though she was beneath all those layers of fabric, she was a fighter, a brave little thing.

With an arm around her, he guided her to the nearest pew. "Sit. Are you hungry? Thirsty? I have supplies in a bag tied to my saddle."

"I'm quite all right." She offered a shaky smile. "Don't let's make a fuss. Being safe is enough for now."

He reached for her hands to warm them, or perhaps to warm his own. Sitting beside her, holding even a small part of her, had an oddly calming effect on him. Christ, earlier he had almost believed he had somehow crossed a barrier in the mist, stepping from the world of the living into that of the dead.

But this girl, this angel, was very much alive and assured him, with her soft, delicate hands and her quiet frankness, that he was still a member of humankind.

He savored each place at which their bodies pressed—hands, shoulders, knees—with an unabashed mingling of thankfulness and pleasure, and wished for little else except a reason to have her back in his arms.

"Were you lost as well?" Her whisper was a caress that sped his blood.

He thought again of the little ghost's message. The woman beside him had been through an ordeal, certainly. She had been alone and frightened, yes. But grieving? Her soul dying? Surely not.

"Come to think of it," he said, "I'm no less lost than I was earlier. I'm not from here. Do you know this place?"

She shook her head. "I'm visiting Penhollow as well. I only know what lies along the main road. If it hadn't been for your light guiding me, I'd still be out wandering." A shudder passed from her shoulder into his.

But it was her words that caused his neck to prickle. "My light?"

"Yes. I saw it shining from the windows."

"But look about you. Do you see a light other than the one you brought?"

Craning her neck, she turned until her gaze settled on the glowing circle thrown by her lantern. "That's not possible. I'm quite certain I saw lamplight."

"What on earth were you doing wandering about on such a night?"

That drew a gasp. She snatched her hands from his and jumped to her feet. "Good heavens, in all my confusion and my utter relief upon finding my way here, I'd nearly forgotten. Sir, you must help me. The reason I'm abroad is because there's been a change in the harbor lights. They're not where they ought to be, and I saw a ship putting in." She seized his arm. "If someone doesn't *do* something, that ship will crash."

"When did you see this?" He was on his feet beside her, gripping her wrists urgently, a bit too roughly. At her startled expression, he loosened his hold and said more gently, "Tell me exactly what you saw. And where."

"It may already be too late. I wandered for so long. . . ." The tip of her tongue darted over her lips. "I couldn't sleep. Something kept nagging at me, so I got up and wandered to my bedroom window. It faces the beach, and as soon as I looked out I knew something wasn't right. The harbor lights . . . they'd been moved, I'm certain of it, lit instead where the rocky coastline juts into the sea. And then I saw the lights of an approaching ship, and I realized the crew would follow the shore lights, would believe they were safely putting into Penhollow Harbor and . . . Sir, please, we must do something!"

"Good God, yes. We'll go immediately."

"What does it mean? Why would someone do this?"

Several possibilities formed in his mind, none of them good, and the fact that he even thought of them said little enough about his character. But he shook his head, unwilling to jump to conclusions until he learned more. "It could mean many things. Are you certain of what you saw?"

"I . . . believe so. It's all such a blur now." A crease formed above her nose. "But yes. I know the harbor lights were extinguished and relit farther south. I'd stake my life on it."

She paused, frowned, moistened her lips. "Could it have been deliberate? I've read of such things. Of evil men who lure unsuspecting boats onto the rocks. They steal the cargo and leave the passengers to fend for themselves."

She might have knocked him a blow to the chest, for how quickly her speculation deflated the air from his lungs. For a moment he thought she might have been speaking directly to his conscience, his soul. But as she awaited his response without any trace of suspicion or judgment, his jostled nerves steadied.

"There's no use guessing," he said. "Come, we'll make our way to the shore."

She regarded the night-blackened windows. "How will we find our way in the mist?"

"You said you saw a light here."

"Yes, but—"

"Then the mist must be parting, and what you saw must have been the moon reflecting off the windows. If so, we'll be able to find the road." He held out his hand to her. "Come. We've little choice tonight but to trust our fate to each other."

Chapter 3

How easily Sophie slipped her hand into this total stranger's, trusting him with her fate, as he'd said they must. It was a risk, an uncertain one. Yet instinct and the comforting warmth of his palm quieted the warnings of a lifetime's teaching; somehow she knew she would come to no harm.

She believed, however, that he would be proved wrong about the mist. She knew what she had seen, and she was certain it hadn't been reflections of the moonlight.

Or . . . had it? Outside in the churchyard she was bemused to discover the air had nearly cleared. The moors stretched in every direction, glinting where the moonlight struck a granite peak here, a pool of water there.

"It seems you were right," she murmured. "This is most peculiar. There is a distinct difference in hue, you realize, between lamplight and reflected moonlight."

"Here in Cornwall, people are forever mistaking one sight for another." He stood beside her, his gaze sharp as he assessed their surroundings. He was a tall man—her head barely reached his shoulder—and solidly built, with broad shoulders, a trim waist and sturdy thighs, the muscles of which created a fascinating topography beneath his snug riding breeches.

But then, she hadn't needed to study him to know

that his was a powerful physique. At the memory of his arms around her, a tingle of awareness traveled from the tips of her fingers to her toes.

"It's a phenomenon having to do with the air currents sweeping in off the sea and mixing with the moor breezes," he continued. He untied his horse's reins from the railing. "It creates a unique sort of light, one that often plays tricks on the eyes."

"Yes, my aunt made a similar claim earlier. About the harbor lights." She frowned at the memory.

"But you didn't listen to her." He walked his horse into the middle of the yard, where he adjusted the saddle and bridle.

"No. Because in this instance she was utterly wrong. And . . . frightened, I believe."

He made no comment as he swung up into the saddle. Did he doubt her? Would he dismiss her claim as summarily as had Aunt Louisa and Uncle Barnaby? The horse danced in restless steps, but with a few soft words his master brought him under control.

"Have you ridden pillion before?" He reached a hand down to her.

Sophie's heart fluttered. Yes, she had ridden pillion—behind her father, her brother, her uncle Peter in London. Oh, but never, ever behind a fair-haired gentleman with broad shoulders and striking features with whom she had not the slightest acquaintance.

Then again, after those rather intimate moments in the chapel, they did have some slight acquaintance, didn't they?

She grasped the offered hand, noticing how wholly it enveloped her own in a sure and steady grip. Warm and firm . . . like the rest of him. He removed his foot from the stirrup. She placed hers into it and gripped the back of the saddle with her free hand. As she hopped up, her body brushed the length of his leg, and as she swung astride behind him, her breasts pressed into his back. The sensations traveled inside her, producing most unsettling results.

"Prince is as sure-footed a mount as could be wished for," he assured her, "but nothing is certain on this terrain. You'd best put your arms around me."

Goodness. Riding in such familiar fashion behind a man not related to her in the least, dressed only in her nightshift, dressing gown and an ill-fitting cloak that was even now half falling from her shoulders—if this were London, her reputation would never recover.

But they weren't in London. They were in the wilds of Cornwall, where such notions didn't—couldn't— hold such sway. Lives could be lost, and that certainly outweighed any notions of proper decorum.

Tomorrow she would be the girl her family wished. Tonight . . .

She put her arms around him, clasping her hands against his hard stomach. Her own stomach nestled against his back, her thighs against his hips, her cheek . . . She held her cheek aloft, but oh, how it longed to yield to temptation and snuggle against one of his formidable shoulders.

"Hang on tight."

Sophie sighed and noticed how her breath stirred the fringe of golden hair across his collar. His hair bore a faint, fresh tang of sea air. Did his skin smell of the sea as well? He turned his face half around to speak to her, and she schooled the wayward notions from her features.

"Can you tell me where you set out from?"

"Oh, er . . . my aunt and uncle's home lies on the main road about a mile south of the village. Theirs is the last farm before the boundary of an abandoned old estate called Edgecombe."

He tensed slightly. She felt it in the various parts of her that were engaged so thoroughly and personally with his.

"Did I say something wrong?" He wouldn't, after

all, be the first person to react adversely to the name of Edgecombe.

"Theirs must be the farm I passed right before I veered off course." She noticed he hadn't answered her question, but the muscles of his back relaxed against her. "Do you see anything familiar yet?"

She glanced out over rolling hills and silver-tinged brush. "It all looks the same to me."

He brought his horse to an abrupt halt. "Bloody unbelievable."

"What is?" She pressed forward, bringing her chin to nuzzle in the solid curve of his neck and trying to ignore the warm sensation that rose inside her. This wasn't at all like riding pillion behind Father or her brother or Uncle Peter.

"I can scarcely believe it." His incredulous words broke into her thoughts. "Surely the chapel could not have been so close to the road."

"How strange." She looked behind her expecting to see the silhouette of the chapel, but detected nothing but the empty moor. Puzzled, she turned back around.

Off in the distance the roof of Aunt Louisa's house stood out as a darker stain against the night.

Her arms tightened around his sturdy torso. "We must find a way down to the beach. I believe we're very near the place where it . . . would have wrecked."

They crossed the road and negotiated their way across an open headland. Leaving his horse to graze at a safe distance, they proceeded on foot, hand in hand at his insistence, to the top of the bluffs. From here both the farm and the village were hidden by the sharp angle of the coastline. Far below, moonlit waves rushed in and out of a narrow cove.

A shallow, boulder-strewn beach hugged the base of the cliffs. For quite some distance out, ocean-worn humps of rock jutted from the water, the currents frothing around them. Sophie's heart contracted as she searched the heaving waters. Doubtlessly she hurt the knuckles of the man beside her with all her squeezing.

Of a certainty no ship attempting to put in here could possibly have survived.

But as she scoured the shore for signs of tragedy, she detected no disturbance of any sort, much less the shattered remains of a ship or the ghastliness of bodies washing ashore.

"I don't understand. Perhaps we're not in the right place after all."

He cleared his throat. "Or perhaps what you saw wasn't—"

The condescension in his voice sparked a burst of irritation. "Don't tell me I was seeing things. Or that I was dreaming." With one hand she tugged her borrowed cloak closed around her. "I was wide-awake. My eyes were not deceived."

"Then where is this ship of yours?"

"It is no ship of mine. How on earth should I know what became of it?"

He swiveled his head to study the coastline, raising his free hand to point to a distant glow lighting the water. "See there. I believe even the harbor lights are precisely where they ought to be."

She gritted her teeth. "I am not making this up."

"I never assumed you were." His voice took on a soothing tone. Maddeningly so, as if she were a frightened child to be mollified. His long fingers caressed her knuckles. "I'm quite certain you believe what you saw was real."

Sophie yanked her hand free and moved away.

He was beside her again in an instant. Moonlight gilded the harsh lines of a scowl as he reclaimed her hand with a strength she found fruitless to resist.

"However solid this ground may appear," he said, "the slightest misstep can send whole chunks sliding into the sea, and you with it. This is no place for dancing about, I assure you. Come; it's time I took you home."

"Yes, well, let me assure *you,* Mr. . . . whatever-your-name-is, that I neither care to dance nor do I require your assistance in finding my way home from here." The wind parted the edges of her cloak. With only one hand at her disposal, she struggled to retain a measure of modesty. "I can follow the road perfectly well, thank you."

"That may be, Miss whatever-*your*-name-is." With a nimble tug he swung her around to stand toe-to-toe in front of him. A gust whipped her cloak open, and with it her flannel dressing gown, exposing the cotton shift beneath. His gaze burned her length as it dipped to take in the view, then just as quickly flicked back to her face. "You are in my care now, and I *will* see you safely home. We'll have no further argument about it."

Indignation sizzled through her. How like her family he sounded. How condescending and superior and overbearing.

But the lips that spoke those words . . . they were full, lush, so very warm and close. . . . Sophie couldn't help staring at his mouth, entranced by what was surely the only soft thing about this man, especially when he spoke so forcefully. Her own intended retort forgotten, she gazed mutely up at him and wondered what his lips would feel like against her own.

He grasped her elbows and lowered his head as if . . . as if he meant to do the very thing she pondered. But he merely peered into her face, then shook his head and made a little scraping sound in the back of his throat, as if he'd reached some disparaging conclusion about her but didn't deign to share it. He compounded the insult by grasping the edges of both her dressing gown and cloak and drawing them closed around her with a familiarity that somehow belittled her, made her feel rather like a strumpet.

He offered his arm. "Come. You've no cause to be angry. What you need is a good night's sleep, and in the morning you'll see that all is well."

Too perplexed to reply, she let him lead her back

to his horse and lift her up behind him, where she did her utmost to preserve as wide a gap between their bodies as possible. That became especially difficult when he clucked the horse to a canter, forcing her to encircle his torso and hold on tight or tumble over the animal's rump. Still, she managed as best she could to sit her tallest and straightest.

Whatever had happened to the solicitous gentleman she'd met in the church? He had been nothing but respectful, even while holding her in his arms. He had shown her patience and concern, had listened to her and been alert to her needs. When had he transformed into a stern stranger eager to be rid of her?

Her fingers curled into frustrated fists against his shirtfront, but she realized he would certainly notice this. She relaxed her hands, which brought her palms flat against a firm, flexed set of abdominal muscles that thoroughly captured her fascination one instant and piqued her temper the next. She was behaving exactly like a strumpet, and like the capricious female Grandfather had accused her of being right before he packed her off to Cornwall.

"I'm not angry," she lied, then drew several calming breaths to make the assertion true. "If anything, I am relieved to have been wrong. I certainly didn't want . . . Oh, but I simply don't understand how I could have been so mistaken. It seemed so vivid at the time, so real. It is most peculiar."

He brought Prince to a halt and half twisted in the saddle. Beneath a tousled shock of hair, the even length of his nose and the square line of his jaw edged a sturdy silhouette against the night sky. "I'd advise you to let it go."

"Have I any other choice?"

He turned farther around, his eyes narrowing as he contemplated her, and suddenly, here in the wide open, with the mist gone and the air crisply clear, his fair hair and aristocratic looks seemed entirely familiar. Before her mind could work it over, he said, "You say one thing, yet I would swear I detect quite the opposite in your voice."

"Meaning?"

"Meaning, Miss What's-it, that you'd do well not to go chasing phantoms in the mist."

"And if they are not merely phantoms?"

"All the more reason to steer clear."

His warning had the opposite effect he had intended, for a little spark ignited inside her. "Earlier you said the change in the shore lights could mean a number of things. Smugglers and wreckers are among them, aren't they?"

A muscle in his cheek bunched. "We've no reason to suspect any such thing."

"Don't we? I've done quite a lot of reading about Cornwall, and about this area in particular. Those lights could certainly indicate smuggling activities."

Yes, a century and more ago, Cornish waters were pirate-ridden. While swashbuckling men—and women—in cuffed boots and eye patches had long since vanished from the seas, smuggling had continued with subtle, yet perhaps more sinister methods.

Her gaze roamed his moonlit features, both smooth and stony, hard and yet possessing an underlying tender quality, or so she had thought earlier. She knew what she had seen tonight. And then this man, who seemed so strangely familiar, turned up as if conjured by the mist. Was he one of those phantoms he spoke of? Did he present a danger she should steer clear of?

For myriad reasons, Sophie rather believed he did.

"I suspect you know more than you are willing to divulge, sir."

"We found nothing amiss tonight. What can I divulge about nothing?"

"You are most perplexing. Please entice your horse to continue our journey. I find myself longing to be home."

"Which is exactly where you belong. Giddyap, Prince."

They rode in taut silence until they reached Aunt Louisa's gate. Sophie hitched her skirts to her knees in preparation for dismounting—without unneeded and unwelcome help, thank you ever so much.

But he was too quick for her, arching a leg over Prince's mane and sliding to the ground. He reached up and caught her hand but made no move to help her down. Instead he pinned her in place with a piercing stare that roused yet another prickle of recognition. "I'm sorry to have angered you, but you'd do well to heed my advice. Go to bed and forget about tonight. And no more indulging in high-seas adventure stories."

"Give me back my hand, please."

He complied, only to grasp her firmly around the waist, his hands finding their way inside both her cloak *and* dressing gown in a manner that sent her belly into a disquieting flip-flop. He lifted her from the saddle as though she weighed nothing at all, and stood her on the ground right in front of him, inches away, with the horse like a wall at her back.

She tried to move past him, but he blocked her path and wouldn't budge. "God, you're lovely," he whispered, "with the moonlight gilding your hair and shining in those enormous eyes of yours. What color are they?"

Was he flirting with her? Did he believe that because she had ventured outside in her shift it was acceptable to take liberties with her?

Or, good heavens, had he somehow recognized her from London, and made assumptions based on the rumors? Oh, but that was silly. If she had encountered this man before, she certainly would have remembered him.

"I hardly see the point of such a question." She tried again to ease out from between him and his horse, but he raised an arm and gripped the saddle, trapping her fast.

"What color, Miss What's-it? Blue? No, lighter than that, I think. Gray?"

"Yes, gray." Damn her voice for trembling, her pulse for racing. "Satisfied?"

He didn't answer. Staring down at her, he traced the pad of his forefinger across her bottom lip. The gesture left her wobbly kneed, short of breath and entirely too confused to raise a protest. He leaned closer, nearly close enough to kiss her. "Promise me you won't chase any more phantoms. It isn't safe."

The velvet murmur of his voice sent a fiery shiver through her, and she wrestled an overwhelming temptation to bring the notion of that kiss to completion. Had the gentle stranger she'd met in the chapel returned? Or was he merely trifling with her again?

She squared her shoulders. "I try never to repeat my mistakes, but I hardly see the point of promising you something when I'll likely never see you again."

His eyes darkened with some inscrutable emotion. "Then do not promise me. Promise yourself you'll be more careful, more prudent in the future. The night holds many dangers, Miss . . . ?"

"St. Clair," she replied before stopping to consider the wisdom of telling this puzzling stranger anything about herself. Was his last comment meant to caution her or frighten her? Of what? Him? If he wished to harm her, he'd certainly had ample opportunity before now. Still, he made her feel crowded, small and very alone with him here in the dark. She resisted the temptation to dart a nervous glance over his shoulder to the house, to judge the distance between her and the door.

"My name is Chad," he said softly.

His tone melted like honey through her. Then she realized what he'd done. She held back a huff of exasperation, but only just. How ill-mannered to introduce himself with his given name only. The impropriety of it slithered through her, once again making her wonder if he considered her a less-than-decent woman.

Suddenly she saw herself through her family's eyes—half-dressed, her hair in shambles, riding pillion behind a man who obviously held her in no great esteem. Her family would be shocked, scandalized, disappointed in her all over again.

"I thank you for your assistance tonight, sir." She put frosty emphasis on the *sir*. "I'm very sorry to have inconvenienced you. Good night."

His eyebrow quirked; his nostrils flared. Stepping around her, he gathered the reins and mounted his horse. "You have been no inconvenience, Miss St. Clair. I bid you good night."

Turning, she intended to enter the house without another look back, but a twinge of conscience slowed her steps. She had wished to quell his arrogance, but perhaps she had made too good a job of it. The odd circumstances of their earlier meeting had foisted a disarming familiarity upon them, which perhaps accounted for his cheek. But he had done her a good service tonight and deserved better than her terse dismissal.

Ready to make amends, even to offer her first name in recompense, she turned back around. He had ridden beyond the gate, but not in the direction she had expected him to go. "Aren't you returning to the village?"

"Indeed not, Miss St. Clair."

"Then . . . where?"

"To Edgecombe, of course."

A shock of realization made her take an unsteady stride backward. It couldn't be mere coincidence, not with such an uncommon name. Chad . . . Chadwell Rutherford . . . fifth Earl of Wycliffe. Now she understood why he seemed so familiar. That day at Edgecombe . . . it had been he who had glared out at her from the window. He who had disappeared again inside the house without a word of greeting.

Openmouthed, she watched him disappear down the dark road.

A crack rent the air as the schooner struck the rocks. The hull split upon impact. From the shore Chad watched helplessly as the ocean rushed to fill the gap. Screams and shouts poured out. Again the tide thrust the vessel against the bluffs. The framework shuddered. Wood splintered. Sails tore as masts toppled. Bodies came hurtling over the rails to splash like feed sacks into the heaving water or thud sickeningly against the rocks.

Chad could only watch the carnage and pray and agonize over the how and why of it. What devilry had lured the craft into the headland?

The answer singed the flesh from his fingertips. In horror he stared at the torch flaming in his hand, and at the other torches dotting the cove. By God and the devil too, he had done this. With his own hands.

Dead for the cargo.

He awoke with a lurch, breath knifing through his lungs. His fingers clawed the bedclothes from his sweat-soaked chest. His entire body throbbed. Stinging pain blurred his vision. He pressed the heels of his hands to his eyes and struggled to rein in the terror of the dream, calm his exploding heart and see past the gruesome images flickering in harsh relief inside his skull.

He lowered his hands and went still, listening. Searching the shadows hunched in the corners of the room, and feeling as though someone were watching . . .

Had it been just a dream? Or a message from the apparition he'd met on Blackheath Moor?

His thudding heart eased to its normal rhythm. Christ, what *had* he encountered last night? He'd been weary, lost, confused by the mist. Perhaps he'd merely stumbled into the chapel, fallen asleep and dreamed the rest. Yes, his own guilt haunted his nightmares— nothing else made sense. To believe he'd actually seen

a ghost was ludicrous. The only true haunting last
night had come in the form of a lovely if somewhat
impulsive young lady, Miss St. Clair.

The warmth of her curves against him, the fragrance
of her hair beneath his nose, the endearing perplexity
in those earnest features as she peered up at him . . .
If he closed his eyes he could conjure those memories.
Could almost conjure *her*. Feel her. Taste her. He
wished he'd kissed her . . . just once. . . .

Remembering her frankness and the damned naïveté that would send a young woman out alone onto
a darkened, mist-shrouded moor, he opened his eyes.
He had no business being anywhere near a female
like that.

He dragged himself out of bed, tugging to straighten
the clothes he'd slept in. He pulled on his boots but
didn't bother buttoning his shirt. Beyond his windows,
deep stacks of clouds were pushing in off the ocean,
their blackened bases glowering over the waves.
Bursts of lightning forked within them, followed by
growls of thunder. On unsteady legs he crossed the
room and heaved open the window. Warm air spilled
into the room, oppressive with the promise of rain.

He caught himself tiptoeing down the staircase as if
afraid of disturbing . . . someone. "Don't be stupid,
Chadwell," he said aloud. "If there were such things
as ghosts, you certainly couldn't hide from them."

Nor could he hide from whoever had summoned
him here. *Go to Edgecombe and wait for instructions.*
What did they want? Watling had claimed that no one
wished to kill him, at least not yet. But what use could
Chad be now, with his money running out and most
of his resources confiscated by the court?

A notion struck him. There had been arrests besides
Watling's. Perhaps the others had already been
caught. The message that summoned Chad here might
have been nothing more than a condemned criminal's
idea of a final jest, a way to torment Chad for having
testified against the ring.

He cringed at the echo of his footsteps against the stonework of the main hall. Moving from room to room, he threw open windows and shutters and peeled the shrouds from furniture. The flitting of his own shadow made him flinch.

The house was too quiet, too empty. When he'd closed up the place following his father's death, he'd dismissed the staff and helped them find new positions. There had been neither the funds nor any good reason to keep them on. More recently his solicitor had arranged for a man-of-all-work who lived in the village and came occasionally to trim the gardens and prevent the place from moldering.

By the fireplace in the drawing room Chad paused, staring up at the black-and-crimson shield that had hung above the fireplace for as long as he could remember. When his father had purchased Edgecombe a single rapier with an uncommonly small hilt had sat mounted at a downward angle over the shield, one half of an incomplete *X*. Supposedly the weapon had belonged to Meg Keating, and the story held that its missing mate belonged to her husband. When Jack Keating went down with his ship just off the coast of Penhollow, the sword presumably went with him.

It had been one of his father's eccentricities that he'd never wished to replace the missing sword, but preferred the lopsided display as a reminder of Edgecombe's turbulent history.

But now the mounting brackets held nothing; the small-handled rapier Chad remembered so well from childhood had vanished. Had his father for some reason moved the weapon? That hardly seemed likely, which left another possibility—theft. His ire rose at the thought of criminals stalking through his father's home, stealing valuables . . . yet a quick gaze about the room revealed Franklin's collection of ivory and gold snuffboxes, a pair of *famille verte* vases, the bronze mantel clock. Why take only the sword and leave the other valuables?

Intending to see if anything else had been stolen, he continued his inspection of the house, but came to an uneasy halt in the adjoining game room. On the far wall the blank face of a closed door all but challenged him to turn the knob and walk through, something he hadn't been able to do in over two years.

The library. The room where his father had died.

When the news had reached him, Chad had raced here at breakneck speed from London, sickened and horrified, racked with regret and knowing he'd be too damned late to change anything.

The memory reeled through him. Blackened walls, charred furnishings, the suffocating bitterness of soot. Since then repairs had erased the evidence of the fire that stole Franklin Rutherford's life, but no amount of wood or paint could remove the anguish that room held for Chad.

Crossing the game room, he stood before the door, wrapped his hand around the knob and told himself it was just a room, that his father's spirit didn't dwell inside.

That Franklin's death hadn't been, in part, his fault.

Chad had received his father's missive only a fortnight before he died.

> Dear Chadwell,
>   It's been rather a long while since I've seen you. Do join me at Edgecombe as soon as you may. We'll hunt, play chess, eat what we wish when we wish and smoke our pipes without apology.
>   I've missed you, son.
>
> —Father

London had been in high Season at the time, and there had been that new actress he'd been pursuing for weeks. The thought of cutting short his exploits and exiling himself to this remote Cornish backwater . . .

well. He'd sent a reply promising to be here by midsummer. By May Franklin was dead.

By autumn of that year, upon discovering his inherited fortune was far too depleted to support the lifestyle he so enjoyed, Chad had shaken hands with Watling and entered into a devil's bargain.

If only he had been here with his father . . .

Bitter bile rising in his throat, he shoved away from the door. He wasn't ready to face that room. God . . . not yet. Half-blinded by memories, by the damned shadows that draped like palls over every room, he made his way back to the main hall. The air felt heavy in his lungs, fetid on his tongue. The very atmosphere of the house pressed down on him like a weight. He needed to get out, to escape the stifling gloom.

Wrestling open the terrace door with a tug that nearly shattered the glass panes, he staggered outside. The blowing, salt-laden air rushed by him, chilling the perspiration rolling down his sides beneath his shirt. The unsettling charge of the approaching storm pricked like needles at his skin.

Vague sensations crawled through his gut. Growing urgency. Uncertain dread. An ominous assurance that whatever he must learn here, face here, he must see it through to the end. There could be no escape, not if he wished to restore even a shred of his honor.

He could sit crouched in this house, watching the shadows over his shoulder and waiting for some unknown enemy to strike, or he could attempt to discover who had ordered him here, and why . . . and strike first. Miss St. Clair's mysterious harbor lights—could there be a connection?

The garden slope fell away beneath his desperate strides until he found himself at the western edge of the property, staring down at the frothing sea a hundred feet below.

"You were not in your room last night."

Sophie started at the rumble of her uncle's accusing

baritone. She had just left the room she shared with Rachel and was on her way downstairs, but Uncle Barnaby stood a few steps below the landing, blocking her way.

His black hair, a mass of tumbling waves that fell below his collar, was held back from his bearded, scowling face by a squat tweed cap, and she could see by his damp trouser hems and the dirt smeared across his shirt that he'd been toiling in the fields for some time already. Time during which she had lain slumbering, making up the sleep she had missed during her strange jaunt on the moor.

"Well, lass? Where were ye when ye should've been abed?"

"I . . . er . . . yes." She drew a breath and swallowed. "I couldn't get back to sleep after what I saw last night. Or thought I saw," she added hastily when something ominous flashed in his eyes.

Apparently he hadn't fallen back to sleep either, or he couldn't have known she'd been gone. What to tell him? Certainly not that she'd lost her way on Blackheath Moor and ended up riding on the back of a stranger's horse, and in her nightgown, no less.

"And?" he prompted in a demanding bark.

"And . . . so . . . I walked down to the beach." A partial truth, after all. She *had*, finally, stood looking down at the water last night, only to admit she'd made a mistake. "I needed to make quite certain it had been my eyes playing tricks on me, as you and Aunt Louisa suggested, and not the tragic occurrence I'd feared."

His features drawing tight, her uncle surged up the remaining steps, crossed the landing and stopped in front of her. "What did ye see?"

Sophie's heart thudded against her stays. She began shaking her head, more out of fear than in answer to the question. Why did he look like that, threatening and angry and . . . afraid, almost? He was like a stray dog that snapped because it was frightened and perceived everybody and everything as a threat.

"I—I saw nothing, Uncle Barnaby. Nothing at all. The waters were dark, the harbor lights where they should be. I . . . must have dreamed otherwise."

He straightened, but held her in his wary sights. "Why were ye gone so long?"

How did he know how long? Had he waited up for her, heard her return? She couldn't help wondering what he had been doing in all that time.

"I fell asleep," she said. "I can't say for how long."

"On the sand?"

"Yes, on the sand. As soon as I awoke I came inside. I hadn't realized you were up as well." She attempted to smile. "Had I known I'd have offered to make you tea."

He didn't respond. His brooding regard lingered on her, his eyes hooded by his heavy lids. Sophie fought the urge to squirm. Footsteps and Aunt Louisa's voice rising from the bottom of the stairs brought a welcome relief.

"Sophie? Are you up yet, dear?"

The woman's soft cotton bonnet appeared first, bobbing as she made her ascent. Then her face came into view through the banister newels and she went still. "Barnaby, what are you doing back in the house? I thought you and Dominic were herding the ewes into the south pasture today."

"Aye." His boots drumming loudly on the bare wooden floorboards, he turned and walked to the top of the stairs. "Tell your niece here it isn't safe to wander about at night, no matter what she thinks she sees outside her window, or she might get hurt."

He and Aunt Louisa exchanged somber glances as he squeezed past her down the steps. Aunt Louisa's chin jerked back toward Sophie. "Goodness, no, Sophie. It isn't safe. Were you out last night? You mustn't think of doing such a thing again." She scurried up the remaining steps. Clutching the top of the banister, she turned alarm-filled eyes to Sophie and breathlessly said, "Promise me, Sophie. Promise me you'll not act in such a foolhardy manner again."

Sophie promised, but the urgency of Aunt Louisa's request, coupled with Uncle Barnaby's stern warning, spiked a keen curiosity and made her wonder if she wouldn't find ample reason to break that promise, and soon.

The restless wind shuddered off the water, plastering back Chad's hair and filling his shirt like a sail. Squinting against the gusts, he peered down at the coastline beyond Edgecombe's boundaries.

What of Miss St. Clair's claims of misplaced harbor lights? Obviously no ship had crashed on the shoals last night. But could one have put in somewhere close by, safely unloaded an illicit cargo and sailed away without detection? And where would they have put such a cargo?

Had the estate been used all along despite Chad's adamant refusal to allow such an insult to his father's memory? As a boy he had combed the cellars and the gardens searching for the legendary tunnel believed to have been used centuries ago by pirates. To his youthful disappointment he had found nothing.

From his vantage point he detected no waters calm enough or clear enough to allow a ship safe anchorage other than Penhollow Harbor. Perhaps from water level he might discover something different. He leaned slightly over, staring down into the pounding waves. Beneath him stretched a hundred feet or more of narrow ledges, razor-sharp ridges and slippery cliff face. The prospect made his senses swim, his vision blur. He felt light-headed, disoriented. . . .

"Lord Wycliffe?"

With a shout of alarm he spun about, swayed precariously and scrambled to catch his balance.

Chapter 4

"Miss St. Clair? Good God, don't sneak up on a man like that!"

"I-I'm so sorry. I didn't mean to startle you."

"Startle me? You nearly sent me tumbling over the edge. What the devil are you doing here? And if you wouldn't mind, you may release me now."

Heart in her throat, Sophie had rushed forward when the earl appeared about to fall over the cliff, and now stood squeezing his arm in both her hands. "Oh, yes . . . sorry. But perhaps you shouldn't stand so close to the edge."

Vexation flared in his eyes. The muscles of his forearm bunched beneath her palms.

She unclenched her fingers and backed a step away. "I . . . came to thank you for last night and . . . to apologize. And . . ." She trailed off, uncertain how best to continue.

"And what, Miss St. Clair?"

His tone made her flinch, while the anger sharpening his handsome features made her wish she had ignored the impulse that had sent her here this morning.

As brooding as the storm gathering behind him, the earl stood waiting with arms crossed, an eyebrow quirked and his gaze boring into her with no small amount of impatience. By day he was even more magnificent than she had realized, his body tall and lean;

his nose, cheekbones and jaw strong slashes in his handsome face; his eyes the rich amber of aged cognac. His fair hair was tousled by the wind, as was . . . good heavens . . . his shirt. Sophie averted her eyes, but not before taking in the astonishing details of a muscled torso sprinkled with whorls of gleaming golden hair.

"Well, Miss St. Clair?" He tugged the edges of his shirt together and began doing up the buttons.

With a blush hot on her cheeks, she attempted to gather her thoughts. "I brought you muffins."

"Pardon?"

"Muffins. My aunt baked them this morning. Quite a lot of them. For the tavern. She sometimes provides the tavern with baked goods. I didn't think she'd miss a few, so I snatched them hot out of the oven and, well . . . there they are."

Dear heavens, she was babbling like an idiot. She turned and retreated a couple of yards, retrieving the basket she had hastily dropped when she had believed the earl might fall.

"Molasses." She extended the basket with an uncertain smile. The wind threatened to seize the bonnet off her head. She held the brim with her free hand and raised the basket another inch. "They're quite wonderful, actually."

With a frown he reached for them, staring down at the linen with which she had covered them, and the sprig of wild heather she had laid on top. When he didn't smile, when his expression remained one of perplexity, a sense of the foolishness of her gift took hold. Muffins? She wished she had at least not included the heather.

What had she been thinking, arriving unannounced, unescorted, uninvited?

She had considered asking her cousin Rachel to come along, but that would have meant having to explain about her foray onto the moors last night. Bad enough that the Gordons believed she had wandered out to the beach and fallen asleep alone. If they guessed the truth . . .

Even before this morning, uneasiness had crept over her whenever she was around them. Whispers cut short when she entered a room; the continual barrage of barely concealed scowls from Uncle Barnaby and Dominic; warnings that she avoid places like Edgecombe—admonitions based, so far, on vague misgivings about curses and ghosts, rather than on rational, concrete evidence that the house posed any true danger.

Uncle Barnaby had demanded to know what she had seen from the beach, and had seemed relieved by her claim that she had witnessed nothing. That she had fallen asleep. And that she was willing to admit the change in the harbor lights had been produced by her imagination.

There was more to learn in all of this; she felt certain of it.

Wishing the earl would say something, anything, she ground the toe of her shoe into the dirt. "I do hope you've a liking for muffins, Lord Wycliffe."

His inscrutable gaze returned to her face. "I do. Thank you, Miss St. Clair." The eyebrow quirked again. "So you know who I am. Is it possible we've met somewhere previously, and I've done you the disservice of forgetting?"

"We have not, at least not formally, but I've done quite a bit of reading about Edgecombe. When you told me your first name last night, it wasn't difficult to make the connection. I've long had an interest in the place. Its history, its previous owners. The connection to the Keatings is fascinating. I've wondered, is your family somehow descended from the Keatings, or was Edgecombe purchased later?"

"We have no connection to the Keatings." His jaw stiffened and clenched. Had she said something wrong? "My father bought Edgecombe when I was a boy."

"I see." She longed for the tension in his features to ease, longed to glimpse something of the tenderness he had shown her in the chapel. Had she merely dreamed that side of him? The strength of his arms around her, the heat of his body against her had been solid, real. She hadn't imagined those things, but neither did she detect anything welcoming or gentle in him now.

"May I do something for you, Miss St. Clair?"

A clear dismissal. *Go home,* a little voice advised. But what welcome awaited her there, among relatives who seemed to have something to hide?

"I . . . wonder, my lord, if it would be possible for me to see the house sometime? Not today, of course. I've taken you unawares, and I won't inconvenience you further. Perhaps I may return with my cousin Miss Gordon?"

His eyes narrowed a fraction. "You may see the house now, if you wish. If you truly care to, that is. And then perhaps you'll be good enough to tell me the real reason you're here."

Her stomach tightened around a ball of apprehension. "I don't understand your meaning. Of course I—"

"Miss St. Clair, you didn't come here merely to bring me muffins, though I appreciate the gesture. Nor are you here to sightsee. You want something, and I've a good notion what it is. I'll tell you right now the answer is no."

"Lord Wycliffe, how can you possibly know what brought me here today?"

In truth, he didn't wish to know. He simply wanted her to leave. Or, at least, to not look up at him so ingenuously with eyes that were not simply gray—not dark and somber like the shadows hanging over Edgecombe, but as deep and vivid as clouds with the sun shining behind them.

Damn her. Why hadn't she sense enough to stay away?

"I'm of no mind to play games, Miss St. Clair. Please just state your business."

"Oh . . . yes, all right. Please, my lord. I need your help."

Christ, no. She mustn't *need* from him. Mustn't believe she could rely on him for anything. He wasn't dependable, wasn't steadfast. He wasn't someone in whom a nice young lady could safely bestow her trust. Couldn't she see that?

He supposed not. He bore no distinguishing scars, no brand marking him a criminal, no sign revealing the state of his finances or that his world was slowly closing in on him from all sides. She saw only the nobleman, a peer of the realm, a man of supposed good breeding and gracious intent.

He thrust out his chin and showed her his sternest expression. "Then you admit, Miss St. Clair, to a motive beyond muffins."

"Yes. No!" A breath slipped past her supple lips, and she said more quietly, "Yes."

"Good of you to clarify."

He set off walking back toward the house, brushing by her without sparing her a glance, but reasonably certain she'd be quick to follow, and that some sort of explanation would be not long in coming.

"Lord Wycliffe, please." Her skirts rustled as she hastened to match his strides. "I realize we found no evidence of a mishap last night, but I do know what I saw. I was not dreaming."

He wished *he* were dreaming. Wished her appearance today were nothing more than a sweet, wistful dream he might indulge in for a few hours' respite before waking to the bleak and uncertain realities of his life.

"Lord Wycliffe—"

"I believe you," he tossed over his shoulder. "And as I advised you last night, let it go."

Her hand came down on his forearm, exposed by the sleeve he had pushed to his elbow. Suddenly there was warmth and the impossibly soft touch of her fingertips sending shards of awareness to pierce him. The dream turned sensual, alarming. Dangerous.

He stopped and turned to glare down at her. To warn her away with callousness, if he must.

Before he spoke she removed her hand and said, "There's more. Last night my aunt and uncle treated my claims with indifference. Today, when they realized I'd left the house, that indifference transformed into anger. And anxiety. And fear too, I believe."

"Your uncle knew you'd left the house? What explanation did you give?"

"I made no mention of you. I told him I'd wandered down to the beach to prove to myself all was well. Which leads me to my point. He asked if I'd seen anything. As if he feared I might have. And as if he might have something to hide."

Chad's pulse bucked. Had she just provided him with his first clue into the mystery surrounding his summons to Edgecombe? Could her family be somehow involved, perhaps part of the very same smuggling ring he had aided?

But no, that would be too easy. He would be a fool to think he could spend one night in Penhollow and have the answers he sought.

"Perhaps you only imagined anger and fear," he said, "where there existed only concern for your safety." She huffed the beginnings of a retort, one he quickly defused by speaking over her. "You still haven't told me what you want of me."

"Last night you were willing to listen when no one else would. I know you doubted me, but—"

"Actually I concede the possibility that something odd may have occurred last night." Shrugging, he turned and began walking. "I went down to the cliffs this morning to inspect the coastline for anything we might have missed last night."

Together they thudded over the footbridge, her stride noticeably quickening until they descended onto the grass on the other side. She came up beside him, bringing with her a flowery fragrance that tantalized his senses. "What did you discover?"

"Nothing."

"Oh. But that doesn't mean there mightn't be something to be discovered. Perhaps at water level—"

"I'd had the same thought," he admitted, then silently cursed himself for encouraging her.

"Perhaps if we went by boat—"

"If *I* went by boat, Miss St. Clair." They reached the terrace steps, and he stopped again, angry with himself for having failed to end the conversation before putting dangerous thoughts into her head. "At the first opportunity I'll hire a vessel and see if I can't discover what this coastline might be hiding, if anything. You, Miss St. Clair, shall remain onshore, where you belong."

She rounded on him. "I *am* the one who witnessed the incident firsthand."

"That makes no difference. Not with the treachery of the seas hereabout."

"I am not afraid of a little water, my lord."

"Perhaps you should be. Perhaps you should be afraid of a great many things." *Such as entering the home of a man you do not know, alone, while being so damnably unaware of the effect you have on him.*

If she only knew the thoughts—urges—her proximity aroused in him, how fiercely he fought the impulse to drag her into his arms and kiss her, to seek relief from the burdensome darkness of his world in the sweetness of smooth, tempting flesh . . . in innocence and the stubborn, reckless naïveté that had sent her here in the first place.

He shoved his blowing hair from his eyes. "Why is this so important to you? You said you are only visiting. Why concern yourself with affairs that have nothing to do with you? Confound it, Miss St. Clair, who *are* you that you are so hell-bent on probing into the secrets, if indeed there are any, of an inconsequential village in the middle of nowhere?"

"My lord, in my experience I have learned that nothing is inconsequential. Not if it involves the lives and well-being of innocent people."

"What of your life? Your well-being?"

"I can take care of myself."

"Then why do you need me?"

She appeared flustered by the question, but his little triumph paled as he found himself holding his breath and wishing her answer held some redeeming truth he might latch onto as he fought to salvage his life.

"I can't be everywhere at once," she said. "Nor can I, due to my circumstances, move as freely about this village as you can. I'm asking for your assistance, my lord, as a second pair of eyes and ears. I've no one else to turn to. And you seem a reasonable man."

"Ah. You wish to use me."

"Yes. No." Flustered again, she frowned. "I mean—"

"Again, thank you for clarifying." He climbed the terrace steps two at a time.

She scurried up behind him, stopping slightly out of breath, cheeks faintly flushed, and he wondered where their chase would end. Here? In the house? He'd carelessly offered to show her the inside, but now he recognized the prospect as a bad idea. How could he trust himself with her when she looked as she did— fresh, windblown . . . and so tempting?

He needed her gone. Not only because of how she tipped his senses on end, but because at some point dangerous men would make demands of him, perhaps even claim his life.

"Will you help me?" she asked.

"Miss St. Clair, you are nothing if not dogged. I . . . Hang on one moment. . . ." It suddenly struck him.

Her tenacity, her inquisitiveness, her impulsiveness. He could think of one explanation. He set her basket of muffins in the low wall bordering the terrace. "St. Clair . . . as in the family who owns the *Beacon*? Are you Cornelius St. Clair's granddaughter? Are you *Sophie* St. Clair?"

A wave of scarlet engulfed her from neck to hairline. Her lips opened, compressed, then opened again with a quiver that made him wish he'd held his tongue. But in the instant it took all of that to happen, the mortification on her face hardened to stoic, proud resolve. "Yes."

A queasy sensation crawled through Sophie, and she felt as though she once more stood before the earl with her cloak flying open to reveal her nightshift beneath.

Tucked away into one of the remotest corners of faraway Cornwall, and *still* she could not escape the scandal. Chadwell Rutherford must have heard about it in London—who hadn't?

"This explains quite a bit," he said, a corner of his mouth pulling into the first hint of a smile she had yet seen from him today.

The gesture made her want to turn and hide. But what good would hiding do? Her family had sent her here in hopes of defusing the gossip, yet her ruined reputation had followed her as faithfully as an old dog. The earl must think her wanton and shameless, must suppose she came to Edgecombe seeking a lurid assignation.

She forced open a mouth that felt as tight and stiff as starched linen. "I assure you the greater portion of whatever you heard about me bears no resemblance to the truth."

He folded his arms across his chest. "Then what is the truth?"

"You wouldn't believe me." No one else had, not even the people who claimed to love her most.

"I do know a thing about rumors, Miss St. Clair.

How they grow and spread and take on a life of their own."

Was he giving her the benefit of the doubt? Finally would someone give credence to her side of what had happened that deplorable night? Not daring to meet his eyes lest the sympathy she believed she detected turned out to be as flimsy as her family's trust, she turned and put a few steps' distance between them. Feeling confined, backed into a corner as she had been that night, she tugged her bonnet strings loose and removed the silk-and-straw contraption from her head.

"It was the night of the Winthrops' annual charity ball. Grandfather allowed me to cover the event for the *Beacon*. My task was to sit quietly in a corner and take notes on who attended, what they wore, the size of the donations . . . that sort of thing. I went there with another story in mind." The wind sifted through her hair, bringing cooling relief to the searing memories. "I'd had a tip, you see, about wrongdoing within the Winthrop Benevolent Society."

"What kind of wrongdoing?"

"The pilfering of funds." She glanced briefly over her shoulder. "By the Winthrops themselves. For years they've effectively been stealing from orphans and widows and men who were wounded in the wars against Napoleon."

She heard his quietly approaching tread. "How does that explain your being in Sir Henry Winthrop's bed-chamber?" The murmured question, almost but not quite an accusation, grazed her nape and made her shiver. "With Sir Henry."

"My tip—from a maid in their employ—was that I'd find proof of their perfidy in files kept in Lady Gertrude's private salon. When the guests sat down for supper I stole upstairs to search. But the house is a veritable maze, and—"

"I see." Did he? Or was that simply what one said when nothing could be done to change a wretched situation? "And the kiss?"

She whirled, a reproach hot on her lips. So the sordid details had made the rounds, had they? Skulking into parlors, shops, private gentlemen's clubs. She had probably been the toast of White's—had the Earl of Wycliffe raised a glass in honor of her supposed exploits?

But as she beheld his face—those strong, even features and cognac-colored eyes—she detected no hint of censure. Only the opportunity for the truth, at long last, to be heard.

She wanted to kiss him for it. Instead she said, "When I realized I'd entered the wrong room, I decided to make a quick search anyway. But Sir Henry had spilled sauce on his neck cloth and came up to change it. Oh, he was furious to find me rummaging though his things. Caught me by the shoulders and propelled me out his bedroom door with promises to summon the authorities immediately. At that moment several guests appeared at the top of the stairs, and before I knew it . . ."

Her throat ran dry as the humiliation of the incident roared through her. "He grabbed me in his arms and forced a disgusting sham of a kiss on me. Behind me I heard the gasps of onlookers. It was hideous. Then he released me and said, 'Sorry we haven't more time now, love. Next week, perhaps,' and pretended to be shocked and embarrassed by our audience."

"Damn the rotten whoreson." The earl's voice plunged with restrained emotion, and tense white lines formed on either side of his nose. "Obviously he guessed what you might be after. By compromising you he effectively discredited any accusations you might have made against him. You would have sounded like a jilted paramour. And as far as his marriage is concerned, it's common knowledge that Lady Winthrop turns a blind eye to her husband's dalliances. She's too preoccupied carrying on affairs of her own." His fists clenched and unclenched at his sides.

"You believe me." It was not a question, not even

a statement, but a palpable outpouring of relief. She closed her eyes to savor the sensation.

She opened them at the warm touch of fingertips beneath her chin. The earl stared into her face with an intensity that made her nerve endings tingle, that made her wonder, as she had last night, if he might lower his head and kiss her.

His thumb brushed back and forth against her lower lip, making it burn, tremble. Myriad emotions deepened with the hue of his eyes and held her motionless while a rippling awareness inside left her wanting . . . as she had never wanted before. Waiting . . . for what she had never experienced before. Thunder rolled across the sky, the sound vibrating inside her and wrapping around a growing, unsettling ache.

Then his fingers fell away and he straightened to his full height, towering over her until he seemed unreachable, removed and distant. "What I believe, Miss St. Clair, is that you are here in Cornwall for no good reason, and that you should contact your family immediately and ask them to bring you home."

"They won't allow it. Not yet."

"Have you told them of your suspicions concerning Penhollow?"

She sighed. "My family wouldn't believe me. They'd think it merely a ruse on my part to return to London. Unless, of course, I found solid evidence."

She couldn't help the hope that entered her voice, or the wistful glance she cast him. But his handsome features had become closed to her again, as shuttered as the windows of his house had once been.

Rippling thunder drew his gaze seaward. "I think it's time I saw you home, if you'll allow me a moment to don a proper shirt and find my coat."

"It isn't necessary. I made a mistake in coming here. After last night I believed you to be the sort of man who was willing to invest his time in the welfare of others. But I see my first impression of you has proved correct." That day she had first come here, he had

been so uninterested in greeting her that he had retreated into his house and pretended he hadn't stared
at her through the window.

He was a stranger, after all. She had no right, really,
to feel such weighty disappointment in him, yet the
sentiment sat heavy on her shoulders. "Good day,
Lord Wycliffe. I'll not trespass here again."

Chapter 5

Feeling like a scoundrel, Chad watched Miss Sophie St. Clair stride down the steps and make her way to the postern gate. He actually took a step with the intention of apologizing for his abominable behavior and asking what she meant by first impressions. He reached the swift conclusion that it was better to let her go.

Safer. For her. For him.

If he let her into his life and something happened to her . . .

The same question continued to batter about his brain: How many innocent victims had suffered as a direct result of his support of smuggling? By Christ, Sophie St. Clair wouldn't be one of them, even if he had to threaten her to keep her away. He only hoped it wouldn't come to that.

Her basket remained on the terrace wall, a mute, unassuming token that pierced him through. The carefully folded linen . . . the sprig of heather . . .

If Henry Winthrop were standing here now, Chad would be sorely tempted to wrap his hands around the man's throat and strangle the life out of him.

Then again, Sir Henry might be a fraud and a villain, but what would Sophie think of Chad if she knew the crimes he had committed?

Carefully he moved the heather aside, peeled open the linen and plucked a still-warm muffin from the pile. At the sweet aroma curling beneath his nose, his stomach growled. He sank his teeth into the muffin.

And immediately spat a gooey lump of batter into the grass beyond the terrace. In spite of everything a smile tugged at his lips. Apparently Sophie should have checked with her aunt before plundering the oven.

An hour later Penhollow's thatched and slate rooftops rose into Chad's view. As he turned Prince onto the village road, he noticed a small gathering in the far corner of the churchyard, in the shadow of the sanctuary. Freshly turned soil was mounded beside an open grave. A plain pine casket waited to be lowered into the earth.

The preacher's soft drone carried on the breeze. Odd, but Chad didn't hear any sobbing, didn't detect any tears. He watched over his shoulder as Prince took him past. As a few scattered raindrops fell, the preacher closed his prayer book. Quietly the somber group dispersed.

Chad remembered from his previous ride through here that Penhollow boasted no mercantile or emporium. Most trade in rural villages still depended on weekly or monthly market days, when traveling merchants set up booths offering goods not otherwise available to the local inhabitants. But he needed supplies immediately, and headed for the only establishment where he would likely find them: the village tavern.

Outside the two-story stone-and-timber building, a weathered sign creaked back and forth on its post. Chipped paint depicted a seagull flying on a background of black clouds above peaking whitecaps, mirroring the view beyond the nearby harbor.

He left Prince in the care of the stable boy and stepped into a dim, cool interior. Murmured conversations sent a raspy hum floating beneath a raftered ceiling. As his eyes adjusted, he made out a handful of rough-clad men hunched over long plank tables. The guttering glow of oil lamps sharpened craggy features, leathery skin. Woolen shirtsleeves pushed to the elbows revealed forearms bulging from years of hauling lines and hoisting sails. No one looked his way as the door closed behind him.

He walked between the tables, heading for the bar. A man sitting nearby happened to glance up, and the tankard in his hand halted several inches shy of his mouth. Almost immediately conversation dwindled to a blanketing silence. As Chad came to an uneasy halt, whispers hissed like wasps from a nest.

"By Christ . . ."

"Can't be . . ."

"Saints preserve us."

"Wycliffe!"

Chairs screeched as the whiskered fellows pushed to their feet—all but one, who watched silently from the corner, his calculating expression a sharp contrast to the bewilderment of the others. Chad exchanged one inquisitive glance with the man, then found himself inching backward from the gawping circle fast closing around him. Who were these men, and why on earth were they so thunderstruck at his arrival? Could they possibly know of his guilt?

Or . . . could whoever had summoned him to Penhollow be among them?

"I am Lord Wycliffe," he said, half in explanation, half in challenge. If his unknown adversary stood facing him, Chad would just as soon have their confrontation here and now, and have it done.

A towering figure filled an inner doorway, a giant bear of a man with a pate as smooth as an egg. He carried a tray of tankards, and as he moved behind the bar his gaze flitted over the tense crowd. Then he spotted Chad. The tray nearly upended in his hands. "Jesus!"

Chad waited for something more to happen, for someone to spring forward and shove a dagger between his ribs, to fire a bullet into his gut. At least to signal to him, with a look or a hand motion, that his days on earth were limited for having turned in fellow smugglers to the authorities.

No one moved. Nothing changed. Through the stares and pulsing silence, he stepped around the men blocking his way and approached the bar. "Are you the proprietor?"

"Jesus," the man repeated. He swept a hand over his bald head. "You're the spittin' image, ain't ye?"

Understanding dawned. "You're remembering my father."

"Aye." The word was a barely audible grind in his throat.

Weak daylight framed Chad's shadow on the floor as the street door opened. "What the devil's got everyone clutched in such a bloody tight knot?" Heads swiveled toward the source of a feminine voice. "I'll tell you now, gentlemen, there'd best be no brawling in my pub today."

The door closed, once more sealing the tavern in gloom. From every direction fingers shot out, all converging on Chad.

"It's *him,* Kel."

"He's come back."

"Returned from the grave, he is."

The man behind the bar blew a short, sharp whistle between his teeth. The men fell silent and one by one faded into the shadows as they resumed their seats.

Holding striped skirts aloft to reveal the sheen of heavy black boots, the woman strolled closer, then came to an abrupt halt. Her eyes snapped wide. "My word! You *are* like him." Recovering quickly, she extended her hand as a man would. "I'm Kellyn Quincy. Welcome to the Stormy Gull, Lord Wycliffe."

He hesitated, taken aback at the bold way she offered her hand, as if his rank were of no consequence here. Her eyebrow cocked as her pale eyes assessed him, as an emerging smile good-naturedly mocked him.

He shook the proffered hand. "Miss Quincy."

"Mrs. I'm a widow." She returned his shake with confident pressure.

"I'm sorry. . . ."

"It's been several years now." She dismissed his condolences with a wave of her hand.

"I take it you are the proprietress, Mrs. Quincy?"

"I am. Kellyn will do. Please have a seat." With a toss of her long, loose hair, so rich a shade of auburn it seemed the flames from the lanterns had gone astray, she gestured toward the closest table. "Reese," she called with the ease of someone used to wielding authority, "a bottle of brandy. Our best."

Chad was about to point out that the chairs at the table she'd indicated were taken when the patrons practically tripped over one another in their haste to vacate their seats.

"Impressive," he couldn't help commenting.

She raised a half-bared shoulder. "It helps to be the only source of good ale and decent grub for miles."

Was it merely the food that sent them scrambling to obey? Or a lingering fear that Chad was, in fact, his father's ghost returned to haunt them?

Or more likely their compliance stemmed from a shared infatuation with a woman whose sheer brazenness held an enticing allure.

Chad couldn't deny it. Under normal circumstances he would have considered Kellyn Quincy an agreeable challenge, and not for her physical attributes alone. He hadn't needed more than a few seconds in her presence to recognize a tough mettle and a fiery spirit. Ordinarily he might have pursued such a woman for the pure sport of it.

Now the very idea aroused nothing but thoughts of Sophie, and as he mentally compared the two women he found himself far preferring earnest gray eyes to frosty blue, rich brown hair to garish red, and a trim, petite figure to the curvaceous one all but spilling from the neckline of her chemise.

He shook thoughts of Sophie away, and with them his fears and regrets concerning her. As long as she stayed out of his life, she'd be safe.

From across the table Kellyn rested her chin in her hand and studied him unabashedly. "You're the mirror image of your father, exactly as he might have been twenty or so years ago."

"Did you know him well?"

"After a fashion, yes." She smiled as if at a memory. "I came to Penhollow and purchased the Gull only some three years ago, but your father was a faithful customer. One who never shrank from bumping elbows with farmers and fishermen."

Reese, the barkeep, set two hammered pewter cups and a bottle on the table, then treated Chad to a look of lingering mistrust before shuffling away.

Kellyn poured out measures of deep russet brandy and held hers aloft. "To the late Lord Wycliffe."

Chad tapped his cup to hers, feeling a sudden and surprising affinity for the woman. He drew courage from the fiery liquor and asked, "Did my father tell you much about his life? Away from Penhollow, I mean. About the family, perhaps?"

"I'll admit owning the local tavern often places me on a par with a priest in the confessional." She flashed a cunning smile, but not an unkind one. "Liquor loosens a man's tongue as nothing else can. But like a priest, I never betray a confidence, not even that of a man gone to his grave." Her expression sobered. "I can tell you how proud he was of you, and what high hopes he had for your future."

"Hope devoured by flames," Chad murmured. He raised his cup and swirled the brandy.

"Aye."

"I suppose you know why those flames failed to rouse him from slumber."

His father had been drinking that night. Heavily, from what Chad had been told. Franklin's valet had been the first to smell the fire devouring the library two years ago. While he and the other servants had been able to douse the flames in time to save the house, there had been nothing they could do for Franklin, who had likely suffocated from the smoke before the blaze engulfed his body.

Without drinking, Chad set his brandy back on the table as images from his last visit to Penhollow assaulted him. He could still smell the charred remains, feel the sting of lingering soot in his throat.

Kellyn's expression held sympathy, but no trace of pity. "One of the last things he told me was how much he looked forward to your visiting him that summer."

Chad's heart gave a sickened twist. Why hadn't he come at the time of his father's request?

Because he had still viewed life with a young man's unthinking enthusiasm. With high-spirited impatience and the certainty that he alone ruled his world, his life, his fate. How categorically wrong he had been.

He cleared his throat and leaned back in his chair. "The reason I came in was to arrange for provisions for my stay in Penhollow. Can you help me?"

She smiled her acknowledgment of his brusque change of subject. "Whatever you need."

"The basics. Bear in mind that I have no servants to cook for me."

"No servants? Perhaps I can remedy that. In the meantime you'll want meat, baked goods and tea, yes?"

"Perhaps coffee instead? I loathe tea."

"I believe I have some I can spare."

"Hay and oats for my horse."

"And a cartload of coal and firewood."

"Yes. Can you send over a few bottles of brandy?"

Her mouth pulled as she considered. "We're running low on brandy just now. Prices have gone up. Perhaps when the next shipment arrives. . . ."

He made mental note to leave ample coin to pay for the brandy she'd served him. "Wine, then?"

"You won't need it."

"The hell I won't."

"What I mean," she said with a throaty laugh, "is that your father kept the wine cellar stocked. It should all still be there. The Cornish might be known for smuggling, but out-and-out thieves we are not. Especially when it comes to one of our own."

Her blatant mention of smuggling jarred him. But of course she would be familiar with this particular Cornish tradition. As a tavern owner, she would have benefited, even profited, from the tax-free wine and brandy smuggled in from France, the whiskey from Ireland and the tobacco carried across the ocean from the Americas.

He wondered if she understood the cost attached to such commodities.

"I can arrange the first delivery by tomorrow morning," she said. When he voiced his agreement, she called out the barkeep's name.

Deep creases formed across Reese's shiny forehead as Kellyn explained. "Edgecombe?" His gaze flicked to Chad and narrowed. "Why, in Lucifer's name? Don't ye know the place is haunted?"

A week ago Chad would have laughed at the claim. Now the hair on his arms bristled. He darted a look to Kellyn, expecting—hoping—to see a rueful shrug, a roll of the eyes. As the barkeep sauntered away, she met his gaze and nodded. "That's what folks hereabout believe. That Meg Keating haunts the house, while her husband haunts the seas in a phantom ship off our coast. Have you heard of them?"

"The pirate couple, yes. But no one has ever proven the link between the Keatings and Edgecombe. I tried myself as a boy, but other than an old sword which may or may not have belonged to Lady Margaret, I found no conclusive evidence."

But the sword had gone missing, and he wondered briefly if that fact held any significance in more recent events. Smuggling, ghosts and a missing rapier . . .

two, actually, if one considered the sword that had supposedly belonged to Jack Keating, missing now for centuries.

"People believe their violent ends forced their spirits to roam the earth," Kellyn said, breaking in on his thoughts, "crying out for retribution."

"Retribution? Good God, their deaths were more than deserved, considering the brutal acts they committed." According to the legends he'd heard, the pair hadn't balked at unnecessary cruelty, sometimes even lashing injured sailors together and tossing them into the sea to drown. Jack eventually went down in one of their ships, the *Ebony Rose,* during a skirmish with a naval galleon. That set Lady Meg and the remainder of their band on a murderous quest for revenge, until she was caught and hanged.

"Thus far," he concluded, "I've seen no sign of either of them."

And he hoped it stayed that way, that his conscience conjured no more accusing specters like the one he had imagined on the moor last night. The little apparition had seemed so real. . . .

He regarded the woman sitting opposite him and took a chance that she wouldn't think him daft. "Do you believe in ghosts, Kellyn?"

Again he expected amusement or surprise at the question. Her brows gathered. "I believe such tales reflect the strength of the human spirit, the lasting desire to redress the wrongs experienced in life. That is a powerful force indeed. Not one to be dismissed out of hand."

He pondered that statement. With her bold demeanor and flirtatious appearance, Kellyn embodied what one would expect of a tavern wench. Yet he detected in her a keen intelligence, a quality at odds with her circumstances.

Outside, figures in black hurried past the rain-splattered windows overlooking the road. Remembering the gathering at the church, he said, "I passed a funeral on my way here. A quiet affair, not many mourners. Did you know the deceased?"

Kellyn shook her head. "A mariner, by all appearances. Perhaps off one of the merchant schooners."

"What of the rest of the crew? The ship itself?" As he asked his questions, his gaze traveled the room—and locked with that of the man who had sat staring at him earlier. By all appearances he seemed no different from the other men here, with his plaid wool shirt and whiskered chin. But there was something. . . .

Several seconds passed as Chad took in lined features, a nose that curved with a slight hook, and colorless lips that held a disquieting air of speculation. Something in his posture, his movements, even the way he wore his clothes—as if he weren't quite comfortable in them—hinted at a measure of refinement that was lacking in the other men.

Or was Chad imagining it?

Finally he looked away, filled with a conviction that the individual had been studying him for some time. Irrational suspicion, or an instinct he should heed? He ventured another glance, in time to see the man's dark, close-set eyes flick in another direction.

He returned his attention to Kellyn and the matter of the deceased mariner. "Were there no clues as to his origin?"

"No." She sipped her brandy and avoided his gaze. "Situated as we are so close to the tip of the peninsula, we see a good deal of wreckage washed in by storms. And"—she lowered her voice—"bodies as well. It's a fact of life here, I'm afraid. We do what we can. If we can identify them, we attempt to contact their kin. If not, we provide a burial. A pauper's grave, but it's the best we can do."

The brandy soured in his stomach. "You speak of storms," he said. "Could something more sinister be at fault?"

He glanced again at the man in the corner, who this time did not return his gaze but sat fingering the brim of the tweed cap that lay on the table before him.

"You wouldn't be the first to ask that question," Kellyn said in an undertone that had him leaning across the table to make out the words. "But it is a question I cannot answer."

He studied her for a long moment and decided to follow his gut in trusting her. "Have you ever noticed changes in the harbor lights?"

She shot two quick glances to the right and left. "Why do you ask?"

However much affinity he might feel toward this woman, he thought better of mentioning Sophie's name. "Something I thought I saw last night. The quay seemed dark, and I thought I detected the glow of torches not far from my property."

"The Irishman."

"Who?"

"Grady. A sailor from Kinsale, on the southern Irish coast. Some say he's mad, given to skulking up and down the coast at night in his sailboat, venturing into areas other mariners avoid at all cost."

"What's he up to?"

"Claims the fish that come in to feed at night practically jump into his nets."

"You sound skeptical."

"I don't know. Some think he's searching for something. Others say they've heard him ranting about mermaids and mystical sea creatures." She ran a forefinger along the rim of her cup. "You needn't worry about him. He's harmless. But it was likely his boat lanterns you saw. Unless, of course, it was after midnight. Grady's always back in port well before midnight."

In truth, Chad didn't know what time Sophie had seen those lights. The odd actions of an addled Irish mariner might well explain things . . . unless that mariner had been seeking something other than fish and mermaids.

Chad thanked Kellyn for her hospitality and got to his feet. He glanced at the corner table. The man and his tweed cap were gone.

Chapter 6

The tabby screeched and darted in a blur of orange fur out of Sophie's hurried path as she circled the feed shed. She kept going, hoping to slip into her aunt's house without encountering any of the family.

Would they ask her where she'd been all morning?

A golden hen flapped its wings and clucked angrily as she passed the henhouse door. Her attention dwelled elsewhere, on features chiseled to perfection, on a pair of cognac-colored eyes. Eyes that held inscrutable secrets in their depths and allowed her only brief glimpses of the man within.

He had seemed to believe her about Henry Winthrop, that Sir Henry and his wife could be capable of fraud, and that the man would sacrifice Sophie's reputation to save himself. No one else had been willing to accept her side of what happened. Or if they had suspected the truth, as Sophie believed her mother did, they still blamed Sophie for involving herself in what was none of her business.

Even now, bitterness rose inside her at that thought. If widows and orphans were being cheated out of a better life, wasn't it every decent human being's business?

She had hoped, for the briefest instant, that she had discovered an ally in the Earl of Wycliffe, but in choosing not to help her he had proved as harsh and inhospitable as the landscape to which her family had banished her.

As she came around the vegetable garden, words hissing through the open kitchen windows stopped her short.

". . . shouldn't have let her come." Her uncle's voice.

"What else could I have done?" her aunt replied. "Obviously they'd packed her off before my sister's letter even arrived."

"Could've sent the shameless hussy straight back, rather than letting the old man's coach pull away without her. Now she's our problem."

"Don't be calling her names. And it isn't as though they didn't send quite a lot of money to help with her upkeep."

Sophie winced at a sudden thud, like a fist hitting a table. "I'm no tenant farmer in need of handouts. I own my land and I can damn well feed my family and a host of guests besides."

"Oh, there's no pleasing you," Aunt Louisa scolded. "And anyway, sending the poor lamb back would have been too great an affront to my sister."

"God's teeth. We don't answer to your family, Lou."

"Well, and after all, it's not *my* family we need worry about," Aunt Louisa returned. "It's those St. Clair relatives of hers."

"High-flown busybodies." Uncle Barnaby gave a snort. "And this one's the worst of the lot."

"No, she isn't, Barn. You'd be foolish to think it. It's to that grandfather of hers we must pay heed. He's the one to fear. His newspaper and his fortune have made him a powerful man. But let it be. The girl shall be gone in a few weeks."

"She can cut a fair scrap of trouble in that time."

Sophie's indignation mounted like a boiling tide. How she wished to push her way into the kitchen, let them know she had heard every bit of their spitefulness, then pack her bags and leave without another word.

If only she had somewhere else to go.

"Don't worry," Aunt Louisa soothed. "I'll keep a sharper eye on her from now on. It's unlikely that while she's here you'll be called upon again to—"

"What the devil do you think you're doing?"

With a gasp, Sophie whirled to discover her cousin Dominic looming a few steps away.

"Oh!" She pressed a hand to her bosom. "You startled me. I'm merely returning from my walk."

"You're eavesdropping. Don't deny it."

"Very well," she said with a shrug. "I won't. But am I so terribly in the wrong when the conversation is clearly about me? Besides, I thought it more prudent to remain outside until the discussion reached its conclusion, rather than embarrass your parents by letting them know how much I'd heard."

"Think you're clever, don't you?" His long stride toward her made her flinch and want to pull back, though she held her ground. At twenty years old, Dominic was tall, broad shouldered, a younger copy of his father in both his endless scowls and his quelling rudeness. "Think you're better than we are, don't you?"

"I don't think any such thing." Still, she couldn't help the downward sweep of her gaze. He had been tending cattle and sheep, and his clothing showed it. Though prosperous farmers, the Gordons were nowhere near as wealthy as the St. Clairs. The lifestyles of the two families could not have been more dissimilar, but in Sophie's mind that didn't make one better than the other.

She glanced back up at his face in time to catch not only an expression of outrage but also, much briefer, a flicker of humiliation sparked by her perusal of his clothing.

If his attire, his way of life, even his family caused Dominic shame, what fault of hers? She would not be bullied; nor would she suffer anyone to put words in her mouth.

She stretched herself taller. "If anyone sees himself as better than others it's you, Dominic. You've been looking down your nose at me since I arrived. And while I fail to understand your aversion to me, let me assure you I shan't lose sleep over it."

Heart beating in her throat, she pushed her way through the kitchen door. Beneath the table Heyworth, a bearded collie too old and blind now to be entrusted with the Gordons' sheep, emitted a soft whine and thumped his tail in greeting. Aunt Louisa stood before the stove, sliding hunks of mutton from a cutting board into a stockpot. At the work counter Rachel plucked feathers from a beheaded chicken. Sophie averted her gaze. In her experience meat was something that arrived at the dinner table on decorative platters and covered in savory sauce.

"Sophie." Aunt Louisa turned, using her forearm to sweep strands of hair from her perspiring brow. "I didn't know you were back."

"Only just, Aunt."

Rachel continued plucking and dropping the feathers into a bucket at her feet and absently humming a tune. Sophie hadn't been aware of the girl's presence during her father's tirade. Did her younger cousin agree with him? She hoped not.

Of Uncle Barnaby she neither saw nor heard any sign. He must have exited through the front rooms while she had been occupied with Dominic. She wondered if he and Aunt Louisa had reached any useful conclusion concerning her, if they had agreed upon a satisfactory course of action to forestall the trouble she was likely to cause.

"Where ever do you wander to, child?" Aunt Louisa washed her hands under the water pump before taking a seat at the table.

"The village, mostly. I've been studying the architecture of the homes and buildings in the area."

Her aunt picked up a new knife and chopped at a milky white onion. "Can't imagine a young thing like you working up much enthusiasm for rough stone and graying timbers." She traded a look with Rachel.

Did Sophie detect more than idle curiosity in Aunt Louisa's voice? Would she find herself having to dodge her cousins, sent to spy on her activities?

Let them try. She was not the only member of this household harboring secrets. Uncle Barnaby wasn't simply irked at the intrusion of a stranger into his private life. Both his and Aunt Louisa's words indicated something more.

It's unlikely that while she's here you'll be called upon again to . . .

To what? Could it have anything to do with last night, and the altered harbor lights both Aunt Louisa and Uncle Barnaby had refused to acknowledge? Perhaps she misread their meaning entirely, but Sophie couldn't shake a nagging suspicion.

With a sigh she opened a cupboard and plucked an apron from the top of the pile. "What may I do to help, Aunt Louisa?"

"Here, dear." She pushed a colander across the table. "Shuck the peas, if you would."

Sophie dragged an empty bowl closer and picked up the first of what seemed an endless number of pods.

Images of rugged strength and aristocratic elegance filled her mind. The Earl of Wycliffe could at once calm her fears and raise her ire, treat her with the greatest respect while somehow awakening her most unladylike sensibilities. The notion alarmed her. *He* alarmed her, or rather, her untenable reaction to him did. She had been sent to Cornwall to escape an undeserved scandal, yet here she was, courting true scandal by entertaining the notion that the earl had wanted to kiss her . . . that she would have let him. . . .

"Oops! Sorry, Aunt Louisa." She bent to retrieve the peas rolling across the floor. If she ever wished to be restored in her family's good graces, it would be in her best interest to stay well away from the Earl of Wycliffe. But he *had* given her an idea. "Aunt Louisa, may I borrow the dinghy this afternoon?"

"Whatever for?"

"It would make for an enjoyable outing." And a good look at the shoreline between here and Edgecombe. Lord Wycliffe was right: closer inspection of the coast might disclose any number of revelations secreted at the base of the bluffs.

"It's going to storm today. Can you not smell it in the air?"

"Tomorrow then."

"It's too dangerous." Aunt Louisa brought her knife down with a thwack that made Sophie blink and Rachel flinch. "You don't know our currents, Sophie. The tide has conquered far stouter sailors than you'll ever be."

"But to have come all this way and miss out on viewing the coastline from the water's edge . . ."

"Well, I suppose if you have your heart set on it . . ."

Sophie experienced a burst of hope until Aunt Louisa continued, "Have Dominic take you."

After trying nearly every key he'd found hanging from the hooks in the former butler's office, Chad finally managed to unlock the boat chain and remove it from around Edgecombe's front gates. Just beyond them the provisions he had ordered the day before were waiting. Of Reese he saw no sign. Nor of anyone else, for that matter; the road was deserted.

He carried in the crates and sacks and took them down to the frigid storage vaults beneath the kitchen. Kellyn had been correct about the wine. One of those vaults served as a wine cellar, its walls lined with shelves holding a variety of his father's favorite vintages from France, Spain and Italy.

Cradling a Bordeaux in his palm, he couldn't help wondering if this or any of the others had been acquired through smuggling. But no, even with his finances diminishing, Franklin Rutherford would never have resorted to illegal means to maintain his lifestyle.

With the sun rising over the moors, Chad set off for the village on Prince. The crisp, almost eye-stinging clarity of the air this morning would suit his objectives perfectly. He stabled Prince behind the Stormy Gull, paid Kellyn for the supplies and made a brief inquiry.

Armed with the information he needed, he trudged down the muddy lane to the quay, where a bracing sea breeze swept his open coat out behind him and filled his mouth with the taste of brine. The salty atmosphere thickened as he approached the piers. Inexplicable knots formed in his stomach.

He'd never feared water, neither while swimming nor boating, which he had enjoyed since his earliest years at the family seat of Grandview, situated on the gentler coast of the eastern Lizard Peninsula. Penhollow's waters were far from mild, but that didn't explain the tension presently mounting inside him like a weed-choked tide.

Upon reaching the first pier, he understood. A mucky, debris-laden swell lapped at the pilings, giving off a pungent stench. Rancid seawater. Briny decay. The odor triggered an image, a flash of horror.

The little apparition on Blackheath Moor.

He scrubbed a hand across his face and shut his eyes to block out the blinding glitter of the sun. An inner voice insisted that once again his imagination, and not angry spirits, dogged him.

He gave his head a hard shake and continued past the few schooners and sloops that had not yet set sail for the day. At the farthest slip a single-sailed vessel some dozen feet long bobbed up and down, tugging at its lines. Onboard a stocky fellow busily made adjustments to the rigging. A shoulder-length mane of red hair and a beard that reached his chest identified him as the sailor Chad sought.

"Aye, I'm Grady." The Irishman's hands went still

over the rigging as he regarded Chad with a squint.
"And who might be wantin' to know?"

"I'm Lord Wycliffe, and I'd like to hire your ser-
vices for the morning." He held out a handful of coins.

The man leaned over the gunwale and peered at
the offered payment. A grin revealed darkened gaps
where his front teeth should have been. "Come
aboard, mate. Grady's your man."

According to Kellyn, the folk of Penhollow considered the Irishman to be bordering on madness. But
she had also told Chad that no other sailor would
likely take him where he wished to go. Only Grady
would brave the currents close to the cliffs near Edgecombe, having done so countless times in the past
without mishap. The luck of the Irish, perhaps.

The mariner rowed out past the moorings and into
the channel before hauling in the oars and hoisting
the sail. The wind filled it and the boat shot forward,
slicing like an arrow through the waves. They rode
the wind currents south, toward Edgecombe. From his
coat pocket Chad drew a wooden spyglass edged in
brass.

"Lookin' for mermaids?" Seated at the stern of the
boat, Grady offered another gap-toothed smile that
made Chad reconsider the wisdom of having placed
his welfare in the man's hands. "You won't find any.
Not by day."

"I wish to learn whether it might be possible to
anchor a boat near my estate." He knew his excuse for
today's excursion would sound preposterous to anyone
familiar with these waters, but better to appear foolish
than to admit he was searching for proof of misplaced
harbor lights and approaching ships at midnight. At
least until he knew for certain whom he could trust.

"I can tell ye the answer to that one, mate. Plain
and simple, no."

"I'd like to see for myself, if you wouldn't mind."
Judging by the size of this craft, Chad simply didn't
believe Sophie would have mistaken its night lanterns

for the glow of shore lights. And even if it had been Grady out prowling the coast, it still didn't explain why the quay had gone temporarily dark, if indeed it had.

She didn't seem the sort of woman to imagine things or to make up tales. Chad raised the spyglass to his eye and perused the coastline.

"Ye've got one hell of a lot o' pluck, mate, stayin' on at Edgecombe." The mariner raised his voice to be heard above the wind and surf. "Never thought to see the place lived in again after your da passed, God rest 'im." He made a quick sign of the cross.

Chad's stomach clenched. He lowered the spyglass. "You knew my father?"

The Irishman shook his shaggy head. "By reputation only. Came here just after he passed."

Chad studied the other man. "Why do you say I have pluck? Do you believe Edgecombe is haunted too?"

Grady crossed himself again. "As surely as the moon haunts the night sky, mate."

"Why? What have you seen?" He held his breath. If Grady spent his time sailing at night, he might know something about Sophie's harbor lights.

"Only know what I've been told. Voices. Lights in the windows at odd hours of the night." Grady held the rudder and steadied the sail through a snapping gust.

Chad's shoulder blades tingled. He had always considered the tales of Edgecombe's haunting to be laughable, but an earlier suspicion returned. Despite his refusal to put Edgecombe at the smugglers' disposal, could they have been trespassing these past two years and making convenient use of those ghost stories?

"I'm told you're willing to sail right past Edgecombe's cliffs, even at night," Chad said. "If you believe the place to be haunted, why aren't you afraid?"

"Don't ye know anything about ghosts, mate? They

don't just flit about in the wind. They need a place to anchor themselves. Somewhere familiar, a place they frequented in life. Usually a house where they lived."

"Is that right?"

"Aye."

Chad thought of his little ghost . . . and of the nearby chapel to which she had led him. But surely that had been nothing but a dream. He regarded the mariner. "I've heard that some people believe Jack Keating haunts the seas as well. What about that?"

"Aye, it's said the *Ebony Rose* sometimes sails the coast. But only after midnight. See, that's when old Jack's ship went down. I'm careful. I always put in well before midnight."

"Not at all curious to see if the legend is true?"

"I mind my business. That's how a man lives to a ripe old age. If something ain't got to do with ye, ye got no need to be knowin' about it. Wisdom to live by, if ye know what's good for ye."

An offhand observation, or a subtle threat blanketed in amiable words? For an instant Chad had thought he heard the latter, but Grady's sunburned features retained their good-natured indifference as he turned his attention to the rigging.

"Do you believe Edgecombe's ghosts could have had anything to do with my father's death?" Even as he asked the question, Chad hadn't thoroughly realized the turn his thoughts had taken. As he waited for an answer, his heart pounded so violently his shirtfront fluttered. Not once since his father's death had he ever considered the tragedy as anything but an accident.

"Ah, now, mate, it's clear ye truly know nothin' about ghosts. They can't kill a body. Can't raise a pistol or shove a bloke out a window."

"Can't start a fire?" Chad suggested quietly.

"Exactly." Grady aimed a wad of spit over the gunwale. "They can only drive ye to do things by goading. That's why they haunt. They can't do for themselves, so they beleaguer the living till we do their bidding for them."

The boat arced through frothing whitecaps, following the curve of the coast. His mind racing with possibilities, Chad raised the spyglass and resumed watching the passing shoreline. They had just passed a stretch of flat, rocky beach bordered by dunes. The farm belonging to Sophie's relatives lay just beyond.

As they rounded a promontory, he aimed the spyglass farther down the coast, where he detected the narrow inlet above which he and Sophie had stood the night before. Sharp projections of granite thrust up from the water, forbidding entry to even a boat as small as Grady's. At least, that appeared to be the case from this angle. Chad needed to go closer to be sure.

A breaker rocked the boat. His gaze shifted, and what he saw caused the spyglass to tumble from his fingers onto the deck. Craning forward, he gripped the gunwale with both hands. The craft teetered and a wave splashed over the side.

"Bloody hell."

"Aye, have a care, milord. We're in dodgy waters now. Locals call this current the Devil's Twirl. Gets worse the further south ye go. I can't be takin' ye much beyond Edgecombe. Ye'll soon see why."

Chad could already see. He had never experienced waves like these before. Cresting sideways, crosswise, and crashing into one another, they surged from every direction at once and created eddies that spiraled downward with a vicious suction.

But that was not what had forced the oath from his lips.

On the shore about fifty yards away, Sophie picked her way along the water's edge, stepping gingerly across the boulders that formed an uneven ledge at the base of the cliffs. The crashing surf raised a spray taller than a man, sending gleaming foam splattering against the bluffs . . . and Sophie. She shrank against the cliff face beside her, only to push onward when the waves receded.

He swore again, while Grady summed up the situation with a colossal understatement: "She oughtn't to be there. Especially not now, with the tide rollin' in."

"How high will it go?"

"See the watermark on the rock face?"

"Good God." It was well above Sophie's head. "How long?"

"Not long a'tall. Half hour at most. That's the other thing about these waters—"

Chad cupped his hands around his mouth and shouted her name. Her head twisted around and she spotted him, but from that distance he couldn't make out her expression. Had she realized her mistake? To Grady he said, "Turn in. We'll go get her."

"Can't be doing that now, can I?"

Chad glared at the man. "What do you mean, you can't? Turn this damn boat and put in."

Grady made an adjustment to the rigging that drained the wind from the sails. The boat stopped its forward momentum and bobbed like a toy. He pointed toward the shore. "See them rocks? Tear the hull to shreds."

Chad supposed he was right. Between the channel and the cliff countless boulders thrust their jagged forms above the water. He peeled off his suit coat and dropped it to the deck. Next he shoved out of his boots.

"Wait here. I'll swim in and get her." He hoisted a leg over the gunwale, rolling into the water as carefully as he could to avoid tipping the little boat. A million icy needles pierced his skin, but he had swum in colder water as a boy. His feet didn't reach the bottom, and as he gripped the side of the boat with one hand, a wave lapped at his face.

Grady leaned out over him. "You'll never get the lass back here. Not unless you strip her naked and knock her out so she don't panic and thrash about. Even then, the current's too strong and the tide's pushing landward, straight into the cliffs. If that don't get ye, the Devil's Twirl will suck ye under."

Chad could feel the truth of those words tugging him downward and toward the rocks at the same time. For an instant he questioned his ability to dodge the saw-toothed rocks standing between him and Sophie.

He had no choice. If he didn't reach her and get her off that ledge, the waves would either batter her body against the rocks or drag her out to sea.

He pushed away from the sailboat and kicked his feet for all he was worth. Water filled his ears as he dove under, blocking out the roar of the surf. The twisting currents plucked and shoved. He pressed on, heaving his shoulders into each stroke. He opened his eyes, grateful for the crystal clarity of the water that would allow him to see the boulders before he slammed into them.

Where he could, he used the rocks for leverage to haul himself forward. Once, he lost his grip and was caught in a vicious undertow that sent him reeling. His back struck stone with punishing force. Disoriented, his breath about to burst, he searched wildly for the brightness of the sky through the water. On about his third or fourth twist he found it and kicked hard, breaking the surface and sputtering for air. Filling his lungs, he pinpointed the shore again. Where was Sophie?

Still pressed tight against the cliff face. The wind whipped her hair across her face and plastered her skirts behind her. She stumbled, and he knew a moment's panic before she righted herself.

He surged forward. His shoulders were burning, his arms shaking with cold and exertion. The currents shoved him into another rock, the force of the water sliding him lengthwise against it. A biting sting along his ribs told him that not only had his shirt torn, but his skin as well. Salt seeped into the wounds with slicing pain, momentarily sapping his remaining strength. He thought he heard Sophie shout his name. Then a wave smashed into him and his head went under.

The slap of hard ground beneath his feet renewed his stamina, his hope of making it. Bracing against the seabed, he broke the surface and stood up tall. The water reached his neck. He moved forward in long strides, using his arms to thrust forward against the swell. Behind him Grady shouted encouragement. Sophie's cries wafted from the shore.

"Go back. Please, I didn't mean for you . . ."

He blocked out the rest, intent only on reaching her. The water swirled around her feet now. The pelting waves splashed higher and higher. Her skirts would soon be soaked through.

He was close. Just a dozen or so yards, though they were perhaps the most dangerous of all. Wave after wave crested over him, and once more chaotic peaks of foam shoved him off balance. He lost his footing, toppled backward, his legs tangling in weeds. Submerged, he sealed his mouth tight and opened his eyes. A face stared at him through the water.

He all but drowned in the terror of believing she had fallen in, that he was too late. His horror twisted on end as he recognized the face, glowing fish-belly white except for those vacant, staring eyes and a raw wound gaping across the brow. A claw of a hand reached for him, and a voice echoed through the water.

Live . . .

The shock of it sent water sliding down his throat. He choked and sputtered as his lungs seized. Then his collar cinched tight around his neck as if someone were gripping him by the back of his shirt. He felt his body being hauled upward until his face broke free of the water.

Chapter 7

Her own fears forgotten, Sophie pressed her balled fists to her mouth as she watched the Earl of Wycliffe flounder in the waves. He had been coming to help her, and now it was he who needed rescuing. If he drowned it would be her fault.

His arms and legs flailed beneath the water, sometimes breaking the surface with bursts of foam. He grappled as though fighting an invisible foe, and then simply heaved himself into shallower water. Sophie couldn't fathom how it happened. He seemed propelled by the ocean itself.

She strained forward from the cliff face, willing his sodden lungs to expel the water as he clung with both hands to the side of a rock. Coughing, he tipped his head back and opened his mouth wide for what appeared to be a painful, life-giving gulp of air.

Relief sent her sagging against the wall behind her. A sob of laughter escaped her as the earl pulled himself upright, steadied his feet beneath him and raised a hand in the air.

"Hang on, Sophie! I'm coming!"

When he reached her she crouched, grabbed him beneath the shoulders and tugged as he climbed up beside her. Doubling over, his shoulder pressed to the cliff face, he stood shivering and panting to catch his breath.

She seized his hand and held it against her cheek.

"I'm sorry. This was so stupid of me. You must be furious."

A single word slipped through his chattering teeth. "Yes."

A hooting cheer rolled across the water. Sophie peered out at the sailboat that had brought the earl here. The boatman waved and she waved back.

"Your friend appears wildly relieved."

"He shouldn't be." The earl straightened. His shoulders fell to their full breadth, giving Sophie the giddy impression of yet another cliff face, tall and rugged and powerful. She felt rescued. She felt safe. Until he spoke again.

"We're both trapped now. As that mariner predicted, there is no way in hell I'll ever be able to swim back to the boat, much less bring you with me."

"We'll return the way I came." She turned in that direction and immediately comprehended the impossibility of the suggestion. The rocks were already submerged, the cliff face gleaming and slick. "The other way, then."

But that proved no better. A wave slapped their ankles. Her skirts were sodden from the knees down, already heavy and cumbersome.

"What can we do?" She shoved strands of hair out of her eyes and prayed the earl had an answer.

"Up."

"What?" Perhaps she hadn't heard him correctly. He was still shivering, panting, gasping past the water he had so recently swallowed.

He raised their clasped hands—she hadn't realized she was still holding on to him—and gestured up at the bluffs. "We'll have to climb. There's no other way."

Alarm bells clanged inside her. Had nearly drowning addled his wits, made him hallucinate ladders where there were none to be found? "It's straight up. We'll fall to our deaths."

"No, we won't. It isn't straight up. There's enough of an incline and plenty of hand- and footholds. Trust me, Sophie. I've done this sort of thing before. Many times. We can do this."

"No. Oh, no, no, no. I've never . . . I couldn't—"

He dropped her hand and just as quickly seized her shoulders, tugging her close until her face was mere inches beneath his. "Listen to me. We have no choice. The boat can't get to us and we can't get to it. Within minutes now the tide will devour this ledge and we'll be swept away. We'll both drown, Sophie, unless we climb to safety."

"I . . . oh . . . all right." Her own teeth were clacking now. She looked up again. Up and up and up.

"I'll be right beside you, showing you exactly what to do." He flattened his hands against the rock, preparing to begin the climb.

Sophie gasped. "You're bleeding."

Blood was oozing down his side, soaking into his already sopping shirt. He brought his arms down, tugged his shirt from the waistband of his breeches and pulled it into view. "Looks worse than it is. Just scrapes, really."

"Oh, but your forehead." That too had begun to bleed, the drops trickling down his temple and onto his cheek. He pressed his shirt cuff to the spot, examining the bright red stains with little apparent concern.

"You can't possibly make the climb," she said. "If you lose too much blood you could pass out. You could . . . could *fall* and then—"

"Sophie." He held her face between his hands. His palms were cold and wet, but even so a steadying influence. She stopped babbling and stared into his rich velvet eyes. "I am not badly injured," he said. "I will not pass out, and neither of us, I promise you, will fall. Now then." He regarded her with a faint frown. "You'll need to take this off."

"My dress?"

"It's soaked. It'll weigh you down."

"I couldn't possibly. Why, that man is still watching from his boat."

Lord Wycliffe spun her about. Before she could react, he gripped her bodice and yanked. The top button popped free, then the next two, and then all the rest in a torrent, pattering around her feet and into the water. She sputtered protests, all ignored as he peeled the sleeves from her arms and tugged the dress down over her hips. Compounding her chagrin, she thought she heard, "Bloody good idea, mate," shouted from across the water.

The yards of green muslin puddled onto the wet rocks, leaving her little option but to kick her legs free. A wave swept the ledge. The water surged to their knees, prompting the earl to pin her with a steel-like forearm to the bluff. When the water receded, her dress coursed with it, blending with the vivid blue-greens of the sea.

"We haven't much time." His gaze swept her. "Tuck your petticoat up into your corset a bit so your feet don't get tangled."

Burning crimson, she did as he said, thankful when he turned to view the cliff face rather than watch. Hugging her newly bared arms around her, she saw him reach over his head and wedge his fingers into grooves in the rock. He then lifted a foot to a small ridge, balanced with his toes and stepped up. "Like this. Slow and steady all the way up. You try it."

Doing her best to ignore the fact that she wore nothing but her chemise, corset and tucked-up petticoat, she tested the cliff surface with her fingertips.

"Oh, and Sophie?"

The somber rumble of his voice made her go still.

"Whatever you do, don't look down. Don't look up either, at least no higher than to find your next handhold."

She gulped and placed the fingers of her right hand into a crack in the stone. She did the same with her other hand before looking down to find her first foot-hold. One step up, then another. Not so bad. With luck she might even make it to the top.

He waited for her to repeat the process once more, raising herself a foot or two higher on the wall before climbing up beside her. "That's all there is to it," he said with a grin. "Just keep at it until we reach the top. So, how about it? You game?"

"You make it sound like a dare, as if I have a choice." Yes, she even detected a twinkle of enjoyment in his eyes.

"It *is* a dare, Sophie. I dare you to do this. I dare you to show me you aren't afraid of a little climb. That you are every bit as capable as I am of tackling this scrap of a challenge. Unless, of course, you truly aren't up to it."

"Excuse me?" She experienced a stab of indignation before realizing his purpose. Yes, of course. The appreciative grin she flashed him quivered a little—she couldn't help that—but she hoped it convinced him, as he had almost convinced her, that she could manage the feat before them.

"Right, then," he said briskly. "Remember, slow and steady. We won't stop again until we reach the top. Ready?"

"Ready." As much as she would ever be, she thought with a grim inner chuckle.

Grip, pull, step, push. Little by little they worked their way up, side by side, the earl waiting for her each inch of the way, though he could easily have proceeded a good deal quicker if he'd wished. Sophie breathed past the gratitude swelling in her chest; she needed all her concentration, all her courage, for the task at hand. Whenever she paused, unsure where to reach next, he was right there guiding her, his voice a gentle but steadfast presence in her ear.

"Yes, there. That's right. Very good. Now here . . ."

Winds gusted off the water and pushed at her back. For the first few yards of the climb she had felt drops of spray splattering her ankles. Now she could hear the waves slapping the bluffs where they had stood. He had been right: to have remained any longer would have meant being swept away.

By now the water must indeed have swallowed the ledge completely, but she never once looked down. Never gave in to the perverse temptation, because Lord Wycliffe had told her not to, and a conviction gripped her, stronger than any she had ever known, that as long as she trusted him and did what he told her, they both would live.

"You're doing just fine, Sophie. Not much farther."

"Child's play," she lied.

Grip, pull, step. It became a rhythm inside her, commanding her limbs when her brain seemed incapable of coherent thought. *Don't think; just climb.*

A screech ripped the fabric of her concentration, and the flashing brightness of a gull's wings flapped at the corner of her eye. Her foot slid out of its notch, sending down a shower of sand. Sophie yelped as she slipped several inches. Scrunching her fingertips into the rock face as tightly as she could, she clung, just barely, while her heart thrashed so violently she thought the force would dislodge her tenuous hold and send her crashing. She attempted to regain her foothold, but her shoe slipped off the rock again. She froze flat to the cliff, the sharp stone biting into her cheek.

Almost instantly the earl's face, strong and confident, was beside hers, so close she could feel the vibration of his voice against her brow. "You're all right. Lift your foot a few inches to the left."

"I can't move."

"Of course you can. You'll find a solid foothold just to the left of where you tried. Do it now, Sophie."

She couldn't. With the wind snapping as if to pluck her free, she couldn't move an inch, not a fraction in any direction. The very thought sent waves of nausea pitching in her stomach, her head. Sky and stone began to spin.

"Sophie." The gentleness gone, he pronounced her name like an order. "Raise your foot and move it to the left. Do it, Sophie. Now."

"I can't . . . I want to, God knows I do, but—"

"Listen to me. Listen to my voice. Don't think about anything but what I'm telling you. You can do this. You've come this far, more than halfway. We can't go down. We must go up. I'm going up and you're coming with me. Now lift your foot and find the foothold. Do it for me, Sophie. I know you can."

"Good thing one of us does," she whispered, and inched her foot to the spot he indicated. The toe of her shoe found purchase.

He gave a soft laugh. "There you are. Now put your hand there, right above mine. And the other one there, do you see?" He gestured with his chin. "Good. No, don't grip the weeds. You don't know if they'll hold. Right, now the other foot . . . and up, yes, that's it."

He literally talked her up, grip by grip, until they had nearly reached the top, where storm erosion had done its job to create more manageable footing with broader slopes and deeper furrows. She resisted the urge to scramble the rest of the way, knowing a single misstep could still send her plummeting. But, oh, she longed for firm ground beneath her more than she'd ever wished for anything; she would have made any bargain for an assurance that she would make no last-minute mistakes.

"Let me go first." Chad's solid thighs came up against her backside as he eased around her, leaving an imprint of heat to penetrate her thin cotton under-pinnings.

He disappeared over the rim of the cliff, and she experienced an instant's panic at being without him, left alone between the distant, snarling water and the garishly bright sky. Then his head and shoulders reappeared. His hand dangled above her. "Catch hold. I'll pull you up."

For this final, dizzying scrap of the journey, her eyes squeezed shut and didn't open until her chin smacked the turf of the headland. Relief poured through her in weakening torrents. She lay flat against the ground, cheek to the grass, arms outstretched as if to embrace the earth and thank it . . . simply thank it for being there beneath her.

"We made it . . . oh, good heavens, we made it. I can't believe we did it . . . that *I* did it." Tears welled in her eyes, rolling off the bridge of her nose and trickling into the grass. She fisted her hands around clumps of weeds, half unable to accept that she was safe. "Thank you, Chad. Thank you. If it weren't for your faith in me, I could never have—"

"It's Chad now, is it?"

Something in his tone, a cold edge she had not heard previously, made her lift her face from the ground. At the sight of him standing over her, she sat up in alarm. His eyes were fierce, fever bright in a face gone deathly pale. His nose was pinched, his lips a thin, grim line. Blood from the cut on his forehead had caked in his eyebrow and was smeared across his cheek. Sophie's gaze dropped to his side, to the scarlet streaks staining his white linen shirt.

"Good heavens, I'm sorry. You're hurt. We had better—"

In a blur of movement he was on his knees before her. He seized her face between shaking hands and shoved his own face close. "Faith in you?" he bellowed. "Do you have any idea how many small deaths I died watching you struggle up that cliff? What the bloody blazes did you think you were doing, strolling along that ledge?"

Before her startled wits could recover sufficiently to form an answer, he crushed his lips to hers in a savage, bruising kiss.

* * *

Sophie St. Clair's mouth tasted of fear and urgency and a passion as riotous as the crashing, foaming ocean below.

But damn it, he hadn't meant to kiss her. Hadn't a clue what he was doing until his lips were on hers and a raging heat filled his mouth, so alternately sweet and fiery he wanted to roll with her across the headland, holding her and kissing her until the sheer exertion of it left them exhausted and shaking and breathless.

On the other hand he wanted to strangle her and make damned certain she never did such a foolhardy thing again.

He tore his mouth from hers and pushed her to arm's length. "How could you have been so reckless? So unthinking? Do you not know the faintest thing about tides, Sophie? They aren't fixed. They move. They change. Did you never once look up at the watermark on those bluffs and realize that ledge would be gone at the high tide? Are you that unbeliev- ably—"

He broke off. His hands had slid to her shoulders, and he realized he was shaking her in emphasis of every shouted word. High color blistered her cheeks. Her eyes were wide and glistening, and her lower lip, crimson with kisses, trembled like the tips of the grass in the wind. The sight of her made his loins sizzle, yet cooled his temper by several degrees.

"Stupid?" came her tremulous whisper. "Is that the word you're searching for?"

"No." He released her and sat back in the grass, ripping out a handful and flinging it to the breeze. He shouldn't have kissed her. It had only made the pros- pect of her death that much more real, that much more horrifying. "I never knew from one moment to the next if you would make it. I only knew I had no choice but to urge you on."

He allowed himself a glimpse of her reddened eyes. Her high, smooth cheeks were mottled by tears and fright. Her small frame shook beneath a scanty layer of cotton. And those lips . . . still bright and swollen from their brief skirmish with his.

He looked away. He didn't want to feel sorry for her. Didn't want to comfort her.

Didn't want to desire her.

No. He wanted to vent his searing anger because of what she had put him through. Not because he had almost drowned. Not even because of the ghastly specter he had seen—*thought* he'd seen—in the waves . . .

No, he wished to rant loud enough to shake this headland because every inch of the way up that cliff his heart had clogged his throat from fear of her falling, of his possibly having to watch her tumble to her death knowing he could do nothing to prevent it. Not a damned, blessed thing . . .

"I'm sorry." She avoided his gaze, contemplating the ground instead. The fingers of one hand smoothed across her lips. "I truly don't know about tides. I grew up in London."

"Even the Thames has tides."

"Yes, but not like this. The sheer speed with which it came . . . I'd never imagined—"

"You haven't answered my question. What the hell were you doing?"

"Aunt Louisa wouldn't let me borrow the dinghy."

"Borrow the *dinghy*?" His anger fired anew. "Of course she wouldn't let you. If the currents didn't send you smashing into the rocks, you'd have been swallowed by the Devil's Twirl, you—" He stopped short of using her own words, of saying, *you stupid, stupid girl.*

"The devil's what?"

He studied her in amazement. Shook his head. Clenched his fists as he tried to tamp his roiling frustration. "Do you never stop to look before you leap?"

Wary defiance sparked in her eyes.

"No wonder," he said very low, very deliberately,

"you came to such ruination in London. You never once stopped to consider the risk of what you were doing."

She recoiled as if he had slapped her. Admittedly part of him regretted the words the moment he'd uttered them. But the part left quaking from their near brush with death couldn't help needing to punish her a little for her blithe disregard for her own welfare.

"I told you I would inspect that coastline," he said to her bowed head and crumpled shoulders. She flinched at his tone, as cold as when he had discovered one of his servants stealing from the collection plate at church. He glared down at her small figure huddled on the grass and knew another moment's regret. His mention of London had opened a painful wound.

Then he pictured that same small frame floating facedown in the water, her skirts billowing with the tide, her dark hair trailing like seaweed.

"I told you I would take a boat out, and I told you that I would do so alone, that the waters were too dangerous for you. What didn't you understand about that, Sophie?"

Raising her eyes without lifting her face, she glowered at him through the spiky wetness of her lashes. "Too dangerous, too complicated, too shocking . . . for a woman."

"What are you going on about?"

"I saw those lights, that ship. I have every right to investigate."

He threw back his head and laughed. "Playing at being a newspaper reporter, are you? Shouldn't you leave that to your dear old grandfather?"

"Don't say it like that. I'm not playing at anything."

"No? Then why these senseless escapades?" He pushed to his feet and offered a hand to help her up. She merely glared at it, then up at him.

"You appeared safe enough in that sailboat," she said, her voice low and slightly shaking. "There would have been little risk in allowing me to accompany you. You speak of danger, but perhaps what you feared was what I might have seen."

Something inside him went still. "What are you implying?"

"What are you hiding?"

The question momentarily robbed him of breath. What made her ask such a thing? What could she have heard about him? Guessed about him? Apparently she could somehow see the guilt he carried inside him, without having the faintest understanding of what it meant.

Oh, he was hiding a great many secrets. Secrets that would turn her blood cold and transform her mildly suspicious gaze into one of fear and hardened loathing.

And yet perhaps fueling her mistrust would help keep her safe.

He extended his hand again. "Come. We had better get you home."

Her mouth pinched, her eyes still holding him in their narrowed gaze, she accepted his help and came to her feet. "You're going to escort me home?" Her tone implied he had taken leave of his senses.

"Yes. We'll have to walk, I'm afraid. I left Prince in the village."

"You're going to take me home," she repeated, "dressed like this?"

His gaze dropped and he took in all he had missed in his anger, in the passion of the kiss, and in his lingering panic at how this day might have ended. Ah, but he saw her now, all of her.

She hugged her arms across the delicate camisole covering her breasts, but not before he glimpsed the dark circles of her nipples beneath. He perused the tiny waist cinched by her corset, the roundness of her hips, the shapely lines of her legs, amply displayed by her damp and clinging petticoat. His insides stirred;

awareness pulsed. She shifted her feet self-consciously and coughed.

"I see what you mean." With difficulty he drew a breath past a constricted throat. "We'll go to Edgecombe. I can at least find you a cloak to put on. It isn't far. We'll keep to the headland and avoid the road. With any luck we won't be seen."

"What of your friend?"

For a moment he didn't know who she meant. Then his gaze lighted on the distant flash of a sail as the Irishman maneuvered his craft back toward the village. "You mean Grady. I paid him rather handsomely this morning. We can only hope it was enough to persuade him to see the sense in holding his tongue. I'll try to head him off later, before he wanders into the Gull."

After that they walked in silence, she in her underthings, he in his stocking feet. He tried to assist her over the rugged terrain, but she would only snatch her hand away, hoist her petticoat and continue on, her gray eyes sparking like thunderheads, her pretty features set and determined.

Her quick steps set her a few yards ahead of him. He watched the twitching of her delectably round backside, certain he detected an eyelet pattern adorning the drawers beneath her petticoat. He studied the vigorous swing of her arms, long like a dancer's, and so slender he wondered how she had mustered the strength to climb.

His eyes were drawn higher, to the inviting curve of her nape and the sweeping line of her backbone dipping into her camisole. He longed to trace his fingers down that line, explore each tender ridge of her spine with his thumbs, her nape with his lips, while burying his nose in her hair.

Such notions crossed a dangerous line. Between his mounting debts, the permanent blotch against his name, and the unknown purpose for which he had been summoned to Penhollow . . . what could he possibly offer a woman like her?

Of all the questions hanging over him, that was the simplest to answer. Nothing. Just being with him posed a risk to her welfare. At some point whoever had ordered him to Penhollow—a member of a murderous gang—would approach him and make demands, the nature of which he could only guess at. He didn't want Sophie anywhere near him when that happened.

When they arrived at Edgecombe he stopped her in the forecourt. "If there is anything to be discovered here in Penhollow, I insist you let me be the one to uncover it."

Her expression became guarded, vaguely defiant, and a sense of urgency rose in him. "I understand your passion for adventure," he said. "It happens to be something we share. But this is more than adventure. The Cornish landscape poses hazards at every turn, most often in the very places one would least expect. Bogs, mist, treacherous tides . . ."

Smugglers. Murderers. Need he speak those words to make her understand? But that would raise questions; she would wonder how he, a nobleman, could know of such things. He resorted, instead, to simple reasoning. "You don't know this country. Can't begin to comprehend it."

"And you do?"

"I grew up in Cornwall, so yes, I understand it a good deal better than you. And you can't but admit that as man I'm better equipped than you to handle the challenges that might arise."

At the indignant curve of her eyebrow, he held up a hand. "As you yourself pointed out yesterday, I am freer to move about this village and ask questions. It only makes sense, then, that you let me. I won't keep anything from you as long as you agree to put your safety first."

She remained silent for a moment, her eyes narrowing. "You wish me to stay safe?"

"By all means, yes."

"You understand my passion for adventure?"

"I do."

Arms folded, she stepped closer. "I am afraid, Lord Wycliffe, that you understand precisely nil. I'll admit I made a near fatal mistake today. You are correct that I do not know this country as well as I might, and this morning I did not respect the land as I should. I failed to take into account the strength of its power, but that is not a mistake I intend to repeat."

She paused, pursed her lips and opened them with a little smacking sound. "You saved my life, and for that I am grateful. I apologize for the risk my behavior posed to your welfare. But it is not your ongoing task to protect me. I am amply burdened with an overprotective father and a domineering grandfather. I need no other males attempting to rule my life. And for your edification, it is not adventure that I've a passion for. It is truth, my lord. *Truth.* A concept you would do well to familiarize yourself with. Now, if you might lend me a cloak, I shall be on my way and inconvenience you no further."

With that she swept past him into the house. Confound the woman. With her pride, her lofty ideals and her stubborn refusal to see his point, she seemed intent on making this situation as difficult as possible. If trying to reason with her wouldn't work, so be it. If she needed frightening, he would comply, though he would loathe himself while doing it.

Her last words echoing in his brain, he shot forward into the dimness of the hall and caught her wrist.

Chapter 8

"Turn around, Sophie, and look at me." His large hand closed around her forearm tightly, insistently. "What the devil did you mean by that accusation?"

Slanting shadows cloaked his brow, his mouth, leaving only his eyes, piercing her with an emotion that frightened her. She wished to yank free of his hold, put distance between them, but what safety would she find in this man's house, this chilly, gloomy Edgecombe, where she had been warned never to go?

"Tell me what you meant about truth," he demanded in a tone that brooked no debate, granted no quarter, "and my need to familiarize myself with the concept."

He had forced those words from her with his condescending notions of safety, with his infuriating arrogance. She had felt justified in speaking them. Now, however . . .

"You all but called me a liar." He leaned over her, his elegant features rearranged into a scowl as black as a gathering storm. "Why?"

His fingers claiming her still, he perused her length, lingering on her state of undress, on the burning, tingling expanse of bosom straining against her camisole as she struggled to breathe air that was suddenly thick and sweltering. A sudden fear squirmed inside her.

Out on the headland he had stolen her breath and shaken her to her very core with his impassioned, punishing kiss. Yes, punishing. He had been furious with her; the pressure of his lips had communicated the magnitude of his anger and left her trembling, confused and not nearly as in control as she would have wished.

And yet . . . in between all his shouting, and beneath the fierceness of the kiss, she glimpsed a very different emotion . . . one she felt fluttering inside herself whenever she beheld his face. But where had that regard gone now? He was like a chameleon, ever changing, his moods ever shifting. As though two entirely different men inhabited the one.

She stood very still, no longer making any attempt to free herself from his grasp. "You lied to me," she said.

"Never."

"Yes. About when you arrived in Penhollow. You said it was the night we met. But you were here before that. I saw you. Here in this very house."

"That's impossible." The sheer bafflement that tightened his features raised a smidgen of doubt.

Doubt she immediately dismissed as the memory of that day returned. "I was in the garden. I saw you looking out at me through the library window."

He released her hand so suddenly that she flinched. His own dropped to his side. "You're wrong about that. Dead wrong. I arrived exactly when I told you I did. And I assure you, even if I had been at Edgecombe sooner, there is no way in hell you would have seen me in the library."

So adamant. Still so angry. Could she have been mistaken?

"Then tell me what you know about the harbor lights and the ship I saw. What does it all mean?"

"I have no answers for you. I was attempting to find some this morning when circumstances forced me to cut my errand short and rescue you. It seems you have a penchant for interrupting me at the most inopportune moments."

He referred, of course, to yesterday morning, when she had surprised him on the cliffs at the base of his gardens. He had been looking for answers then too.

A nagging conviction persisted that he had left something of great significance unsaid. To protect her? Or did other reasons motivate his reticence?

"I'll find you a cloak," he said, "or whatever else may be stored away upstairs." Looking suddenly weary, he moved past her and started up.

She watched him go, then surprised herself by hastening to follow. It was this place. The chill. The damp, slanting shadows and the ghost of his anger shuddering in the air.

"Lord Wycliffe?"

He seemed equally surprised to discover her behind him on the winding stair. He stopped at the half landing and waited. A dusty stained-glass window behind him draped him in a murky rainbow.

"I . . . didn't wish to wait alone," she stammered, realizing how foolish she sounded but not caring.

He regarded her blandly, as if the altercation of moments ago hadn't occurred. "My father always kept a full wardrobe here. My mother visited only occasionally, but perhaps she left a thing or two as well."

Sophie trailed him into a bedchamber appointed with dark furnishings and heavy draperies. Catching a glimpse of herself in a dressing table mirror, she experienced a moment's shock. How scandalized—and how deaf to her explanations—her family would be to see her now, keeping company with a man while in her underpinnings. How deeply they would lament her ever being the proper young woman they wished.

He opened the double doors of a wardrobe. "We might find something for you in here."

The room was dark, the contents of the wardrobe

indiscernible. She went to the window and drew the curtains aside. In the distance beyond the gardens the sea flashed silver in the sunlight. She stared out at it, caught by a singular realization: if not for the earl, for Chad, she would be out there now, drifting on the tide, fodder for the creatures that lived beneath the waves.

She turned back to the room, her attention seized by the tug of his shirt across his shoulders as he closed the wardrobe doors and moved to a dresser. It barely contained him, that shirt, especially now, with the fabric tight and stiff with dried seawater. The linen seemed to have shrunk to his proportions, adhering like a second skin to every line and muscle.

Without warning he turned. A quirk of his eyebrow told her he had caught her staring, though his gaze remained shuttered, indefinable. She blinked and groped for something, anything, to say.

"Was this your father's room?"

"My mother's."

That surprised her. She drifted to the bed, wrapping her hand around one of the thick, carved mahogany posts. There was nothing the least bit feminine about this room. "No wonder your mother rarely came to Edgecombe. It is a man's place through and through, isn't it? I suppose your father must have enjoyed coming here to hunt and enjoy the peacefulness of being alone."

"Wait here while I search the other rooms," he said with a sharp look. Tight-lipped, he disappeared into the hallway. With a sigh she perched against the edge of the bed to wait for him.

The down mattress proved too tempting. In defiance of the dust coating the coverlet, she stretched out. A stack of pillows lay piled at the headboard. She tossed the topmost ones to the floor and laid her cheek upon a relatively clean one beneath. Her limbs trembled with fatigue. Her back ached with it. Her eyelids felt weighted with lead. The climb. The fear. They had taken their toll. Just for a moment she would close her eyes.

When she opened them again, stars winked timidly above her from behind a sheer veil of cloud. Frigid water lapped at her body, tugging like an impatient child at her skirts, her hair. She was drifting in the middle of a vast, black ocean, with no point of reference but the impossibly distant pinpoints of the harbor lights. In a surge of panic she tried to sit up and was swallowed by the swell.

Chad nearly gave up his search after opening an empty wardrobe in the third bedchamber he tried. He hadn't bothered rummaging through his father's former chamber or the one he himself had chosen for his stay. But in the sixth and final room he came upon a small assortment of gowns he felt reasonably certain had never belonged to his mother, or to any other woman of his acquaintance.

As he contemplated the collection of dresses, a vague uneasiness crept through him. His mother had not been as tall as these dresses suggested. Nor did they in any way reflect the styles she had regularly commissioned from her personal modiste.

He rifled through cheap muslins and satins, regarding each with growing resentment. The sensation in his gut now resembled the queasiness often brought on by cheap brandy and stale cigars. He went to the dressing table and scoured the drawers. There wasn't much in them. Ribbons and hairpins. Stockings and garters. A brightly embroidered shawl. A crystal bottle of some earthy, musky scent, nothing his mother would ever have worn.

He kicked the stool back into place and glared into the mirror, breathing heavily, gritting his teeth.

With a favorite hunting hound in tow, Franklin Rutherford used to ride off from Grandview claiming he needed a week or two at Edgecombe to relax, hunt and smoke his pipe without offending his wife. Chad's mother had never complained, had always seen him off with serene smiles and sincere wishes that he enjoy his time away.

As a youth Chad had accompanied his father on many of those respites, but as the years passed his visits here had become less frequent. Chad had felt guilty about that, but had his father been secretly relieved, happy to be able to steal time alone with . . . ?

His mistress. Or whore, judging by those dresses. Chad glared at the wardrobe, then sank onto the edge of the bed and dropped his head in his hands.

Had Marianne Rutherford ever guessed the truth? Or had Franklin remained an honest husband until after his wife had succumbed to fever six years ago? By Christ, Chad prayed it was the latter. To think of his father as the kind of man who would betray his wife pierced him to the core, as did picturing his dignified mother as a woman who would have silently borne it.

But those were answers he would never have. If only he had remained close to his father in those final years and not allowed such an indifferent, if cordial distance to grow between them. Perhaps Franklin would have confided in him.

A harsh truth struck him a sickening blow. He had never truly known his father, neither as a man nor as the friend Franklin might have become. Had Chad only deigned to spend more time with his aging parent, for good or ill, at least he might have understood what drove his father, what motivated and inspired him.

What had prompted him to imbibe so much brandy one night that encroaching flames had failed to wake him?

Like splintering ice, pain crisscrossed Chad's chest, leaving soul-deep fissures. He gripped the bedpost, pulling as though to rip it from the frame. The past could not be changed. Only he could change, become a better man.

His mind filled with thoughts of Sophie, and the pain lifted. Sophie in her corset and petticoat, her rich brown hair blown about her lovely face. Sophie, small and vulnerable and brave. Brave enough to stand up to him. To call him a liar because for some reason she believed it to be so.

He was almost glad she believed it. Most women of his acquaintance concurred with his every opinion, his every wish. Not because they thought so highly of him, but because he was the Earl of Wycliffe, titled, landed and, they assumed, exceedingly wealthy. An excellent catch for the lucky young miss who finally managed to hook him.

He returned to the wardrobe. There may have been one . . . yes, the mossy satin with short puffed sleeves and a pleated skirt. The most decent of the bunch. The color wasn't far off from the one he had cast out to sea, and with luck Sophie's family mightn't notice the difference. He tossed it over his arm.

"I believe I've found something suitable. . . ." He left off as his gaze fell upon the four-poster in the room where he had left her.

She lay on her side, cheek plumped against the pillow. Her eyes were closed, her lips softly parted. Her petticoat had tangled around her knees, revealing shoes and stockings encrusted with salt, ruined, yet somehow unable to detract from the sleekness of her legs, the enticing contour of slender ankles and small feet.

But it was the view higher up that arrested him, that sent his senses reeling. Her breasts had all but spilled from her camisole, the valley between them a deepened, darkened promise of velvet heat, sumptuous heaven.

His lust fired. He went to the bed and stood over her. She was all sweetness and warmth and soft, sensual curves. He could hear her breathing, little sighs catching in her throat in response, perhaps, to a dream.

She was a dream, and he couldn't take his eyes off her. He wanted to place his hands on her, on all of her, wished to strip away his clothing and hers, take her in his arms and forget . . . everything.

She must be exhausted. Of course she was, after fighting her way up that cliff so bravely, only to become the brunt of his ranting anger. Yes, she had endangered them both, but he should have shown more forbearance. He should not have shouted.

Nor, he saw now, should he have grasped her wrist downstairs. Reaching out, he touched a fingertip to the pale pink imprints that had resulted from his boorish behavior. Oh, he hadn't gripped her roughly, had used nothing of the full strength he possessed. She simply was that delicate, her skin that tender.

Perhaps it was those marks, or simply that she slept so peacefully beneath his roof, within his protection, that wrapped itself around his lust, turned it on end and transformed it into overwhelming tenderness.

"Reckless, Sophie," he whispered, "to so let down your guard with me."

His throat tight, he removed her shoes and placed them carefully on the floor. He gazed down at her for a moment longer, allowing his eyes the pleasure he denied his hands—hands that did not deserve her. Then he circled the bed and eased into the overstuffed chair by the window, from where he could watch over her while she slept.

The little girl, no more than six or so, swung Chad's hand back and forth in hers as they walked along the road. She chattered away, giving a tug whenever he lagged to survey the surrounding miles of heather and gorse.

"Come on, come on!" she urged. Her bright auburn hair was parted in the middle, plaited into braids and held with bright blue ribbons that matched her eyes. She grinned up at him and started to skip, forcing him to lengthen his strides. "We'll be late if we don't hurry."

"Late for what?" he asked, wondering where they were going and who she was. And why she seemed to know him, to trust him so completely.

"Oh, you know, silly."

"I don't. Perhaps you'll be good enough to tell me."

She was a pretty child, with a pert slope of a nose and a smattering of freckles that made her eyes glow all the brighter. *"Today is my birthday, of course. We mustn't be late for my party."*

"Where is your party to be held?"

"Oh, you know."

"I don't." As they topped a rise an endless vista fell before them, edged in the distance by the jagged peaks of a granite ridge. *"Is it nearby?"*

"You are *silly. We're almost there."*

"But who are you? Won't you tell me your name?"

"Oh, you shouldn't tease a lady on her birthday." Releasing his hand, she skipped around him. He became a little dizzy as he tried to follow her flouncing movements. She veered off to the side of the road, returning a moment later with a handful of roses. *"For you."*

Gathering the flowers from her outstretched hands, he gazed out onto miles of soft purples and browns and fading golden gorse, but detected no sign of the bloodred blossoms she'd gathered. *"Where on earth did you find roses?"*

"Roses are my favorites." She tipped her small face to his, her gaiety and laughter fading into vacant darkness, hollow despair. *"She shall bury me with roses."*

The odor of brine wafted beneath his nose. He pulled back with a start, heart knocking against his ribs.

"We'll be late," she whispered. *"Too late."* Her gaze rose to a sky that had suddenly lost its brilliance, that growled now with an approaching threat. *"A storm's brewing. Come!"*

She darted away, pink skirts and snowy petticoats swirling madly as she bounded not down the road but across a rock-strewn headland. Chad took off after her,

*shouting for her to stop, pumping his legs in a desperate
attempt to catch up to her, to stop her before . . .*

*He didn't know what. He only knew he must reach
her. Rain began falling, a pelting downpour that
drenched him instantly. The drops splattered in his
eyes. He raised a hand to wipe them away, and when
he looked up again the child was gone.*

*Panic clogged his throat. He pushed on furiously,
skidding to a stop at the edge of the promontory. Where
was she? Had she fallen? Shielding his eyes from the
rain, he searched the thrashing waves, dreading to find
a glimmer of pink in all that churning blackness. A
deathly chill stole over him. His breath frosted before
his lips.*

*Somehow—he didn't know how—he slid down the
bluffs, landing unscathed at the bottom. Waves lashed
at his feet, his ankles, sucking, dragging, reaching to
pull him in. God, where was she?* Where?

*A thin arm rose up from the water. Then another.
Groping, floundering against the surf. Her head pierced
the surface, her lips gaping. She went under again. He
staggered forward into the raging water, surrendering
to its force and letting it haul him out.*

Almost there. So close. Hold on, little one!

*She came up again, and the shock of it racked his
bones. Limp, lifeless, she was sapped of color; her lips
were blue, her dress torn to rags. And her eyes, her
once bright eyes, stared vacantly back at him, filling
him with despair and hopeless remorse.*

*His hands closed around her wasted frame. His
strength draining into the heaving, malevolent sea, he
towed her to shore, spurred by a single resolve: the sea
could not have her. He would not let it. He was shivering, quaking, his grip on her slipping. . . .*

*He pulled her to him. Tears stung and blurred his
vision, blocking out the storm, the waves, everything
but those eyes. Those earnest* gray *eyes . . .*

*No longer the little girl's bright blue eyes. No longer
the little girl at all. The howl of disbelief and rage*

erupted from the deepest part of him, from his core, his soul. It was Sophie in his arms, Sophie he hugged to his chest, Sophie he cried out to, a ferocious wailing that tore through the snarl of the waves and the pummeling thunder of the storm.

Consciousness exploded through Sophie's mind. A shout rang in her ears. She bolted upright, hands gripping her throat. She sputtered for breath, choking, trying to draw air into lungs gone sodden and heavy, as if filled with frozen seawater.

Where was she? What had happened? She trembled all over, grappling with her skirts as she tried to disentangle her legs and make sense of the images even now flashing grotesquely behind her eyes.

Beside her, the mattress dipped beneath the weight of someone climbing onto the bed. A pair of arms closed around her. A familiar solidity pressed against her cheek, and a deep voice rumbled in her ear.

"Sophie? Oh, God. Sophie. You're alive. You're all right."

Desperation lent a frightening intensity to Chad's embrace, to the way he surrounded her with his body and crushed her to him, to the way his lips dragged across her brow, her cheeks, through her hair, endless kisses in a frenzied show of relief. She felt the same desperation as she let him go on holding her, kissing her; as she used all her strength to tighten her arms around him and bury her face against the frantic pulse in his neck.

Like her, he shivered violently, his heart pounding so wildly she could feel its thrash against her breast. But then, her own heart beat so furiously her entire body throbbed with it. She burrowed against him, seeking his warmth, sharing her own.

Like that night in the chapel.

"The most horrific dream . . ." he began.

"Me too," she whispered. "An awful dream. I can't begin to describe . . ."

"You were drowning. . . ."

"You were trying to save me. . . ."

"There was a storm. . . ."

"Fearsome waves . . ." This last they uttered together, and each suddenly realized what the other had been saying. Sitting up, they broke apart and went still.

The fierceness in Chad's eyes belied the gentleness of his touch as his hands smoothed up and down her bare arms. "It isn't possible."

Despite his caresses, goose bumps erupted on her flesh. What they had each been describing . . . he was right. It wasn't possible. And yet . . .

"We had the same dream," she whispered, hands clamping around his forearms.

"How could we have?" A muscle in his cheek ticked as his mind worked it over, even as she groped for some logical explanation. In the end, one didn't exist. There was only the force of the energy crackling between them, the blaze in his eyes and the need that sent her back into his arms.

They closed like steel around her, and the room tipped as he pressed her to the mattress and covered her body with his. His lips burrowed at the edge of her camisole, claiming the exposed tops of her breasts with urgent kisses. Over and over he spoke her name, between smoldering kisses and the fiery stroke of his tongue.

Through billowing relief, desire burgeoned in her, stark and powerful. "You came for me." She held on to him, needing to feel the heated certainty of his body against hers. "You were there, and I knew I was saved. I knew I would live."

"I thought I'd come too late." His whispered confession splintered in his throat. "Too damned late. I tried, but—"

"No. It's over. Just a dream. Nothing but a dream." She raked her fingers through his hair, closing them around a handful and tugging until his head came up and his lips met hers. Flames of longing licked through her, igniting the tips of her nipples and the juncture of her thighs, burning at her core.

"Just a dream," he said. "Thank God." He kissed her and crushed her in his arms with a force that alarmed her; yet his desperate show of relief whispered of the man she had met in the chapel on the moors, the one who had rushed up the aisle to take her in his arms and shield her from the eerie night with its bewitching vapors.

Through petticoats and camisole his hands trailed fire across her skin, and she found herself parting her legs for him as he sought out her most intimate places. His touch felt somehow right, fit perfectly along each quivering inch of skin he explored.

A ribbon came free and her breasts spilled into his waiting hands. She gasped aloud as he swept his palms over them, brushing his thumbs in feather-soft caresses across the nipples. The sweet agony released a torrent of longing, a twisting surge of physical sensation and roiling emotion.

And something more . . . an urgency not only to take, but to share this astounding pleasure, even as they had shared the terror of the dream.

She thrust her hands beneath his shirt, her breath hitching at each startling discovery made by her trembling fingertips: the impossibly hewn lines of his chest; the fascinating pattern of muscles rippling across his back; the tight, stony curve of his buttocks beneath his trousers. Across her body his much larger hands roamed everywhere, her breasts, her thighs, her buttocks, branding her with the fever encompassed in his palms. Desire mounted, became frenzied.

At the line of crisp hair that disappeared into his waistband, she paused. Dare she follow it?

His rumble of consent sent her fingers dipping beneath the fabric. Oh, there *was* nothing soft about this man, nothing but his lips that nipped encouragement across her flesh. He was as solid and as rigid as the

Cornish landscape. But it was his *smoothness* that fascinated her, the velvety hardness of his shaft throbbing in her palm.

A growl vibrated against the breast he was kissing, pleasuring with his tongue. She closed her fingers around him, and his deep groan set off a quickening inside her, a yawning desire that demanded to be filled.

She released him and used both hands to unbutton his trousers. His arousal sprang forward, thudding against her belly. He moved his mouth from her breast to her lips, breathing his desire into her through a deep and insatiable kiss.

Her petticoat became bunched around her waist. His hands were on her, between her thighs, spreading fire through her lacy drawers. One hand slid to cradle her bottom, while the other eased her thighs apart and caressed her through moist fabric. Tendrils of need shot through her, undulating in surging waves but never quite breaking, carrying her along on an uproar of sensation.

"Do you want this, Sophie?"

"I . . ."

Be a nice girl, Sophie. A proper young lady.

She went still. Oh, God, would she never be free of her family's censure? Why now, of all times? They were not here; they didn't—couldn't—understand the circumstances that had led her into Chad's embrace. They had effectively abandoned her, banished her. Why should she let them continue to dictate her life?

She shut her eyes, pulled his head down and kissed him. "Yes. I want you."

"And I you. But open your eyes, Sophie. Look at me." When she obeyed he stared down at her for a long moment, his large hands gone still between her thighs. Slowly the desire written so plainly across his face receded into an expression of regret. "We mustn't. It would be wrong. I would never forgive myself."

Sophie's thumping heart stilled. Had he sensed her inexperience and been seized with a bout of conscience? Or had her eagerness put him off?

Within the tangle of confusion and aching need, the answer formed, plain and simple. Even here, now, with no one to see, she would have been ruined, besmirched. No one else might ever know, but she would know.

She would know how far short she fell of being a proper young lady.

Shame crawled through her, making her want to slink away and die. She covered her breasts with her hands and started to sit up, but he pressed her down, moved her hands away and kissed her, a sweet, redemptive touch of his lips.

"There are other ways . . ." he whispered.

He pressed kisses down her length, starting at her breasts, moving along the ticklish ridges of her rib cage and across the trembling stretch of her belly. With each moist offering she released more and more of her discomfiture and gave herself up to rapture. He reached her inner thighs and kissed each one, nipped them, trailed his tongue over flesh that quivered at his touch. His hands closed over her hips, lifting her to the heat of his mouth.

His lips pulled and suckled the sensitized flesh. The tip of his tongue teased; the length of it scorched with sizzling heat. As it entered her in earnest, liquid fire raced to her core. Letting go, she crested on wave after wave of sheer bliss, surrendering to the shimmying upsurge, higher and higher, until her cries filled the air and her body bucked and shattered like storm-ridden surf against the cliffs.

Several minutes passed before her racing heart calmed and her wild panting ceased; before she once more felt herself to be part of the physical world, rather than a dervish of passion and sensation. He came up beside her, gathered her in his arms and rolled until she lay cradled on top of him. His hands burrowed in her hair and lifted the damp weight off her back. She shivered, pressed closer to him and wondered.

He had brought her to heights of pleasure she had never imagined, yet knowing he had not shared in that pleasure diminished her own, or at least dulled the lingering glow. "Why did you deny yourself?"

His breath stirred her hair. "The truth?"

She nodded.

"I have no damned idea." Tipping his head back against the pillows, he threw an arm across his eyes.

Had he simply lost his desire for her? Needing to know, she slid a hand toward the juncture of his legs. Her fingertips met with stony heat for the briefest instant. Then his free hand closed over hers and drew it aside. "Do not tempt me, Sophie. You've been reckless enough today, tempting the sea."

The admonishment prickled in her ear, and she felt a measure of his warmth recede beneath her. Lifting her head, she gazed up at the hard line of his jaw, the rigid set of his mouth. His hewn forearm continued to shield his eyes—and his thoughts. A strange foreboding came over her, so at odds with the tender passion of moments ago.

She longed to reassure him, to banish his enigmatic mood and see his rare smile return. "I'll be more careful in the future. I shan't go chasing danger again."

"You had best not." Arm sliding from his face, he gripped her shoulders, rolled until her back was pressed against the mattress. He held himself above her.

"Remember this: each time you endanger yourself, you endanger me. Because I intend to be there. Wherever you are, whatever foolishness you devise, I shall be right behind you. Or, if I'm lucky, one step ahead of you."

Lying trapped between his arms, his fisted hands, she stared up into a stranger's eyes and shivered in the fierceness of his promise. A promise that resounded with the discordant tones of a threat. Was it intentional on his part? Was his sternness meant to coax her to safety, or dissuade her from interfering any further in his affairs, and the affairs of Penhollow?

She had thought to tell him about the conversation she had overheard yesterday between her aunt and uncle. Now . . . she thought better of it as insidious suspicions she hadn't quite dismissed reemerged. His refusal to admit his presence here that day she saw him . . . his unpredictable moods . . . his bouts of reticence . . .

She loathed doubting him, loathed believing he might be hiding something.

He eased away from her and sat up. She rose beside him, her breasts exposed by her open camisole, the nipples pink and beaded from the attention he'd shown them. She quickly gathered the ends of the drawstring and pulled the garment closed.

"As I told you," she said quietly, "I thank you for what you did today, but I do not need another—"

He yanked her close, cupped his palm over her breast through the cotton and claimed her mouth with a kiss that stole her breath. "I am *not* your father, Sophie. Or your grandfather. Don't ever be foolish enough to believe it."

Good heavens, no. He had made that more than clear.

Chapter 9

Standing on the headland, Chad watched until Sophie made her way down the road and disappeared into her relatives' farmhouse. He lingered a few moments longer, as if he could possibly see inside and know whether she'd gotten in without mishap, without any of the family confronting her about her long absence this morning or the unfamiliar dress in which she returned.

Not that he could have done anything to improve matters. Showing up there now would only make things worse for her. He only hoped he could find Grady in time to line the sailor's calloused palm with enough additional coin to induce the man not to spread gossip about the lady in her underthings climbing bluffs with the Earl of Wycliffe.

Clucking to Prince, Chad continued along the village road, still shaken by the near disaster of the previous hours. The climb, the dream, but worst of all, how close he'd come to being villain enough to rob Sophie of her innocence. Good God, he had wanted her. Painfully. Selfishly. Had wanted to bury his fears and guilt in sweet, virginal flesh and seek forgiveness in her guileless gray eyes.

Doing so would have rendered him irredeemable, so much worse even than the Henry Winthrops of the world. He knew he had hurt her with the sudden cooling of his passion. In those final moments, nestled in rumpled sheets and her warm scent, he had pretended anger and disapproval to warn her away, both from investigating those damned harbor lights and from him. Better she believe him erratic, a cad.

Better she remained free to walk away from him and look elsewhere for a more deserving man.

Just outside the village he stopped, his progress arrested by a niggling sensation of being watched. The wind had suddenly dropped. The birds had become too quiet. The very landscape seemed tensed, as if waiting. . . .

The latter notion restored a modicum of sense, while a quick look about assured him that no lurking entity, living or otherwise, held him in its sights. Shaking off his apprehensions he continued on, retrieving Prince from the stable yard behind the Stormy Gull, his coat and boots from the bottom of Grady's skiff.

The Irishman assured him he'd spent the remainder of the morning fishing, and hadn't spoken to a soul since. Chad flipped him a sovereign to ensure the man's continued silence, more than willing to part with his little remaining silver for Sophie's sake.

He donned his own boots immediately, glad to exchange them for the toe-pinching pair he had found in his father's dressing room. His next stop brought him to the vicarage at the top of the village road.

Walking Prince along the mossy cobbled drive that led around back, he noted the unusual number of fresh graves dotting the churchyard. Most of them occupied the rear corner, the paupers' section, as Kellyn had said. Yesterday's newest grave had been filled in to form a low mound marked by a plain wooden cross.

Arriving at a small carriage house, Chad dismounted. Within a stone courtyard built off the back of the residence, the man who had presided over the funeral crouched between the neat rows of a garden.

Chad called out a greeting. The vicar glanced up, removed his hat and swiped a shirtsleeve across his brow. "One moment, if you please." With a pair of pruning shears he snipped a handful of drooping, verdant leaves and dropped them into a basket beside his knee. The mingled scents of fresh herbs wafted on the breeze. "My vervain has reached perfect ripeness today," he said. "It must be harvested before the temperature drops."

While Chad waited he studied the little parish compound his father had funded. It consisted of the church, which doubled as a school, and the modest dwelling, both composed of formidable granite block and shielded from the ocean gales by sturdy slate rooftops. These structures would withstand both time and the elements, unlike his father, who had succumbed to both.

The sudden silence of the clippers drew his attention back to the garden. The vicar pushed to his feet, sunlight flashing off a pair of silver spectacles. "Welcome to St. Brendan's. May I help you?"

His gaze meeting Chad's, the man went suddenly still, wide-eyed. His clippers dropped to the ground. Hand clutched to his chest, the vicar took a backward step right onto one of his well-tended herbs. "Franklin . . ."

Several more plants suffered as Chad rushed to his side and gripped a trembling forearm to steady him. "I'm *Chad* Rutherford. Franklin's son."

The vicar's eyes appeared glazed, held Chad as if to stare clear through him. He blinked several times, dragged a breath into his lungs and released it slowly. He shoved a hand through his thinning brown hair. "Forgive me . . . the resemblance is . . ."

"I know. Extraordinary."

"Uncanny."

Chad released his grip. "I'm sorry I startled you. I should have sent word of my arrival."

"No, no, my lord. It is I who am sorry. I had heard you were in Penhollow, was even told you bore a striking resemblance to your father. But . . ." His spectacles had slipped halfway down a short, round-tipped nose that reminded Chad of a ferret's. He pushed them back up and offered a tentative smile. "I never quite imagined this. But do forgive me. I am Tobias Hall, St. Brendan's vicar."

Chad shook the man's hand. "An apt name for a seaside church, St. Brendan's. He is the patron saint of sailors, no?"

"Indeed, my lord."

"And would you say he brings Penhollow's sailors good fortune?"

He had asked the question lightly enough and expected a reply in similar kind, but the vicar frowned. "I'm afraid our saint has shown us but fickle favor in recent years."

Chad gestured toward the paupers' section of the churchyard. "I see you had a funeral yesterday. Any word on the man's identity?"

"Poor soul. No." The man gave his head a little shake. "Will you stay for tea, my lord? I'll send my man out to tend your horse."

Chad made himself at home in the vicar's modest parlor while Hall disappeared into an adjoining room to prepare the refreshments. Chad couldn't help wishing he had encountered the man at the Stormy Gull instead, where they might have indulged in brandy or a pint rather than the one brew he abhorred. He forced a smile as Hall reentered the room and set a tray on the table in front of him.

Chad balanced his cup and saucer on his knee. "You mentioned vervain, Mr. Hall. Are you a physician as well?"

"I did study medicine for a short time at Cambridge, but I discovered my calling in the church instead. Still, with no medical doctor in Penhollow, I often tend the sick and bind wounds when the occasion calls for it."

"Wounds?"

"Farming, fishing . . . people injure themselves rather readily, I'm afraid."

"Saint Brendan's fickle favor?"

"Quite right. My herbs help dull the pain and prevent festering. I grow cooking herbs as well. Parsley, mint, sage. Perhaps you taste the mint in your tea?"

That seemed to demand that Chad venture a sip. Suppressing a sigh, he raised the cup to his lips. A pungent flavor filled his mouth. He forced himself to swallow, conjured an expression of appreciation and changed the subject. "Have you been at the parish long?"

"Some four years now."

"You must have known my father."

"Indeed, my lord. The late Lord Wycliffe often came by for tea and chess in the afternoons. We sometimes hunted together, though I confess he brought down far more fowl than I can boast."

Remorse gave a sharp tug. Franklin had mentioned chess and hunting in his final letter, hoping to entice Chad to visit.

"I only wish I hadn't been away when he died," the vicar said with a sigh. "Sorry too that I wasn't on hand to be of service when you came to retrieve his body."

"You needn't apologize for what you could not have foreseen." Yet how many times a day did Chad berate himself for just that—for not being here when he should have been, for not anticipating the disaster that occurred in his absence?

"If it brings you any comfort, my lord, your father loved this part of the country. His last days were happy ones. Do you . . . ah . . . share his enthusiasm for rural life?"

Something in the man's tone prompted Chad to ask, "Is that your way of asking how long I intend to stay?" When the vicar's fair complexion reddened, Chad smiled to set him at ease. "I haven't yet decided. I suppose until the Keatings drive me out."

Hall didn't return the smile; in fact he looked distinctly uncomfortable. "You've been speaking to some of our locals."

"Yes, and their warnings have set me wondering. My family has owned Edgecombe since I was a boy, and we have always been aware of the Keating legends. But I don't remember this blatant fear of ghosts circulating among the villagers. This seems to have arisen much more recently. Can you enlighten me as to why?"

The vicar stirred his tea, clinking his spoon lightly against the porcelain. "These are tense times here in Penhollow. The funeral you mentioned . . ."

"Kellyn explained about tides bringing in wreckage and bodies."

"Did she tell you how such occurrences have increased lately?"

"No, she didn't mention that. Do you suspect foul play?"

The vicar hesitated, then shook his head. "There's no proof of such. Storms hit year-round. Even in the best weather the currents surrounding the peninsula are fierce. Perhaps we see more mishaps now because there are more people than ever sailing these seas. But the rise in the death toll has frightened our villagers. They want a reason they can point to, something they can then vow to avoid."

"Such as . . . ?"

"The lanterns of a phantom ship sailing the coastline in the dead of night."

The hair on Chad's nape spiked. Sophie's approaching ship lights? But if sailors were dying, it could be no phantom ship attacking them, but a very real, very solid one.

"Mr. Hall," he said, "isn't it possible such stories were concocted for the express purpose of frightening people into minding their own business?"

"Perhaps." Hall avoided Chad's gaze.

He set his teacup on the table and pressed forward. "Let us speak plainly, vicar. I am talking about smuggling. Or more accurately, piracy. Not something that happened three hundred years ago, but right now."

"I won't deny that our sailors and fishermen have been known to slip goods past the customs cutters.

These are poor, hardworking folk, my lord. One can hardly blame them for—"

Chad held up a hand. "I neither blame them nor begrudge them their tax-free brandy. But if such activities have turned violent, that does concern me. Very much."

Hall squinted at him through his wire-rimmed spectacles. "I can't help but wonder why a nobleman such as yourself would wish to involve himself in such unpleasantness."

Chad opened his mouth, then snapped it shut. How could he possibly explain that he didn't *wish* to involve himself; he already *was* involved. He had provided both the funds and the means for smugglers to ply their trade. He'd helped brigands who ran goods past the customs authorities, yes. But had he also helped those who scuttled ships and murdered innocent passengers? How could he explain that his future depended on finding the information that would put those murderers out of business once and for all?

"I feel an obligation toward Penhollow," he said, resorting to a particle of the truth. "And to my father, who made his home here in his last years. If some unpleasantness, as you call it, has attached itself to this village, I intend to uncover it."

"My lord, you venture on dangerous ground." A current of warning resonated beneath Hall's well-mannered tone.

Did the vicar mean to imply that Chad would regret his inquisitiveness? Such an admonition might work on a man with something to lose. As it was, Chad stood to lose much more by not taking action.

"Understand this, Mr. Hall: I do not frighten easily, and I will not be complacent."

A veil seemed to fall away from the vicar's face, revealing a cunning that again reminded Chad of a ferret. "I believe there is something you should see," the man said. "It may prove . . . enlightening."

*　　*　　*

As Sophie closed the front door and turned, a shadow fell across her path.

"Where in the world have you been?" With a frightened look Rachel grabbed her hand and cornered her against the wall of the small foyer.

Her urgency took Sophie aback. Four years her junior, Rachel rarely questioned anyone about anything, much less initiated a confrontation. In fact the girl's gentle nature seemed an anomaly in this family. Even Aunt Louisa, though not nearly as coarse as her husband and son, had lost much of the gentility Sophie remembered.

At present there was nothing genteel or placid in Rachel's demeanor. And that raised Sophie's apprehensions. Had the man in the boat this morning told tales in the village? Tales that had found their way to her relatives' ears?

Unblinking, she met her cousin's gaze. "I walked to the village. And then I—"

"Shh!" Rachel cast a glance over her shoulder into the dusky parlor doorway. "No, you didn't. That's what we all assumed when you were nowhere to be found after breakfast. But Father had errands in the village this morning. He asked after you, and not a soul remembered seeing you. He's in the kitchen now, waiting to speak to you."

Sophie's involuntary step backward brought her shoulders up against the wall. "Simply because no one noticed me doesn't mean I wasn't there."

"Please, Sophie, you mustn't lie. Father is angry enough."

"Why should he be angry? What difference does it make where I go or what I do?"

At the approach of booted footsteps her confidence plummeted.

"The difference, girl, is I'll not have a chit under my roof wandering the countryside like a common strumpet."

She and Rachel both flinched at her uncle's harsh

indictment. He filled the parlor doorway, his black hair and beard an unkempt tangle about his scowling face. "Where were ye this morn?"

Beside her Rachel froze, her features washed pale. Sophie felt a surprising urge to hold out an arm to protect the girl, to shrink with her further into the corner.

Instead she mustered every ounce of false bravado she possessed and squared her slightly trembling shoulders. "With all due respect, Uncle Barnaby, I am no child." Eyes as black as sulfur snapped but she hurried on, altering her story in accordance with Rachel's warning. "However, if you want to know, I strolled the beach as far as I could, then climbed to the headland and circled back here."

"Ye were gone for hours."

She schooled her features carefully. If Uncle Barnaby guessed even a morsel of the truth . . . The memory of Chad's chiseled features, his splendidly carved body and strong hands flooded her, even now, with an astonishing sense of yearning, even if they *had* parted with an awkward, uncomfortable silence hovering between them.

She compressed her lips and again summoned a partial truth. "The countryside is breathtaking. As long as I am here I mean to enjoy it. Besides, I'm working on a piece about Penhollow for my grandfather's newspaper."

Uncle Barnaby made a noise ominously like a growl. A morsel of fear skittered through her. With his hulking frame, nearly feral features and the temper she had witnessed several times since her arrival, she believed he might be capable of anything. Of course, those displays of ire had usually come in short, admittedly harmless bursts typically directed at Dominic for minor annoyances. Still, she had no desire to test her uncle's limits.

He spared a brief glance at his daughter. "Rachel, go."

The girl didn't hesitate in ducking behind him and disappearing into the next room. Uncle Barnaby stepped closer, and Sophie smacked her shoulder blades against the wall in a vain attempt to escape him.

Dust motes danced in the shafts of sunlight streaming through St. Brendan's narrow windows. Chad blinked against the contrasting brightness and shadow until his eyes adjusted.

"I'll just be a moment." The vicar preceded him up the aisle and disappeared through a doorway behind the altar. He returned holding a lighted lantern. He set it on the floor and gripped the pulpit with both hands. Digging in his heels, he pushed against the oak podium.

Chad stepped onto the dais. "What are you doing?"

"My lord," Hall said with a grunt, "if you wouldn't mind stepping aside."

As he did, a grinding sound issued from the floor. The vicar gave a forceful shove and, to Chad's astonishment, the entire pulpit slid sideways. Within moments he saw that the base had been built upon two wooden tracks fitted with grooves on either side of an opening in the floor.

"What the devil?"

Hall retrieved the lantern. Crouching, he dangled it over the hole. "Have a look, my lord."

Chad hunkered down, peering to make out a wooden stepladder that disappeared into shadow. The vicar lowered his lantern, and a natural bedrock floor some ten feet down came into view.

"A tunnel?"

"Yes, and a storeroom."

"With access to the harbor?"

"Of course."

"Beneath the church?" The question required no reply. This revelation changed everything about Chad's perspective on Penhollow. It meant no one was above suspicion, no one ignorant of the truth. Not the local cleric. Not even . . . Franklin Rutherford, whose money had built this church.

Chad lowered himself to the floor and swung his legs into the opening. "My father knew of this?"

The vicar nodded. "But you mustn't think ill of him, my lord. While he might not have approved of this entirely, he understood the often dire needs of these villagers. He simply turned a blind, benevolent eye."

"And what of you? Does fair trading have your blessing?"

"My church has expenses, repairs the parish funding cannot cover, not to mention poor families who rely on St. Brendan's largesse." The defensive gleam faded from the vicar's eyes. "But that is not the point I wished to make in bringing you here."

"I don't understand."

Hall gestured to the vault. "See for yourself."

Puzzled, Chad gripped the ladder and climbed down. A salt-tinged draft fluttered his sleeves and cooled the perspiration that had gathered across his brow. Opposite the ladder murky blackness filled a narrow opening framed in timber beams. A tunnel angled out of view, he presumed toward the harbor.

The vault itself lay empty. No crates, casks, not so much as a crumb to be found. Chad climbed back up to the dais. "There's nothing to learn from an empty storeroom," he said.

"Isn't there? I should think its very lack of stores would speak volumes."

"Do not talk in riddles, Mr. Hall."

"My lord, since time out of memory, unfair taxes have been levied against the people most unable to pay them, and impoverished families learned clever ways to stave off hunger through unlawful means. Without those means many would not last through a single winter." The man removed his spectacles, peered at them in the light, polished the lenses against his sleeve and set them on his nose again.

Chad's impatience neared its limit. "Your meaning, sir."

"Despite this village's desperate needs, our people are forced to pay full price, taxes and all, or go without. Virtually all smuggling has stopped. Our sailors no longer bring in illicit goods."

"Why would that be?"

"Because in recent years nearly every ship that has attempted to run goods into Penhollow has either disappeared or washed up—in pieces."

Chad felt the blood drain from his face. "The authorities?"

"No, my lord. Most definitely not the authorities."

"Then . . . who?"

Hall tipped his head. "According to these villagers, the Keatings' *Ebony Rose*."

Chapter 10

"It's just you and me now, lass. You had best listen, and listen good."

Sophie flinched as Uncle Barnaby's finger jabbed at the air near her face. Cliff climbing suddenly didn't seem quite so dangerous. If she could only wish herself back to the headland. Or better yet, to Edgecombe, and into the sheltering strength of Chad's arms.

But then she remembered how those arms had trapped her fast against the mattress while his censure had rained down on her. His warning that she stay out of danger had carried sure notes of anger. Her lips still bore the sting of that reprimand; beneath her bodice her breast burned with the imprint of his demand.

More than ever she felt alone, cut off from all that was familiar and comforting and . . . safe.

"I won't be made out a fool," her uncle was saying, "nor have folk prattling that Barnaby Gordon can't control his own family." His hovering hand fell away, only to become a fist that tapped against his thigh. "What would that high-flown grandfather of yours have to say if he learned of your ramblings?"

Oh, Sophie knew exactly what Grandfather—and her parents—would say about her recent escapades. Her gaze dropped to the floor.

"Then from now on, my pet, ye'll abide by my rules.

Ye'll be where I say, when and as I say. We'll have no more mischief out of ye."

A surge of indignation sent her hands, however ill-advisedly, to her hips. "Perhaps therein lies the problem, Uncle. No one has asked for my assistance other than to shell the peas for supper. You can hardly blame me for attempting to fill my days with activity more engaging than staring out the parlor windows. Provide me some gainful employment and I shall set myself to it happily enough."

The man's seething silence made her feel jostled, despite his never lifting a hand to touch her. Despite a frantic little voice urging caution, she returned his glare unblinking, though her chin felt no steadier than a butterfly's wing.

"God's teeth," he murmured at length, "ye make a valid point. Though I can't imagine ye're good for much."

"Give me a chance to prove my worth."

His ironic smirk could not, in fact, be termed cordial, but it was the closest thing to a smile she had yet seen on him. "Ever milked a cow? Collected eggs? Mucked a barn? Pulled thistles from a lamb's coat? I'll wager you can neither card wool nor spin it into yarn."

Sophie's eyes narrowed. She raised her chin. "What do you wish me to do, Uncle Barnaby? I'm more than willing to learn. I might even make you proud of your high-flown London relation."

Tossing his own words back at him produced an unexpected result: a slight easing of his typically harsh expression. The change lent a startling hint of youthfulness to his face, and Sophie thought perhaps she had just glimpsed the ghost of the man who stole Aunt Louisa away all those years ago.

She longed to know what had happened to that man, how he became such an ill-tempered brute. Were the trials of a difficult life responsible, or the burden of his own conscience? How she wished to fire off a

barrage of questions concerning his life here in Penhollow, and what he knew of errant harbor lights.

"You want employment, lass?" The cool mockery
in his tone reminded her that they were not suddenly
friends. "I'll put ye in Rachel's keeping. Lord knows
my wife has made a blasted sorry job of keeping track
of ye."

With that he exited through the front door, leaving
her regretting the past moments and mourning the loss
of her freedom. Instead of holding her tongue, she
had given in to pride. Now her days would be regi-
mented and supervised. She would have no choice but
to acquiesce to Chad's plea and allow him to be her
eyes and ears while she remained safely under her
cousin's wing.

Part of her missed Chad already, missed his courage, his tenderness and his ability to talk her through
impossible feats. She missed his rare smiles and his
dashing good looks and the anticipation that fluttered
through her whenever he was near.

But another part of her conceded that the man she
had met in the chapel, who patiently urged her up a
cliff this morning and later roused such unimaginable
passion in her, possessed another, darker side. One he
had quite deliberately allowed her to glimpse; she was
sure of it. To protect her, or to hide the secrets he
harbored?

Oddly it was that enigmatic side of him that in-
trigued her most.

During the next days Sophie helped Rachel weed the
kitchen garden, card the wool the family saved for its
own use, clean the stalls where the two tremendously
large draft horses were kept, and dip long wicks into
melted animal fat to make the tallow candles they
burned each night. She helped prepare the meals and
clean up afterward. She rose early each day and fell
into bed exhausted each night. And during that time she
could not erase the Earl of Wycliffe from her thoughts.

Far too often she wondered where he was, what he was doing. Did he sit alone and brooding in that chilly, murky house of his? Had he made any discovery concerning the harbor lights? Perhaps he had decided she'd been imagining things and given up. She regretted not telling him about her aunt and uncle's conversation.

It's to that grandfather of hers we must pay heed. He's the one to fear. She wondered what threat Grandfather St. Clair could pose to the Gordons.

It's unlikely that while she's here you'll be called upon again to . . . To what? If only Dominic hadn't interrupted her eavesdropping and she had heard the rest. Perhaps then she might have been able to put her suspicions about her relatives to rest. But judging by her uncle's subsequent behavior toward her, she didn't think so.

On the fourth day she managed to rise early enough to follow Rachel out to the still-dark barnyard and have her first lesson in collecting eggs, which resulted in her hand being pecked to virtual mincemeat by outraged, squawking hens. Halfway through the chore she deemed scaling cliffs a far more comfortable venture.

"How can they *possibly* lay so many?"

Rachel didn't bother answering.

After Sophie snatched the last egg with only a minor peck on her little finger, they returned to the kitchen, where she washed off her bleeding knuckles. Heyworth greeted them with affectionate sniffs, then shambled after Sophie as she drew a kitchen chair closer to the hearth. Sinking into the delicious warmth cast by the fire, she let her eyelids droop. In the corner the black iron stove gave off tantalizing waves of muffin-scented heat that made her stomach rumble.

Her eyes sprang open as Rachel thrust her cloak back into her hands. "No sleeping yet, Sophie. We have to deliver the eggs and milk to the Stormy Gull before sunup. Dominic has the 'cart loaded and ready for us."

She eyed the younger girl wearily. "You do this every morning?"

Aunt Louisa entered the kitchen. "You'd best get on to the tavern before the first patrons begin drifting in."

"Patrons? At this ungodly hour?"

"They're fishermen," Rachel said with a look that chastised. "Some aren't married. They break their fast at the tavern before putting out to sea for a long day's work."

Sophie had never set foot inside a tavern before, had never entered any establishment other than London's finest restaurants. A growing curiosity kept her tired feet apace with Rachel's as they trudged beneath a granite sky flecked black as crows and stout, long-fingered ravens took wing.

They were met at the kitchen door by a great, bald hulk of a man Rachel addressed as Uncle Reese. He ushered them inside, handed them each a steaming mug of tea and bade them stand by the roaring hearth fire while he unloaded the cart.

The stone-and-timber kitchen was the most primitive Sophie had ever entered, with neither a proper stove nor even the convenience of a water pump. Reese returned, and as he transferred the eggs from their baskets into waiting bowls, he and Rachel spoke of the weather, the Gordons' herds, and how the recent wet weather would affect the quality of the pastures. Apparently too much rain could introduce a damaging rot into the soil, and Rachel seemed concerned. Gradually Sophie gleaned that this man was married to Uncle Barnaby's sister.

More than once she felt his eye upon her, and wondered what tales Uncle Barnaby, Dominic or the mariner, Grady, might have told about her. Did Reese expect to find horns beneath her bonnet? It came as something of a relief when Rachel gathered up the empty egg baskets and they said their good-byes.

Sophie gladly followed her cousin to the door, only

to discover the source of the hissing sound she had largely ignored these past several minutes. Pelting rain churned the stable yard to mud and blended the dawn landscape into muted blurs of gray.

"Stop right there." The order, issued in a female's voice, came from across the room. "You two are mine until this deplorable weather clears."

Sophie turned to behold a woman with shockingly red hair and clothes so bold and brazen that the street-walkers she had occasionally glimpsed near Covent Garden sprang to mind.

"Ladies, close that door and join me in the common room. Reese, oatcakes, blood sausages and a good warm draft of small ale. These two look as hungry and bedraggled as freshly hatched sparrows." Turning, the woman disappeared through a doorway.

"There's no harm in waiting out the rain," Rachel whispered to Sophie as she sealed the kitchen door against the weather. "Mother will expect us to."

In the common room they took seats around an oak trestle table. As in the kitchen Sophie felt as if she'd stepped into an earlier century. Inhaling the jumbled scents of ale and oak-aged wine, cooking aromas and the acrid smoke of the peat fire burning cheerfully in the hearth, she experienced a sudden contentment, her first since coming to Penhollow that wasn't directly linked to Chad. Whatever the tavern lacked in re-finement it made up for in snug warmth and solid security, especially with the driving rain streaming down the windows and fogging the panes.

As Rachel made the introductions, the street door burst open to admit four men who hurried in out of the weather, followed almost immediately by three more, their oilcloth overcoats glistening wet. The red-head, who insisted on being addressed as Kellyn rather than Mrs. Quincy, greeted them heartily and called their orders in to Reese.

"How splendid," Sophie couldn't help blurting when

she learned that Kellyn owned the Stormy Gull. "I've never met a woman who owned a tavern. Or any sort of business, for that matter."

Kellyn laughed softly. " 'Tis no great feat, I assure you."

Oh, but to Sophie it was, and a bubble of envy rose up inside her.

The street door opened again upon a blast of wind and another handful of men. They bade the ladies gruff good mornings and shuffled around a table. Reese returned carrying a tray loaded with steaming oatcakes, blood sausages still sizzling from the pan and three pints of mulled ale. Sophie's stomach rumbled in appreciation of the tempting aromas.

After filling a plate with food, she sipped her ale. Small ale, Kellyn had called it, meaning it was less potent than regular ale and wouldn't make her tipsy. The brew was warm and thick, and bore a sweet hint of apples.

"This is wonderful. Thank you," she said, and sliced into a sausage. Kellyn questioned her about London, but Sophie's own curiosity soon steered the conversation back to what she considered Kellyn's extraordinary circumstances. "Was this tavern left to you by a member of your family?"

"In a sense. I purchased the Gull myself with money left to me by my maternal grandmother and my husband, who had been a sea captain."

Then Kellyn was a widow. Sophie exchanged a glance with Rachel, whose downcast expression revealed her knowledge of the unhappy story. Around them the gravelly drone of conversation afforded them a measure of privacy. "May I ask what became of your husband?"

Kellyn set down her knife and fork. "Rob died as many a Cornishman does, on the deck of a storm-racked ship. Most of his crew died with him."

Sophie gasped. "I'm so sorry."

"My husband's was not the only schooner to go down in the tempest. Many a widow was made that day. And other days as well."

"Then . . . it's something that happens often here?"

"Often enough." Kellyn raised her mug but didn't drink. "Our seas are fraught with danger."

The woman's voice held a faintly bitter note, and prompted Sophie's next question before she judged the wisdom of saying it aloud. "Is it true what I've heard, that even in these modern times sailors sometimes run afoul of pirates and wreckers?"

When Kellyn didn't answer, Rachel murmured, "To Cornwall's shame, it has been known to happen. Never openly admitted, but not unheard-of."

"Has such a thing ever happened in Penhollow?"

Rachel exchanged a guarded glance with Kellyn. Before either offered an answer, the tavern door opened. Rain blew in on a squall of wind, quickly doused when a figure in a dripping cloak stepped inside and slammed the door.

Sophie's heart gave a lurch as Chad stamped the water from his boots and blinked in the gloom. Raising both hands, he swept his drenched hair from his brow, sending a shower of drops sprinkling the floor behind him.

A tense silence blanketed the pub as the other patrons fell silent. Subdued conversation slowly resumed. Chad swung his cloak onto a hook beside the door, revealing snug breeches and snowy shirtsleeves. Yearning flared, heating Sophie more than the fire behind her.

His gaze alighted on their table, meeting hers with a spark of surprise, a smolder of awareness. Her name formed on his lips, and for the length of a heartbeat, it seemed no one else inhabited the room but the two of them.

"Lord Wycliffe," Kellyn said, "what on earth are you doing out in such weather? You'll catch your death."

Outside, the frantic clanging of a bell pierced the pattering rain. Abandoning their meals the sailors came to their feet in an urgent cluster and pushed outside. Sophie saw them through the window, all heading in the same direction—the harbor. Kellyn rushed to the window and stared after them, then turned and grabbed a cloak off a hook.

"What is it?" Chad asked.

"Trouble on the quay." Her features were taut, her brow ribbed with furrows. "Reese," she called across the room, though she needn't have. He'd already sprinted from the kitchen. "Get Tobias," she said, and hastened out into the rain.

Chapter 11

"What kind of trouble?"

Chad stood at the open door, trying to determine the answer to Sophie's question. Kellyn and Reese were already gone. About a dozen other villagers streamed down the road behind them.

"It could be anything." He turned to Sophie and started to reach out, to frame her face in his hands and offer comfort, reassurance. He let his hands fall to his sides, knowing it wasn't his place to offer her anything. As she herself had told him, it was not his ongoing task to protect her.

Nor was it his right to care about her.

Her cousin hovered at the window. She turned toward them, her eyes huge in a face that glowed ghostly white. Outside, the bell rang discordant notes that could herald nothing good. "There's been a death at sea," Miss Gordon said in a trembling voice.

Her certainty confirmed Chad's worst fear, or at least part of it. Lives were lost in countless ways on the seas. Accidents, storms, illness . . . Why had a stifling certainty crept over him that none of those were to blame?

"I'll go and find out what happened," he said. "You two stay put."

The rain hit his face and he broke into a run.

A throng of villagers choked the entrance to the

quay and spilled down onto the main pier. A schooner's lines were being secured to the moorings. As soon as the gangway had been let down, Kellyn climbed its length. Reese's glistening bald head moved through the crowd. Onboard, a small knot of sailors shouted and gestured. Ranged about the deck, others of the crew stood shivering, arms hugging their sides as rain dripped off their bent heads.

The gleaming wet brim of a familiar tweed cap caught Chad's eye. He craned his neck and searched the crowd. A gap between the close-pressed bodies opened to reveal a slightly hooked nose and a pair of sharp, close-set eyes—the man who'd sat watching Chad in the Stormy Gull on his first morning there.

The crowd moved again and the gap closed. Chad pushed forward, but when he could again see the spot where the man had stood, he was gone.

Under his feet the dock's wooden planking shuddered beneath the weight of so many people. More kept arriving, their necks craning, their shrill speculation forming into names, questions, cries of blatant fear.

"Is it one of ours?"

"Bill—has anyone seen Bill today?"

"My Stephen—where is he?"

"Has Josiah returned?"

The reek of sodden wool and panic mingled sharply with ocean brine. A sickening dread spread in Chad's gut until he half expected gruesome apparitions to rise up and point their rattle-boned fingers at him.

Kellyn descended from the schooner to the pier, singling out a woman in the crowd. A moment later a scream filled the air, and Kellyn's arms went around a pair of wrenching shoulders.

The crowd shifted, thickened. An elderly couple pushed their way through. They shouted a name— Randolph—to which Kellyn solemnly nodded. The couple fell against each other, hands clutching, groping for purchase. In their distraction they might have plunged off the side of the pier had not their neighbors formed a barrier around them.

A lanky youth, all arms and legs and dark, curly hair spilling from beneath a tattered wool cap, called out a third name.

"Gregory?" Even before an answer came tears spilled down his freckled cheeks. He turned to Chad with unseeing eyes and wailed, "I should have gone out with them, but he wouldn't let me. I'd been ill, and he said I'd only be underfoot. They'd gone out to . . ." His tearful gaze landed on Chad, and wariness flickered behind his anguish. "They'd gone out fishing. I should have been there. I should have gone. . . ."

No, Chad thought with a sinking dread, they hadn't gone out fishing. They had gambled their lives on a much more valuable cargo—and lost their wager.

A man approached from behind and slipped an arm around the youth's shoulders. " 'Tis all right, lad. You couldn't have done aught. 'Twas God's will."

Sorrow swept the villagers like a rushing tide, engulfing Chad in its wake. Three men dead. Three families devastated. Otherworldly fingers pointed at him, whispered his name. . . .

"Lord Wycliffe, can you tell me what happened?" Tobias Hall's query roused him, and he turned, trying to calm his erratic pulse. The vicar came up beside him, a leather bag dangling from his hand, a pile of blankets draped across his arm.

Chad shook his head. "I know only that three men will not return to their homes today."

Kellyn threaded her way down the pier. Her pale eyes told a grim tale. "We can use the blankets, Tobias, but I'm afraid your herbs will do no good."

Familiar voices prompted Chad to search the quay. Near the entrance to the road he spotted Sophie and her cousin. Sophie had caught hold of the other girl's wrist and was attempting to restrain her. At the sight of their soggy clothing and streaming hair, the horror of the other morning's dream came rushing back to him—his struggles to save the little girl in pink from drowning . . . only to watch Sophie die in his arms. . . .

Breathe. Stand steady. Know that Sophie is alive and unhurt.

"Let me go!" Her cousin yanked to free herself of Sophie's grip. "I have to see. I have to know who it is."

Chad worked his way through the crowd to them. "Miss Gordon, is there someone you wish to inquire after?"

She stopped squirming and peered at him through red-rimmed eyes. "Ian," she whispered.

"Then be reassured. I heard three names, and Ian's was not one of them."

"Oh, thank God!" The girl's knees wobbled and Chad made a swift move to catch her. Sophie cried out and reached to steady her cousin as well. But already the girl was pushing out of his arms, determination burgeoning behind her tears. "Thank you, Lord Wycliffe."

He nodded. "I'll see if I can find out more. I wish you two would go home. This is no place for either of you."

The vicar now stood at the bottom of the gangway. "Stand aside. Make way."

Above him a half dozen crewmen lifted three blanket-wrapped bundles from the deck and started down. The crowd parted, flanking the narrow walkway in stunned curiosity. Whispers fluttered, little louder than the hissing rain and the murmuring ocean.

"Meg Keating, that's who."

"And her husband, Jack."

"The ghostly crew of the *Ebony Rose* . . ."

By Christ, could these people believe such a thing? That phantoms had murdered these men?

As the mournful procession reached him, a hand slid from beneath the blanket, dangling like a dead fish on a line. Blue. Bloated. Fingers missing. Stinging bile rose in Chad's throat. He clutched at his shirt-front, wanting but unable to turn away.

Around him the faces of the villagers blurred. Harbor, sky and the schooner's long hull began to spin. Beneath his feet he felt the slap of the waves against the pilings, the sway of the dock. He pressed his hands to his temples and attempted to crush the images, block out the condemning words.

Killed for the cargo.

"Chad? Are you all right?"

A hand closed over his shoulder, a delicate pressure with power enough to anchor him. Out of the spinning visions Sophie's concerned features came into focus. Heedless of the onlookers, he closed his arms around her, knowing he shouldn't, but letting his quaking guilt dissipate into the calm compassion of her sweet body.

Sophie knew they were creating a spectacle, albeit one likely to go unnoticed under the present circumstances. As the last of the three bundled bodies passed, she pressed her cheek into Chad's shirt collar and spoke soothing words in his ear.

Whatever had taken hold of him moments ago had alarmed her enough to steal her from Rachel's side. What could have unsettled him so? The bodies, yes, but she sensed something more.

"What is it? What happened?" She ran her fingers through his sodden hair, tarnished nearly russet by the rain. "You looked as though you were about to keel over into the water."

"I'm all right." His lips moved against her dripping hair. Then he released her and eased back a step. "And you? Did you . . . see it?"

"The hand?"

Head bowed, he nodded.

"It was horrible. All of this . . . it's like a nightmare." Almost like the nightmare they had shared. A bout of shivering racked her, and suddenly she was against him again. His hands rubbed up and down her back, instilling the only warmth she could hope to glean from this wretched day. "Who are those men?"

"I don't know. Villagers. Sailors." He held her at arm's length and scowled. "Why did you come? Why didn't you do as I told you and stay at the tavern?"

Despite his stance, his tone, she felt the lack of true anger in his words. "Rachel took off running. What else could I do but follow?"

Pushing wet hair out of her eyes, she searched for her cousin. Most of the crowd had dispersed onto the road, slowly making their way into the village. The quay was nearly deserted. "Do you see her?"

He pointed, not toward the road, but down the wharf. "There she is."

Half-hidden behind the stern of a neat little clipper ship, Rachel stood with her arms around a man. A shock of surprise went through Sophie. Her cousin's black hair whipped bannerlike behind her as she pressed her lips to his, then laid her cheek against a broad chest clad in the dark woolen jersey and oilcloth coat of a fisherman.

"That must be her Ian. I never knew he existed. She never gave so much as a hint."

"Have you hinted at your acquaintance with me?"

The sharpness of his question startled her. "Of course not. But this is different. Poor Rachel, to feel she must keep such a secret from her family."

"Yes . . ." His attention wandered over her shoulder to the road. Sophie followed his gaze, seeing nothing but the backs of the villagers receding from view. When she turned around, a steely glint had entered his eyes. "Perhaps they have reason to disapprove. Perhaps Miss Gordon would do well to stay away from the young man."

"Why on earth?" Sophie searched his face. It was back again, that shuttered expression that kept his thoughts a mystery. Sophie shivered but tried not to let him see. "At least he arrived home safely."

He nodded absently, his focus pinned somewhere

beyond the quay. "I don't suppose it would do any good to order you home?"

"No, it wouldn't."

"Come, then," he said, and set off toward the road at a brisk pace.

A somber gathering milled outside the Stormy Gull. Sophie followed Chad as he shouldered his way through the crowd, doubling back more than once as he seemed to search for someone. From listening to the scattered conversations they soon learned that, at Kellyn's insistence, the bodies had been laid out in one of the upper rooms.

"Grady!" Chad gestured to a man in the crowd, and Sophie recognized the red hair and unkempt beard of the man who had captained the sailboat that brought Chad out to the cliffs to rescue her.

The man joined them, shaking his head sadly. "Milord. Miss." His accent identified him as an Irishman. He offered a respectful nod to Sophie, but gave no indication that he recognized her, for which she was grateful. "This is a sorrowful day for Penhollow."

"I heard some of the villagers speaking the Keatings' names." Chad lowered his voice as he spoke. "How could anyone believe such an atrocity could be the work of ghosts?"

The man ran a hand over his beard and shuddered. " 'Cause o' the way the bodies were found."

Chad exchanged a puzzled glance with Sophie. "What do you mean?"

Sophie noticed heads turning in their direction. Grady noticed as well and shook his head. "I've said too much. Wait for Kellyn and the vicar. They're sorting matters out now with the captain o' the schooner." He started to move away.

Chad stopped him with a hand on his shoulder. "Someone's got to notify the authorities."

Grady hesitated, then nodded. "You're right, mate. I'll do it. Soon's the weather clears, I'll take me skiff up to Mullion and let the coast guard know."

Just as he turned again to go, Sophie stepped in his path. "Do you have any idea who might have killed those men?"

"That I don't, miss." Again he made as if to leave, and Sophie placed a hand on his forearm.

"These people. They seem grief-stricken, but not entirely shocked." She leaned closer and asked in a whisper, "Has such a thing happened before? Often?"

An imperative hand closed over her shoulder, yet Chad said nothing as they both waited for the mariner's answer.

"Aye, but not like this. Not with this kind of warning attached."

"What do you mean, warning?"

The mariner didn't answer Sophie's question. Hunching his stocky figure against the rain, he eased through the crowd and scurried down the road. Sophie followed Chad into the tavern. They met the vicar just inside the door, donning his overcoat.

"Give them all proper burials," Chad said to the other man. "I'll pay the expenses."

Sophie's throat tightened. The vicar nodded his thanks.

Near the hearth a handful of men sat wrapped in blankets, drinking steaming ale and passing around a bottle of whiskey. Kellyn stood quietly talking to them.

"This is Daniel," Kellyn said when Sophie and Chad crossed the room to her. She placed a hand on the shoulder of the sailor nearest her. "He captains the schooner. Dan, tell Lord Wycliffe what you told me."

The sea captain took a swig from the bottle his neighbor thrust into his hand, wiped his beard and said, "We were out well before dawn this morn, but when the storm kicked up I decided 'twould be best to haul in the nets and put in. Those three we found— Randolph, Gregory and Peter—they were caught in the webbing."

Chad's handsome features hardened with something akin to pain. "Did you see any sign of their vessel?"

"No. The three of them manned a small sloop, sometimes with Gregory's brother. We saw no sign of it, only the bit of wreckage we hauled in along with them." Daniel gave a forlorn shrug. "But that could have been anything, from anywhere."

"Can you estimate how long they might have been in the water?"

"I'm no physician, milord. . . ." Daniel traded looks with his companions.

"The vicar thought three, maybe four days," Kellyn interjected.

Chad's jaw worked, then squared. "I've one more question. I'm told this could not have been the result of a storm or an accident. Can you tell me how you know?"

Every man at the table gave a shudder. The captain tipped the bottle to his lips again. Then he said, "Because when we pulled them in, they were all three tied together."

Chapter 12

Sophie . . .

Sophie bolted upright in the darkness, certain she had heard something, someone. A voice no louder than a whisper, yet one whose eerie echo shivered in the air around her.

Had she dreamed it? Then she had felt it too—a chilly breath against her cheek, like that day at Edgecombe. The thought brought her fully awake. She trembled, gleaning neither warmth nor comfort from the coverlets. After a glance beside her to be sure she hadn't disturbed Rachel, she slipped out of bed and went to the window.

After today's grisly developments, no wonder restless dreams thrust her from sleep. Those men . . . tied together. She shuddered. Meg and Jack Keating had used such brutal measures against their victims. But why would anyone nowadays emulate such cruelty? What could they hope to gain from it?

Her gaze was drawn lower, and she gasped as movement on the beach caught her eye. A shadow. A glimmer of reflected moonlight. Pressing her forehead to the cool glass, she strained for a better view. Was she still dreaming?

Silently she slipped through the house, tiptoeing past a slumbering Heyworth beside the cookstove. She was taking an awful chance, she knew. And she might be very much mistaken. But, tossing a cloak around her nightshift, she darted out the kitchen door.

With only a hazy moon and the pale wash of the dunes to guide her, she followed the downward slope of the property to the beach. The rain had stopped and the winds abated, yet the sea remained a churning, foaming blackness. She looked up and down the sand in either direction and saw no one.

A sense of foolishness rode fast on the heels of disappointment. With a shake of her head she started back—and collided with a wall of chest.

A hand came over her mouth, muffling her involuntary yelp, but even as her heart exploded against her ribs, a soft but steadying warmth brushed her forehead.

"Shh. It's me."

Relief coursed through her. Feeling weak, she nodded against the hand at her mouth, the lips heating her brow. He released her and stepped back. No wonder she hadn't seen him standing among the dunes. He was dressed all in black—shirt, breeches, boots—a shadow crowned in gold.

Desire poured through her at the sight him. Her knees wobbled as his hands framed her face. In the moonlight glinting off the water she saw the shock and grief of that morning etched in stark relief around his eyes, in the hard set of his mouth. Stretching tall, she pressed her lips to his in a kiss meant to tell him she understood, that she felt what he felt and welcomed it, no matter the pain.

"I heard you call me," she whispered, knowing even as she spoke the words that they could not be true. How could she possibly have heard him from all the way inside the house, over the roar of the waves and the keening of the wind?

Yet, when she had looked out her window, she had seen him. Known he would be here, waiting for her.

"Yes . . . perhaps I did call you." His open fingers swept the hair from her face in a way that made her feel possessed. For this moment, at least, she was his. "I'll admit I wished for you." He pulled her close. "I wanted to feel you against me."

His hands slid under her cloak, and as he took her in his arms his touch fired her flesh beneath her shift. Once more it seemed the man from the chapel had banished the aloof stranger. An insatiable ache grew, fueling a yearning to feel his lips follow where his fingertips traveled.

"Sophie . . . you make me forget. Only you can do that." Nibbling at her neck, he left a scalding trail from her ear to her shoulder. "Only you make me feel whole again."

She pondered the meaning of that puzzling statement. Then her thoughts drowned in his kisses and the thrust of his tongue. Her senses became keenly attuned to him, to everything about him. The heat of his mouth. The musky scent of his skin. The hardness of male muscle against the softer places of her body. The solid pulse of his arousal against her thigh.

"God," he said as he dragged in a breath, "you feel so good. Taste so wonderful. But . . ." The pressure of his lips lessened; his body retreated a fraction. "Forgive me. I shouldn't be—"

"No." She tightened her arms and kissed him harder. Whatever he was about to say, she didn't wish to hear it, not if it created so much as an inch-wide gap between them.

"Sophie, this isn't why I'm here."

She lurched a step backward. Had she completely misread him?

He caught her shoulders. "Don't look like that. Do you think I don't want you? Christ, I wish I didn't. Wish I could erase you from my thoughts."

The words cut. She started past him. "Then do so."

"Damn it." He caught her hand and drew her close again. "So help me, I *will* have you someday. Somehow. But not here, Sophie. Not on the ground, with sand in our hair and God knows where else."

Surely her pride must have dissolved into their kisses or been sucked out to sea, because all she could think to say was, "I wouldn't care."

"Confound it, I would. I'd never forgive myself if I did that to you." His mouth dipped, drank greedily of hers.

The assurance did little to soothe her aching disappointment. If he hadn't come here for her, then . . . "Why *are* you here?"

"I'm patrolling. Looking for the lights you saw." The frothing waves tossed illuminated patterns across his face. "I believe a connection exists between the ship you saw that night and what happened today. The timing is too close for coincidence."

She clutched the smooth cambric of his ebony shirt as the disturbing revelation of that morning tumbled back. "The Keatings used to tie their victims together before throwing them overboard. Especially Lady Meg, when she went on her rampage."

"I know that, but this was the work of human hands, not ghosts."

"Of course, but it seems someone is using the legend to frighten people. To keep them from searching out the truth."

His hands dug into her sides. "Stay out of it, Sophie. It's a treacherous game, hunting for smugglers. They're too clever by half at covering their tracks and removing whatever or whoever stands in their way."

"I've no intention of getting in anyone's way. But if we—"

"Shh!" His hand clamped over her mouth. He tucked her to his side and lunged into the dunes, taking her with him in a small explosion of sand.

She experienced only seconds of confusion before she heard what had spurred him to action: the swish and scatter of approaching footsteps.

Chad did his best to cushion Sophie from the fall. Then he rolled to cover her, pinning her with his weight to prevent her from making any telltale movements. They lay in a depression between the dunes, camouflaged by weeds and shadow but by no means completely hidden from view. If their unexpected guest happened to turn in just the right direction, he might very well spot them. Only by lying utterly motionless did they have any hope of remaining concealed.

Quicker than he would have thought, Sophie quieted her breathing and blinked her understanding up at him. Still, he dared not ease off her for fear of the shifting sands making too loud a hiss, especially when the intruder halted mere yards away.

Chad could make out a tall, broad-shouldered figure with an unkempt pelt of black hair that reached below his collar. Sophie's uncle. Chad had met him briefly at the tavern that morning, after Sophie and her cousin had set out for home.

Barnaby Gordon stood at the edge of the splashing waves, hands on his hips, staring out at the churning water. Seconds ticked by.

Beneath Chad the soft planes and hollows of Sophie's body embraced his harder contours. Her cloak lay open, spread out on the sand. Despite the coolness of the night, heat gathered between them, coating her skin with a sheen that beaded in the valley between her breasts.

Desire stabbed, all the more excruciating because he could do nothing to alleviate it.

Her lips touched his ear, her voice no more than a sigh. "Who?"

In her position she could not turn without shifting her shoulders as well. He lowered his head until his nose submerged in her loose hair. "Your uncle."

A furrow formed above her nose; she shook her head in a wordless query. In reply he retuned the gesture. He had no idea what brought the man outside, fully dressed, in the middle of the night to simply stare at the sea.

He lifted his head for another look. The man braced his feet wide and raised a spyglass to his eye. His torso swung in a slow half circle that encompassed the black horizon.

Raised precariously on his elbows above Sophie, Chad watched for several more minutes. It wasn't until he felt her hips give an infinitesimal wiggle that he realized his weight must be digging into her.

He lowered his arms and came cheek-to-cheek with her. Perhaps that didn't relieve the pressure sufficiently, for her mouth closed on the corner of his lips, her teeth digging into his skin with what felt more like a reflex than a deliberate attempt to bite him. He felt a whisper of arousal. Under any other circumstances . . .

Gordon turned. Folding the spyglass, he slipped it into a trouser pocket and trudged back toward the dunes. Chad communicated to Sophie with an emphatic expression. She held her breath. Grains of sand kicked up by the man's stride pelted Chad's hair. Gordon couldn't be more than two yards away. Chad dared not so much as flinch, even when one of those tiny particles lodged in the corner of his eye.

The footsteps faded to a distant thudding. Chad rose up onto his elbows again, then eased off Sophie to crawl forward and peer around the dunes. The top of Gordon's head bobbed out of view. Chad sat up and offered a hand to help Sophie do the same.

Her relief breezed from her lips on a long but nearly soundless sigh. He kissed her. "You all right?"

She nodded.

He rubbed at his eye, hoping to dislodge the irritating grain of sand. She shook out her hair and ran her fingers through it. Sand showered the ground. Hand in hand they made their way past the dunes.

"Where is he going?"

Chad followed the line of Sophie's outstretched arm. Gordon appeared to be skirting the house.

"He's heading for the road," she said, and took off at a run.

The only way to stop her would have been to call out, something he didn't dare do. Chad sprinted to catch up, but even as his fingertips brushed her arm, she shook free and kept going. "Sophie, stop," he hissed.

"No time to argue. We don't want to lose him."

Damn the woman for being right. They kept the sheds between themselves and Gordon as long as they could, stopping to spy around each corner before hurrying to keep him in their sights. As they reached the front garden they saw him step through the gate onto the road.

"The village," Chad murmured, but Sophie shook her head.

Her guess proved correct. Instead of turning north, her uncle crossed and entered the pasture across the road. Sophie moved as if to surge forward. Chad wrapped an arm around her waist and stopped her cold.

"We'll be too close, with nowhere to seek cover."

"Don't you wish to know what he's up to?" Her eyes gleamed with eagerness, and with the recklessness that sometimes terrified him.

"Go back to the house," he said. "I'll follow him."

Her attention shifted back to her uncle. "He's cutting across the fields. There are other farms in that direction, though I doubt he's off for a friendly visit. Come, we can stay back a good distance and still keep him in our sights."

Further argument would only have given them away. Not liking this development a bit, he reclaimed Sophie's hand tight in his. Quickly they scurried across the flat, all-too-open expanse of road.

Gordon led them across his pastures. The sleepy murmurs of the cows and the bleating of the sheep helped mask their tread. Where the land rolled away to the north, points of light stood out like stars in the sky, marking other farms and shepherds' cots on Blackheath Moor. They left these behind and trudged on. The grassy turf gave way to the wild heather, brambles and heath rush of the moor.

The rocky terrain sent Sophie teetering into Chad's side on more than one occasion, once bringing her to her knees when brambles snared her hems. Her breathing became labored, and he began to feel the strain of their trek in his own lungs. But if the scrub-fringed hills and stony outcroppings made for unsteady footing, the landscape also provided cover to help mask their pursuit. Keeping low and scrambling from one craggy hillock to the next, they trailed her uncle to a lonely farmstead huddled at the edge of a bog.

There wasn't much to the place. A tumbling wall wound its way around a sagging barn, a couple of dilapidated sheds and a stone shack. The shack's roof emitted feeble beams of light through moldering patches in the thatch. Thready smoke rose from the chimney. Gordon rapped twice on the door and stepped inside.

Sophie started up from their hunkered position beside an outcropping. Chad grabbed a handful of her cloak.

"We don't know who else might come walking up."

"I hadn't thought of that."

"When will you learn to look before you leap? Come. We'll circle to the rear."

Keeping low to the brush, they steered a wide berth around the property. There were no proper windows at the rear of the shack, only narrow openings in the stone wall on either side of the hearth. Both were presently stuffed from the inside with wads of raw wool, perhaps to keep out not only the damp mist, but also vermin. They crouched beside the nearest aperture.

". . . no sign of 'em." Gordon's voice.

"Shoulda been back by now."

". . . the lights . . . They must have seen 'em and stayed away. . . ."

". . . mighta missed the signal." Gordon again.

The words bore a combative timbre. Gordon seemed to be accused of something. Of not performing his job to satisfaction, from what Chad could make out. Again he heard Gordon's distinctive snarl, then a string of oaths, a scuffle and a crash. When the voices resumed they were quieter but no less antagonistic.

Who had these men been waiting for, and what signal had Sophie's uncle supposedly missed? Ship lights on the midnight horizon?

He'd counted three voices in all. Slurring drawls, coarse and uneducated. At a reference to that morning Sophie's eyes widened and she gave him a significant nod. Another word drifted through the opening, one that halted Chad's heart in midbeat and raked the hairs on his arms.

Edgecombe.

Were these the men who had ordered him to Penhollow through Giles Watling's message?

He stole a glance at Sophie, but she gave no indication of having heard. Had he been mistaken? He bloody well hoped so. In frustration he regarded the paltry gap in the stone. If he could only shift the wool aside . . . But he didn't dare risk someone noticing, especially not with Sophie there.

Footsteps thudded across what sounded like an earthen floor, and the door of the shack creaked open. Chad pushed to his feet and darted to peer around the corner. Over his shoulder he answered Sophie's silent question with a nod. Her uncle had just left.

She started to rise, but Chad quickly made his way back to her and stilled her with a shake of his head. He resumed his crouch near the opening.

". . . bloody nuisance."

". . . get rid of him."

"Soon enough . . ."

Pressed tight to his side, Sophie let her mouth fall open. Wishing with all his being that he hadn't brought her along, Chad wrapped an arm around her and waited to hear more. Were they considering murdering her uncle?

". . . handle it myself." The voice became a vicious grind. "Tonight."

"No." The reply was equally fierce, equally guttural. "Not yet."

Then came a whack like a fist hitting a table.

Beneath the shelter of Chad's arm, Sophie trembled. On impulse he pressed a silent kiss to her hair. For several moments he wavered between stealing away immediately and waiting to hear more that might reveal the plans of the two inside. The first action would ensure her safety now; the second her safety and perhaps that of her relatives in the days or weeks to come.

Then again, he wasn't entirely certain Gordon was the nuisance they spoke of. Those brigands had mentioned lights, ones that warned off whoever they were waiting for. And they had mentioned Edgecombe, where Chad lit lights each night.

The shack's door swung open. Unsteady footsteps skimmed the dirt in their direction. Alarm surged over Sophie's features. Chad pulled her to her feet and tugged her into motion. He vaulted the stone wall, then helped her over. Together they took off onto the darkened moor.

They had gone only some two dozen paces when mud sucked at their feet. They had stumbled into a bog. Chad brought them to an abrupt halt, held on to Sophie and listened for sounds of pursuit. In the scant moonlight he could just make out the shadow of a man hunching, apparently relieving himself by the farm's boundary wall. When he had finished he secured his trousers around his waist, then propped a foot on the wall and stared out over the landscape.

By Christ, Chad thought, what a time for stargazing. Sophie shivered, and he realized that while his boots would keep out the water for some time, her thin slippers would not. Looking back over his shoulder, he found himself staring directly into the moonlit gleam of the man's gaze.

A shout, footsteps and the slamming of the door tumbled on the wind. Chad didn't linger to see what happened next. He and Sophie splashed through the bog, raising a loud squelch with each step.

"Someone's here! I saw 'em."

"Probably a deer. Gordon's gone."

". . . not taking any chances."

Sophie began to lag. Her cloak, several inches too long, dragged in the mire, sucking her back until she gave a great heave that lifted it free of the muck. Chad considered tugging the thing from her shoulders and leaving it, but he realized that if found the garment might be identified, and then Gordon would know she had been here.

With a swift two-word prayer—*please, God*—that he was making the right decision, he veered hard right. Somehow Sophie managed to keep up, matching him stride for stride. For one heady moment admiration filled him. Then the raw fear returned. Within seconds their feet hit solid ground, their footsteps reduced to a dull thudding through the vegetation.

They were headed south now, back toward the Gordons' farm. That would bring them into open pastureland, make them easy targets. Sophie realized it too, for she caught his eye and shook her head. They turned eastward, farther out onto the moor.

In the distance behind them, their pursuers hit the bog; Chad heard the clamor of their splashing. Up ahead the land heaved in a rocky upsurge, visible as a jagged density against the night sky. Hope billowed when the sounds of splashing behind them ceased.

Had their pursuers given up? Thank God Sophie had worn a dark cloak over her white shift and he'd had the foresight to dress in black. He could only hope the night had swallowed their forms sufficiently to convince the outlaws they had heard nothing more than a startled animal or two.

The tors were close now, the safety of their granite shelter almost within reach. Chad propelled Sophie on. So close . . .

An explosion split the night—a flare of light, a deafening crack, the ricochet of fracturing stone. His heart crashing into his ribs, Chad surged forward on a burst of speed, yanking Sophie with him. A second explosion roared, and down she went.

Chapter 13

"Sophie? Oh, God, wake up. Please, please wake up." Choking on desperation, Chad tapped her cheeks with the backs of his fingers, then laid his palms against either side of her face. Her head flopped to the side like a doll's. "Oh, God, Sophie, wake up."

Why had he brought her? *Why?* He might have seized her back at her relatives' farm, held her down until Gordon was well out of sight. He might have kept hidden among the dunes and not revealed himself to her at all. Not held her, kissed her, nor sought to relieve his guilt in the sweet temptation of her mingled innocence and passion. Passion *he* had awakened in her. Because he couldn't do what was right. Couldn't leave her alone.

He ran a hand over her torso, then slid it between the ground and her back, feeling for a wound. His fingers came away dry, unstained, which brought only a small, uncertain measure of relief.

He pricked his ears. Silence. He hooked a trembling arm beneath her knees, slung the other around her shoulders and struggled to his feet. Cradling her, he staggered into the shadow of the tor.

He picked his way through the night-blackened heather, around brush and scrub, over rocks, careful not to jostle her. While choosing his footing with exceeding care and listening for signs of pursuit, he remained ever alert for what he dreaded most—the sensation of hot moisture seeping through her clothing. Her cheek bumped his shoulder in rhythm with his stride. Her eyes remained closed, her features relaxed as if she were merely asleep.

As if she weren't wounded. Weren't dying. *Please, God.*

The air grew frigid and a thick mist surged across the ground. His breath clouding before his lips, Chad quaked from his bones outward. His heart throbbed; the hair at his nape bristled. He clutched Sophie tighter, imparting to her as much of his body heat as possible. He refused to let the cold mist claim her, as it had claimed him on his first night in Penhollow.

"I will not let you have her. Do you hear me?"

Follow.

The word was no more than a hiss of wind that breathed frost against his face. He strained his eyes as fury rose up inside him, as he held on to Sophie with every ounce of strength he possessed. But he saw nothing in the darkness. No hideously decaying face, no vacant, hollow stare.

Yet a few yards away a gaunt spire pierced the fog.

He blinked, unable to trust the evidence of his own eyes even as relief flooded him. The chapel. *Their* chapel. It was impossible; surely they hadn't come so far in their madcap flight from the shack. The stone steps felt solid enough beneath his feet as he climbed them, the door substantial and creaking as he shouldered his way inside.

Halfway down the nave, he laid Sophie on a wooden pew and knelt on the floor beside her. He swept the tangle of hair from her face. Was she pale? Her lips white? In the darkness he couldn't tell. He lifted her hand to his cheek. Still warm. He turned it over and pressed the underside of her wrist to his lips. The pulse was steady, strong.

Unclasping the cloak and peeling it away, he again ran his hands over every bit of her, her bare arms, her legs. He sat her up against him to be certain no stains blossomed on the back of her shift. With every inch of her that revealed no wound, no blood, his heart rejoiced.

A whimper escaped her throat.

"Sophie. Oh, thank God. You're safe now." The relief was almost more than he could bear. It throbbed and pulsed and stung. It stole the strength from his limbs. It made his head swim and left him dizzy . . . and happier than he ever thought he could be.

His arms encircled her. Gently he rocked her, stroking her cheek with his fingertips until her eyes blinked open.

"Wh-what happened?" Through the dark fringe of her lashes, her gaze flickered over their surroundings. "The chapel? How did we get here?"

His emotions rendered speech impossible. He kissed her instead, drinking in the sweet taste of her lips, filling his mouth with the heat of her breath and savoring the pliant, living warmth of her body.

"I can answer your first question," he finally managed through a blistering throat. He pressed his forehead to hers. "Once again you've managed to cheat death. As for the second question, I can't for the life of me conceive of an answer."

A ridge formed above her nose. "I fainted, didn't I?"

He nodded.

She groaned and buried her face in her hands. "I've never fainted before in my life. I despise females who faint."

He tried, unsuccessfully, to raise her chin. When she wouldn't budge, he leaned closer and spoke in her ear. "We'd run ourselves breathless through a bog. And then they shot at us. I believe they were shooting blindly, but if you hadn't been able to keep up with me, they might indeed have hit one of us." His chest constricted painfully.

Her hands slid away. She shivered. "Did I lose my cloak along the way?"

"No. It's here." He grabbed the garment off the floor and draped it around her. "When you fainted I feared you'd been shot. I carried you here, not knowing whether you were dying or not. I had to see . . . know for certain. . . ."

She offered her pardon in the form of a smile. "It isn't as if you haven't seen me in my nightshift before." Beneath the cloak a violent trembling possessed her, and she gave him an imploring look. "Would you do something for me?"

"Anything."

She held out her arms. The cloak fell open to reveal her tempting outlines and the dusky shadows of her nipples peeking from beneath her shift. "Forget for a moment that we're in a chapel, and hold me."

However wrong or inappropriate, however much her family would shake their heads, Sophie needed him. She needed the beat of Chad's heart against her breast to banish the stony chill that would not release its grip.

Before he woke her she had been cold, so cold. She'd wandered, lost and despairing of finding her way through a bewildering mist.

He moved onto the bench, drew her into his lap and closed his arms around her. Gladly, gratefully, she pressed her length to his torso. Given the sheerness of the cotton covering her, she was all but naked against him, but the contact wasn't enough. She needed more of him.

One by one she unfastened the buttons of his shirt and burrowed against him, relishing the hardness of muscle and the coarseness of chest hair against her skin. Did this make her shameless? The notion seemed not to exist. Neither did disapproval or regret. There was only this stark physical need to be close, to feel connected, to be as much a part of him as she could possibly be. Shifting in his lap, she straddled a leg on either side of him and wrapped all of herself around him.

She didn't know how long they sat enveloped in silence and relief and the heat of their bodies. Through his trousers the undeniable evidence of his desire pulsed against her, sending its echo inside her with a promise of something yet to happen between them.

Inevitable, but not here. Not in this place.

Against his shoulder she spoke softly. "Do you think they'll find us?"

He shook his head, stroked her hair. "We're safe."

She nodded, having already known the answer. There was something perplexing and otherworldly about this chapel, inexplicable yet dependable. They both knew it, even if neither understood it.

"We can't stay here indefinitely, though," he said. "We'll wait for first light and set out for Edgecombe."

"But I must return to the farm."

His chest turned to iron against her. "Do you think I'd return you to those people? To that uncle of yours?"

"If anything he is the one in danger. Those men he met tonight are surely criminals, and he seems to have displeased them somehow. You heard their plan to be rid of him."

"We don't know for certain they meant Barnaby."

"Who else?"

His arms tightened around her. "I don't give a damn right now who they meant, as long as you're safe."

"I will be. No one knows we were there tonight. It was too dark for them to identify us, and we had a good running start." Resolve sat her up straighter, although she was still in his lap, still straddling him. "My failure to return home will only raise suspicions. What if those men in the shack hear of it? How long before they put two and two together?"

"Assuming they can count that high."

"They shot at us. They've no fear of murder."

"Precisely why I insist you come home with me."

"But don't you see? As long as I slip back into the house before anyone notices I've gone missing, I'll be safe. And free to continue observing."

"You'll do no more observing." His voice was rough, edged with emotion. "Leave this to me."

"Is it not as dangerous for you as for me?"

"That doesn't matter."

She heard bitterness in his words, a hint of despair. His eyes glittered as he stared straight ahead into the darkness of the altar. She felt him slipping away again. Helpless to understand why, she gripped his shoulders so tightly she knew she must be hurting him. "It matters to me," she said with quiet fierceness.

His amber gaze caressed hers with sadness. "Don't, Sophie. Don't let it matter so much to you."

The beginning of tears pricked her eyes, pinched her throat. She pulled back, letting the cool air flood the space between them, even as a cold despondency filled her heart. "Why do you do this? Why do you reach for me, then push me away?"

"Because I have no right to reach." Pain etched his features in sharp relief.

"How can you say that? Why . . ." A disquieting suspicion slid from nowhere to silence her questions. She tried to shove it aside, tried not to think ill of him, but an insidious doubt quivered through her.

Lies. Half-truths. Evasiveness. He refused to admit being at Edgecombe the day she had seen him staring out the window. She couldn't help wondering what he might have been doing there that he didn't wish her to know about. Then this morning on the quay he had seemed overcome by a desperate, personal grief, though he had not known any of the victims brought ashore.

"What are you hiding?" She seized his face in her hands. "Have you . . . done something . . . something that makes you afraid?"

For an instant his startled reaction took her aback. Then he gained control of his features and locked his thoughts away behind a blank expression. He encircled her wrists and lowered her hands from his face. "Yes, I am afraid. *You* frighten me, Sophie, with your unthinking recklessness and your stubborn refusal to listen to reason. You might have gotten us both killed tonight."

The allegation stole her breath, sliced her to the core. Tears threatened once more, blurring his image. She blinked them away and realized what he had just done.

He had avoided her question. Avoided having to trust her or confide something about himself by turning the conversation back to her. Her faults. Her failings. As if she hadn't already been more than open with him. As if he didn't know far more about her than she did about him.

More evasiveness. More half-truths.

"You're lying." She raised her chin to meet the outthrust angle of his. "I don't care if that angers you; I'm not afraid to say it. You are carrying something around inside you, and it's destroying you."

"You know nothing about me."

She shook her head sadly. "Oh, but I do. The night we met, here in this very chapel, I saw who and what you are. A good and decent man. A man of courage and principles. A man I could easily . . ."

This time she was grateful for the rising sob that quelled a confession she might have regretted. "I believe I met the true Chad Rutherford that night, and I've been searching for him ever since."

"Have you considered that, like everything else that night, that man might have been a figment conjured by the mist?"

She wanted to shake him out of whatever miasma held him in its grip. Instead she moved off his lap, came to her feet and closed her cloak around her.

"I am returning to my aunt's house," she said. "I

have no choice. If I go to Edgecombe with you I'll only raise my uncle's suspicions. It is safer this way."

He stood up beside her, tall, brooding and still so desirable. She marveled that she could be so drawn to him, want him with such aching intensity, despite the barrier he maintained between them. Yet it was shaky at best, that barrier, and she knew that if she moved the necessary few inches, his arms would encircle her again, surround her in strength and protection. Oh, but not with the truth of what seethed inside him.

She resisted the urge and walked to the end of the pew. "Are you coming, or shall I make my way back alone?"

She started down the aisle, expecting him to follow. At the front door she stopped, listened for his footsteps, heard nothing, and pushed her way outside. Amid the jumble of leaning headstones she came to another uncertain halt. Would he let her stumble home alone across the moor? Had she pushed him away for good?

At a creaking behind her she whirled to behold him standing in the doorway. No part of him moved but his chest and shoulders, heaving up and down as if he'd run the length of the nave. He simply stood there with a wild, tumultuous look that pierced the darkness and prompted her to turn back around and shut her eyes.

His approaching stride pinned her to the spot. Her knees went weak as he came up behind her, as he snaked an arm around her waist. He pushed her hair aside and spoke against her nape.

"You want to know why I reach for you? Here's your answer." He pressed his length to her back and buttocks, his hard planes digging into her soft flesh. The restrained energy quivering in his muscles aroused her senses.

"No matter how strong I resolve to be, when I am near you I lose all sense of what is right." His whisper both scorched her flesh and raised goose bumps. "I forget who and what I am, and who and what you are. You wish to be reckless? To stand up to the likes of me? Then be warned. Despite my birth I am no gentleman. A lady like you should never put her trust in a rogue like me."

Before she had time to think, to either resist or acquiesce, he turned her around and crushed his mouth to hers. Confusion, shock and raging desire collided with the forceful thrust of his tongue, and the whole of her melted, surrendered to him without a struggle. As the kiss went on and on, she spiraled into the glory of it until the chapel and the graveyard dissolved around them, and reality became nothing more than their joined mouths, hot breath and pummeling hearts.

Then his hand was beneath her cloak, her shift, gliding between her thighs. Even as she sank into the compelling temptation of his palm a dangerous fear filled her, not of losing herself to him but of *relinquishing* herself, handing herself over without heeding the consequences. Consequences she sensed, feared . . . yet continually defied.

His free hand tunneling into her hair, he tipped her backward, robbing her of balance and exposing her throat to the heat of a blistering promise. "Were we anywhere else but on hallowed ground, I'd make you mine this instant and teach you a thing or two about risk and adventure."

His head came up, his eyes glinting with irony as he took in the churchyard. "Bless us, Father, for we have sinned. . . ."

"No, we haven't." Her voice caught. Giddy, reeling, she swallowed, trying to clear away the hitch and only half succeeding. "Not yet."

"But we will. We both know it."

A shiver went through her at the truth of those words.

He released her. They left the churchyard and made their way across Blackheath Moor, coming finally to the pastures, the road and her aunt's farm, where he kissed her quickly and disappeared into the night.

Chapter 14

It was all Chad could do to let Sophie go, to wait in the roadside shadows long enough to make certain she got inside without mishap, and then, when nothing disturbed the quiet farmhouse, to turn and walk away.

He left her at the hands of an uncle who could not be trusted, yet staying would only have endangered her further. She still didn't comprehend that. She thought she knew him, understood the kind of man he was. Good God, she had no idea how readily he could point to those men who had shot at them tonight and say, "I have conspired with fiends exactly like them. I am one of them."

But like a fraud and a cheat he had held his tongue, because part of him—perhaps the very worst part of him—could not let her go.

For her, then, in the effort to someday deserve even a shred of her regard, he doubled back onto Blackheath Moor. Using the stars and familiar rock formations to guide him, he approximated the path Gordon had followed and returned to the isolated farmstead.

All lay dark, as still as a crypt. Climbing over the outer wall, Chad crept close to the largest of the outbuildings, a sagging barn roofed with ragged tufts of thatch. A whiff of the air revealed no scent of dung, nor the pungent odor of perspiring hides. The barn held no animals, hadn't for quite some while.

So what *was* inside?

The wall facing him had no windows, no openings but the ventilation holes beneath the sloping thatch. He circled to a pair of wide plank doors held closed by a padlock. A heavy rock might break it, but he didn't dare risk the noise.

After another look about him he sprinted across the barnyard to the stone cottage. He approached the door gingerly and set his ear against the wood.

He heard nothing. Were they asleep, or gone?

He tried the latch. It stuck, then gave a click that arrested the beat of his heart. Breath frozen in his lungs, he waited. Then he opened the door an inch and moved his eye to the gap.

He both smelled and heard them before his eyes adjusted to the denser gloom inside. The place reeked of foul breath, sour whiskey and odors he would sooner have associated with the barn. The wheezy gusts of deep breathing and the occasional snort marked the rhythm of drunken slumber.

Gradually their outlines took shape. One lay stretched out on his stomach on the floor, his feet sprawled beneath a kitchen table, his head pillowed on what looked like an old boot. Near his half-curled hand, shards of glass caught the faint gleam of light from the open door. Bottles and tankards, some knocked on their sides, littered the tabletop. A second man sat in one of several mismatched chairs, head tipped against the wall, mouth open wide.

Despite the prudence of retreating, Chad lingered, squinting to make out their features. The merest phantom of familiarity stirred his memory. Had he encountered them at the tavern? On the docks this morning? He couldn't be sure. He studied the color of their hair, the shape of their features.

Rage released a scalding rush of blood into his veins. Whoever they were, their dirty hands had fired guns at Sophie. He found himself wishing he were capable of standing as judge and jury, of stepping across the threshold and making bloody certain neither of those miserable bastards ever again fired a gun.

A tiny glint banished his murderous thoughts. His pulse kicked but he hesitated, disbelieving the sight before him. Then he shouldered his way inside.

The offensive stench enveloped him. A cough threatened, but he swallowed against it. Moving with deliberate care he stepped over the body slumped across the earthen floor. He resisted the urge to give a good hard kick, instead bracing his feet and reaching toward the table. His fingers closed over cool metal.

A snore ripped through the silence. Heart crashing, Chad nearly dropped the ring of keys. They clattered in his palm. He froze, gaze zigzagging back and forth between the men. Inches from his feet a hand shot out, fingers grinding over the broken glass before once more falling limp. Chad backed toward the door.

"Wha . . . ?"

Halting in midstep, Chad stared into the open eyes of the man in the chair. With the clamor of a thousand bells hammering inside his skull, Chad stared back, unmoving, not breathing, praying for a miracle.

The drooping mouth formed another incoherent word, then went slack. The eyes dropped shut. Wasting no time, Chad cleared the threshold in two swift strides and eased the door closed behind him. His prize clutched tight, he dashed across the open ground to the barn.

His pulse careened the moment the doors swung open and he stepped inside. He had been right. No animals inhabited this barn. He didn't know where to turn first, which part of the piled mound to explore. Crates, trunks, barrels, casks . . .

Evidence. Scads of it. Enough to put away these drunken swine for many years to come. But for what? Smuggling? No great revelation there, except it contradicted the vicar's claims that smuggling in Penhollow had all but ceased.

From where had this plunder originated? And under whose orders? He considered the two men in the cottage. Would they show up at Edgecombe one day soon to issue the commands the condemned pirate, Giles Watling, had told Chad to await? How, exactly, did Sophie's uncle fit into the mix? Instinct told him all three constituted a workforce, and that their leader remained elusive. If he summoned the authorities prematurely, his efforts might merely serve to send other, more blameworthy culprits into hiding.

He retraced his steps, relocking the barn doors and stealing back into the shack. He dared not leave the slightest trace of his presence. He wanted the bastards to remain confident.

Repeating his earlier actions in reverse, he leaned over the sprawling form and placed the keys on the table. Then he set out for Edgecombe, intent on forming a plan.

Following breakfast the next morning, a bleary-eyed Sophie returned to her bedroom to discover Rachel kneeling on the floor and pulling something out from under the bed they shared. Sophie's heart stilled as the younger girl tossed her curly black hair over her shoulder and glanced up, her hands filled with the stained folds of broadcloth she had just drawn into her lap.

Knowing she could not have returned the cloak to the kitchen with mud and vegetation clinging to its hem, Sophie had bundled the garment beneath the bed with plans to set it to rights at the first opportunity.

An opportunity she had apparently missed.

"Where were you last night?" her cousin asked.

Guilty heat suffused Sophie's cheeks, until she remembered she was being confronted by a girl four years her junior, one who not only bore her own secrets, but whose father consorted with criminals.

"I couldn't sleep, so I went for a walk."

Rachel pushed to her feet and held out the cloak. "Where? Across the moors?"

Sophie swallowed. "Of course not. I took a shortcut through one of the holding pens. I'm sorry. I'll do my best to clean it. If need be, I'll purchase another."

Rachel ran a hand back and forth across the soiled lining. "Still damp. A walk across a holding pen would not have soaked it so."

"I went as far as the beach. I must have strayed too close to the water's edge. What does it matter? Why all these questions?" She regretted the query immediately. Better to have let the subject drop.

She retrieved the cloak from her cousin's arms. "A good, stiff brushing will dislodge most of this mess," she said with false brightness. "If not, I'm certain your mother will know an effective remedy."

"Supposing I ask Father how best to clean it?"

Sophie met her gaze. "Don't."

"Why not?"

"Because I'm asking you. Just don't." She drew a steadying breath and searched Rachel's pretty features, shadowed now by apprehension. Was Rachel debating her loyalties? Could Sophie hope to prevail against the girl's own father?

"I'm worried about you, Sophie. I'm . . ."

"You're what, Rachel? Frightened? You are, aren't you? I see it in your eyes."

"Don't be silly." The girl blinked, looked away. "I have nothing to be frightened of. I simply don't wish to see you land in yet another scrape."

The reference to Sophie's London disgrace sent her chin inching higher. "Am I the only one with a penchant for scrapes?"

It was Rachel's turn to bristle. "What do you mean?"

"I'm referring to the fisherman you were so desperate to find at the quay yesterday. The rather strapping young man with sandy hair. What was his name, Ian? You shed a good many tears over him before you learned he was safe, yet you didn't so much as acknowledge his presence once we reached the tavern and you were surrounded by people again. Nor he you, come to think of it."

A guilty blaze flooded Rachel's face. She swept to the window, her back to Sophie. "Ian and I haven't done anything wrong. It's just that . . . Father doesn't approve. Not yet, at any rate. Mother suspects, but only Dominic knows that Ian and I find opportunities to meet. And now you, of course."

"I won't tell a soul," Sophie promised quietly, "but surely you're not going to wait for your father's approval. Not if you love your young man."

Rachel didn't reply. Sudden indignation sent Sophie to her. She grasped her cousin's shoulder and spun her about. "Why won't you answer me? Are you going to allow your father to rob you of happiness? Will you sit in his house silently carding wool for the rest of your life?"

Rachel wrenched away. "I card wool, and dye it, spin it and weave it, because it is among my duties to do so. Because my first allegiance is to my family, not myself."

The hurt in her voice doused Sophie righteous anger and stabbed at her conscience. If Sophie's loyalties to her own family had matched her cousin's, perhaps she would have taken greater pains to ensure that the incident at the Winthrops' never occurred.

But she hadn't. She had set her own ambitions first, with disastrous results.

She grasped Rachel's hands, usually so steady as they performed intricate chores, but now trembling and damp. "I'm sorry. I didn't mean to belittle your life; truly I didn't. I have nothing but respect for you and for all you do here."

The truth of those words resonated. Had she initially believed Rachel to be docile, lacking in ambition? For all her reticence, Rachel possessed a strength

Sophie could never hope to attain, the sort that allowed the younger girl to put the needs of others well before her own without a word of complaint.

Humbled, she drew Rachel with her onto the edge of bed. "Our lives have been so different. Perhaps I do not—cannot—fully understand what yours has been, but I'd like to. If you'd give me the chance."

Rachel gave a half shrug, a sad smile. "Our mothers are sisters, but as unalike as these moors from a London street. Your mother married into wealth and privilege, mine into hardship, at least by comparison. But my father wooed her, and she fell in love with him. Loves him still . . ."

"Yes. I suppose I can see that." In their harsh way, Aunt Louisa and Uncle Barnaby did share a tenderness of sorts. Did her own mother love her father? Sophie had never considered the question before. She discovered she didn't know the answer.

"My parents have both changed so much through the years," Rachel said sadly, "especially these last several—"

She seemed to catch herself and went silent.

"What about these past years?" Sophie prompted. "What changed? Have they become unhappy?" *Is that when your father became involved with brigands?*

As if contemplating making her escape, Rachel regarded the bedroom door with longing.

Sophie squeezed her hand. "Forgive me. I have no business prying."

Rachel's face became pinched. "Promise me you'll do as Father says and stay out of trouble. Promise me that, Sophie, and I won't mention the cloak to anyone. I'll even say I dirtied it myself should anyone ask. Just swear to me you won't go sneaking off again."

This last ended in a whisper fraught with anxiety, and Sophie knew with a certainty that Rachel's warnings were not given out of a general concern for her welfare. The girl *knew* something, perhaps more than

her family suspected she did. Wasn't it always the
quiet ones who rooted out everyone's carefully
guarded secrets? Perhaps Rachel even knew where
her father went last night, and why.

How Sophie yearned to forget civility and grill the
girl for answers. Yet she knew pressing Rachel would
do no good. That strength she had detected moments
ago would keep those answers locked securely away
until Rachel was ready to divulge them.

By the same token Sophie didn't think she could
fool her cousin with a blatant lie. "I wish to neither
find trouble nor stir it up," she said. "But I am who
I am. My family hoped my being here would help
quell my natural tendencies to delve into affairs that
shouldn't concern me. I'm afraid it isn't working."

"No, indeed. They were wrong to send you to Penhollow." Rachel stood up from the bed and went to
the door. "Dreadfully wrong."

"Rachel, wait." When the girl paused with her hand
on the knob, Sophie hopped down from the bed. "I
can't promise I'll stay out of trouble, but I'll try if
you'll promise me something in return."

"Yes?"

"Never give up on the man you love, even if your
father disapproves."

Rachel merely stared back, then turned and left
the room.

Deep within Edgecombe's foundations, Chad lowered his lantern, illuminating the stone and tile flooring as he made his way through the chilly vaults. One
by one he inspected the meat and dairy larders, the
ice and coal closets and, at the end of the whitewashed
corridor, his father's wine cellar.

Long ago, in his childish zeal for adventure, he had
scampered through these cellars, dodging busy servants as he searched for the Keatings' legendary tunnel. He had found nothing. His father had chuckled

at his disappointment and told him that if the Keatings *had* built a tunnel, they certainly wouldn't have made its access so obvious that a child could find it.

Remembering what the vicar had revealed to him beneath the pulpit, Chad examined more than the walls. He pushed against cupboards and counters to see if they moved. He tapped the flooring with his feet. If those men at the farmstead had been talking about Edgecombe—and Chad would swear they had been—then there had to be a tunnel . . . somewhere. There was simply no other way to bring in cargo from the sea, no other way past the cliffs lining the coast beyond the harbor.

The Gordons' farm . . . He ruled out the possibility. True, the beach and sloping property provided easy accessibility to the water's edge, but it was also too visible from both the village and the road to offer any real privacy to anyone unloading illicit cargo from a ship.

As soon as Grady returned from Mullion, Chad intended to have another look at the coastline from water level. Until then, however . . . he stepped down into the wine cellar.

Bottles glinted in the surrounding shadows. Placing his lantern on the floor, Chad ran his palms over the damp walls and pushed against the stone shelving. All felt and appeared as solid as the rock from which it had been quarried. He retrieved the lantern and started to leave, planning next to try the laundry cellar. A whisper of a breeze stopped him.

Turning in a slow circle, he studied the play of light and shadow on the walls and bottles. At a faint skittering sound, his head snapped to the left, toward an alcove once used for storing casks, but empty now.

He stepped down into the recess and felt an infinitesimal shift in the tiles beneath his feet, so slight that anyone else would have assumed that age-loosened grout had caused the movement.

Heart racing, he fell to his knees to examine the

clay tiles. With the flat of his hand he pushed down, then from side to side. As one solid unit the tiles shifted again. He bent lower, brought the lantern closer and could just make out the infinitesimal gaps running around the centermost tiles to form a square some three feet wide.

A trapdoor.

Excitement rippled through him. He jiggled the tiles again and realized he would need a tool to wedge them open. Remembering the collection of tongs and picks hanging from the wall of the ice chamber, he bolted to his feet. In the corridor he heard a thud penetrate the arched ceiling above his head.

He went still, head raised to listen. He heard it again. Someone was above, in the kitchen.

Sophie? As eagerly as he grasped at the possibility, it didn't make sense. Not after their time at the chapel. He had all but warned her to stay away from him, had practically threatened her, then substantiated his admonitions by pawing and groping her.

No, surely not Sophie. Then . . .

Get rid of him . . . soon enough.

The men from the farmstead?

Blood pumping, he grabbed a wine bottle off the nearest shelf and headed for the steps. At the top he paused to listen. The partially open door offered a slim view of the main pantry. He saw no one, but heard movement in the adjoining kitchen. His fingers tightened around the neck of the bottle.

The shuffling nature of the individual's gait perplexed him, as did the creaking of cupboard doors. Not an assassin, then, but a thief? Not necessarily any less dangerous.

He pushed the door wider, freezing when the hinges whined. Sweat beaded across his brow. When no one rushed in to discover him, he swiped a sleeve across his forehead, pushed the flat of one palm against the door and stepped through.

A sudden clatter suggested the intruder was rummaging through a cutlery drawer just to the right of the pantry doorway. Chad listened for signs of a second individual, but heard none. Raising the bottle above his head, he set a foot on the threshold.

With a howl he leaped through the doorway. A shriek filled his ears; a flurry of motion blurred in his vision. A mug flew at him, sailing over his shoulder and smashing against the brick hearth behind him. He caught an image of wild eyes, grizzled hair, a pair of gnarled hands. Then he lunged.

Chapter 15

Chad rammed a lean, stooping figure up against the work counter. The cupboard below shuddered from the impact of booted calves. A glass went over and shattered. Cutlery fell with a clatter onto the floor. Chad bent the man over backward, pinning his gaunt shoulders to the countertop. A haggard face gaped up at the bottle hovering in Chad's raised fist.

His other hand circled the intruder's neck. "Who the hell are you and what the devil do you want?" A sputtering reply prompted him to ease his grip a fraction. "Who are you?"

"N-Nathaniel."

Chad regarded terrified features, wide, rolling eyes. The intruder's remaining resistance drained away, and Chad concluded that whoever Nathaniel was, he posed little threat to anyone. The poor man was frightened out of his wits.

Chad released him, set the bottle on the counter and backed away. "What are you doing here?"

Nathaniel unfolded his gangly length from the counter. He pointed a crooked finger toward the cast-iron cookstove. "Preparing breakfast."

Chad saw a frying pan on the stovetop. Beside it a coffeepot gurgled, emitting jets of steam. On the worktable beside it sat a jug of milk, several eggs and a rasher of bacon.

"Did Kellyn send you?"

"She said I was to do the cooking and the cleaning, look after the horse and whatever else milord requires."

Chad took in Nathaniel's leathery features, the befuddlement clouding his faded brown eyes. The fellow stood clutching his hands, shifting uncertainly from foot to foot.

The gesture touched a chord of sympathy in Chad. For all his advanced years, Nathaniel seemed little more than a child. Chad smiled to set the man at ease. "You're a man-of-all-work, then?"

"Aye. Been doing the trimming."

"Trimming? You must mean the gardening. Are you the groundskeeper hired by my solicitor?"

This was met with a look of confusion. Nathaniel shrugged. "I do the trimming and the sweeping." Frowning, he shuffled backward, his heels thwacking the cupboard doors. "Only by day. Ain't safe by night."

Seeing the man's agitation, Chad held up his hands in a gesture of reassurance. "That's quite all right, Nathaniel. I won't ask you to come at night, and I'll always be sure to release you well before dusk. Did Kellyn discuss your wages?"

Nathaniel shrugged.

"Well, we'll arrange something." A sudden notion prompted Chad to ask, "Nathaniel, since you've been looking after Edgecombe for me, have you ever encountered anyone in the house or on the grounds?"

Wide-eyed, he gave an adamant shake of his head. "Ain't seen no one."

"You're quite sure?"

"No one." Boot heels struck the cupboard doors again.

It was an awfully quick answer, in Chad's estimation. As if Nathaniel had been instructed by someone to make such a denial. Thinking it unlikely he'd glean much useful information from his new manservant, he gestured toward the stove. "You continue cooking breakfast, Nathaniel, and then put it in the warmer for me. I like my bacon crisp. In the meantime, I'm going below again for a little while."

"Never go below," he heard the man murmur to his back.

Chad turned. "Who told you that? Kellyn?"

Nathaniel only stared, his faded eyes unreadable.

"Chad? Are you here?"

The echo of Sophie's own call made her jump, while the resounding silence of the house raised a shiver of unease. Going to the staircase, she placed her foot on the bottom step and craned her neck to view the corridor above. "Chad? It's Sophie."

Was he upstairs in his room? A wayward tendril of longing curled about her apprehension. The last time she had climbed these steps she had discovered the rapture of forbidden pleasure in Chad's arms. A rapture that might have been repeated last night, had they been anywhere else but the chapel.

Had she made a mistake in coming here? Of being alone in this deserted house . . . with him? Desire stabbed, evoking the scent of him, the taste of him, the heat of his touch on her bared flesh. At the same time an unsettling fear of something she could not name breathed caution against her nape.

Be warned . . . I am no gentleman.

Oh, that was what he would have her believe, and perhaps there was truth to it. But something more lurked inside him. Something he feared . . . and feared her knowing. . . .

But she had not come here for seduction, or to confront him about his secrets. She called his name one more time, then turned away from the staircase and chose a direction at random. She entered a drawing room, long, elegant in a masculine fashion, but revealing no sign of Chad.

Moving on into the next room, she came to a closed door, and once again her heart gave a thump. Could

this be the room from which she had first spied Chad?
She pressed her ear to the door. Hearing nothing, she
knocked and spoke his name. With a quick look over
her shoulder, she turned the knob, peeked . . .

. . . and gasped. That day she had seen Chad she had
crossed the terrace to have a look through the window.
She had seen furniture, countless books and every indication that someone used this room as a library.

Now empty bookshelves gaped from the walls, and
no furnishings remained. She ran her hand across the
nearest bare shelf, blew dust from her fingers, and
moved to the window that overlooked the terrace.
Closed shutters obstructed the view. She raised the
window, opened the wooden shutters, and pushed the
window closed again.

Yes, this had to be the room. The waviness of the
panes blurred the gardens, but she could make out
the unkempt rows of pear trees, dogwoods and the
wilder, native rowans. That day Chad had looked directly at her, long enough to have remembered her.
Yet when they met at the chapel he had shown no
hint of recognition, and later denied having been here.

Why?

The design of the window seized her attention. She
backed up to study the diamond-paned mullions and
stone sill. Details of that morning tumbled back.

The window had been a *bay,* not flush to the walls
as it was now, but bowing gracefully outward beneath
the slope of a slate overhang.

A whisper at her shoulder made her jump. She pivoted, expecting to find Chad behind her. There was
only the empty room, the strangely yawning shelves.
A hiss raked her spine.

Mmmurrrrderrrr.

Whirling, she once more confronted the window, to
find nothing but the view outside, the trees and hedges
shuddering in the sea breezes.

Quickly she retraced her steps into the hall.
"Chad— Oh!"

Her hand flew to her mouth but not in time to stifle a yelp. Moving from the slanting shadows of a formal dining room a figure emerged, tall and thin and stooped. As he moved in front of the terrace door, the light behind him threw his features into dark relief. She could make out only deep-set eyes and a grim slash of a mouth.

Heart lodging in her throat, Sophie backed into the bend of the staircase. With a swift glance to the front door, she gauged her chances of escaping. She might make it out, but he could easily catch her in the fore-court.

She thrust out her chin and conjured her most commanding tone. "Who are you? Where is Lord Wycliffe?"

"I'm Nathaniel." He made no move toward her. "Milord's below."

"Below as in where? The kitchen? The cellars?"

A freshly dug grave?

"I insist you tell me exactly where Lord Wycliffe is," she said. "This instant, and don't simply say 'below.' "

Sharp shoulders hunched beneath a worn tweed coat. "Dunno."

"Don't know, or won't tell?" Her misgivings kicked up like a sea breeze. "H-has anything happened to him? W-why are you here?"

"Cook the meals, tend the horse, trim the garden."

She blinked. "What?"

"His horse needs oats and a good brushing down." He started to turn away.

Her apprehensions realigned into sheer bafflement. She stepped out from the staircase. "Good Lord, you're his servant, yes?"

Wariness crept over his face. "By day. Only by day."

The odd comment piqued her curiosity. "Why only by day? What happens here after nightfall?"

Nathaniel's bristly eyebrows converged. "Milord promised I may leave before dusk."

"I see. Well, if his lordship promised, then you needn't worry." No longer fearing him, she strode past the bewildered servant and entered the dining hall. "I suppose this way eventually leads to the service staircase and down to the kitchen? Is that where I'll find the earl?"

Nathaniel didn't answer. As Sophie reached the middle of the room, a faint rumbling shook the floor beneath her feet. Above the dining table the crystal chandelier tinkled.

"What on earth?"

She felt another shudder; then all went still. Nathaniel stood braced in the doorway behind her, hands pressed to the lintel on either side.

"Not safe." His eyes rolled upward, exposing the whites. "Must go."

Before she could object, he scurried through the terrace door and was gone.

The quiet pressed in around her. Chad was still somewhere below. . . .

She forced her legs to move despite their trembling. One empty, silent room followed upon another until she found the service corridor and stairwell. At the bottom she came upon a scullery, where pans and dishes dripped on the drain board beside the water pump. Seeing no signs of a disturbance she stepped into the main kitchen, where the aroma of cooked bacon permeated the air.

"Chad?" She cleared her throat and spoke louder. "Your man told me I'd find you down here. Please don't jump out at me or anything."

How stupid of her; of course he wouldn't do any such thing. In a walk-in pantry a door stood partially ajar. Beyond the threshold stone steps plunged away into inky darkness. She leaned in and called his name. The downward spiral of her voice twisted her stomach into knots of reluctance.

"I suppose if I'm going to leap," she whispered

shakily, "I should at least be able to see what I'm leaping into."

Doubling back into the kitchen, she snatched a lantern off a windowsill and lit it with a piece of stove kindling. Then she returned to the stairs, steeling herself for the descent.

A subterranean chill greeted her at the bottom. Her lamplight flickered over whitewashed walls and arched ceilings, and sent shadows dancing in the doorways of workrooms and larders. Her footsteps raised a clamor on the tile-and-stonework flooring and made her cringe.

The corridor ended at the entrance to a wine cellar, where her lamp reflected dollops of light on countless bottles. Detecting no sign of Chad, she turned to go.

Sophie.

"Chad?" She spun full circle.

Nothing in the room moved; not a sound drifted from the corridor. Perhaps a rustle of her petticoats had deceived her ears. She arced the lantern, chasing the shadows from an alcove in the corner. In the tile flooring a hole gaped.

She dangled her lantern over the opening. A set of steps that appeared to be carved into the natural bedrock led down to an earthen floor. Sophie's pulse leaped. A tunnel leading out to the sea?

"Chad? Please answer if you can hear me."

Her words echoed back at her, ending on a hollow, far off note. Did the rumble she'd felt upstairs mean he had been hurt? With the lantern clutched in one hand she gathered her skirts and climbed down into a colder, damper, exceedingly *darker* place than even the cellars had been. Goose bumps peppered her arms. The floor sloped sharply downward.

After several minutes of picking her way along a narrow passage, she suspected she could no longer be beneath the house, but somewhere under the gardens, under the trees and grass and earth and rock.

Like a grave.

The tunnel tapered, became cramped. Loose stones slid out from beneath her feet, and the sounds of sliding earth and dripping water echoed around her. Her ankle turned on the uneven ground, and she stumbled across a pile of stones. Pressing a palm to the wet wall, she caught her balance and steadied the lantern. A few feet farther on, a wall of rock and broken timbers blocked her way. She raised the lantern. Gouged ridges of earth that had once been the tunnel's ceiling disappeared into blackness.

Her thrashing heart froze. Then she filled her lungs and shouted his name, until a new fear silenced her. She gaped at the earth above her head. Could loud sounds bring down more of the tunnel's ceiling? She'd have to take that chance. Feeling about she found a stone small enough to wrap her fingers around. With a little prayer that she wasn't making a terrible mistake, she tapped the stone against another, larger one.

After several moments she stopped. Her heart and the whole of her insides went still as she listened. And then, as if from a great distance, a faint knocking sounded. A cry tearing from her lungs, she rapped her stone again, harder. Three beats, then a pause, followed by three more beats.

She heard the pattern repeated, muffled and weak, from the other side of the cave-in. In her excitement she forgot about being careful and scrambled over the boulders, pressing herself up against the dividing rubble.

"Chad, it's Sophie. Can you hear me? Are you hurt?"

"No . . . don't think so . . ." Clenching his teeth, Chad pulled himself to a sitting position. Wooziness rolled through him. Sophie called his name again, and he realized his response had been too weak for her to hear. He drew a breath. "I'm all right."

He wasn't. Pain stabbed his right ankle. Stones bit into the backs of his legs. He touched his fingertips to his temple and winced. How long had he been out?

A memory flashed in his brain, and revulsion sent him shoving up against the rock wall beside him. Earlier he had come upon the cave-in and judged it to have occurred long ago. But he had discovered a gap preserved by the fallen cross timbers and had heaved himself through. Lantern in hand, he had maneuvered only three-quarters of the way when sediment began raining down. He'd only just managed to pull himself clear before the gap closed. If he had moved any slower he might have been crushed.

He had landed headfirst on the cavern floor. His lantern had toppled over with a crash, but not before a harrowing sight greeted him. Though he couldn't see them now in the dark, he keenly felt the presence of the two skeletons lying a few feet away.

"Sophie," he called. "Shine your lantern as close to the wall as you can. Try to find a gap."

When she did, spears of light pierced the cavern. A metallic object glinted on the ground close by. He reached, closing his hand around the hilt of a sword. He pulled it close, a shock of recognition running through him as he examined the hilt. The weapon seemed to vibrate with a cold current against his palms, or was it merely his own reaction to the find?

"I think I've found a way through," she shouted. "Do you see it? I'll reach through. Try to clasp my hand."

He lowered the sword to his side. "No, Sophie. Just set the lantern down and back away."

"Don't be ridiculous. Can you make out where I am?"

Realizing she wasn't going to listen to him, he searched the fissures penetrated by her light, and crouched beside the largest one. He stretched his arm through until his shoulder stuck the edge of the opening. His fingertips came up against softness, warmth, hope. Her fingers hooked around his, and for one giddy moment he thought she might magically pull him through. He couldn't see her, yet a vision of her filled him—her face, her smile, her wide, earnest eyes. A sense of purpose and empowerment surged through him.

"Sophie, move away. I've an idea I can try from my side."

Gripping the sword hilt in both hands, he rammed the weapon into the gap. The steel rang out, sending a jolting vibration up his arm. But he felt the slightest of shifts, and sediment and pebbles clattered to the ground.

"Do it again," she urged.

The grinding of the steel reverberated through the cavern. By agonizing increments he dug away at earth and stone, widening the gap. As he worked, his insides ran cold at the thought of another cave-in, of Sophie being hurt, but he had little choice. Without a lantern of his own he'd have virtually no chance of making his way to the other end of the tunnel. In such utter darkness he'd be stumbling blindly, perhaps into another wall of debris, or a chasm in the ground, or he could miss a turn and wander into an impossible maze.

"I can see you!" Sophie's triumphant cry echoed from the other side of the wall. "Try to slip through."

"Stand back." Sword in hand, he squeezed into the opening, which was barely wide enough to accommodate his shoulders. His shirt tore. His skin stung as the jagged stone scraped him raw. Contorting, twisting, he pushed on toward Sophie's light, her encouraging voice.

His momentum stopped. He was stuck. Wedged in tight. Trapped in a wall of rock that threatened to crush him, he could budge neither his arms nor his legs. Couldn't move ahead or go back the way he'd come. Hopelessness filled him until a force from behind, like a shove, thrust him forward.

Chapter 16

"Chad, have you hurt yourself? Can you reach out your hand to me?"

Sophie's throat closed around a sudden terror. Why had he stopped? Her arms ached to hold him, to save him as he had saved her last night.

A glimmer of golden hair winked in the lamplight, and surging relief made her giddy. His shoulder came next. Then an arm extended beyond his head, dragging an object toward her. Metal clanged, scraped. Chad grunted. What was he holding?

The answer came as he thrust the basket hilt of a rapier at her. Mystified, she took the weapon and placed it on the ground.

"Grab my hands." He sounded drained, his energy nearly spent, "and pull."

Sophie did. Pulled as though her life, his, everything she held dear depended on it, drawing on the same borrowed strength that had gotten her to the top of a seaside cliff and across a moor when men were chasing them.

Pulling him through seemed akin to the birth process as Sophie imagined it might be. Pain. Difficulty. Fear. The sheer sweat of effort. Little by little, with her help, he maneuvered his body past flesh-scraping stone until his head and shoulders cleared the opening on her side. With a final heave he fell out, his arms wrapping her waist and his weight propelling her off balance.

Together they toppled among the rocks in a tangle of arms and legs. She was half on him, half under him, with the rocks biting into her thigh, his solid torso snug against the rest of her and the fingers of her hand fisted in a shank of his hair.

Tears streamed down her face, sopping his shoulder where her cheek pressed it. She didn't know why she was crying. Despite a bevy of minor injuries he seemed well enough. So was she. Truly, this had been nothing compared to fleeing armed brigands in the black of night. But the tears flowed regardless, riding upon hiccupping sobs.

His breath came in hot puffs against her neck. "Are you all right?"

Frenzied laughter bubbled in her throat. She buried her face in his shirtfront and held on tight until the trembling subsided, though which of them shook more she couldn't say. Gently he unfolded his length from around her, eased to his feet and helped her up.

Holding her face in his hands, he peered intently at her and smiled. "You look and sound the way I felt last night when I realized you hadn't been shot."

She responded with weepy laughter, a fresh surge of tears. He wiped them from her cheeks with his palms.

She gestured toward the rock slide. "Is this a smugglers' tunnel?"

"If it was, it hasn't been used in a long time." With the toe of his boot he nudged a loose stone. "I didn't cause this cave-in; I only roused its anger." He shook his head and rolled his left shoulder. "Let's get the hell out of here, shall we, and then I'll explain."

"Not a moment too soon for me."

Sophie took the lantern. Chad carried the sword, looking like an embattled warrior in his torn and bloodied shirt. His sleeve had nearly ripped away from his left shoulder, revealing zigzagging abrasions that scored the muscle beneath. The soldier image carried over to his face in the stony set of his features and the brutal exhaustion in his eyes. He limped as well, favoring his right ankle.

A brief glimpse down at her muslin dress revealed dark blotches gleaming wet in the lamplight. Chad's blood. Far from being repulsed by the sight, she pressed her free hand over one of the stains and experienced an odd sense that his blood forever connected them with a bond that surpassed anything the future might hold.

Her stomach turned an unsettling flip-flop. A connection to Chad, to the man who scaled cliffs, outran bullets, defied cave-ins . . . and who awakened in her startling, exhilarating sensations. Yes, the notion of being with that man filled her with an elation as bright and glorious as the hair on his head.

But that man also harbored another side, one swathed in secrecy and darkness, hidden behind walls he would not allow her to breach, no matter how hard she tried. And she was not the sort of woman to cease trying, to be content with the limited, incomplete part of himself he offered.

Then again, he had offered nothing. No matter what they had been through together, what they had shared, she must not forget that he had made her no promises. He'd made no mention of a mutual future of any kind. It was just that sometimes, because of the intimacy they had shared after so short an acquaintance, she felt as if he had.

Her gaze pinned with regret on the broad sweep of his shoulders and, yes, the tight arc of his rear, she followed him through the tunnel and up the steps. After offering an arm to help her safely into the wine cellar, he stopped to examine the bottles ranged along the nearest shelf.

Still clutching the sword in one hand, he grabbed a bottle and continued on. Before they reached the doorway, he tossed her a rueful look, tucked the bottle in the crook of his elbow and snatched another.

"Are you going to tell me about that thing?" She gestured at the weapon.

"After I get a good measure of this wine in me."

They both blinked in the comparatively bright light of the kitchen. Sophie cringed at the amount of blood smearing Chad's linen shirt. "I'll tend to your injuries." She opened a drawer at random, hoping to find dishcloths.

His hand came down on her wrist. With his hip he pushed the drawer closed. "Later. It'll sting less after a bit of wine."

He rummaged through the cupboards for glasses and a corkscrew. These he handed to her, retrieved the bottles, grabbed the sword and half limped, half sauntered into an adjoining room. The long oak table and its flanking benches declared this to be the former servants' dining hall. Chad straddled the end of a bench and plunked the bottles and sword on the table.

"Hand me that corkscrew." He dragged out the ladder-back chair at the head of the table and patted its seat. "Get comfortable. We may be here for a while."

Hunching over the table, he said nothing more until he'd consumed the whole of two glasses of claret and poured a third. Sophie nursed hers carefully until her first glass became two-thirds empty. Then she found herself nearly matching him swallow for swallow. A headache that had been threatening since the tunnel now began to fade. Her body felt lighter, her mind calmer. For the first time in weeks her soul felt freer.

Chin propped on her palm, she watched him tip the glass to his lips, following the path of the wine as his throat constricted, the sharp peak of his Adam's apple twitching beneath the skin. His torn and bloodied sleeves were shoved to the elbows, displaying bruises on his forearms.

Her gaze darted back to the chiseled features—the intelligent curve of his brow, the strong length of his nose, and his mouth, that single, devastating hint of tenderness borne with such unthinking confidence, such poise. Her insides stirred. He was so beautiful. So male. So perfect.

Why *couldn't* she have a relationship with this man? After several more sips of wine she couldn't quite remember the reasons.

At the clunk of his glass hitting the tabletop, those reasons came hurtling back. She flinched as her reflections scattered, and felt ashamed to have lost herself in such inappropriate yearnings when she should have been focused on his welfare.

He wiped the back of his hand across his mouth and pinned her with a glare. "On one hand I'm grateful as the dickens you happened by today, and on the other I'd like to wring your lovely neck."

He reached over, laying his open palm against her collarbone, caressing her throat with his thumb while his long fingers raised tingles at her nape. "What in bloody hell were you thinking wandering here alone after what happened last night, not to mention venturing into a tunnel where you had no inkling what the conditions might be?"

"Are you going to berate me for saving your blasted hide?"

"No." His hand slid to her shoulder. He gave her a gentle shake. "I'm going to berate you for risking yours."

"Ah. *That* again."

"Yes, *that*." Another shake. "Can you deny the foolhardiness of your actions?"

"They were no more foolhardy than yours. What were *you* thinking, traipsing through that tunnel alone? What if I hadn't been hell-bent on finding you? Believe me, I entertained several notions of giving up." She shuddered as she remembered the whisper that had spurred her on. So like his voice it had sounded . . . yet it could not have been. "Do you think your servant would have come looking for you?"

"Nathaniel? God, no." His hand fell away. He

snatched up his glass and took a long swallow. "But men shot at us last night. Does that not suggest a need for caution? Not to mention the risk you're taking in testing your uncle's limits by sneaking away from the farm."

"Uncle's Barnaby's threats are pure bluster. I realize that now. His association with those men proves he has more to hide than I do, and he daren't risk attracting my grandfather's attention, neither by hurting me nor by reporting back on my behavior. Besides, it is because of what happened last night that I came."

He lowered his glass so quickly that the scarlet liquid nearly sloshed over the rim. "You've learned something else? Has something more happened?"

"Nothing like that. But my aunt and uncle left Penhollow immediately after breakfast this morning. They're riding up to Mullion on business concerning their farm, and won't return until quite late."

"Mullion, you say?"

"Yes. They might even spend the night." She leaned forward. "Dominic should be busy with the herds for hours. I thought we might take the opportunity to poke about the farm to see what my uncle might be hiding. I could distract Rachel while you—" She broke off and ran a quick gaze over him. "Oh, but look at you. You're bleeding and limping. You've no business traipsing about anywhere, much less sneaking about a farm."

"At least not by day." His eyebrows pulled tight as he considered. "You say they'll be gone until late. If you could manage to distract both your cousins, I'll have a look about. Though it's doubtful Gordon will have anything illegal stashed on his property. That's what the moorland homestead is used for."

"How do you know that? We didn't—"

"I did. After I brought you home I doubled back. The barn is filled with cargo. Illegal, undoubtedly, for I can think of no logical reason for legitimate merchandise to be stored anywhere but at the warehouses along Penhollow Harbor."

His first statement had snared Sophie's attention and she barely heard the rest. Her hands snapped to her hips. "And you call *me* reckless."

At the combative expression gathering on his features, she decided she would gain nothing now by raising an argument. If anything a tender gratitude grew in place of her indignation. Dear man, of course he had returned alone rather than risk her being shot at again. Her thoughts must have shown on her face, for his scowl deepened as he splashed more wine into his glass.

She changed the subject. "Uncle Barnaby might not have a cache of stolen goods hidden on the farm, but he might very well have the equipment needed for guiding ships away from the harbor at night. I *know* he had something to do with those shore lights I saw. Last night convinces me all the more."

"I'll concede that you may be right."

"Then we should—"

She flinched as his glass slammed the table. Wine spattered onto his shirt, her dress. His free hand slid into his hair and fisted. "Can you never let anything rest? *We* should not do anything."

Nothing of tenderness resonated in his outburst, only sharp, prickly anger. Resentful frustration pinched her throat and forestalled any rejoinder she might have made. Seconds passed in taut silence, marked only by the strained rhythm of his breathing. The guarded stranger had returned, and once more she felt pushed away, cut off.

With a resigned sigh, she stood up beside him and quietly said, "I'll tend to your wounds now. Take off your shirt."

Sophie returned from the main kitchen moments later bearing cloths and a washbasin filled with water.

Chad had not removed his shirt. He had done nothing but brood and drink wine and wonder if she would ever be content to stop probing.

He might not have recognized those men at the farmstead last night, but he felt fairly certain they belonged to the same smuggling gang with which he had involved himself over the past two years. And someday soon their leader would come for him, either to embroil him deeper or to make him pay for testifying against their cohorts.

Good God, what if today was that day, while Sophie was here?

As she set the bowl and linens on the table, he wrapped a hand around a bottle and tipped the remaining contents into his glass. "Not now."

"Yes, now." She leaned over him and summarily began unbuttoning his shirt.

Her fingertips sparked his flesh and prompted him to suck in a sharp breath as a pain of sorts shot through him—the lancing of acute desire, of wanting her, all of her, and knowing he didn't deserve her. His hands closed over hers. "I'll do it."

She nodded, her cheeks mottled pink. Her blush deepened as he peeled the shirt from his arms and draped it over the bench beside him. Cool air grazed the web of scratches covering his shoulders, arms and chest. In contrast the heat of her gaze scorched him raw.

"Good heavens." Eyebrows knitted tight, she wet a cloth, wrung it out over the bowl and pressed it to his rib cage. He winced, hissing through his teeth. "I'm sorry," she whispered.

Delicate, graceful hands bathed the wounds clean. The torn flesh stung where the cloth touched, but her fingertips roused excruciating pinpoints of pleasure. Her repeated apologies for hurting him feathered across his skin. Desire wrestled with pain until the two entwined to become one aching, single-minded resolve.

He seized her wrist. "Stop."

"I'm sorry, but you don't wish an infection, do you?" Held in midair, the rag dripped water onto his trousers. Her cheeks flamed; her eyes mirrored his own riotous emotions.

"Infection be damned. You'll be the death of me, Sophie St. Clair."

With a yank he pulled her onto his lap. She cried out, a yelp he quickly swallowed when he pressed his mouth to hers. He felt the slightest hesitation before her fingers raked through his hair and her body melted against his. Her lips opened and she returned his kisses, panting into him and meeting each thrust of his tongue with equal force.

Throbbing desire strained his trousers, a thunderous need intensified by the mingling of her sweet taste and the wine he'd consumed. He was drunk—drunk with wanting her, with impatience to be inside her. He knew right from wrong but reached, nonetheless, for the bliss he had hungered for since that very first night at the chapel.

And this was no chapel. This was Edgecombe, where he was master.

"I shall tell you this once." He opened his mouth against her chin, biting down, dragging his tongue across the soft angle until she shivered against him. "You are not safe here, Sophie. Not safe with me. Go if you wish. But do so quickly."

"You're forever telling me to go. To be safe." Her lips traveled over his brow, leaving moisture, tender fire. "Haven't you learned that I've no liking for safety?"

Words dissolved into the joined heat of their mouths, dissipated on their twining tongues. His abrasions stung where her fingers roamed his skin, breath-stealing pain that heightening his senses. Given the passion seething inside him, she flirted with a far greater danger than any they had thus far faced. Cliffs and bullets and cave-ins. Danger, passion . . . inescapable temptation.

"So be it." His arms around her, he surged to his feet. She hung on, her legs wrapped about his waist. He moved forward until her bottom hit the table edge. Then he set her down upon it and shoved her skirts to her thighs.

Her breathy "Yes" fired his blood, his lust. Right and wrong? Holding her, drinking her in, burying his rigid length in her luscious flesh seemed entirely right. Within the madness consuming him, tugging open the buttons down her back and peeling away her bodice to expose her breasts seemed the only reasonable act.

Her breasts sprang from her camisole into his palms, the nipples erect with passion, begging to be touched, kissed. He eased her backward onto the table until she lay half propped on her elbows, head back, neck straining, breasts thrusting like the peaked hillocks on the moors.

He bent over her, took a nipple in his mouth and sucked, teased, pulled. Not gently. No, while his scruples urged restraint, Sophie's moans of pleasure persuaded him to do otherwise. With the seasoned skill of the rake he had once been, he unhooked her corset, whisked it out from under her and tossed it away.

Her hand came up, wrapping around his nape and pulling him down. She smiled as she tugged him to her lips, went on smiling as their tongues engaged in a sweet battle and her fingers hooked onto the waistband of his trousers. An inferno raged as she slipped each button free, as she stared into his eyes with a deliberation that turned his knees to jelly and his shaft to granite.

Their groins met at the edge of the table, his pulsing and exposed, hers encased in eyelet cotton dampened by desire. The room around them, heretofore lost to a blur of passion, sharpened into focus. His conscience gave a shout.

"Sophie, we can't. Not here."

Her smile subtly challenged. "Where then?"

"Upstairs." He dipped his lips to her breasts. "My bed."

She shook her head, hands fisting in his open shirt. "Too far. Too much time to think. On the way you'll devise a dozen reasons why we shouldn't."

"Perhaps we *should* think."

"No." Her ankles crossed behind him in a slender-legged embrace that pulled him flush against her. The all-too-thin layer of cotton between them did nothing to stop her heat from flooding him. Dragging his head down again, she pressed her lips to his ear and with a lick whispered, "Together we've defied bullets and the forces of nature. We don't need pillows and down."

In that instant he knew she was right. All his life he'd been a risk taker, a cavalier who had never met his match. Not until Sophie St. Clair pushed her way through the mist and into his life, armed with nothing but foolhardy courage and a wide-open heart.

Yes, he had met his match and it terrified him . . . humbled him . . . and filled him with an overwhelming need to believe he might somehow, someday, be worthy of her.

Using both hands he smoothed the tangled hair from her face, spilling it over her shoulders and onto the tabletop in a pile of dark, glossy ribbons. "You are right. We don't need pillows and down." He thrust the tip of his shaft against her, delighting in the tremor that shook her frame. "Nonetheless I insist you have them."

He spared a moment to secure his trousers well enough to keep them on his hips. Then he swept Sophie into his arms and carried her up the stairs.

Sophie shut her eyes and burrowed her face in Chad's neck. A dizzying fear swept her as he raced up the stairs. "Chad, your ankle."

"Is giving me no pain now, I assure you."

She didn't know how that could be, yet his steady hold and sure footing assured her they wouldn't both go tumbling head over heels. No, he would never drop her, never let her fall. Hadn't he already proved that beyond all doubt?

As they reached the dining hall she wondered fleetingly where his manservant might be, but they encountered only the echoes of Chad's hurried steps and the frenzied harmony of their audible breathing. He dashed through the rooms and up the main staircase. At the top he shouldered his way through a doorway. With a gentle hiss her bottom landed at the center of his four-poster bed.

He stood over her, golden and chiseled and beautifully male. A sheen of perspiration accentuated his perfect features; his broad chest, crisscrossed with scratches, rose and fell sharply.

"We made it, and I haven't changed my mind." His voice bore a dangerous rumble, like a warning from the earth. "I haven't thought of a single reason why we shouldn't."

"No, nor have I." She held out her arms to him. He hesitated only long enough to peel off his boots, unbutton his trousers and step out of them. Her breath caught at her first-ever view of all of him. Words like *rock* and *stone* and *granite* flew through her mind but were dismissed as inadequate as he stood, naked and erect, displaying not the faintest trace of self-consciousness.

He eased onto the bed and filled her beckoning embrace with the ruggedness of his body, with flexing muscle, with the heat of his desire throbbing like a living thing against her thigh.

"These must go." He stripped away her chemise, then tugged the drawstring of her drawers. Together they shoved them from her legs and kicked them to the floor.

His lips followed where the fabric had been, sparking the sensitive places between her legs and sending intense little shocks through her. Her fingers tangled in his hair, clenching to the rhythm he created against her with his skillful mouth.

Gasp after gasp spilled from her lips. Pleasure twisted, then streaked like lightning when he cupped her breast and closed his fingers around her nipple. She cried out, and suddenly his mouth was on hers, soft, melting, consuming.

"My darling," he whispered into her, "this will hurt, and will be irrevocable. Are you quite certain?"

Her eyes, shut tight in response to excruciating pleasure, flew open. His face filled her vision; his tender expression encompassed her soul.

His words echoed in her heart. *This will hurt. . . .*

How did he know? What made him so certain? Oh, but he *was* certain. She heard it in his voice, saw it in the sorrow-tinged joy burning in his eyes.

No one, but no one, had ever shown such faith in her before.

Gathering her breath, she paused to quiet the sensual chaos frothing inside her. She wished to assure him her answer was forged in sincerity and not mindless passion.

She braced her hands on either side of his beautiful face. "I've never been more certain of anything."

A lustful murmur slid from the deepest part of him, and a desperate aching gripped her thighs, her womb, her very being.

He positioned himself above her. "Trust me?"

Her reply rushed from her heart. "Oh, yes."

"Then hold on tight, my Sophie."

As her name rumbled from his lips, he eased against her with a tenderness she had never imagined, that seized all of her and made her his. She wrapped her legs around his waist, crossing her ankles and holding on tight, as he'd commanded. Gradually she felt herself parting, opening, his impossible width stretching and filling her. And then . . . the halt of a barrier.

The last barrier between them.

"You mustn't stop."

"I couldn't if I tried."

Drawing back, he slid his length nearly out of her. His head dipped and his tongue speared past her lips in a kiss that mimicked the act of lovemaking. Sophie took his tongue into her mouth, holding on to it as her body held on to him. He thrust again and she felt the break, the splintering of her maidenhead.

All movement stopped. Tears rolled from her eyes, pooling in her ears. She clung, not knowing what would come next, but trusting utterly. Slowly he began to move. His eyes opened and locked with hers. From somewhere within passion and pain she summoned a smile. For him. For this gift they gave each other.

Rapture and relief flashed in his eyes. His movements quickened, intensified, sweeping thought and sensation in a violent surf. Realizing that the pain, or most of it, was gone, she moved with him, rocking her hips to meet his thrusts. Her ankles uncrossed and her legs slid from around him until her feet hit the mattress.

Higher, harder she drove herself against him, helping him to fill her. Their bodies advanced and retreated like the tide against the shore, while he moved inside her with the fierceness of the Devil's Twirl.

"Let go now, my love. Give yourself up to the pleasure. To me."

With those words her very self shattered into a thousand glittering shards of sunlight on splashing waves. As her being broke apart again and again his seed surged into her, filling the tender, throbbing places. Screams tore from the deepest part of her to converge with his raw cries.

Together their bodies pulsed and squeezed until all had been given and taken and returned. Until his beautiful form blurred behind the salty sting of her tears, tears that mingled with those trickling from his eyes. Exhausted and sated, they turned on their sides with their arms wrapped around each other and drifted off to sleep with his length buried inside her.

Chapter 17

Chad awoke with a start. He could have dozed only a few seconds, but he hadn't meant to sleep at all. Admittedly Sophie's slumbering form tucked against him provided an almost irresistible temptation to do just that. Sleep and forget about everything but the incredible joy she brought him.

But sleep brought dreams, and dreams brought demons, and once again Sophie might have shared the horror, as she had the last time they'd fallen asleep together. He couldn't let that happen.

The depth of her trust humbled him. She'd given him her virginity, her heart. What would happen to that trust if she learned the truth of what he was and what he had done; if she realized she'd given herself to a man who didn't come near to deserving her?

A man who was guilty of the very thing they had been investigating these past days?

His chest constricted with a painful, overwhelming emotion he had no right to feel for a woman he had no right to claim. Yet claim her he had, and he couldn't find it within himself to regret any part of his actions.

She didn't sleep long before her soft sigh murmured against his skin. Her warm body stirred, rousing his desire anew. Not blazing and urgent as previously, but sultry and languid, a beast stretching its limbs in the sun.

Her eyes opened and she reached her arms around him. Her smile beckoned. When she hooked a leg over his hip, he eased between her thighs. Their earlier lovemaking had left her moist and ready; he needn't fear hurting her again. He rode her gently, hands splayed on her bottom to press her fully to his hips. Only when he'd carried her over the edge and set her safely down did he allow the predator inside him to satisfy its hunger.

Afterward, as he raised her hand to his mouth and kissed each of her fingers in turn, he realized he might never be satisfied. He wanted her, needed her that badly, that entirely. Perhaps that was why he had done the one thing he *never* did, not once, but twice.

Experienced as he was with lovemaking, he knew at least a half dozen methods to prevent pregnancy: French letters, herbal rinses, withdrawal. . . .

Ah, yes, he'd always relied on that last strategy when none of the others were at hand. It was the easiest, if the least enjoyable, and though reputed to be less-than-dependable, it had always worked for him. At any rate, no mistress or demirep had ever come knocking at his door with an infant in her arms.

He'd used none of those safeguards today. And what unsettled him most was the utter and appalling lack of dismay on his part. Quite the contrary, the thought of their actions resulting in a child produced a flutter of elation.

Good God.

"What's wrong?"

He shook away his musings and kissed the tip of her nose. "Not a thing. Wait here."

Leaving her looking puzzled and slightly out of sorts at his hasty retreat, he pulled on his trousers and bounded down the two flights to the kitchen, where he drew fresh water into the basin she'd used earlier. He gathered up the clothing that littered the floor and tossed it over his shoulder.

A glint of reflected light sent him back to the table.

He lifted the sword, and as he had felt in the cavern, the metal shivered with an unsettling energy. The sensation traveled up his arm and spread into his chest, seeming to curl like a cool hand around his heart.

He wrapped his shirt around it, tucked it beneath his arm and, carrying the basin of water, returned to Sophie.

When she realized what he intended, she clutched the bedclothes high beneath her chin. "I'll take care of it. You needn't."

Moistening a cloth, he settled on the bed beside her. He distracted her with a kiss and dragged the sheet aside. "You've nothing to hide from me. Not ever."

"Oh, but . . ." Her face flamed at the sight of the rusty stains marring her thighs. She made a grab for the coverlet.

"Stop it." He placed his hand very deliberately on one of those blotches. "Don't you know how beautiful this is to me? How beautiful *you* are? Especially now that you're mine. Oh, hang it . . . don't cry. I'll stop if you wish. I didn't mean to upset you."

Her quiet sob rippled into laughter. "You didn't. I could cry buckets right now and I haven't the slightest idea why. Absurd, aren't I?"

"No. Not in the least." He touched the cloth to her thigh and gently wiped. With a sigh and a brimming gaze she parted her legs for him in yet another gesture of trust that gripped his chest. "What we did binds us, Sophie," he whispered. "Binds us as nothing else can."

Near the entrance to her sex her hand came down on his wrist. The tears magnified her lovely gray eyes. "How did you know? After the debacle at the Winthrops' ball, dreadful rumors about me spread through London society. People called me loose, shameless . . . a strumpet. How were you so certain . . . ?"

He couldn't help a quiet laugh. "No one who has met you could possibly believe such nonsense. I certainly never did." He tossed the rag into the washbasin, sending up a splash. Then he kissed her gently.

"From the moment you walked into my arms in the chapel, I knew what sort of woman you are. I tried not to want that woman. Tried to stay away."

"Why?"

The answer lodged in his throat as a sudden fear rose inside him. Fear of her tenacity, her unquenchable desire to root out the truth of everything.

Her probing gaze held him for another moment. Then she blinked and leaned back against the pillows, stretching her naked body in a way that made the clothing he had donned feel exceedingly uncomfortable. "Never mind," she said. "I've no wish to argue. Not now."

Palpable relief left his heart thumping.

"I'd forgotten all about that." She pointed to the sword he'd placed on the dresser. His shirt had fallen open around it. "You found it in the tunnel?"

He retrieved the weapon and held it flat in his hands, feeling the slight vibration against his palms. "This isn't the only thing I found in that tunnel. There were two bodies, skeletons draped in the remains of what once had been clothing, lying not far from this sword."

"How ghastly!" She shuddered. "And there you were, trapped along with them." Sitting upright, she leaned closer to run her fingers over the curly silver brackets that enclosed the hilt.

"The odd thing is," he said, "this sword is nearly the duplicate of the one that used to hang over the shield downstairs in the drawing room."

"Used to hang?"

He nodded. "It appears to have gone missing. I don't know if my father did something with it or if it's been stolen."

She leaned closer to examine the hilt. "My word. Do you know what this sword is?"

"Only what I've been told. According to legend, the Keatings owned identical rapiers made to fit each of their hands perfectly. This larger hilt would have been

Jack's, except that it should have gone down with him and his ship."

Her startled gaze met his. "Could one of those skeletons . . . be Jack's?"

"Good God. If it is, that means Jack made it home before he died." He turned the sword over and back, trying to ignore the hum traveling through his hands and into his wrists. "I suppose it's possible he escaped his ship before she went down, and someone pursued him into the mouth of the tunnel. They might have fired guns at each other, causing the ceiling to fall in. And then both died there, trapped."

"To think Jack might have been mere floors below Meg in the end, but unable to reach her, and she never knowing." Sophie shivered.

"Then again, you know how legends grow and take on a life of their own. Both swords might have belonged to anyone at any time during Edgecombe's history."

"Not any time." Sophie took the sword from him, cradling it in her hands with an air of reverence. Then her expression changed, became perplexed. "Such a strange sensation . . ."

"You feel it too?"

"So peculiar . . ." She gave her head a shake, as if to dismiss a nonsensical notion. "This is an *espada ropera*. Spanish-made, probably of Toledo steel, judging by how little it has warped or rusted even down in a damp tunnel." She frowned and murmured, "Perhaps the steel is reacting to the metals in the cavern rock, and that's why—"

"What makes you so certain of what it is? What did you call it?"

"An *espada ropera*. See the hilt, how these thin silver bands are curved to form a decorative webbing? It's a primitive design by later standards, but even so it made an effective guard around the hand. The *espadas roperas* were among the first basket-hilt swords in Europe. Solid baskets weren't devised for another hundred years or so." She looked up and met Chad's gaze. "This sword hails from the early to mid-sixteenth century. Exactly when the Keatings lived."

"And how the devil would you know all that?"

Tossing her dark hair behind her, she wiggled to the edge of the bed, hopped down and moved to the window. "I know quite a lot about a great many things. Comes with being in the newspaper business." As she held up the weapon to examine it in the light, Chad used the opportunity to study the exquisite silhouette of her naked body.

Unaware of his perusal, she flipped the rapier over. "Can it be possible? Can this truly be Jack's, and the missing sword Meg's? It would all make sense with what's happening now, wouldn't it?"

He pushed off the bed and went to stand beside her. "I don't see how. What difference whose swords these were, or if the Keatings once owned this house or not? I'm not searching out sixteenth-century pirates; I'm looking for smugglers here and now. Surely you're not suggesting the ghosts of the Keatings are at large." He reached for the weapon. She whisked it aside.

"Don't be absurd." She treated him to a scowl, but a short-lived one. "But what if there is a connection? Couldn't the incidents of today be a continuation of the piracy begun by the Keatings, taken up generation after generation all this time?"

"That's far-fetched and you know it."

"Do I? So much would make sense. We need to go back into that tunnel and follow where it leads."

"Not on your life. Or mine." He grasped her shoulders and pulled her close. Her rosy nipples grazed his chest, but he bit back desire and scowled. "It's too dangerous. Besides, if someone has been smuggling goods through Edgecombe, they haven't been doing it through that tunnel. Not for a good long time."

He expected her enthusiasm to wane. Instead excitement illuminated her gray eyes. "According to the legends, the Keatings built a maze of tunnels. There's likely another entrance elsewhere on the property or close by. Perhaps the farmstead . . ."

"Too far inland."

"Then we'll need to search the shoreline again." She tapped a finger against her lips. Lips he had a good mind to still with kisses, to stop her from making plans that could get her killed. "I cannot believe this is all an incredible coincidence."

He fervently wished it were, wished those men last night had no connection to Edgecombe . . . or to him. But he knew better than to hope for the unlikely. As he watched her ruminate over rapiers and tunnels and ancient pirate legends, regret stabbed deeper than he knew it could. Soul deep. Heart deep. If only he had made different decisions two years ago. If only . . .

"Chad." She stood glaring out the window. The light from outside gilded the delicate lines of her profile, the inviting curves of her breasts and belly. One elegant hand pressed the glass; the hand holding the rapier had dropped to her side.

He moved beside her, seeing nothing but the usual vista of gardens, headland and sea.

Her finger pointed. "The hothouse."

He looked again and saw nothing remarkable, not even Nathaniel.

"We're seeking another tunnel entrance, one that could be used today." She faced him, features taut. "As you said, according to legend, the Keatings owned identical swords. Chad, look at the weather vane on the hothouse roof."

They were dressed and outside in a matter of minutes, armed with a garden hoe, a lantern and a small canvas sack containing flint, steel and a tinderbox. A crisp wind had kicked up, scattering intermittent raindrops. Sophie had tossed her dress over her head without bothering with corset or petticoats, and her bodice twisted uncomfortably on her torso as she descended the gardens. The rainy gusts penetrated the thin muslin of her day gown, the chill blending with her excitement and raising shivers.

She hurried to keep up with Chad's long strides until he noticed her exertion and slowed his pace. Little knots in her inner thighs clenched and ached with each step, a sharp reminder of what they had done, of how her life had changed today. Irrevocable, he had called it. Yes. And though perhaps that made her as wanton and rash as her family believed, she didn't regret a single moment in his arms.

Of letting herself love him.

Did he love her? Knowing him as she did, she believed that yes, he loved her, or at least *had* loved her through every caress and every inch of the passage of his body into hers.

Would that love last? He had said their lovemaking bound them as nothing else could, but when they no longer lived with danger, when he no longer felt the need to protect her, would he seek his freedom?

She pushed her blowing hair from her eyes as they reached the hothouse. Perched at the apex of its sloping roof, the weather vane with its two crossed swords topped by a sail squeaked as the wind sent it spinning. She touched Chad's shoulder as they came to a halt and pointed up at it. "Still think everything is merely a coincidence? The harbor lights, the approaching ship, the cargo you found secreted at the farmstead . . . and let us not forget those poor sailors, killed by the same means once used by the Keatings."

When he didn't answer she moved forward and gripped the door handle. The door stuck, shuddered twice from the force of her tugs, then swung open. The wind caught it, threatening to slam it into the glass panes of the outer wall. Chad moved quickly to catch the door before it struck and shattered. With a roll of his eyes that accused her of undue haste, he strode past her and entered the octagonal structure.

Little remained of the plants that had once flour-

ished there. The planters stood empty but for stalks
and rotted remains. Sophie wrinkled her nose at the
putrid odors of decomposed vegetation.

Chad turned to study the door behind them. "I'll
admit the opening is wide enough to allow easy access
in and out."

She nodded her agreement. His focus shifted to the
floor. The planters began wide at the perimeter of the
hothouse and tapered inward around a statue of a
mermaid at the center. In between, flagstones paved
the narrow walkways.

"Search for the illusion," he murmured.

"Sorry?"

"In the wine cellar the tunnel's trapdoor was concealed beneath a layer of tile to match the rest of the
floor. I'd never have noticed it unless—" He broke
off, toeing the nearest box frame that held the planting
soil in place. "If there's anything here to be found,
my guess is it'll be right under our noses."

Upending plant stands, rapping their garden hoe
against countless flagstones, they searched until the
sun pushed through a break in the clouds and flooded
through the hothouse windows. Inside the glass the
temperature climbed until Sophie's back beaded with
perspiration.

"It's grown as airless as a catacomb in here." With
a grin, she pointed at the carved marble mermaid. "No
wonder she wears so little."

Leaning as he tapped the hoe along a footpath,
Chad froze. Sophie regarded him in puzzlement as he
slowly straightened and leveled an alarmed expression
at the statue. "In most hothouses of this sort, wouldn't
that have been a fountain?"

"I couldn't say. We only have a conservatory at
home. Perhaps the brook isn't near enough to power
a fountain."

Dropping the garden hoe, he strode up the pathway,
stopping in front of the mermaid's curving fin. "Like
the altar."

"What altar?"

"In the village. The vicar showed me how his pulpit can be moved aside to reveal the entrance to a tunnel."

"I don't understand." She hurried down the aisle to his side. "The smugglers are using a tunnel right in the middle of the village? Beneath St. Brendan's?"

"No. At least, not the smugglers we're looking for. The tunnel beneath the church was used by Penhollow's sailors and fishermen who occasionally ran goods in from France. But those men we encountered last night are of a far more dangerous variety of smuggler, and their methods are obviously much more insidious." He sank to his knees, feeling frantically about the statue's pedestal. "Help me push."

Standing, he leaned and gripped the top edge of the plinth. Sophie moved beside him. Together they dug in their heels and shoved. To her astonishment a shrill grinding chafed her ears as the pedestal slid across the flagstones. Her amazement grew tenfold when she found herself staring down through a hole in the floor nearly identical to the one in the wine cellar.

"This is it." Chad's fingertips trembled against the marble base. "I'll get the lantern."

While he did, Sophie glanced up at the vaulted ceiling, thinking of the crossed-sword design of the weather vane above. "It's almost as if the Keatings were deliberately trying to send us a message. How *did* you find the tunnel entrance in the wine cellar? One would have to be crawling on hands and knees and have known where to look."

He set the lantern down by the opening and crouched. "An odd turn of luck, I suppose." He drew the flint, steel and tinderbox from the bag he had brought. He struck the flint to the steal, but no spark fell into the tinder. He tried again with no success. After a third try he slammed the flint to the floor. A chunk went flying. "Blasted thing."

"Oh, here, let me." With a doubtful shrug, he relinquished the steel and flint into her hands. A few strikes sparked the tinder, and within moments the lamp was lit. At his reluctant thank-you, she smothered a smile and closed the tinderbox to douse the tiny flame.

Her pulse pattered in her wrists as she held the lantern over the shaft. "Let's see where this leads, shall we?"

He grasped the lantern handle and took it from her hand. "I think I should do this alone."

"Chad, please—"

"You saw what happened in the other tunnel."

"Yes. You might have been killed because you foolishly ventured down alone. If I hadn't come along when I did . . ."

He raised his free hand to cup her chin. His thumb brushed across her lips, evoking the sensual memory of his kisses. "You saved me and I'm grateful. But things easily might have gone quite differently. More of the ceiling might have fallen in, and—"

He broke off, set the lantern on the floor and roughly pulled her into an embrace. "Damn it, Sophie, tides, cliffs, bullets . . . I won't risk you again. Please grant me the peace of mind of knowing that no harm will come to you."

She pressed her cheek to his shirtfront. "But what if something happens to you?"

His arms tightened, imprisoning her against his solid length. The places at which their bodies met pulsed, throbbed with a frantic, rising need. The pressure of his lips filled her mouth with the taste of him, and with a heat that spoke of urgency . . . and fear.

"It is my task, Sophie. Not yours. You must allow me to do this alone."

Her heart squeezed. Was his anxiety a result of their making love, of her relinquishing her virginity to him so recently? Or did his concern stem from something more lasting?

"I shall wait for you up at the house," she said.

"No. Go back to your relatives' farm and wait for me there. Later tonight we'll carry out your plan to search the premises."

She felt his embrace begin to recede and wanted to hold on to him all the more tightly. Instead she reluctantly allowed gaps to open between them. "I'll find your man Nathaniel before I go and send him here to keep watch. I don't think the hothouse will frighten him as the cellars did."

Chad's fingers grazed her cheek. "Yes, send Nathaniel. Or better yet, have him escort you home first, and then tell him to come down to the hothouse."

Again the ghost of a now familiar emotion flickered in the downward cast of his eyes.

Apprehension gathered like a growing storm inside her. "It's there again. The fear. I can see it."

"Yes, I'm afraid. As I was last night and again this morning. Terrified you might be hurt, or worse." His hands gripped her shoulders, fingers digging in. "I don't wish to carry that fear around inside me any longer. That's why I want you to go home."

"No," she said. "That isn't the sort of fear I'm taking about, and I think you know it." Despondency wrapped itself around her. After what they had done, all that they had shared, he still held back, refused to be completely honest. She saw it in his face, and felt the harsh truth of it as keenly as she had felt the piercing of her maidenhead. That pain she had welcomed. This one splintered her heart.

She grasped his sleeves. "You said our lovemaking connected us. Look me in the eye, then, and ask me to trust you."

"Sophie . . ."

She would not back down. If there was some dreadful thing hidden inside him, no matter how dark or shocking, she must know of it. "Tell me I can trust you with my life, my heart, and everything I hold dear. If you can speak those words I shall gladly do as you say."

"Go home, Sophie," he whispered. His hands slid from her shoulders, down the length of her arms, and swung to his sides.

"You cannot say it, can you? You cannot reassure me." She released him. Her hands, her heart, all of her let him go as she stepped back. The man she had met in the chapel . . . who had saved her life countless times . . . and taken her virginity with breathtaking gentleness . . . this man she could love with the whole of her being.

But that man was not the whole of Chad Rutherford. Another part of him existed, aloof, isolated, swathed in shadow. That man was not hers and never could be.

"If I see Nathaniel I'll send him down," she said, and turned to go.

Chapter 18

Through the hothouse windows Chad watched Sophie climb the garden lawns, and used every ouce of willpower he possessed not to set off after her.

What could he have said? With his silence he had lied to her, denied the very thing she so clearly perceived in him, though she did not have the facts that would enable her to understand what she saw.

With each passing day Edgecombe became a more dangerous place for both of them. Eventually the person or persons who had summoned him here would make known their demands. He'd been mad to risk keeping her here for so long today.

He had spoken from his heart when he told her their lovemaking connected them as nothing else could. But someday, perhaps soon, she would learn that she had forged that extraordinary, sacred bond with a criminal, with the sort of villain from whom he had claimed to wish to protect her.

The truth would horrify her, not merely because of what he had done in the past, but for letting her believe that he was an honest man. A man who deserved the precious thing he had taken from her.

Stolen, essentially, with his lies.

He might have used the opportunity moments ago to tell her everything. Have it out and done with, and grant her the justice of slapping his face, calling him every unpleasant name she could think of and wishing him to the devil.

He simply hadn't found the courage—not to watch her walk away from him forever, nor to rip the joy of their lovemaking out from under her. He might deserve that sort of pain, but she did not, especially not today.

His chest constricting, he watched her climb the sloping gardens and disappear into the house. *Good.* She would find Nathaniel and go home where she belonged. God willing, she would be safe there. Her uncle might not be the most trustworthy of men, but Chad didn't think he would deliberately harm a member of his family. The Cornish were fierce when it came their kin.

He started to return to the tunnel when a stooping figure exiting the carriage house sent him hurrying outside. "Nathaniel!" he called. The servant halted with a bemused expression.

"I have a guest up at the house," Chad said when he reached him. "Miss St. Clair. I want you to wait for her in the hall and escort her home when she leaves. Can you do that?"

"Aye. The horse is tended. I'll escort the lady home."

"See that she arrives safely. Afterward you may go home also, even if she bids you to come back to Edgecombe. I won't need you again today after all."

Without another word the servant shuffled away. Chad returned to the hothouse and, with the lantern in hand, lowered himself into the tunnel. Gripped by a sense of the morning's events repeating themselves, he proceeded slowly through the moldering darkness. Trying to muffle his footsteps, he hunched as he walked, his muscles coiled to run if need be—if he discovered he was not alone or if the timbers holding up the ceiling suddenly gave way.

This morning he might have been forever sealed in

a tomb already inhabited by two souls from long ago. Sophie had saved him then, but what could happen now, in this tunnel? If he became trapped, what cries might he hear echoing from the past? Those of desperate, dying pirates? Of victims? Would his own shouts of remorse blend with theirs to ride the ocean winds and frighten the villagers in their beds at night?

He pressed on, trudging much farther than he had in the previous tunnel. Fifty yards, a hundred. He lost count of his paces. Without his lantern the darkness would be profound. Even with its scanty glow the walls and ceiling closed around him as if to swallow him whole.

A stale whiff of brine wafted from ahead. He had come to associate that odor with death, and with the gruesome image of a drowned girl rising up to demand his help. Again he thought of the other tunnel, and of the odd, wispy noise that had drawn his attention to the hidden trapdoor.

Sophie had wished to know how he had found that entrance, and in truth he didn't know. Since that night on Blackheath Moor he had tried to convince himself he'd dreamed the little ghost. But more than once these past few days he seemed to have been guided by a force he couldn't explain. It had led him to the chapel last night with Sophie in his arms. It had even, perhaps, helped him crawl through the gap in the cave-in. He'd gotten stuck, then suddenly slid through as if pushed. . . .

Could his little ghost be real? Could she be guiding him? But to what end?

In midstep he froze, his lantern illuminating crouching shapes some dozen yards ahead. His heart careened into his chest as one of those shapes seemed to move. No sound came but for the distant hiss of the sea, and, creeping closer, he realized the movement had been an illusion created by the erratic beams from his lantern.

Continuing onward, he reached out to tug draping

fabric from a pile of crates. A yank on another cloth revealed a cluster of barrels crowded against the wall. His pulse raced. On either side of him, countless containers of various sizes lined the passage, leaving a walkway down the middle wide enough to admit one man at a time.

So much for a cessation of smuggling in Penhollow, as the vicar had claimed. How long had this cache been here? Had Sophie's midnight ship brought it in, while Chad's unexpected arrival at Edgecombe had foiled plans to transfer the goods inland?

When he had entered into the smuggling conspiracy, part of the bargain had been that Edgecombe would not be used. What a fool he'd been to think his wishes would be respected, as if the men he'd dealt with possessed a sense of honor and fair play.

Another thought rose up to grip him around the throat. Had his father known? Had he given his permission, as with the vault beneath the church? Or had whoever used this tunnel done so only after Franklin died? Then another, more disturbing doubt arose, one he had contemplated days ago but had found no good reason to pursue.

Had his father's death been an alcohol-induced accident, as reported, or something more sinister?

Chad knelt to shine his lantern on the letters stenciled across a cask. CHATEAUROUX, it read. The names of other French towns emblazoned the crates and barrels around him. Had the goods been smuggled in from France through the age-old Cornish practice of fair trading, or had they been seized by more violent means?

Killed for the cargo.

He lurched to his feet as the whisper curled about his ear. Holding his lantern high, he looked up and down the tunnel, searching for . . . a ghost? He lowered the lamp, knowing he should feel foolish for entertaining the notion, but unable to shake the sudden chill that raised gooseflesh down his back.

The far-off lapping of waves drew him past the stacked booty; he followed twists and turns until the tunnel gave way to a natural cave. Shrill winds coursed in off the nearby water to shriek along the jagged walls. The reek of seawater became stronger, more pungent. Brightening light from ahead rendered the lantern unnecessary. He set it down and kept going.

In the bend of a sharp turn a half dozen torches set on poles leaned against the cave wall. He picked one up and sniffed the scent of oil emanating from the charred rushes. Were these Sophie's altered harbor lights?

An opening ahead brought him out onto a rocky ledge. Beside it a high natural breakwater curved inward toward the cliffs to form a tiny inlet, concealed to boats passing in the channel waters.

Beyond the rocks on which he stood, a narrow, pebbled beach spanned the inlet. Where the cove opened onto the wider expanse of the sea, the treacherous currents of the Devil's Twirl churned the waters. Such a tide would persuade most, but perhaps not all sailors to steer a wide berth around this area, rendering the inlet that much more invisible. Invisible enough to hide a small boat, such as the one that filled Chad's vision and raised a maelstrom of questions.

Chained to a spike driven into the rocks of the breakwater, Grady's sailboat bobbed up and down in the waves.

Sophie averted her gaze from Chad's four-poster bed as she struggled into her petticoats and corset and stepped back into her dress. She had no wish to confront the twisted jumble of coverlet and sheets that marked the deepest connection and most genuine trust she had ever shared with another human being. Though glorious beyond imagining, neither the connection nor the trust had proved any more enduring than the fading golds of a moorland sunset.

The truth that had dogged her from the hothouse

draped like a shroud across her heart. Lovemaking had brought her and Chad no closer than before, had banished none of the brooding shadows that so often fell between them. He continued to present as enigmatic a facade as ever, his inner self protected behind a sheer cliff face she could neither breach nor scale.

The grim fact left her bereft and made her wonder how she could have relinquished her maidenhead so blithely to a man of whom she knew so little.

What was he hiding? What did he fear? Or did he simply not feel for her what she felt for him? *Would* feel, if only he'd stop pushing her away.

She thought back on their time together . . . and realized something that made her sink onto the edge of the bed. Always his dark moods erupted in response to her probing into the matter of harbor lights, mysterious ships and the question of possible smuggling here in Penhollow.

He had found the tunnel beneath Edgecombe's cellars, but refused to explain how. Could he also have known the location of the tunnel in the hothouse, and only pretended to discover it today to deceive her?

He continued to deny being at Edgecombe on that day she first saw him.

Glancing up, she regarded her reflection in the dresser mirror, beholding features that in the past hour had lost their blissful glow and taken on a wary pallor. Could Chad possibly . . . be involved . . . ?

No. Wrenching her arms behind her to secure the buttons down the back of her dress, she gave a vehement shake of her head. How could she consider such a notion about a man who had awakened her to the most tender, breathtaking passion?

She could not believe ill of such a man. *Would* not. If Chad harbored secrets, she must believe he had good reasons, ones he would eventually share with her as long as she continued to have faith in him.

Standing, she regarded her reflection again and experienced a ripple of censure. Her dress showed clear signs of having lain in a crumpled heap on the floor. Her hair fell in a tangled mass halfway down her back. She certainly couldn't return to Aunt Louisa's in her present state.

Remembering the dress Chad had found for her following their cliff-climbing escapade, she left his room and began searching the others, hoping to find any semblance of ladies' toiletries or accessories that might help set her to rights. She discovered them in a room hung with deep crimson draperies accented with gold.

A dressing table drawer yielded hairpins and a ribbon. Running her fingers through her hair to smooth it, she sat before the mirror and approximated the simple coif she had arranged that morning. Curiosity prompted her to open other drawers. She found silk stockings, brightly colored garters, an elaborately embroidered shawl.

If this hadn't been his mother's room, whose hairpins held her twisted chignon in place? She went to the wardrobe. Dismissing a niggling qualm concerning the ethics of snooping, she threw open the doors. Several dresses hung inside.

As she sifted through them, her brow wrinkled at the odd variety. There were some whose gaudy fabrics she dismissed as simply being in bad taste. Others were hopelessly out of fashion. In fact, the slashed sleeves and quilted petticoats spoke of an era long past, of a time when the Tudors ruled England and pirates roamed the seas. A notion shivered up her spine. She fingered the stitching of the brocade designs.

These were no relics from Meg Keating's day. The fabrics were too fresh and vivid. These dresses had been made much more recently, intended to mimic the antiquated styles. She couldn't imagine why, unless the wearer knew of Edgecombe's history and enjoyed playacting, hardly something one would expect of a countess.

A mistress, then? Perhaps the late Earl of Wycliffe

and his paramour had indulged in acting out strange
fantasies in his isolated manor. Or . . .

She clenched her fingers and squeezed her eyes
shut, but could not block out the wretched possibility
that today she had become merely one more conquest
for the present Earl of Wycliffe. Dear God, no, she
far preferred to salvage some small part of the day's
joy, rather than be left with nothing but the knowledge
that she had acted the fool.

Yet no matter how hard she tried, she could not
entirely dismiss the suspicion raised by those garish
dresses.

"You don't belong in here."

With a shriek she slammed shut the wardrobe doors
and turned to see Nathaniel hunching in the doorway.
She pressed a hand to her throat. "You startled me.
I didn't know you were in the house. What are you
doing above stairs?"

"Looking for my lady. Milord said I must escort
you home."

"I see." The man unnerved her, but she felt fairly
certain he wouldn't harm her. She cast a glance at the
closed doors of the wardrobe. "Nathaniel, how long
have you worked at Edgecombe?"

"I did the trimming. Now I cook and tend the
horse."

"Would you know who has used this room? A rela-
tive, perhaps?"

He shrugged, but a twinge of anxiety flickered in
his craggy features.

"You've nothing to fear," she said. "I'm simply curious. Has the earl had any . . . lady visitors other
than me?"

The gaunt shoulders shrank inward. "Little roses,"
he whispered. His gaze flitted erratically, as if he
saw visions invisible to Sophie. "No one knows about the
roses. Only me."

"What about the roses, Nathaniel?"

"Roses gone now. All gone."

His puzzling words and his unfocused gaze raised a frisson of fear. He seemed cut off, lost in a world of his own imagining. If she could no longer reason with him, what might he be capable of doing?

"It's all right, Nathaniel. We needn't dwell on it."

"Dead and gone to the ground." His attention swerved suddenly back to her, piercing in its intensity. "Little roses gone away, never to come back."

"Of course they'll come back. We'll plant more."

"No!"

His shout set her feet in motion. Ducking around him, she darted into the corridor and scurried down the staircase. She didn't slow her pace until she'd cleared Edgecombe's boundary walls and a backward glance assured her the servant hadn't followed. She paused to catch her breath before continuing on.

A gauzy fog blanketed the moors, pooling in the bottomlands, muting the landscape to a dull haze and spreading an eerie calm. The continuing drizzle numbed her face and hands to match her spirits, but she was grateful the weather would be blamed for any dishevelment in her appearance. In a constant reminder of what she had done—of the part of herself she had given away—her thighs smarted with every step. No amount of rain could wash away the discomfort or ease the weight of the doubts pressing in around her.

Had Chad played her false, not just today, but all along?

As she rounded a bend in the road, her aunt's farmhouse rose into view.

"Sophie! Sophie, come quick!"

Rachel stood outside the gate, waving her arms above her head. At a second shouted hail Sophie broke into a run.

"It's Dominic and Ian," Rachel blurted when Sophie reached her. "Something's happened to them. They should have been back by now. Oh, Sophie, it's been more than an hour. Where can they be? It's my fault if they've come to harm."

Sophie placed a hand on her cousin's shoulder. "Slow down and tell me why you believe anything has happened to them."

"Because I sent Dominic to bring Ian back to the house."

"Isn't your father opposed—"

"Yes, but you know he and Mother rode up to Mullion today. So I thought . . ." She grabbed Sophie's arm and started her walking in the direction of the village. "I know something has happened. I keep thinking of those poor dead men caught in the schooner's nets yesterday."

Lengthening her stride to keep up with Rachel's frenzied pace, Sophie believed she understood. With her parents away, Rachel had planned to meet with her beau. But their tryst had never occurred.

"Whatever has detained them, I'm certain it can have nothing to do with what happened yesterday. Calm yourself on that account. You know how young men are. They're probably at Kellyn's right now, warm by the fire and filling their bellies with oatcakes and ale."

"No. Not Ian. He would not have wasted a moment after receiving my message."

At the reference to her brother's part in the events, Sophie couldn't help suggesting, "Perhaps Dominic didn't deliver the message."

"Of course he did. He promised. Father might not approve of Ian, but Dominic does. They're the best of friends."

Sophie said nothing, but she didn't doubt that her surly cousin would break a promise, even to his sister.

As if reading her thoughts, Rachel bristled. "I realize you and Dominic aren't fond of each other. And perhaps for good reason. He's so like Father. You wouldn't be the first person to take a dislike to him. But in his heart of hearts he is a decent man, and he loves me. If anything has happened to him because of me . . ."

"It hasn't. I'm sure he's fine."

Rachel chewed her lip. In tense silence they walked on through the misting rain. Smoke from the village chimneys curled into view, rising like dark threads being sewn into the clouds. Movement on the stretch of moorland several yards up ahead drew Sophie's attention. Expecting to see a deer, she was surprised when a man materialized from the soupy vapors. On unsteady legs he ran onto the road.

"It's Ian!" Rachel sprinted forward.

"Rachel, stop." Sophie took off after her cousin. At such a distance, and in the rain and fog, the girl couldn't possibly identify the individual with any certainty. In oilskin and homespun woolens he might have been any ruffian in his cups from an all-night sojourn at Kellyn's. Or someone to be feared even more.

Yet in the next instant Sophie realized that had the figure been Chad's, she would have recognized every line and plane of his physique, the set of his shoulders, the way he moved, even from dozens of yards away.

Rachel's instincts proved correct. As they reached the young fisherman, he lurched forward, striking the road hard with his knees. He caught himself from landing on his face by wrapping his arms around Rachel's waist. His cheek pressed up against her belly, his visible eye swollen shut amid a mass of ominous colors.

"Ian! What happened to you?"

He took a moment before answering, fingers clutching the back of Rachel's cloak. When she tried to lift his face to her, he kissed her hands and shut his good eye.

Rachel crouched before him. "Please tell me what happened."

"We were attacked. There were two of them. One had a gun, the other a fishing knife. The jagged kind we use to gut the catch. They dragged us onto the moor."

A queasy sensation rolled through Sophie's stomach. Two men. The moor. She leaned closer to speak to the young man. "Who did it? Did you know them?"

He nodded. "I've seen them before. In the village. They come sometimes on market day, and go into the Gull for a pint. But I don't know who they are. They don't belong in Penhollow. Not like the rest of us."

Rachel took gentle hold of his face, raised it and gasped at the sight of his blackened eye.

"I'm all right," he assured her. "But Dominic . . ."

"Where is he?"

"Where they left us. I couldn't move him, not on my own. Rachel, they had come for him; I'm sure of it. I demanded to know what they wanted, and their reply was a pistol butt to the back of my head."

Rachel ran her fingertips through his hair, pulling back when he winced. "You've a lump the size of a raven's egg."

"It doesn't matter. Dominic needs us."

"Take me to him. Can you walk?" When he nodded, she gripped his forearms and helped pull him to his feet. He teetered, and she steadied him with an arm around his waist. "Is it far from here?"

Ian pointed to where the moor rose to a craggy peak some quarter mile beyond the road. Beside it a thin stand of rowans stood bent against the wind. "Just past there."

Rachel turned to Sophie with a calm fortitude that raised every bit of Sophie's admiration. "Go to the vicar. Tell him my brother and Ian have been injured. Ask him to drive here in his carriage, and direct him to the other side of that hill. Please hurry!"

Chapter 19

Through the drizzle, Chad cantered Prince into the village, sending up a spray as he veered into St. Brendan's. Collar upturned to the weather, the vicar's manservant lumbered out from the carriage house to take the reins.

"Is the vicar in?" Chad asked as he dismounted. Without waiting for an answer, he headed for the house.

"He is, milord," the servant called to his back. "Shall I announce ye?"

"I'll announce myself, thank you."

"He's not alone. . . ."

Chad didn't care if the vicar was presently entertaining the Archbishop of Canterbury. He'd not be announced because he intended granting the vicar precisely zero time to think before he fired off his barrage of questions. As his father's onetime friend, Tobias Hall surely harbored a great deal more information than he had been willing to divulge when Chad last saw him.

Such as, how much had Franklin Rutherford truly known about Penhollow's smuggling activities? Tolerating a tunnel beneath the church was one thing, but the passages beneath Edgecombe were quite another.

Chad pushed his way into the little house. "Hall? I need to speak with you." The sight he met in the parlor brought him up short. "Sophie. What are you doing here? Is the vicar home?"

Shivering beneath a dripping cloak, she looked pale and bedraggled, half-drowned.

Chad's stride swallowed the distance between them. He grasped her hands; they were cold and trembling between his own. She seemed about to speak, but her throat convulsed and she pinched her lips together.

She could only be thinking of their parting words at the hothouse. The memory tore at his conscience. Their lovemaking had been a first for her—for him as well. With Sophie there had been no sense of sport, none of the triumph he had felt with the other women he had lured into his bed over the years. With her there had been only passion and need and a heart-gripping sense of rightness.

Even so, he had not been honest, and his omission of the truth hovered between them like a double-edged rapier. With uncanny perception she sensed his secrets, enough to confront him outright. His denials had hurt her; one look at her revealed to him how deeply. But how much more acutely would he hurt her with the truth?

"I've gathered bandages, splints and medicinal herbs." The vicar entered the room, a leather sack dangling from his hands. His gaze shifted from Sophie to Chad, and to their clasped hands. A twitch of his thin ferret's nose betrayed his surprise and speculation. "Lord Wyclffe. I didn't realize you were here. Have you come to help?"

Chad supposed that with Hall looking on, he should have released Sophie. He held on tighter. "Is something amiss at the farm?"

"Not the farm, but my cousin Dominic has been attacked." Sophie's voice shook. "Rachel's young fisherman, Ian, as well. It happened on the moor near the road."

"How badly are they hurt?"

"Ian is sore and bruised." Her forehead puckered. "I don't yet know about Dominic. I left Rachel and Ian to tend him and came straight here."

"Do you know who did this?"

Her eyes were huge, tempestuous. She shook her head.

"I'll return there with you," he said, and followed her and Hall outside to the carriage yard, where the vicar's curricle stood waiting.

As they readied to leave, a voice hailed them from the road. Kellyn made her way across the churchyard, her vivid red hair hidden by a thick shawl draped over her head and shoulders. Other than that she seemed as oblivious to the weather as a seasoned deckhand.

"Tobias, before you leave, may I trouble you for a few sprigs of sage? We're all out, and Reese is stewing some . . ." She trailed off and stared into each of their faces in turn, Chad's atop Prince, the vicar's and Sophie's through the rain-smeared carriage window. "What's wrong?"

Hall opened the carriage door. "There's been another attack, this time on land. The Gordon youth and his friend, Ian Rogers. We're on our way to them now."

"Good heavens." Kellyn ducked her head inside the carriage to speak to Sophie. "Are you and Rachel all right?"

"We're both fine. We weren't present when the attack occurred."

"Thank God for that." Kellyn pushed out a sigh of relief. "I'll tell Reese what happened. He's Rachel and Dominic's uncle," she explained to Chad. "We'll meet you at the farm in a little while."

As she turned to go, a notion prompted Chad to call her back. He dismounted from Prince and said to Sophie and the vicar, "Go on ahead. I'll catch up in a few moments." Sophie regarded him with puzzlement, but said nothing as the vicar rapped on the ceiling for his servant to drive on.

"I'll walk you back to the tavern. I've a question to

ask you." He and Kellyn fell into step together, hunching slightly against the rain. Prince followed close at his shoulder. "It's about Grady."

Lifting her skirts, Kellyn picked her way over the stream of rainwater running along the edge of the road. "He sailed up to Mullion yesterday, didn't he?"

"So he told you that too? I don't understand it, and I was hoping you might supply an explanation. Grady couldn't have sailed to Mullion. His boat is tied up in an inlet not far from Edgecombe." He hated the two most likely possibilities that had sprung to mind upon finding Grady's sailboat outside the tunnel: either the affable mariner had met with foul play, or for unknown reasons he had never intended to go to Mullion at all. "He didn't mention a change in plans?"

Kellyn stopped short and faced him. "He said nothing to me. How do you know this?"

"I saw the boat." The surprise in her pale blue eyes reminded him that offering up too much information would only encourage more questions, ones he might not wish to answer. Behind him Prince snorted, and Chad rubbed a hand down the length of his damp muzzle. "It was just visible from the cliffs, but I'm fairly certain it was his."

"Really. From the cliffs?" They reached the door of the Stormy Gull, and she moved into the sheltering overhang of the second story. "I told you Grady is a bit on the barmy side. I'll keep an eye out for him and let you know if I learn anything."

Was Grady simple-witted, and therefore an easy mark for someone wishing to do him harm, or was the Irishman more astute than anyone guessed? Frustrated at his lack of answers, Chad nodded his thanks and swung up into the saddle. As he did he glimpsed a face staring out at him from one of the upper windows. The hair on his neck bristled as he recognized a pair of close-set eyes above a slightly hooked nose.

"Kellyn, wait."

Halfway through the door, she turned.

He gestured with a lift of his chin. "Who is that man staying above the common room? The one who dresses like a fisherman but carries himself as though he were something more."

Kellyn glanced up at the building. "I hadn't thought of him that way. I don't know who he is, really. Name is John Hayes, and he came in off one of the traders a couple of weeks ago."

"What's he doing here?"

"Hires himself out as a deckhand. Other times he does odd jobs about the farms." She shrugged. "I assumed he might be hiding out from someone. He wouldn't be the first. But he pays his bills, so I don't ask questions."

As Chad set off down the road, he felt the man's gaze following him, prickling his back.

"His arm is fractured, and he appears to have sustained several broken ribs as well," said the vicar. "We must convey him home immediately. I dare not attempt to set his arm here."

Kneeling at Dominic's side in the sodden heather, Sophie held on to Rachel's hand, feeling the other girl's fingers convulse as the vicar gave the diagnosis. Ian crouched at Dominic's other side, looking as though his world were crumbling. His eye was blacker now, with a stormy purple hue blossoming around the upper lid. Between his hands he clutched a green woolen cap he'd retrieved from the ground.

"We'll wrap him in these blankets and lift him into the carriage seat." Mr. Hall cupped his hands around his mouth and called to his servant, waiting near the base of the crag. "Bring the curricle in from the road."

Moments later the vehicle came into view, jostling over the moor's bumpy terrain. Sophie's pulse gave a lurch at the sight of Chad following the carriage on horseback. She pushed to her feet, walking a little distance away from her cousin's prone form.

As she watched Chad dismount she felt a stab of

guilt and thought perhaps she had been too hard on him at the hothouse, issuing demands she had no right to make. What business of hers were his secrets, if he actually harbored any? Perhaps she only imagined them. A guarded look in his eyes, a misunderstanding about when he had arrived in Penhollow—did that constitute evidence enough to distrust him?

But as he made his way toward her, her doubts persisted. He hadn't denied her accusations. He had only urged her to go home.

"How is he?" he asked when he reached her. The rain had slicked back his hair and rendered his white lawn shirt nearly transparent, displaying the smooth skin and rugged muscles beneath. Lacking both coat and neck cloth, he looked not like an earl born to luxury and privilege, but like a dashing, half-wild rogue who had lived his entire life on the moors and sea cliffs of Cornwall.

Her heart fluttered. She swallowed and cleared her throat to gain control of her voice. "Mr. Hall says his arm is broken. Some of his ribs too. His face is all welts."

"Christ." Chad's hands fisted; his jaw hardened. "When I discover who did this I'll see that they pay."

Behind her Dominic let out a moan.

"He's coming to," the vicar said.

Chad took her hand—or had she been the one to reach out to him, an instinct formed these past days that simply refused to die? Together they returned to the others and knelt beside her cousin.

Dominic's discolored, bloated lids quivered, then opened to slits. His cracked, bleeding lips parted. "Rachel?"

"I'm here." The girl placed a hand gently on his shoulder.

"Are you . . . Did they . . . ?" His fingers fisted on the edge of her skirt.

"I'm fine." Rachel skimmed her palm across his brow. "I was home waiting for you as promised."

"And Ian?"

"He'll be fine too."

Dominic gave a weak nod. His hand uncurled and fell limp on the ground.

"Miss St. Clair," the vicar said, "please find the smallest of the vials in my sack. The one with the brownish liquid."

Sophie rummaged through the contents and found the corked vessel.

Instructing Rachel to raise her brother's head, the vicar uncorked the vial and held the rim to Dominic's lips. "Drink this. It'll dull the pain."

Dominic's bruised forehead creased in response. He compressed his lips. Rachel bent over him, wisps of black hair trailing to frame his face.

"Don't be cheeky. There's no call for sham heroics. Now drink it down, ox."

Sophie's heart gave a twist at the girl's brave humor, and at Dominic's attempted smile. The effort contorted his face in a grimace, which worsened as he swallowed Mr. Hall's concoction. Less than a minute later his head lolled back in Rachel's arms.

"Good Christ, Hall." Chad made a sound through his teeth. "What the devil did you give him?"

"A tincture of laudanum and valerian root. With the dose I mixed a cart pony could trample him and he shouldn't wake up. Now let's lift him into the carriage and get him home before he catches his death in this rain."

When they arrived at the farm the men brought Dominic into the parlor and laid him out on the settee. He did a fair bit of groaning along the way, but mercifully didn't fully regain consciousness.

"We'll need to get his coat and shirt off," the vicar said in a take-charge manner. He set his leather sack on a table and took out bandages, a splint and more herbs.

Sophie's stomach clenched at the thought of what was coming. Her brother had once dislocated a shoulder. She cringed at the memory of his scream when the physician had manipulated the arm back into the socket. She caught the vicar's eye. "Will it hurt much?"

"He shouldn't feel a thing. Lord Wycliffe, will you assist?"

Chad crossed the room to the vicar's side. "What do you need me to do?"

"Hold him still while I work the fractured bone into place." Mr. Hall gestured for Chad to lean over Dominic and hold his shoulders down. "And if anyone is of a mind to pray, you might consider asking the Almighty to guide my hands. It's been rather a long while since I've had to do this."

Sophie said a quick, silent prayer.

Dominic groaned when Mr. Hall ran his fingers over the arm to feel for the break. At the click of the splintered bone realigning, he let go a raw cry and then slumped into deep unconsciousness. Sophie's stomach flip-flopped.

Rachel wiped away tears with her sleeve and held out a roll of bandages to Mr. Hall. "Thank heaven that's over. I'll help you bind his ribs."

Reese and Kellyn arrived at the Gordon farm soon afterward and listened with stoic calm to the scant facts Ian could supply about the assault. His description of the two attackers fairly well matched what Chad remembered of the two men at the moorland farmstead, and as each violent detail fell into place, the conviction grew that this was not a random occurrence, but part of an ominous net tightening around Penhollow, these people and himself.

Kellyn poured out a round of brandy from the bottle she and Reese had brought with them from the Stormy Gull. "Drink it down. 'Twill do you all a world of good."

Sitting in a corner, Ian nursed his slowly. The vicar took a perfunctory sip, then continued searching through his bag for more herbs. Rachel and Sophie wrinkled their noses but gulped small portions. With a shudder Rachel set down her cup and returned to the chair she had placed close to her brother's side. Sophie went into the kitchen. Taking his largely untouched brandy with him, Chad followed.

He watched as she made tea. Upon arriving home she had changed into a dry frock, a pale blue muslin that accentuated the roundness of her bosom and the graceful sweep of her shoulders. A bosom he had kissed . . . shoulders he had caressed. . . . Had it been only this morning?

His loins tightened around a yearning to take her in his arms, tip her backward and crush his lips to hers; not a kiss tainted with the desperate uncertainty of what the future might bring, but one imbued with laughter and the simple, unthinking happiness of two people who belonged together.

In the warmth of the kitchen her cheeks had resumed their glow, and her lips had lost that bleak, pinched look he'd witnessed on the moors. A look that would haunt him from now on, because he knew it would return, would be aimed at him.

For now she looked . . . beautiful, elegant and poised. A sudden image flashed in his brain, one of a dark-haired, gray-eyed countess, smiling as she stood at his side.

A hollow dream, one he'd do best not to dwell on.

The family's dog, an aging bearded collie that had been asleep in the corner near the stove, limped over to him and with an inquisitive whimper rested its graying muzzle on Chad's knee. He stroked between the animal's ears and focused on a new resolve.

Only by discovering Penhollow's secrets could he guarantee Sophie's safety. He had been going about his investigation all wrong—acting with stealth, poking about, asking leading questions but rarely coming right out and demanding what he needed to know.

The time for subtlety had passed.

Several minutes later, when the vicar announced his intention of returning home to mix more of his herbs for Dominic, Chad followed him outside to his curricle.

"Tobias, a word, if you please. Privately. I'll accompany you back to the vicarage."

Waning daylight tinted the western clouds a yellowish hue that reflected in the vicar's spectacles as he opened the carriage door. Chad folded his length into the tight confines, made more awkward by the other man's obvious discomfiture. Tobias sat stiffly against the squabs, hands wrapped tightly around his sack of medicines.

The carriage lurched forward, listing sharply as it turned onto the road. Without preamble Chad said, "How much did my father know about the smuggling in Penhollow?"

The vicar visibly jolted, and not from a shudder of the carriage wheels. "Only w-what I told you. He understood and sympathized."

"Are you quite certain? The vault beneath St. Brendan's is not the end of the story. Far from it. What of the tunnels beneath Edgecombe? Did he know of those? Were they used with his permission?"

"Tunnels? Beneath Edgecombe?"

"Don't play games with me, Hall. With all the legends of the Keatings bandying about this village, the idea is nothing new. What do you know of the passages that lie beneath the estate, and what did my father know?"

Beads of sweat glistened across Hall's brow. The man's mouth opened, closed, opened again. "But . . . they are only stories. No one knows for sure—"

"I know. I've seen them." He studied the quiver in the man's cheek, the twitching of his nose. "Are you hiding something? Protecting someone? Have you been threatened, told you'd better not speak of these matters?"

"No, nothing like that." Hall's face took on a resigned look as he stared out the carriage window.

"Penhollow's silence is enforced by far more substantial means. Those three sailors yesterday. The attack on Dominic and Ian. These are not isolated events."

"Then why the hell don't you do something about it? Why not call in the authorities?"

"The authorities?" Hall spat the words. "They show up periodically to inspect our warehouses, to see what we might be hiding. When they find nothing but legitimate goods, they consider their job well-done. As for ships wrecking, they blame storms and shake their heads at the villagers' tales of ghost ships. In cases where men have been beaten, as Dominic was today, the officials cite flaring tempers and refuse to interfere."

"Interfere? By God, is that what they call administering justice?"

"I'm afraid so. This is not London. Other than imposing the taxes to which the crown feels entitled, this part of the country has long been left to its own devices."

Chad leaned back against the squabs. "That is about to change. The authorities cannot ignore three men tied together and thrown overboard to drown. And while Penhollow's warehouses may stand empty of smuggled goods, the tunnels beneath Edgecombe and an isolated farm on the moors do not. This is not the work of ghosts. Someone is responsible, and it's time we discovered who."

The carriage bucked over a rut in the road, and the vicar's teeth clacked. Chad regarded him, wondering how far he could trust the soft-spoken, herb-tending minister. Hall had been his father's friend, or so the man claimed.

"You knew my father. Did he habitually drink himself into a stupor?"

"No, my lord, not in my experience, but who can say with any certainty what men do in the privacy of their homes?"

Chad considered that. "Perhaps we cannot know, but we can damn well surmise."

"What are you implying?"

"Nothing for certain. But between tales of ghosts and phantom ships, someone is perpetrating a debilitating deception on this village. A deception that seems centered on Edgecombe. I wonder whether my father hadn't simply been in the way, and needed to be gotten rid of."

The sound of his own voice pronouncing those hideous words seared Chad's chest. If only he had been here when he should have been, how much tragedy might have been avoided?

"Dominic is awake."

At Ian's announcement, Sophie wrapped a dishtowel around the iron handle of the teakettle and removed it from the stove. Since returning home she had prepared countless pots of tea, a task that had kept her hands and her mind occupied while Rachel and Ian kept their vigil at Dominic's side.

She exchanged a glance with Kellyn, who had remained behind when Reese returned to the Stormy Gull. "How can he be awake? The vicar said he'd be out for hours. He had enough sleeping draft to bring down a horse."

"He's groggy," Ian said, "but I reckon the vicar underestimated this particular horse."

The three of them entered the parlor to see Dominic struggling against his sister's restraining hands in an effort to sit up.

"Stop being so stubborn," Rachel countermanded with an authority that took Sophie aback. From minute to minute she never knew what to expect of her quiet cousin.

Dominic gave an unintelligible grumble. His eyes were still swollen nearly shut, his lower slip split, his skin mottled with bruises.

Rachel flattened her hands against his shoulders. "You'll loosen the bandages, and then your ribs will heal crooked. Is that what you want?"

He tried levering up onto his good elbow, but the

splint on his other arm threw off his coordination. The arm struck the back of the sofa. A pained expression twisted his countenance, and a gasp slid from his throat. Upper lip awash in perspiration, he fell prone onto the cushions.

"Ribs don't . . . heal crooked," he hissed between clenched teeth. The words were thick and halting, as if his mouth were stuffed with cotton. As with his sister, Sophie experienced a reluctant appreciation for his headstrong resilience.

"The devil they don't." Kellyn poured water from a nearby pitcher into an earthenware cup. She handed the cup to Rachel, who held it to her brother's lips and supported his head while he drank.

He murmured his thanks. Rachel draped a damp rag across his forehead.

"Do you know what those men wanted?" Ian asked, crouching beside the sofa.

Dominic nodded, then shook his head.

Ian angled a concerned expression at Rachel. "Maybe his wits haven't cleared. The beating and Mr. Hall's tincture—"

"I can hear you . . . even if I can't . . . see you . . . so don't . . . talk as if I'm not here." Dominic's chest heaved with the exertion required to speak each word. The uninjured hand fisted against his leg. "They threatened . . . if Father or I ever again . . ."

Ian and Rachel exchanged looks. "If you or Father what?" she asked gently.

"Didn't make sense," Dominic said. "They accused us . . . of spying. Said . . . if we did it again . . . they'd . . . kill us both."

A cry rose in Sophie's throat, but she clamped her lips and bit it back. On trembling legs she moved past Kellyn and approached the settee. The color had drained from Rachel's face, but she sat unmoving beside her brother, her head barely turning as she darted a somber look at Sophie.

Sophie pulled back with a start. "Dear God," she

whispered to the other girl. "You aren't shocked by this. You know what he's talking about, don't you?"

Rachel's silence prompted Sophie to grip her shoulders. "You know who those men are, and I'll warrant you know why your father traipsed across the moors last night to see them."

Dominic lifted his head from the pillows. He pinned Sophie with as fierce a glower as could penetrate his swollen eyelids. "What would you know . . . about where Father went last night?"

Sophie realized she had spoken unwisely. But, unable to take back her rash disclosure, she returned her cousin's glare with defiance. "I followed him."

Rachel bolted to her feet. "Sophie, what on earth were you thinking?"

"That it's time this family's secrets came out in the open," she said. She hefted her chin. "I guessed something was amiss here ever since I saw those errant harbor lights. Your parents feigned ignorance, but it was a flimsy act. Whatever indiscretions you have committed, don't you all think it is time you came clean and did the right thing?"

Dominic's uninjured hand clenched. "Why don't you ask that . . . of your friend the earl?"

"Dominic," his sister warned.

"Aye, I know where you've been . . . disappearing to lately," he persisted. "I've seen you walking along the road to Edgecombe . . . on more than one occasion, this morning included. Go ahead, Sophie, ask the earl what he knows. I assure you . . . it's more than Father or I can tell you."

"Say what you mean," Sophie demanded.

"I mean . . . that if Father and I watched for signals . . . and lit shore lights to guide an incoming ship . . . the earl did far worse. He helped finance that ship . . . and the stolen cargo it carried."

"That is enough." Rachel stepped between Sophie and Dominic. "I'll have no more of this talk until Mother and Father return."

Sophie ignored her. "You're lying," she said to Dominic, but her shaking voice lacked conviction. She shivered as a clammy chill enveloped her, leaving her fingers numb, her heart frigid. She wanted to believe her elder cousin spoke out of spite, or from confusion fostered by the vicar's medication, yet his insinuation echoed her own fear since the hothouse.

Secrets . . . denials . . .

No. Every part of her rebelled against the notion that Chad could be involved in any wrongdoing that resulted in innocent people being hurt, or worse. Perhaps he hid something inside him, some darkness that flickered sometimes behind his eyes, but surely such gentle hands could not turn suddenly ruthless; surely she had not given her virtue to a villain.

Rachel was speaking, but Sophie could make out nothing past the roar of blood in her ears. Needing to find Chad and learn the truth—force it from him if need be—she fled the parlor and stumbled, half blinded by fear, misgivings and a stubborn refusal to give in to either, out into the gathering twilight.

Chapter 20

"**D**rink this before you go."

The vicar pressed a steaming cup of tea into Chad's hands and stood watching expectantly until he grudgingly took a sip. Chad longed to be on his way and return to Sophie, but the vicar had made a request that delayed his departure.

"Drink it all, my lord. We can't have you taking ill. Stand near the fire while I mix more herbs and laudanum for Dominic." Hall poked at the glowing embers in the hearth until flames kicked up. Then he tossed on more wood. "I'm much obliged to you for agreeing to take the medication back to him. I'll check in on him first thing in the morning."

The man bustled into his tiny kitchen, leaving Chad alone in the parlor. He swallowed another bitter mouthful of tea and made a face.

"I say, Hall, what is in this potion of yours?"

"Yarrow, feverfew . . . an infusion to ward off colds and fever."

"I'll take my chances," Chad mumbled under his breath. A potted plant on a stand beside the writing table presented a convenient means of disposal. With a quick glance over his shoulder, he poured out the remaining contents of the cup. "Sorry, old boy. This will either kill you or make you invincible."

"There, now." The vicar reappeared, holding out a small flask. "When Dominic wakes, his sister must see that he drinks all of this down. It'll help him sleep through the night. I'll have my man bring you back in the carriage."

"And tomorrow you'll personally accompany Miss St. Clair and her cousin to Mullion?" Chad said, reminding the man of the request he had made as they arrived at the vicarage. "After what's happened these past two days, I want both women gone from here as soon as possible."

Hall agreed but eyed Chad quizzically, no doubt pondering his interest in a woman with whom he should barely be acquainted. By the time Chad returned to the Gordon farm, the sky had darkened to tarnished silver, and a light drizzle glazed his face as he alighted from the carriage. Across the road billowing mist veiled the pastures.

Inside he found the parlor oddly empty except for a slumbering Dominic. He moved on into the kitchen, where Kellyn stood before the stove.

Wooden spoon in hand, she turned from the pot she had been stirring. "I thought I heard someone come in."

"Where is everyone?"

"I sent Rachel upstairs to rest while Dominic sleeps. Ian is out in the barn, seeing to some of the chores that went undone earlier."

When she elaborated no further, a foreboding gripped him. "What about Sophie?"

Kellyn studied him for a moment. Concern burgeoned on her face. "You look dreadful."

She tapped the spoon on the edge of the pot, set it down on the counter and went to the table. Lifting a glass in one hand and the bottle of brandy in the other, she poured a small measure and held it out to him. "Here, you look as though you need this. If I didn't know better I'd think you'd been attacked as well. You weren't, were you?"

He supposed nearly being buried alive in a tunnel had left its mark on his appearance. "Not in so many words," he murmured, and tossed back the brandy in one gulp. "Now, then, about Sophie."

"I'm sure she's quite all right. Sit down and I'll tell you what went on here while you were gone, though I'll admit I'm not certain I understood it all. Dominic made some accusations . . . about you."

He swore under his breath. "Tell me exactly what he said."

Sophie came to an uncertain halt as the mist thickened around her. She had headed down the road toward the village, believing she would either find Chad at the vicarage or meet him on his way back to the farm. But darkness had fallen with startling speed, augmented by the blanketing fog.

Her dry clothes were fast becoming as wet as those she had changed out of earlier. Her feet squelched inside her ankle boots. With a sinking sensation she scanned the starless sky, the rolling fog, the utter absence of familiar landmarks. The house should still be visible, a dark huddle framed by a charcoal glimmer of sea. Both were now gone.

She had set off from the house, desperate to find Chad and hear from his own lips that Dominic has spoken nonsense, that Chad had nothing to do with smuggling or murder or even misplaced harbor lights. That he was a good and decent man, and she had not been a fool to place her trust and her heart in his keeping.

But somehow, in her haste and perplexity, she had wandered off the muddy road and onto the moor. Her panic rising, she listened for the bleating of sheep, the lowing of cattle. She pricked her ears for the distant tolling of the buoy bells.

Only eerie silence greeted her. Mist, shadow and the vastness of sky and moor merged into a giant emptiness with Sophie at its center.

Fear smelled of rain-soaked peat, salt-tinged air, and the rank muck that coated the bogs. She hugged her arms around her. Turning and trying to approximate the direction from which she had come, she began walking. Forlorn and shivering, she pushed on until a low rock wall appeared before her, encircling a forest of headstones.

A flicker of shadow sent Chad tearing up the hillside, catching himself on his hands when roots and rocks thrust from the turf to break his stride. Pushing upright, he scrambled around boulders, dashed through brambles and stinging nettle, and not for a moment did he slow his pace.

A cramp stabbed his side. He shouted Sophie's name, but received no reply except the echo of his own voice slung back at him from the moor.

Why didn't she answer? Surely she couldn't have strayed so far from the road so quickly? Perhaps it hadn't been Sophie he had glimpsed, but merely the brush thrashing in the breezes. Perhaps she had already returned home, was even now sitting in the farmhouse kitchen enjoying a cup of tea.

No. He knew her. She would not ignore Dominic's accusations. They would gnaw at her and she would seek answers, demand them with the same tenacity that had driven her since that first night at the chapel.

The chapel. He would find her there; he felt the certainty of it down to his bones. But where *was* "there"?

Always where they needed it most.

The saturated ground sucking at his boots, he slowed to a halt. The exertion of his climb had torn his breath ragged, leaving him giddy, unsteady, as around him the moor began to spin. At the edge of his vision the streak of a ragged hem disappeared around a gnarled rowan tree. He took off at a run, only to stagger wildly and come splashing down onto his knees. A bolt of lightning-sharp pain sent his hands pressing against his eyes. When he opened them, a face ravaged by death and decay hovered in front of him.

He blinked, and the face was gone. Had he imagined it—again? Pulling slowly to his feet, he struggled to master his galloping heartbeat. What had he seen? What had led him to the chapel not once but twice now, and shown him the entrance to the tunnel beneath Edgecombe's cellars?

"Do you exist?" he murmured aloud. He threw back his head and shouted, "Are you real? Have you been guiding me all along? Then guide me now. Help me find Sophie."

The air grew as sharp as hoarfrost. A tendril of mist curled, and in it a wan face materialized. The sight sent a shock rippling through him, and toppled a lifelong conviction that ghosts did not exist.

"Help me." His plea steamed in icy clouds before his lips. "She's lost, and I must find her."

The little ghost tipped her disfigured face to him, held him with her vacant eyes. *You love her.*

"God, yes."

I was loved. So very loved. Her voice quavered like the windblown heather blossoms. *Yet I died. Was swallowed by the sea.*

Every instinct demanded he continue his search for Sophie, yet he could not ignore the little ghost's sorrow. "Tell me what happened to you."

Papa took me to sea. 'Twas my birthday. We went to France. We went to sea, and I died.

"Yes, but . . . how?"

A storm came. The ship foundered. And the people . . . they rowed out, rowed out to save the cargo. All were not off. I screamed and screamed. No one came. Not even Papa. The ship was swallowed . . . swallowed by the waves.

"What people? Who saved the cargo and left you to die?"

She gave a forlorn shake of her head, and the horror, the sheer terror of what her final moments must have been, pushed him back down onto his knees. "I'm sorry. I'd have saved you if I could. If I had known."

You can save her. The evil is killing her. Killing her soul.

"I'll do anything I must. Just help me. Guide me to her. To the chapel. I'm certain she's there."

She shook her head. *She is safe for now.*

"I don't understand. How can she be safe?"

There is another.

"Another what?" he shouted in frustration. "What are you trying to say?

She cannot see me. Cannot hear me. Her soul is dying. You must help her.

"Who must I help?" He got to his feet, standing tall despite the unsteadiness spreading through his limbs. "I'll do whatever you ask. Just tell me who she is."

Mama.

"That isn't enough. She could be anybody. What is her name? What is *your* name?" He strode forward, reaching into the icy mist. "Damn it, don't go yet."

The wraith faded away. A glimmer of moonlight pierced the clouds, briefly illuminating the sloping hillsides, the granite crags and the crest of a lonely spire.

"Sophie!"

Her cloaked figure huddled against the newels of the iron railing. Relief sent him dashing between the headstones. She didn't move, barely raised her head as she peered at him through sodden ribbons of hair.

He sank to his knees on the step below and took her in his arms, rejoicing when she didn't resist him. His mouth found hers and devoured it, like a single warm blessing to a man lost at sea. Her fingers tunneled into his hair, tugging with sharp little pains that somehow anchored him, brought him comfort. Again and again he kissed her, suckled her lips and tongue until he drowned in the relief of having found her.

He crushed her in his arms and felt desire streaking through his loins. Even here. Even now. He couldn't hold her without wanting all of her, without yearning for the haven of being inside her.

He drew back, yet remained so close their shared heat steamed between their lips. "What are you doing out here? Why didn't you go inside, out of the cold rain?"

The questions burst out harshly, his voice grating with the awful fear of losing her, of believing he had already lost her.

"I couldn't bring myself to go in alone, without you." Her sobs trembled into his chest, touched him soul-deep. "This place is ours, where we have always been safe together."

"You're safe now; I swear it."

"Am I?" She leaned away, eyes brimming with a despondency that stilled his heart, his breath, the blood in his veins. Her arms slid from around him, and her back came up against the chapel door with a thud of finality that echoed inside him. "Dominic said—"

"I know. Kellyn told me about his accusations. I can explain."

"Can you?" Her chest heaved; her nostrils flared. "How many times have I entreated you to do just that? To explain your sudden scowls and silences and the darkness that so often shadows your eyes. Always you pushed me away. For my safety, you said."

"It *was* for your safety. You must believe that."

"Must I?" She surged to her feet, a glimmer of hope peeking through the bewildered anger that claimed her features. "Tell me I can trust you. Tell me I haven't been a fool to believe in you thus far."

"You're no fool, Sophie." He stood and reached for her again.

"Aren't I?" She strode past him and down the steps. Then she whirled to face him, hands fisted at her sides. "Dominic said you know those brigands at the farmstead. And that you not only helped finance the ship I saw approaching the coast that night, but that you are partly responsible for the stolen cargo it contained."

Against the surrounding darkness her tearstained cheeks glowed ghostly pale, while in her eyes challenge and outrage burned fiercely bright. And he realized his Sophie was gone, vanished like a wraith. The Sophie he might have had, the beautiful, smiling countess he had imagined earlier in her relatives' kitchen, would never be his.

Stepping down from the stoop, he filled his lungs with damp night air. "Dominic was mistaken about my knowing those men," he said miserably. "I have never seen them before. Nor can I identify the ship you saw, or the men who sailed her. I dealt with a limited number of contacts, which is a way to ensure that no one man knows enough to bring the entire operation down."

He moved closer to her, stopping short at the revulsion and alarm on her face as she backed away. He shoved his hands in his trouser pockets to assure her that he posed no threat. "But yes, I may well have financed that ship. For two years, after inheriting a nearly bankrupt estate, I put my warehouses and private property at the disposal of smugglers. I provided funds to bribe customs inspectors to sign off on bills of lading that didn't match delivery destinations and look the other way when black market or stolen goods were slipped through depots along with legitimate freight."

Her eyes narrowed. "And wrecking?"

She meant the deliberate scuttling of ships. *Killed for the cargo.* His guilt lashed at his temples, making him dizzy. "Yes," he whispered. "That happened too, though neither by my hand nor, at the time, to my knowledge." He clutched a fist to his chest. "I swear it."

"My God." Her hoarse whisper iced his soul. And there it was, the look he'd dreaded, the scathing abhorrence inscribed in the slash of her mouth, the steely glitter of her eyes.

He reached out to her. "Sophie—"

"Don't." She backed away another step. A grim laugh escaped her. "Each time I ventured too close to a discovery, you came charging to the rescue, or so I believed. In truth you were merely diverting my attention. Oh, what an inconvenience I must have been."

"I'd have given my life to keep you safe. Would still give my life for you."

"I didn't want your life. Only your heart."

If only he could tell her his heart was and would always be hers, but what good would it do to offer the very thing she scorned?

A dismal silence stretched between them. The air grew colder, the churchyard dimmer, and for a moment he feared the little ghost had returned. But his shaking hands told him it wasn't the outer temperature dropping, but a stony chill inside him, beginning at his extremities and marching steadily through him.

Sophie strode between the gravestones, pulled up short and, with a swirl of her hems, faced him again. "The tunnels. They were too cleverly disguised for anyone to simply stumble upon them. You must have known where they were all along. I suppose you reasoned that by revealing them to me you might continue to use them under the pretense of investigating."

"I swear to you that before today I didn't know where those tunnels were, or even that they existed. I found them because . . . I was led to them."

"By whom? Surely not Nathaniel."

"A ghost."

Her expression told him he sounded insane. And how could he argue otherwise? He didn't believe in ghosts—or hadn't until tonight. But looking back on everything that had happened since his arrival in Penhollow, it was the only explanation that made sense.

He plowed his fingers through his hair, pulling it on end until the roots ached. "The night we met a ghost led me across the moor and to this chapel. It—she—prevented me from drowning the day we scaled the cliff. It was she who guided me to the tunnel beneath the house, and who helped me slide free of the gap we created in the cave-in debris."

Sophie's eyes turned as cool as the mist. Beneath her silent scrutiny Chad burned, writhed, died.

"Liar." Her eyes filled with fresh tears, fresh bitterness. "To think—God forgive me—I gave myself to you today. I threw myself away for a lie, for a phantom pleasure I foolishly believed could be real."

Her words sliced at his soul. The trembling energy fluttering beneath her cloak alerted him to her intention of fleeing. Before she could take more than a step, instinct born of a frantic and stubborn refusal to give up sent him after her. He knew he should let her go; she'd be better off without him. Still he reached across a peaked granite marker, catching her wrist and halting her flight. "My feelings for you are real, Sophie. Never doubt it."

"They cannot be, for the man I believed in isn't real. If any ghost has wandered these moors it has been you, haunting me with an illusion that doesn't exist." She struggled to yank free of him, but he held her fast. The headstone stood as a half barrier between them, preventing him from stepping closer or pulling her into his arms.

"The man who made love to you today does exist; I swear it," he said. A resounding pain thundered inside his head, but he pushed past it, struggling to find the right words. True words, even if she would not accept them. "That was me, Sophie, not a phantom. I despise the things I've done—the crimes I've committed. I came to Penhollow to make amends. To try to discover the name of the individual at the center of the crimes, and stop them once and for all."

"Why should I believe you?" Her voice sounded far off, echoing in his ears with a watery timbre.

"I'm sorry . . . so damned sorry . . . you were caught in the middle. I tried to send you away." The pain traveled beneath his skull. He blinked and raised his free hand to wipe icy perspiration from his brow. "I tried to stay away from you. I couldn't . . . I . . ."

"What's wrong with you?" The words undulated as if spoken beneath heaving waves. Her image blurred as a dark haze obscured his vision. He swayed.

Reaching out, he caught the edge of the tombstone. He released Sophie in the process, but she didn't run. Though poised for flight, she eyed him with uncertainty. He shut his eyes and fought for balance, opening them when a light pressure closed around his shoulders. Her hands.

His own hands clenched the biting granite of the headstone. Somehow her gentle but steady grip lent him the strength to fight past whatever illness had taken him so unawares. Drawing in huge drafts of air, he straightened. The pain receded and his head began to clear.

"Are you ill?" she asked with a reluctant concern he hoped to God he didn't imagine.

Did she—could she possibly—still care?

Chapter 21

Sophie's mind reeled with the turmoil of the past days. Death. Guns. Tunnels. Assault. And now this dreadful confession and Chad's implausible explanations. They crashed over her like a deadly tide yanking the solid ground out from under her and leaving her floundering.

The Earl of Wycliffe, a peer of England . . . a smuggler? A criminal no more trustworthy than those ruffians at the farmstead? And now on top of it all a ridiculous tale of ghosts—as if some other hand and not his own had guided his wicked actions. How could she have so misjudged him?

As his trembling shoulders steadied beneath her palms, she snatched her hands away, fearful that even scant contact would leave her once more vulnerable to his lies.

Her insides withered around a pulsing regret. She had given her virginity to a man who, despite his present protestations, thought nothing of trifling with her. Humiliation left her throbbing with tears she refused—*refused*—to shed. The wind plucked frigidly at her cheeks. With fisted hands she wiped away the last traces of moisture, shook her streaming hair out of her face and raised her chin to him.

"You speak of ghosts," she said evenly. "Everything you have told me, every experience we have shared, has been but a specter of the truth. Perhaps it has been my own fault. You are right. You tried sending me away more than once, and I wouldn't listen. I believed in a dream and refused to awaken. But I am awake now. And for the first time I see you plainly."

With rapid steps she strode to the end of the row of stones and gazed out onto the rolling moor. She felt more than heard him come up behind her, and cursed herself for experiencing an aching tenderness that seemed to exist of its own volition. Even now he haunted the deepest places of her female yearnings.

She jumped at the spark caused by his fingers on her nape.

"Don't turn away from me, Sophie."

She heard the plea in his voice, the desperate hope. Unable to resist, she stole a glance at him from over her shoulder. It seemed the very life had drained from his features, and she experienced a moment of crushing doubt.

Could he care so little for her and still look so gray, so dashed in spirit?

"It is cold," she said, "and there is nothing to be gained by lingering in this abandoned place."

"It is not abandoned as long as you and I are here together." He moved around her until they stood toe-to-toe. He touched her cheek, a graze of his fingertips that set fire to her flesh. "Can you deny the magic of this chapel? Always where we need it, though never in exactly the same place?"

She raised her hand to her face, as if she might rub away the longing aroused by his touch. "The moors confuse, trick the eye. This chapel does not move about like some living, benevolent creature waiting to serve us."

"Doesn't it?"

She ached to believe such a prospect could be true, but the logical part of her refused to give the notion credence.

"I hurt you today," he whispered. "God, I'm sorry for that. This morning meant more to me than—"

"Don't you dare speak of this morning." Her heart wrenching, she squeezed her eyes shut, blotting out the sight of him—and trying to overcome the devastating desire his very image evoked. Even after all these hours, soreness pinched her inner thighs, bittersweet stabs that conjured the passion of him inside her, the length and breadth of him filling her, impossibly, miraculously.

"Sophie, I . . ."

"You what? Say it and have done."

He parted his lips—those velvet, sensual lips—and drew a breath. But when she believed he might speak, he instead released a rasping sigh. The familiar shadows filled his eyes, once more shuttering his thoughts and rendering him a stranger.

She swallowed a sob, but not before it tangled audibly in her throat. "I wish to return to Aunt Louisa's."

"Yes, we should both return to your aunt's farm."

She opened her mouth to tell him that he was unwelcome there, but he held up a hand to forestall her.

"By your cousin's own admittance he and his father are involved in Penhollow's smuggling, and they might very well have some of the answers I seek. I intend to wait for your uncle to return and question him about what he knows. One way or another, Sophie, I will put an end to this, beginning tonight. Before the passing of many more days, the men who attacked Dominic—and, more important, their leader—will be apprehended. Or dead. Or I—"

He broke off, but his words left her with the disquieting impression that he had meant either his adversary would be dead . . . or he would.

"Lord Wycliffe, please come into the house. It'll do you no good to stand outside in the damp night air."

In a gesture that felt as hollow as a freshly dug grave, Chad smiled his thanks at Rachel, who beckoned from the kitchen doorway. He made no move to comply with her request. He would not offend Sophie any further with his presence.

His confession had hurt her as irrevocably as their lovemaking had changed her. Should he have held his tongue and let the truth be damned? The longing to turn back the hours and undo his wretched honesty bored a veritable hole through his chest.

But could he have continued to live with lies hanging between them? The man he used to be, prior to coming to Penhollow, might have. But he wasn't that reckless, unthinking young rogue any longer. He understood now, all too well, about responsibility, and consequences, and the price of one's actions. Not just the outward costs—loss of fortune, privilege, freedom. Those he could shoulder. The inner costs were another matter. Honor. Self-respect. Love . . .

In those final moments at the chapel Sophie had challenged him to "say it and have done." And, dear God, he'd come narrowly close to doing just that, to blurting the whole of what he had come to feel for her. How ironic that those very feelings had forced him to hold his tongue. With nothing to offer her in life but desperate straits and tainted honor, he had seen no other choice.

Her cousin had disappeared into the kitchen. Now she returned to the threshold and held out a bottle and cup to him. "Kellyn left this earlier, said it might do you good. Have some now. It'll help prevent you from catching cold."

A wry smile curled his upper lip at how like the vicar she sounded. Would that his concerns were so simple. He went to the stoop and accepted the offered items from her hands, thanking her again for her kindness. She too would soon find her world altered, probably not for the better. If her father refused to cooperate, the man might eventually land in prison, or worse, depending on the depth of his involvement with the smuggling ring. Changing the harbor lights to guide an illicit vessel to shore was one thing. Chad hoped to God neither Gordon nor his son knew of, or had any hand in, the scuttling of ships.

Abandoning the cup by the doorstep, he gripped the bottle and strode past the kitchen garden. From the stable he heard Prince's soft whickering, and from the henhouse a few sleepy clucks. The distant bleating of sheep drifted from across the road. Hoping the elder Gordons arrived soon, he tilted the brandy to his lips, allowing a small measure to burn its way down his throat. Then, in a burst of frustration, he sent the bottle hurling into the side of the Gordons' barn.

Liquor would do him no good, could not banish a single one of his demons. Not the ones inhabiting his soul, and not the small one that now inhabited his life. She had charged him with protecting someone, but whom? Not Sophie. The little ghost had made that clear tonight. Why wouldn't the apparition simply tell him what he needed to know?

The brandy dripped in amber streaks down the whitewashed barn wall. Shards of glass littered the ground. Turning his back on the mess, he shoved his hands in his pockets and shivered as the cold air and an irrepressible desolation took hold. Protecting a nameless individual, rooting out a nameless villain, preventing nameless, countless others from falling victim to the crime of piracy—his life seemed filled with one impossible task after another.

The crunching of wheels on the drive sent him sprinting to the yard at the side of the house. A cart drawn by two huge, smoky draft horses turned in from the road. The elder Gordons had finally returned.

As Barnaby Gordon descended from the plank seat, Chad strode up behind him. His sudden appearance wrenched a startled shriek from Louisa Gordon, her face pale within the dark folds of a shawl.

Her husband rounded on Chad. "God's teeth!"

"I've got questions for you, Gordon."

The man squinted, his expression incredulous. "Lord

Wycliffe? What the devil are ye doing here? And at such an hour?"

"Helping collect your broken son off the moor, that's what."

His wife scrambled down from the wagon. "Dominic's been hurt?"

"He was attacked. By friends of your husband's."

"What friends, Barn?" The woman clutched her shawl tighter beneath her chin. "What is he talking about?"

"Damned if I know."

"Oh, you may well be damned. And that will make two of us." A twist of fury and guilt drove Chad at the man, who stood taller and nearly twice his width. Using surprise to his advantage, he caught the broad shoulders in a vise grip, backed Gordon up against the cart shed and pinned him to the closed doors with a teeth-grinding jolt that rattled the hinges.

"Who told you to alter the harbor lights?" Chad demanded. "Don't deny it; your son admits as much. I want names, Gordon. And I want to know what other crimes you've been paid to commit."

As the questions seethed from his lips, a commotion broke out behind him—the thwack of the opening front door hitting the wall of the house, then footsteps and a raised clamor of voices.

A hand gripped his sleeve. "Leave my father alone."

Rachel's appeal penetrated Chad's rage. He looked down into her eyes, large and frightened, and decided that no matter what Gordon had done, Chad could neither threaten nor thrash the man as he'd like to in front of his daughter and wife.

He eased his grip on Gordon but didn't release him. Ian appeared at Rachel's shoulder. Louisa Gordon followed, her high-pitched entreaties creating a shrill harmony to her husband's rumbled curses. A shout came from the direction of the house.

"I'm coming, Father." It was Dominic. He stood on the threshold, gripping the jamb for support.

"Go back inside," his sister cried. "Oh, what are you thinking?" Her hems flurrying, she dashed back across the yard. Sophie appeared in the doorway, and Chad immediately regretted losing his temper and causing this scene. He didn't want her caught in the middle; didn't want her hurt any further.

With a stoic expression she stepped outside, slipped an arm around Dominic's waist and set a hand beneath his good elbow.

He seemed not to notice her. "Don't let the blighter bully you, Father," he shouted.

Chad knew an instant's indignation, one that cost him his hold on Gordon. The farmer broke free and headed for the house with a formidable stride.

"She's to blame." He thrust a finger in Sophie's direction. "Miss hoity-toity with her nose in everyone's business."

Sophie's cry of alarm launched Chad into pursuit before he had time to contemplate her uncle's intentions. Sprinting forward on a burst of speed, he grabbed Gordon's arm from behind and spun the larger man around with a momentum that robbed them both of balance. Chad hit the ground with a jolt that sent lights dancing before his eyes.

Landing half on top of him, the other man let out a grunt as the air left him, but he recovered quickly enough. Before Chad could ease free and roll to his feet, Gordon pinned his shoulders. Face framed in wild black hair, the farmer glowered down at him.

Though at a clear disadvantage, Chad met the man's scowl with one of equal venom. "Let me up and try listening to reason. I came to Penhollow to discover the identity of the individual responsible for ordering innocent ships scuttled. Sophie has nothing to do with any of it. But I think you do, don't you, Gordon?"

He felt a slight lessening of the force in the man's brawny arms as Gordon peered over his shoulder. "What did ye tell him, boy?"

Chad took advantage of Gordon's momentary distraction by gripping both of his arms, bracing his own feet on the ground and putting every ounce of his strength into heaving Gordon over onto his side. Then Chad bolted upright and pushed the other man onto his stomach. He wedged a knee at the small of Gordon's spine, reclaimed one of the farmer's arms and pinned it behind his back.

That didn't stop the larger man from struggling. Chad wrenched the arm another notch. "Care to hear it snap?"

Gordon growled, but shook his head.

"Then calm down. You may be larger than I, but I excelled in both boxing and wrestling all through my school days. Shall we put it to the test?"

The fight drained from Gordon's limbs.

"Good. I'm going to let you up now. Remember, this is between you and me. Leave Sophie out of it."

The farmer turned his bearded cheek to the ground and seethed from the corner of his mouth, " 'Sophie' is it now? What's she to ye?"

Chad ignored the question as he eased off the man and stood up. What could he have said? He didn't know what Sophie was to him.

Gordon shook his disheveled hair out of his eyes and continued complaining as his wife helped him to his feet. "Poking about where she don't belong. If the girl don't learn her place good and quick, she'll come to a right sticky end."

"And if you don't come clean and help me, Gordon, you'll find yourself swinging from a gibbet."

At her brother's side, Rachel gave a cry. Louisa Gordon treated Chad to a resentful glare. He angled his chin toward the house. "I want everyone inside. Now."

It irked him no end that they all looked to Gordon for approval before filing into the house.

Chad's questions had to wait, however, until after Sophie's aunt exclaimed her dismay over her son's plight, examined his pulverized face and broken arm, tucked him back onto the sofa beneath several blankets, comforted her daughter, inquired after Sophie's health and made tea.

The bearded collie, called Heyworth, clambered up onto the sofa, taking up a good portion of space as he stretched out beside Dominic and set about nosing and licking his injured arm. The animal seemed to have a calming effect on the young man, for Dominic made no interruptions as Rachel explained the circumstances of the attack to her parents.

Ian, meanwhile, attempted to make himself invisible by hovering silently in the farthest corner of the room. Eventually he retreated into the kitchen. Chad had forgotten that the young fisherman might not be a welcome guest in this house, particularly not by Barnaby Gordon.

Sophie, too, kept her distance, sitting alone on a wooden settle against the wall on the far side of the fireplace. Chad yearned to go to her, longed to hold her in his arms and ask forgiveness for all the wrongs he had done. A single question tormented him: Would being honest from the start have made a difference? As soon as the subject of smuggling came up—that first night as they searched the coast for her mystery ship—should he have confessed his reasons for coming to Penhollow, and all that had led to his arrival here?

She might have run from him then, as fast and as far as possible, but at least she would not now have to bear the dismal burden of his deceit.

I threw myself away for a lie, for a phantom pleasure I foolishly believed could be real.

Those words slashed at his conscience in a relentless punishment he deserved.

He turned to Gordon, and to the one matter he might still rectify. "Who paid you to change the shore lights? Those men at the moorland farm?"

"Don't tell him anything, Father," Dominic mumbled as he scratched Heyworth's shaggy ears.

The hulking farmer lumbered across the room and

settled into a chair he dragged close to the sofa. His large hand draped his son's forehead in a simple gesture of affection utterly at odds with the man's rough exterior. Gordon rose a notch in Chad's estimate, renewing his hopes that his efforts here would not be wasted.

But when Gordon remained silently brooding, Chad stood before the man and gestured toward the sofa. "Two fiends thrashed your son. Supposing your daughter is next? Or your wife?"

Gordon paled. His dark gaze leaped from one family member to the next, even lighted on Heyworth. His coal-black eyebrows converged above his nose.

"Still tongue-tied?" Amid a surge of impatient anger, pain lanced Chad's gut, at the same time thundering inside his skull. The sensation felt akin to the illness that had struck him earlier at the chapel. Determined not to display weakness in front of the farmer, he purposely braced his hands on the armrests of Gordon's chair and curled back his lips in a show of ire he hoped masked his distress.

"You're consorting with murderers, Mr. Gordon." He bit down against the pain and hoped the gesture appeared threatening. "Their actions against Dominic suggest they consider you both a liability now. We know how scoundrels dispose of liabilities."

The man glowered up at him through his bristling eyebrows. "Tell me, Your Lordship, how did I come to be such a bloody liability? It weren't me out there spying last night. My son, neither."

"No, it was Sophie." Dominic pointed a finger in her general direction.

"And me," Chad said quickly. The pain subsiding, he pushed upright.

"Bloody hell." Gordon's features turned ruddy. He surged to his feet, sending Chad back a step and prompting the dog to let out a whine.

"Are we going to tussle again, Gordon, or are you going to decide to be useful?" When the man made a snarling sound in his throat, Chad said, "I watched you scan the sea last night through your spyglass. You were looking for a signal; I gleaned as much as I pressed my ear to the back of that ramshackle farmhouse last night. You've been waiting for the return of a ship, no?"

"None of your sodding business."

"Father, tell him." Rachel hopped down from her perch on the arm of the sofa. "Lord Wycliffe, through the years everyone in this town has benefited from goods brought in from France and beyond. Fair trading is a way of life for us and always has been."

"Yes, Miss Gordon. But the circumstances have changed recently, haven't they?"

"Aye," she whispered. "It's no longer fair trading, but something much more sinister." She turned to her father. "You must tell Lord Wycliffe everything you know. For all our sakes."

Behind his mane of black hair, a pulse ticked in Gordon's cheek. He sank back into his chair. Reaching out, he took his daughter's hand and rubbed his thumb back and forth across knuckles reddened from her daily toils on the farm. He sighed, a sound like an ocean gust hitting the cliffs.

"My son and I are paid to keep watch for ship signals on the horizon. Three flashes, followed by two, then four. Always after midnight, and only in the days of the waning moon, when the night skies grow darker. We take turns at the watch. When the signal comes, he or I take our skiff down the coast and ignite a row of torches.

"In the inlet near Edgecombe."

Gordon nodded.

"Have you followed the tunnel to its inland source?" Chad asked.

"God, no. We did what we were told. Put in, light the torches and leave. The ship sails in close and sends a lighter to shore with the cargo. It's unloaded, and the crew snuffs the torches and stashes them back in the cave before they row back out."

His palm rasping against the growth of beard stubbling his chin, Chad contemplated whether the other man could be speaking the truth. "You mean to tell me you were never tempted to return afterward and examine that cargo? Perhaps snatch a thing or two for yourself?"

A shadow fell across the farmer's face. "Tempted? Aye. But daft enough to swindle a swindler?" Gordon shook his head. "How long do ye think I'd have lived if I'd tampered with any of that plunder?"

An airy little outburst behind him drew Chad's attention to Sophie. Her hems briskly sweeping the floor, she crossed the room. " 'A trick of the light. Go back to sleep. All is well.' How *could* you tell such bald-faced lies?" She whirled to face her aunt. "Aunt Louisa, how could *you*?"

"I'm sorry, child. We were only trying to protect you."

"Protect yourselves, you mean." Outwardly she appeared calm, her hands folded primly at her waist, her head at a slight tilt. But Chad saw the storm tossing in her gray eyes, and felt the anger emanating off her in turbulent waves. "Trying to protect your ill-gotten gains," she went on quietly. "No wonder you didn't want me here. No wonder you fear my grandfather. Can't you simply imagine your guilty faces plastered on the front page of the *Beacon*?"

Rachel gasped. Through his bruises Dominic approximated a fair rendering of a scowl.

Chad went to Sophie's side and touched her arm. She flinched and turned that tempestuous gaze on him, but he refused to move away. Couldn't, once the heat of her skin imbued his palm. Of their own volition his fingers closed around her arm. "They're making an effort to cooperate. This is hardly a time to threaten them with your grandfather."

"Threaten them?" She glared at each Gordon in turn. "Those three sailors were murdered to line *your* pockets, by men *you* have aided. Why did you do it, Uncle Barnaby? How could you?"

"I believed 'twas the same game of fair trading we've always played." Gordon folded his arms across his chest as if to shield himself. "Did as I was asked and minded my business. When I realized 'twas more than the crown's revenue lost, but lives, 'twas too late to back out. I knew too much, they said."

Sophie regarded her uncle for another moment, then turned her accusing gaze on Chad. She said nothing, didn't have to. Like her uncle, he had lined his pockets by abetting murderers, and being unaware of the full truth didn't excuse him. He should have made it his business to understand exactly what he was getting into at the time. Instead he had let himself be duped into complacency by the lure of easy profits. He was as culpable as Gordon; as guilty, in the end, as the men who wielded weapons and preyed upon others.

A cold comprehension seeped through him. He might yet help to set things right, but he could never be completely absolved for the role he had played. Perhaps that was what his little ghost had been trying to tell him the night he arrived in Penhollow. *Can you understand what torment is?*

God, yes. Torment was knowing he could never escape what he had done. Torment was seeing the wounded look in Sophie's eyes, and knowing he put it there.

He shifted his attention back to Gordon. "How are you able to douse the harbor lights with no one in the village knowing it's you doing it? Or are they all in on your secret?"

"I don't douse the harbor lights. I told you. Dominic and I watch for the signals and light the torches near Edgecombe. That's all."

"Then who is responsible for the lights at the quay?"

The farmer shrugged. "I get my orders from Joshua Diggs and Edward Wiley, the men I went to see last night. There used to be a third, Giles Watling. But he's dead now."

"Yes, I saw Watling the morning he died." Chad's disclosure seemed to catch Gordon off guard. "He had a message for me. He said I must come to Penhollow and wait to be contacted. Do you know anything about that?"

Gordon's scowl eased to a look of uncertainty.

"Am I to be contacted, or killed?" Chad persisted. "Perhaps by your friends Diggs and Wiley?"

Gordon gave a shrug. "Your arrival at Edgecombe interfered with their plans."

"Yes, I gathered that. Did my father's presence at Edgecombe interfere with their plans as well?" Growing wrath put a tremor in Chad's voice. "Did they find it necessary to dispose of him?"

Gordon's features registered genuine surprise. "A fire killed your father."

"Perhaps." Chad tamped down an urge to strike something. "Diggs and Wiley will get their comeuppance, but ultimately it isn't them I seek. Give me a name, and I'll do everything within my power to see that you and your family aren't harmed again."

Gordon dismissed the assertion with a cynical grunt and rubbed a hand over his beard. "I can't tell you what I don't know. Whoever is in charge might not even hail from the village. He could be anywhere along the coast."

"Then why was I told to come to Penhollow?" Pacing, Chad sifted through all he had learned so far, admittedly scant information. Someone had wanted him here, yet that someone had yet to make contact. Meanwhile his presence seemed to pose an intolerable inconvenience to everyone else involved in the piracy ring. It didn't make sense. Still, he didn't entirely disbelieve Gordon's claims of ignorance about the man in charge. Beyond Giles Watling, Chad hadn't known many other names either.

His thoughts returned to the matter of the harbor lights. Any inhabitant of the village would have quick and easy access to the quay at night, but who might have gotten away with it without anyone else knowing?

A sudden thought ushered in another bout of dizziness. As the sensation wafted through him, he braced his feet, pressed a hand to his temple and said, "What about Grady?"

Chapter 22

"The Irishman?" Sophie's uncle emitted a bark of laughter. "He's stark raving mad."

"Is he?" Chad shot back. "Or is that what he wishes people to think?

Uncle Barnaby's expression became serious, but in the next instant he waved a hand in the air and made a dismissive sound.

"You supposedly went to Mullion today." Chad's voice plunged to an accusing baritone. "Why?"

"To arrange to sell off some of our lambs before the cold sets in." Aunt Louisa held out her hands. "Why else?"

Chad swung about to face her. "And did you happen to run into Grady there? He left for Mullion yesterday to report the deaths of the three sailors to the coast guard."

"Why, no . . . we never saw him." Aunt Louisa's nervous glance wandered to her husband, then darted back to Chad. "But Mullion is a larger town than Penhollow. We simply didn't cross paths."

Something in her aunt's demeanor prompted Sophie to wonder if the couple was indeed hiding something. "Are you certain, Aunt Louisa? The time for secrets is long past."

"We did not see the Irishman," the woman said without blinking.

"And I suppose neither of you would happen to

know," Chad said evenly, "why a man who claims he's sailing to Mullion would leave his boat tied up in the inlet where you, Gordon, light the torches at night?"

Uncle Barnaby shoved to his feet. "I don't know what you're implying, but I swear on the lives of both my children I've no knowledge of the Irishman's whereabouts, nor that of his blasted boat. If it's moored in an inlet south of here, I'll be damned if I know why."

Several long moments passed as the two men regarded each other, rather like two bulls debating whether to charge. Sophie half expected fists to begin flying, until the rigid line of Chad's shoulders relaxed. "Perhaps I'm a fool, but I believe you."

Like a pair of conspirators, he and Uncle Barnaby reached an uneasy truce and began making plans to apprehend the villains at the moorland farm. Chad insisted they would learn much from those men. Uncle Barnaby agreed, though he stubbornly maintained that an earl had no business taking part in such a confrontation. He suggested enlisting the help of his brother-in-law, the powerful, baldheaded Reese, instead. Chad balked at the former notion, but concurred with the wisdom of bringing the Stormy Gull's barkeep along.

As the men alternately plotted and argued, Sophie watched Chad intently. He wasn't well—she'd stake her life on it. He made a first-rate job of covering, but she detected minute details the others wouldn't notice—the sleeplessness smudging his eyes, the pallor of his skin, the slight tremor in fingers usually as steady as the granite crags on the moors.

He'd shown symptoms of illness earlier at the chapel, and twice again since returning to the house. No, more than that. She considered the countless times his features had suddenly tightened for no apparent reason. The others wouldn't have caught it, wouldn't have known how to interpret it. But she did. She had seen such signs of distress in him before, such as when he'd battled the Devil's Twirl and been heaved against the rocks, or when he'd fought his way through the gap in the cave-in.

Though he soldiered on now, she knew something continued to ail him, and she couldn't force herself to turn away and cease to care. Even when she tried convincing herself that her regard went no further than that of any decent individual toward another, a pain beneath her breastbone and the constant gnawing of worry in her belly belied the assertion. As did a constant desire to take his face in her hands and touch her lips to his.

What a fool she had become when it came to this man.

Sometime after midnight her aunt suggested that everyone snatch a few hours of sleep before the men put their plans into action come dawn. Ian had fallen asleep in a kitchen chair, his head cradled in his arms on the table. Sophie had nudged him, but he had let out a snore and slumbered on with a sailor's ability to sleep in any position, under any conditions.

As Uncle Barnaby helped Dominic to his feet and the family headed for the stairs, Chad approached Sophie.

"At first light the vicar will take you up the coast in his curricle."

"Up the coast? Why?"

Looking as though his eyelids were weighted, he blinked and pinched the bridge of his nose. "He'll bring you as far as Mullion, and from there you can arrange transport to Helston and anywhere else you wish."

She struggled to maintain an impassive expression, to betray none of the emotions clashing inside her. She should be glad to leave this place—a place she had never wished to be. And glad to leave him, a man who, despite their shameless familiarity, remained little more than a stranger to her.

Yet the prospect of continuing her life without him left her feeling utterly empty and as though the future could not possibly hold a single meaningful moment.

"Why send me away?" She attempted to inject enough haughtiness into her voice to mask the quiver in her throat. "Especially now, when we're certain I'm in no danger here in my aunt and uncle's house. Or are there more secrets you wish to prevent me from learning?"

"Damn it, Sophie, I'm not asking you to trust me. I want you gone from here—do the reasons matter so much?" He rubbed a hand across his eyes. "Nowhere in Penhollow is safe. Take your cousins and your aunt and go with the vicar. There must be other relatives you can go to. I'll provide the fare for all of you."

"I, for one, am not going anywhere." Dominic, having made it to the foot of the stairs with Uncle Barnaby's help, gripped the banister and pulled up straighter. "Damned if I'm about to run off on Father."

Uncle Barnaby shook his head. "What good do ye think to do me here, boy, in the shape you're in?"

"Would you be rid of me so easily, then?"

A sigh rumbled from the man's broad chest. "Nay, son, I suppose I wouldn't at that. Stay if ye've a mind to. You're a man grown and may do as your conscience advises."

"Then I'm staying."

"As am I," Aunt Louisa said from a few steps above them.

"I'm certainly not leaving, then." Rachel descended from the upper landing to meet the censure of the others.

"Don't be silly, child; you're to go with Sophie," her mother said.

"Better you're somewhere far from here, for now," her father agreed.

"You'd be daft to stay, you witless chit." A wry, half grin took the sting from Dominic's rebuke.

His sister stood above them, arms crossed and feet braced. "I hardly see why it would be silly, daft or witless of me to do exactly as you three mean to do. I'm part of this family, and I'll not desert the rest of you."

The girl's quiet courage filled Sophie with admiration, with sudden pride in these obdurate relatives of hers. Though she never would have expected it, she realized she would miss the Gordons, even surly Dominic and dour, brutish Uncle Barnaby. Theirs was a fortitude born of the rocky crags and the unremitting sea. Yet what had happened to Dominic today proved they were not invincible, that they were as vulnerable as anyone else.

For her brave but gentle cousin's sake, she knew what she must do. Walking to the staircase, she reached up through the newels and clasped Rachel's hand. "I think you and I should leave. This is not my quarrel. Nor is it yours."

The younger girl whisked her hand free. "I won't run away. My family needs me."

"Of course they need you," Sophie said as kindly as she could. "But our being here will only be a hindrance. If your father and Chad are going to work together to apprehend murderers, they oughtn't to be fretting over our safety, ought they?"

A portion of Rachel's defiance faded from her features. "Oh, I hadn't thought of it that way. . . ." She aimed a questioning glance at her father.

"She's right, lass."

"Please listen to them, Rachel, and go."

All heads turned toward the parlor, where a tousle-haired Ian stood staring up at Rachel, a fierce expression burning in his eyes. Sophie's breath caught. She knew that look, had seen it countless times on Chad when he had feared for her safety, when he had held her in his arms, when he had entered her body and made her his.

But she had also seen another look on Chad's face,

a shadowy mask of secrets and guilt. She hoped her ingenuous cousin would never see such a look on her young fisherman's face, or experience the heartache of learning its meaning.

"Please, Rachel," he said again in a whisper.

And as Rachel nodded her acquiescence, Sophie's heart swelled with affection for the couple, but not without a twinge of envy. Barnaby Gordon disapproved of Rachel's attachment to Ian, yet here the youth stood, willing, for her sake, to incur her father's anger.

If only Chad had possessed the same quiet courage, he might have at least spared her from the pain of his lies.

And from the pain of loving him.

Sophie shivered in the dawn chill. Her bags were packed, waiting alongside Rachel's to be loaded into the vicar's curricle as soon as he arrived. While the others finished Aunt Louisa's hastily cooked breakfast of eggs and blood pudding, she stood alone on the beach, draped in the elongated shadows of the dunes.

Restless waves hurled whitecaps to break against the sandy shore. Dots of foam spattered her dress, occasionally her cheeks. She didn't bother wiping the moisture from her skin, but let it mingle with the tear or two she could not blink away.

Leaving brought a sense of finality she suddenly couldn't bear to face. If she could only convince her heart of what her mind knew; that Chad Rutherford was not the man she had met in the chapel on Blackheath Moor, not noble and honorable and true. She wondered, had the mist conjured the illusion of him, or had she done that herself, with her loneliness and her yearning to find something exciting and worthwhile in this harsh country?

Perhaps in this he could not be blamed.

"I thought I'd find you here."

A shiver went through her at the velvet rumble of his voice, but she did not turn away from the churning sea. That he found her here didn't surprise her. He had remained at the farm last night, cramping his tall frame onto the same settee Dominic had abandoned when he went upstairs to bed. She had slipped down to the shoreline this morning wishing to avoid useless arguments and final, pointless appeals, but it seemed he could not let her leave without parting words.

She wished he would. She wished he had returned to Edgecombe, or anywhere, rather than force her to endure the mutinous desire stirred by his presence. The memories of every kiss, every touch—and the painful longing they evoked—would haunt her for the rest of her life.

Why wouldn't he walk away and grant her a moment's peace?

"Sophie, I . . . I wished to . . ."

The heat of his palm hovered at her nape. He stepped closer, until the graze of his chest against her back set her skin aflame. She lurched and spun about to face him. He stood in shirtsleeves, the linen plastered to his muscular frame by the raw winds.

"To what?" she demanded. "Apologize?"

"I would, if it were possible. I know I've lost your trust, probably for always." The breeze plucked his golden hair from his brow, exposing a healing abrasion across the fine arch of his temple. The circles beneath his eyes mirrored the gloom of the clouds scudding over the water. The rasp of his tired voice echoed the restless ocean gusts.

Unwilling to give in to the tugs of sympathy and concern pulling tight across her heart, she looked away, following the flight of a storm petrel as it swooped over the waves. "How can you speak of trust? I trusted you with so much. So *very* much. Why could you not show the same faith in me?"

"If I'd told you the truth from the beginning, would you have understood? Forgiven me?"

"Your transgressions are for the law to forgive. But your lies and your theft—those I find unforgivable."

"Theft?" His brow creased in genuine puzzlement. "Isn't that also a matter for the law?"

"I mean what you stole from me." Her heart. Her virginity. Yet, in truth, he had stolen nothing from her. She had given herself gladly and eagerly. A trembling certainty rose up inside her that if they stood together much longer on the deserted, windswept beach, she might give herself again, walk into his arms and surrender her heart, her being.

"I am a scoundrel, Sophie. And yes, I stole from you what my own life so desperately lacked: your courage and your spirit, and your sweet, stubborn determination to do the right thing, no matter the cost or risk to yourself." His arms came up as if to reach for her, then dropped to his sides. "Is it any wonder I could not resist you?"

His voice had softened to a murmur that both caressed and tormented her. She allowed herself a glimpse of his cognac-colored eyes, expecting to see shadows and obscurity but finding only anguish—and regret so deep she feared she might drown in it if she looked at him a moment longer. She stared out at the sea.

"Please believe I never wished to hurt you," he whispered behind her.

"If only you hadn't lied, perhaps we might have found some way to breach the rift between us. But even as you finally confessed the truth of your involvement with smugglers and wreckers, you lied again."

He circled her, a denial plain on his face. "I told you everything last night. I swear I left nothing out."

"It isn't what you left out," she said, "but what you included."

He shook his head, held out his arms. "What?"

Her anger rising, she clutched her hands to keep herself from grasping his shoulders and shaking him. "Ghosts. Your ludicrous assertion that a ghost has been leading you through Penhollow, dictating your actions. I suppose next you'll tell me a ghost made you break the law. Perhaps ghosts murdered those three sailors caught in the nets of Ian's fishing boat."

"God, no. The mistakes I made were my own fault. And as for murder, human hands did that."

"And what of your hands? Whom have they hurt? Whom have you—"

She couldn't say it. She had trusted those hands on every part of her body; their touch had propelled her to unimagined heights of ecstasy. Were his hands also capable of murder?

"I swear to you, I've never laid a violent hand on anyone. My crimes were ones of complicity, of facilitating something I didn't fully comprehend. And because I didn't take the time to understand the repercussions of smuggling—that lives are often sacrificed—I shall never fully escape my guilt."

"You are doing an inordinate amount of swearing. I wish I could believe in your sincerity. . . ." And yet part of her feared doing just that: being taken in by him again and letting him manipulate her.

"At least believe this," he said. "The ghost is real. I denied the possibility at first, but after what I saw and felt last night before I found you, I have no choice but to heed the apparition that has been dogging my steps since I arrived in Penhollow. That is why I'm sending you away with the vicar, rather than taking you to safety myself. This ghost has charged me with a task, and I must stay and see it through."

More lies, even now? Painfully, unbearably, her broken heart turned to ice. "You must think I'm the greatest fool ever born."

Kicking up a dervish of sand, Sophie pushed past Chad. Even before his mind fully formed the intention, he strode after her and caught her by the shoulders.

"Let me go."

"Not yet, Sophie. I cannot let you leave with so much still unspoken between us." Perhaps he couldn't let her go at all. The thought terrified him. He'd fancied countless women over the years, shared his bed with many of them, but forgotten them easily enough once they'd gone.

Oh, but not Sophie, the one woman he *should* forget, who should be allowed to forget him. He could never deserve her, and the life he might once have offered her—that of a wealthy, respected countess—might never again exist. But for all that, he could not command his fingers to open their grip and release her.

Nor could he allow her to go away believing there had never been an honest moment between them, that he had played her false at every turn.

"Think about it," he urged, "and you'll see I'm telling you the truth. Yesterday morning when I pushed my way through the fallen debris in the tunnel I caused a further cave-in. Yet later you and I were able to shove rocks out of the way without raising so much as a rumble of complaint from the earth."

"We were lucky."

"We had help. The morning I swam to you from Grady's boat, my strength had run out from fighting the current. I went under. I thought I'd drown, but it was as though something or someone reached in and dragged me from the waves."

Some of the tension drained from her shoulders. "I saw you struggling. . . ."

"That's right. I'd have drowned without help, but apparently I'm needed alive for now."

"And that day at Edgecombe . . . and the other night, when I heard you calling me from the beach . . ." Indecision raged a stormy battle in her gray eyes. Silent questions formed on her lips—tempting lips he wanted more than anything to kiss. But then they stiffened with stubborn resolve. "It can't be true—it *cannot*. There are no such things as ghosts."

"If you can't believe what I'm telling you," he said, "then believe this."

No longer able to resist the temptation he drew her against him, wrapping her tight in his arms and holding on until her struggles became less insistent. Soon the fight flowed out of her on a long sigh. Her body yielded against his, and a fierce and primal need roared through him. He dipped his head and pressed his lips to hers as if to devour them, devour her.

Through their clothing, their hearts pounded one against the other in unison. Her breath filled him, and the sweet sound of her whimpers traveled through their joined mouths to echo inside him.

The taste of salt permeated their kisses. Tears—both hers and his. A single word reverberated through him, the force of it causing him to stagger backward in the sand while still holding fast to Sophie, still kissing her.

"Irrevocable," he said against her lips. "It isn't over between us."

Her mouth came away as she tilted her head to look up at him. For an instant bewilderment shimmered in her eyes. Then her hands slid from around his neck and shoved at his chest.

"No."

Without releasing her, he held her at arm's length. "You know it's true."

She wiped her tears away with her palms. "I don't wish it to be true."

"You cannot change the truth by wishing."

"Release me. I cannot think with you so near. I cannot breathe."

"Am I holding you against your will?"

That drew a frown, a glare of resentment. But when she didn't stir he pulled her close again, pressing his lips to her brow, dragging them across her cheek. She didn't fight him, remained utterly still but for the heavy rise and fall of her bosom and the trembling of her body in his embrace.

"Let me go." It was a tear-choked plea, little more than a breath against his ear. Still she made no move to escape him, as if she couldn't find the strength to do what her will demanded. "Don't you see? Without trust there cannot be love. It *is* over."

Feeling as though she had wrenched his heart from his chest, he forced his arms to open and stepped back. "Go for now, then, Sophie. But know that someday, when I am free, you and I will meet again."

She made no reply. Raising her hems, she strode past him, then came to an abrupt halt between the dunes, her back still to him. "When you go after those men . . . be careful. Don't get yourself killed."

Then she continued her trek back up to the house.

Less than an hour later Chad moved across the rain-soaked moor, fingers gone numb around the steel butt of the pistol he'd borrowed from Gordon. Though he couldn't see the others, he knew he wasn't alone. Reese's bald head and Barnaby's shaggy one had disappeared only moments ago beyond the rise to the west. Ian had circled around to make his approach from the south. Chad waited to the north, while, to the east, the moorland bog closed the noose they formed around the farmstead.

When the edge of the cottage's thatched roof came into view, he crouched among the vegetation to await Gordon's signal. The plan called for the farmer to approach the shack first, confirm that Diggs and Wiley were there, and devise some way to separate them from their weapons before giving the whoop that would bring the others running.

Chad didn't relish sending Barnaby Gordon to do the job he felt should have been his. His task and his risk, one he would take on willingly and deservedly. But Gordon knew the brigands, and his appearance would not immediately put the bastards on their guard.

As on the beach earlier, brooding clouds huddled over the moors, scattering occasional bursts of rain.

Chad settled in to wait, trying to ignore the vague queasiness that lingered from last night.

Instead, Sophie filled his thoughts.

She had been so adamant in her refusal to believe his claims about the little ghost, not that he could blame her. His assertion demanded a complete suspension of her belief system, and how could she be expected to do that for a man who had just confessed to the very crimes they had been investigating?

Yet her denials had brimmed with hesitation, as if she too had experienced bizarre visions. What had she said, that she had heard him calling out to her from the beach?

A faint rumble of thunder rolled through the clouds, and a dull cramp pinched his gut. *Damn.* He thought the illness had left him. Clenching his teeth, he tried to breathe through the pain as he thought back on what he had eaten yesterday and this morning. He couldn't think of much, despite Mrs. Gordon's attempts to ply him with tea and oatcakes. How could he have eaten, knowing Sophie's plate had gone untouched, that she had fled the house rather than have to face him?

The ache pressed again, accompanied by a thudding in his temple. Perhaps he should have asked the vicar for one of his herbal cures, like the infusion in his tea that warded off colds—

The vicar's vile-tasting tea. Hall had insisted he drink it. The man and his herbs . . .

The late Lord Wycliffe often came by for tea and chess in the afternoons. The vicar had told him that. The vicar had also claimed to be away when Franklin Rutherford died.

His father was said to have been drunk the night the fire took his life . . . but Chad had never seen his father more than slightly flushed from liquor, and rarely at that. Why would he suddenly take to overindulging?

Chad's encounters with Tobias Hall raced through his mind. The man had seemed interested in how long Chad might stay in Penhollow. . . .

A possibility sent him staggering to his feet. Could the vicar find Chad's presence at Edgecombe an inconvenience . . . as perhaps he had found Franklin's presence there equally inopportune?

Tobias Hall, with his soft-spoken manners and his carefully tended herbs, was even now driving away from Penhollow with Sophie and her cousin.

Clutching the pistol, Chad traced a wide arc through the damp moor grasses to avoid being seen from the farmstead. Dizziness, whether from illness or sheer panic, dogged his steps, but he gritted his teeth and pumped his legs harder. From behind an outcropping Reese craned his neck and gaped at Chad's frantic approach.

"What the devil are ye doing?"

Barnaby was a dozen or so yards away, heading toward the farm. "Gordon," Chad hissed. "Stop!"

The farmer didn't hear him and kept walking. Beefy hands tightening around his rifle, Reese strode out from behind the crag. "Have ye taken leave of your senses, my lord?"

Without halting his charge, Chad swerved and headed for Gordon. Reese barreled after him. The man hit Chad from behind and took him down with a soggy crash that soaked him to the skin and sent stars dancing before his eyes.

"Ye'll get us all killed."

"Get off me. I've got to stop him. His daughter and niece may be in danger."

"What the devil's going on?" To Chad's enormous relief, Gordon had circled back and stood glowering down at both him and Reese. "Are ye daft? I was almost in sight of the shack. What if they'd seen me, and heard you?"

Chad scrambled out from under the barkeep's tree-trunk legs and pushed to his feet. "Those brigands can wait. Sophie and Rachel might be in danger."

"They're with the vicar."

"Yes, and I just realized it might be the vicar we're after."

Reese sat up, rubbing wet grass and grit from his bald head. "Tobias? Bah! The man's afraid of his own shadow."

Gordon echoed the sentiment.

"Is he? Or is that what he wishes everyone to think? I believe it's possible he used his herbs to poison my father before setting Edgecombe on fire."

The two men exchanged incredulous looks. Skepticism grated in Barnaby's throat. "What in God's creation would make ye think a thing like that?"

"Because he tried to poison me as well. Last night. Made me a cup of his lethal tea and insisted I drink it. I didn't ingest enough to kill me, but it's made me ill."

"Could be illness is putting wild thoughts in your head."

"Are you willing to take the chance? You daughter and niece are with Tobias at this moment."

That set them in motion. Within minutes they collected a dumbfounded Ian and raced back across the moors.

Chapter 23

The vicar's curricle jostled like a boat in a storm as it clambered down the muddy road. Beside Sophie on the narrow seat, Rachel clutched the door handle to steady herself. On her other side Mr. Hall gripped the hand strap.

Rachel stared out the window at the drenched countryside streaming by. "Are we right to leave, Sophie?"

"Of course we are," Sophie replied with more bravado than conviction. She clutched her hands in her lap. Since her confrontation with Chad, her fingers had not stopped shaking. Nor had a single word ceased winding through her thoughts: *irrevocable.*

Had she, through her heart and body, bound herself to Chad irrevocably?

The part of her still clinging to her outrage rejected the notion. But the rest of her trembled with need and with anticipation.

You and I will meet again.

How long before that happened? Long enough for the wounds to heal? Would they ever heal sufficiently for her to be able to trust him?

Yet as the distance stretched between her and Penhollow, it wasn't the deception or the lies or the crimes he'd committed that filled her mind. Not anger or indignation or even the relief of finally escaping him that quivered through her.

Rather, her mind's eye conjured the tenderness, the

repeated kindnesses, the courage it had taken for him to risk his life, more than once, to save hers. She remembered too the thrilling passage of his body into hers, the glorious pain of becoming his. It was those things, and the desperate plea burning in his eyes and trembling in his voice as he had formed those parting words, that haunted her now.

As they stood together on the beach she had believed his lies would always stand between them. Now she couldn't be sure. *Had* he lied? Or simply not been able to speak the truth to her? How did one, after all, admit such things to another individual, things that made one cringe to acknowledge silently?

On the heels of that question came another: Had she already begun to forgive him?

The voices on either side of her brought her hurtling back to the present, to the close confines of a northbound curricle.

"There is no doubt you are both doing the correct thing," Mr. Hall assured them. "The only sensible thing."

"I don't like this scheme Father and Lord Wycliffe concocted, stealing off to confront those men." Rachel frowned. "When I think of what those monsters did to Dominic . . ."

Sophie squeezed her hand. "They'll be fine. They will have Ian and Reese with them. That makes four against two, and they are four rather formidable men at that."

Again sheer bravado fueled her assurances, along with a pang of guilt. She couldn't help suspecting that, in part, Chad's eagerness to apprehend the smugglers lay in a desire to prove his worthiness to her. However angry she might be, however hurt by his deception, she didn't wish him to risk his life again. Not for her. Not at all.

The curricle hit a rock in the road, tossing Sophie into the vicar's side and Rachel against the vehicle's door. The window beside her dropped open a few inches, letting in a splatter of rain and a shriek of wind.

Sophie.

She started and looked about. "Mr. Hall, did you say something?"

"Not I, Miss St. Clair. Is everyone quite all right?"

"Fine, Mr. Hall, thank you." Rachel turned the crank and raised the window. The glass sealed out the whipping wind, but not the murmur in Sophie's ear.

He needs you.

Her heart leaped to her throat. "Did either of you hear that?"

"Hear what, Sophie?" Rachel peered into her face. "A growl of thunder, perhaps?"

Sophie strained to listen, hands braced against the seat. Were her senses playing tricks on her, as they had that morning when she had trespassed into Edgecombe's gardens, and again the night she heard Chad calling to her in her bedroom at Aunt Louisa's?

Through her glove a tickling sensation traced its way across the back of her hand. *The answers are at Edgecombe. He needs you there.*

She went rigid. Who spoke to her? Her conscience? Her heart?

"What is it, Sophie, dear?" Rachel's hand closed over her wrist. "Why, you're trembling. And you're pale as a ghost."

"I'm sorry, I thought I heard . . ."

He'll fight for you, Sophie. A current of energy traveled up her arms, standing the hair at her nape on end.

She gaped at her cousin. "You had to have heard *that*."

"I hear nothing, Sophie, beyond the rain and the rumble of the carriage wheels."

For himself alone he won't battle hard enough. Without you he may die.

A gasp rose to choke her, but instead of a sputter a command broke from her lips. "Turn the curricle around."

"Miss St. Clair?"

"Have your driver turn around at once, Mr. Hall. I am going back to Penhollow."

Rachel compressed her lips and studied her. "I believe you should do as she says, Mr. Hall. What is it, Sophie? What's wrong?"

"Perhaps nothing. Perhaps everything." She didn't know how to explain without their thinking she'd taken leave of her senses. Perhaps she had. Perhaps she wished so badly to believe in Chad that she was imagining things. But . . .

That day in Edgecombe's gardens, when she had first seen Chad through the window, she had also heard a voice as she crossed the footbridge, as though he had spoken in her ear. And she had felt the touch of a fingertip across her hand.

Just as she had a moment ago.

Chad . . . He had deceived her. But each time she had needed him, at each threat to her life, he had been there, willing to put himself between her and danger. And now he needed her.

"I can't explain. All I know is I must go back. To Edgecombe. Immediately."

"Edgecombe? Good heavens," the vicar said, "that would be most unwise, Miss St. Clair."

Choosing to ignore him, she rapped on the ceiling to signal to the driver. When the horses lumbered to a halt, she leaned over Rachel, cranked down the window and called out, "Turn the carriage around. We're going back."

Mr. Hall's hand closed around her forearm. "Miss St. Clair, I must insist you stop this foolishness. We are going to Mullion, as we promised Lord Wycliffe, and there's an end to it."

She raised an eyebrow at him, and then turned to her cousin. Though no words passed between them, Rachel nodded. "Mr. Hall, either order your man to turn around, or Miss St. Clair and I shall get out and walk back to Penhollow on our own."

*　　*　　*

The air clawed Chad's lungs as the Gordon farm came into view. Louisa Gordon stood at the gate. Even before they crossed the road she waved her arms and yelled to them.

"The vicar's curricle . . ." She pointed with an out-stretched arm. "Went that way."

Her husband sprinted the final yards to her. "They went south?"

Chad panted to catch his breath. "How long ago did they pass?"

"Not ten minutes." Agitation made Louisa's voice shrill. She pointed in the direction of Edgecombe. "Did you not see it from the rise?"

Barnaby wiped a sleeve across his sweating brow. "God's teeth, why would they have returned, and why continue on south?"

Without waiting for an answer, Chad vaulted over the stone border wall and tore across the property to the stable. At his approach Prince stretched his neck over the half door of the stall and gave a reproachful snort.

"Sorry to have left you alone so long." Chad ran a hand down his neck, grabbed the harness hanging from a nail and slipped it over the horse's head. "No time for a saddle, old boy. We're needed at Edgecombe, and fast."

As if reading Chad's mood, the Thoroughbred lurched out of the stall. Outside, Chad swung up onto the broad back, detecting Prince's restive excitement trembling in his flanks. "Gordon and Reese, follow me when you can."

Ian pressed forward. "What about me?"

Chad took in the youth's urgent expression and the eager way he bounced on the balls of his feet as he awaited Chad's answer. Chad would rather have sent the lad to safety than involve him further, but as the possibilities of what they might find at Edgecombe pummeled his mind, an idea struck him. "Most of the fishing vessels will have sailed by now, but can you requisition a boat at the harbor and a crew to man it?"

Ian glanced at the other two men, then back at Chad. "I can try, but—"

"Do it, and make your way down the coast. Look sharp for a narrow, rocky inlet just north of Edgecombe, and put in as close as you can." With that he gave spur to Prince. As the horse shot forward to a gallop, Chad shouted over his shoulder, "Come armed and ready for a fight."

The answers are at Edgecombe. He needs you there.
With Rachel and the vicar following close behind, Sophie pushed open Edgecombe's front door, cringing at the whine of the hinges. Even from the road, the place conveyed an air of abandonment. As they entered, a profound hush enveloped them, sending them gingerly to their toes as they made their way into the cool darkness of the hall. Rachel's fingers closed around the hem of Sophie's carriage jacket, and when Sophie came to a halt near the bottom of the staircase, the other girl bumped up against her back.

"Sorry."

"It would appear no one is home." The vicar remained in the doorway. "I think we should be going."

Sophie tamped down her irritation with the man. "Chad? Nathaniel? Is anyone here?"

"Shh!" The vicar shuddered so violently his spectacles slipped down his nose. "Miss St. Clair! I would thank you not to shout."

"Who are you afraid of awakening, Mr. Hall? The ghosts?"

"Really, Miss St. Clair—"

"I asked you both to wait in the curricle," Sophie said, "but you insisted on coming in with me. If you're frightened, I'll be neither hurt nor inconvenienced if you choose to wait in the forecourt."

"No, Sophie, we'll stay. Won't we, Mr. Hall?" Rachel's gaze darted over the shadowed walls and the dusty staircase. "Perhaps now you'll tell us why it was so important we come here."

Sophie wished she knew what to say. She had no proof, only the warnings of a disembodied voice and an inability to deny her feelings for an admitted rogue.

"I need you both to wait here," she said. "I'm only going as far as the library, which is the farthest room in the north wing. I'll be able to hear you, and you'll be able to hear me. I should be only a few moments."

"What do you hope to discover?" Despite the faith Rachel had shown in Sophie on their journey here, the girl's voice rang with puzzlement.

"The truth, I hope. About Chad, this house and its past . . . many things."

Rachel didn't question her further. She sat at the foot of the stairs, settling in to wait with elbows propped on her knees and chin in her hands.

A dark object in the vicar's hand halted Sophie in midstep. "Mr. Hall, what on earth are you holding?"

"An assurance, Miss St. Clair."

"A pistol is no assurance. Wherever did you get it?"

"From my pocket, of course. Lord Wycliffe charged me with the responsibility of your welfare. I always take my responsibilities with the utmost seriousness."

"Yes, well, put it away." She gave a dismissive flutter of her hand.

"I can hardly protect you and Miss Gordon with my weapon in my pocket."

"And neither can you make a tragic mistake and shoot Lord Wycliffe or his manservant."

"Oh, I . . . yes . . . perhaps you're right." He tucked the gun away.

With a shake of her head, Sophie turned in to the north wing.

At the library door a little voice of reason proclaimed the folly of her intentions. What could she hope to learn here? The truth? Of what? Her uncle and Dominic, and not ghosts, had ignited false shore lights. Chad had admitted his involvement in smug-

gling crimes. As for those three poor sailors murdered
at sea, Chad and her uncle were working to uncover
the guilty culprits. What was left?

"Sophie, can you hear me?"

She jumped at the sound of Rachel's call. "I hear
you. It's quite all right. I'll be a few minutes at most."

She opened the door to find the library exactly as
she had seen it last, with its gaping shelves, lack of
furniture, and the wide window overlooking the gardens. The window was flush, not a bay, as it had appeared to her from the garden that first day.

*Gather the facts and let their conclusion form as it
may, without biasing the outcome.* Grandfather always
advised his journalists to do just that. But what facts
could she gather from an empty room? Closing the
door behind her, she went to the window and pressed
her palms to the frame.

And whisked them back with a cry when the case-
ment burned her flesh. Her hands came away un-
marked, yet images of flames rose behind her eyes.
She could hear the crackle and smell the charred flesh.

For some moments she battled the urge to collect
Rachel and Mr. Hall and put as much distance as possible between them and Edgecombe's secrets.

But the voice had told her the answers would be
found here.

Teeth clamping her lower lip, she steeled herself
and flattened her hands to the cool glass. Instantly
flames leaped around her. She held her ground, clinging to the notion that it was merely an illusion.

She forced herself to peer over her shoulder at the
burning room. A blaze engulfed the shelves. Books
curled and disintegrated, their pages dispersing
through the air like swarms of fireflies. An inferno
encased the furniture. As she watched in horror, the
ceiling beams crashed in a shower of embers.

Against her palms the glass panes of a bay window
exploded from the heat. The lead mullions glowed
molten. The stone embrasure crumbled. Her hands

were blackened, hideous. Her hair sizzled and her clothing adhered to her melting skin.

In the raging gusts of the fire, a voice hissed, *Murder.*

A scream rose inside her, but she forced it down and clung to her last shred of reason. A face filled her vision, a countenance eerily familiar and filled with agony. With a shock she realized the features she had once mistaken for Chad's were not his, but those of another man. An older man who bore a startling resemblance to his son.

He raised a burning hand to point. *Murder . . .*

In the licking flames another face formed, one distorted by rippling heat waves and half obscured by tangled locks of hair. From within the tousled strands a pair of eyes, searing in their malevolence, gleamed out at Sophie.

Heaving backward with all her might, she broke free from the conflagration.

Once more the silent, empty room surrounded her. The window before her stood intact and flush to the wall. Though a lingering sensation tingled through her fingers, the illusory flames had done no damage.

In startling contrast to the burning heat, a cool breath grazed her nape. She gasped and spun about. "Lord Wycliffe?"

"Sophie."

Low clouds glazed the landscape and swallowed the tips of the distant crags. Chad had ridden only a few minutes beyond the Gordons' farm when a sense of unease crawled up his spine. To save precious seconds he had set off across the headland, intending to intersect with the road about a half mile before Edgecombe, but he found no road where it should have been, only an empty, misty stretch of moor.

He urged Prince on. Even if he had somehow missed the road due to the fog, as long as he continued southward, the rooftops of Edgecombe should push into view. As he emerged from a tangle of whitebeam and heath rush, a badger scurried across his path. Prince shied and reared.

Without a saddle Chad felt himself slipping. He gripped with his knees and leaned far over the horse's neck for balance. "Whoa, boy. Easy now."

With a jolt all four hooves connected with the ground, but Prince's jittery dance continued. His ears twitched. His tail swished nervously. Chad shortened the reins and squeezed with his heels.

"Come on, boy. Sophie needs us."

The gelding swung about, sidestepped, kicked with his rear legs. A sudden wind that smelled of the sea pummeled across the moor. Though the rain had abated, charcoal thunderheads mushroomed across the sky. Chad urged Prince to a walk. The horse took two steps and halted as though encountering a solid wall.

Chad leaped to the ground and tried to lead Prince on foot. Though he could see nothing in front of him but the mist-coated moor, his chin struck an icy barrier. He tried shouldering his way through, only to stumble backward.

"What is this?" he cried out. "Would you stop me now, when she most needs me?"

He waited for the answer, senses pricked, nape bristling, nerves humming with impatient energy. Beside him Prince stared with wild, glassy eyes.

"Confound it to hell." He considered brandishing his pistol, for all the good it would do. His anger mounting, he searched the mist. "Show yourself and let's get on with it."

This way.

The voice seemed to emanate from the moor itself, from the endless skein of bracken and heather. The breeze turned frigid. Prince whinnied, a sharp, raw cry of distress. At the sound of a mournful sigh Chad pivoted. A small, transparent figure wavered a few feet away.

Chad suppressed an inclination to rant at the little

ghost, and instead forced a calm tone. "What do you want of me?"

Come.

The little ghost took off running, gossamer rags flying out behind her. Her feet neither made a sound nor raised a splash on the saturated terrain. Leading Prince on foot, Chad followed at a half run. He kept his gaze pinned on her, afraid of losing her in the mist. Never before had she appeared to him this way, as insubstantial as vapor.

Her flight ended at the barrier of a low stone wall. "The chapel? It can't be. . . ."

Drifting clouds obscured the spire. The corners of the structure too appeared softened by the haze, melting into the surroundings. Even the headstones seemed vaporous, not solid at all.

Urgency overpowered his bewilderment at finding the place in such a state, and where it could not possibly be. "I'm needed at Edgecombe. Don't you understand?"

She raised her vacant eyes to him, immobilizing him with her stare. A thin arm gestured at the rows of headstones.

Foreboding raised gooseflesh on his neck. "No. She isn't here."

A gaunt finger pointed.

"You want me to go into the churchyard?" He swore under his breath. Leaving Prince outside the wall, he stepped through where the gate had once been. The stunted forest of headstones surrounded him, seeming to float above the ground. Merely a trick of the mist, he knew, but . . .

The chapel walls were fading, revealing the moor beyond.

"What is this devilish place?"

My home.

"You?" His glance returned to the headstones. "You're buried here?"

She no longer tends my grave. No one tends my grave. I am forgotten.

"It isn't actually here, is it?" he said with sudden comprehension. "The chapel. The churchyard. It exists elsewhere, but somehow you've conjured its form here on Blackheath Moor. Is that it?"

The wind scattered a few raindrops. He wiped them from his eyes, and when he opened them again his pulse ricocheted at what he saw. Dropping to his knees he reached out to trace the carving at the top of the granite stone in front of him.

Rosebuds. Seven of them.

She shall bury me with roses.

She had told him that in a dream. A little girl in braids and a pink dress, hurrying him along for her birthday party. Leading him to the sea. To Sophie, drowning in the waves.

Here were those roses, etched to mark her grave. He gripped the sides of the stone and bowed his head to read the engraving.

BORN 6 MAY 1819, DIED 13 MAY 1826
BELOVED DAUGHTER
ELLIE ROSE QUINCY

"Good Christ. I understand now. You're . . ."

He looked up to find her gone, in her place a gathering of darkness that was denser than shadow. A nothingness that radiated hopelessness and pure, cold despair.

"Ellie Rose, come back. Where are Sophie and Rachel? Is your mother with them? They're in grave danger. You can help me . . . please . . . come back. . . ."

"Lord Wycliffe!"

The shout brought him to his feet. Around him the headstones fell away like toppling dominoes to disappear into the ground. The low stone wall dissipated. The glistening chapel gave a final glimmer and was gone. On the rolling terrain where the stones had stood, the breezes swept the heather and the deep browns and faded greens of the moor grasses.

The road to Edgecombe stretched only yards away from where he stood. Gordon and Reese pushed through the thinning mist on horseback.

"What happened?" Gordon called. "Were ye thrown from your horse?"

From the way they regarded him, Chad knew neither man had seen anything unusual, only him kneeling in the wet grass, surrounded by miles of empty moorland. He shook his head, collected Prince's reins and hopped up onto his horse's back.

"Why are ye here, man?" Gordon's exasperation was plain to hear. "Why aren't ye at Edgecombe looking for the lasses?"

Chad ignored the question. "Reese, have you seen Kellyn this morning?"

"Earlier, at the Gull."

"Not since?"

"Of course not since. Why?"

"Because I've reason to believe she may be in danger too." He clucked Prince to a canter, trusting the two men to follow.

At the sound of her name Sophie whirled, a hand flying up to clutch her throat. The ghastly images no longer filled the empty room, but the horror of Lord Wycliffe's death lingered. Her heart pumping against her stays, she turned to confront a familiar figure standing in the open doorway.

"Kellyn! Good heavens." She pressed a trembling hand to her breast. "Why, for a moment I thought . . ."

"That you saw a ghost?"

A glint in the tavern owner's blue eyes commanded the truth. "How did you know I'd say that?"

Kellyn tilted her head. "Because it doesn't surprise me. This house fairly pulses with the echoes of the past."

"You feel it too. But . . . why are you here?" She offered a shaky smile. "Not that I'm not pleased to see you."

"I'm sorry I startled you. With Chad occupied I thought it prudent to check up on Nathaniel. He's a hard worker, but he needs a certain amount of looking after."

"Is he here? I called but he didn't answer."

"Aye, he's belowstairs, doing what he does best—cooking. He helps out at the Gull sometimes." Kellyn pushed off the door frame and sauntered a few steps into the room. "I sent your cousin and the vicar on down to him for a bite to eat."

"Did you?" Sophie frowned. It seemed unlike Rachel—and the vicar, for that matter—to have left her without a word.

"You're flushed," Kellyn said. "I hope you aren't feeling out of sorts."

Sophie's reply burst out before she could stop it. "Did you know that Lord Wycliffe was murdered?"

Crossing to her in a flurry of shocked concern, Kellyn grasped her hands. "Chad? He's dead?"

"No. I mean his father. The fire was deliberately set."

Her relief palpable, Kellyn released Sophie and shook her head. "Franklin had been drinking that night. He passed out and knocked over a lamp. It was a wonder the entire house didn't go up."

Sophie glanced over her shoulder at the window. "They replaced the old bay when they rebuilt, didn't they?"

"The masonry had crumbled from the heat. How did you know?"

Sophie didn't explain. There were no words to describe what she had experienced. Only Chad would understand. Only he would believe her.

"Franklin Rutherford was well liked in Penhollow," Kellyn said. "Why would anyone wish him harm, much less end his life?"

Sophie hesitated in answering, then remembered that Kellyn had been at the farm for much of yesterday, had learned about the men at the moorland farm and their connection to the piracy that plagued Penhollow. "Supposing Lord Wycliffe was murdered by smugglers who wished to use his property, as the Keatings once used Edgecombe long ago?"

"A fanciful notion." Kellyn drifted away, strolling the length of the room and occasionally running her hands over the mahogany shelving. "The elder Lord Wycliffe loved this room. It was his favorite. He loved standing at that window and surveying the gardens and the sea beyond."

Her slow circuit continued. "*His* gardens, *his* view of the sea. He took great pleasure in his right of ownership. As if an individual could ever lay claim to such things, preserve them as his alone." Her mirthless laugh startled Sophie. "He hardly understood this place at all. Never appreciated it for what it truly is."

"What do you mean?"

"This room, and everything destroyed in the fire . . . none of it mattered."

"No, I . . . suppose you're right. What is a house compared to a man's life?"

"That isn't what I mean." Kellyn continued pacing. "The wings of this house aren't original. They were added by later owners, tiresome aristocrats who felt the need for drawing rooms and fancy dining halls, parlors and libraries. Did you know that?"

From across the room Sophie regarded Kellyn and saw what she had previously failed to notice.

In place of the woman's usual shoulder-baring chemise and boldly striped skirt, a gold-and-russet brocade gown draped her figure, the hems of the overskirt tucked up to reveal a quilted satin petticoat and a pair of polished tasseled boots. The molded surface of a stomacher pushed at her breasts and tapered to a downward point at her waist. Sophie immediately rec-

ognized the dress; it had hung in the wardrobe upstairs.

Her perplexity grew. Had Kellyn shared so intimate
a relationship with Chad's father that she kept clothes
in his house? And such outlandish clothing at that?

"Is something wrong, Sophie?"

Her gaze darted back to Kellyn's face in time to
perceive her cunning grin. "I . . . no. Of course not.
I was simply admiring your gown. It's lovely and . . .
unique."

"Do you think so?" A mocking quality in her voice
made Sophie's apprehension rise. She nodded in reply,
confused by this abrupt change in the woman. She
found herself inching toward the doorway and wishing
for the return of her cousin and the vicar.

Long strides brought Kellyn to the threshold before
Sophie reached it. "Let me show you something else
unique. Come."

With little choice but to comply, Sophie followed
her into the adjacent game room, where Kellyn lifted
an object from the felt-topped card table. "Do you
know what this is?"

Sophie's eyes went wide as Kellyn arced a familiar
weapon in the air. "The *espada ropera*," she answered.

"Very good. You impress me."

"Chad discovered it in an old tunnel beneath the
house." A sense of foreboding sent her backward until
her spine pressed against the wall. "What are you
doing with it?"

A feline smile curled Kellyn's lips. "He didn't discover this in any tunnel." Assuming a fencer's stance,
she flourished the rapier and sliced at the air in front
of her. "Such balance. The craftsmanship is extraordinary. Look at the hilt. Have you ever seen such a
perfect fit?"

"I think you should put it down. It belongs to
Chad."

"Oh, no, Sophie, you're wrong about that. This

sword never belonged to Chad. Never truly belonged
to his father, either. How could a thing of such beauty
ever belong to any man?"

Sophie felt the walls of the room close in around
her, cutting off the supply of air to her lungs. Her
stomach clenched around a dawning dread. The rapier's hilt appeared custom-made to the size and shape
of Kellyn's hand. A *woman's* hand.

This was not the sword Chad had found in the tunnel. This was its mate, the one he said had gone missing from the house. The one that had belonged to the
ruthless pirate Meg Keating.

Chapter 24

"There's the vicar's curricle." Barnaby Gordon extended a muscular arm to point. "They must be inside."

The other two men following behind, Chad spurred Prince through Edgecombe's open gates. Before the horse came to a full halt Chad's feet hit the cobbles. He burst through the front door and shouted Sophie's name.

A feeble voice answered. "Lord Wycliffe?"

"Rachel!" He bounded to the foot of the stairs. Lying diagonally across the steps, she reached for the banister and attempted to sit up. Her other hand cradled the back of her head. She groaned. Chad slipped an arm about her shoulders and helped her upright. "Don't try to move too quickly. What happened? Where are Sophie and the vicar?"

"My head . . ." Fingers rubbing back and forth through her hair, she winced. "Where am I?"

"You're at Edgecombe. Don't you remember?"

"Oh . . . yes. I . . ."

Gordon's heavy footsteps drowned out her words. The farmer let go a string of curses as he crossed the hall and knelt at his daughter's feet. "Are ye all right? What's the bastard done to ye, girl?"

She winced and let out another groan.

"It appears she's been knocked unconscious," Chad said.

"I'll kill him," her father vowed.

"Kill who?" She blinked several times.

"Whoever hit ye, lass, that's who."

"Someone came up behind me. I didn't see who it was."

Reese strode into the hall and took in the scene. "Where is that bloody vicar?"

"Do you know where he and Sophie went?" Pushing to his feet, Chad stood poised to run. Every moment mattered; every second he lingered potentially placed Sophie in greater danger.

Rachel shook her head. "Sophie left us first. She went in there." She pointed toward the drawing room. "And then Mr. Hall went that way." She gestured toward the dining hall. "He heard a noise and went to investigate. I waited a few moments and wandered after him. I didn't like being left alone. But then I heard a sound on the staircase. I didn't even have time to turn around. I felt a dreadful pain, and . . . and all went black."

"What was Sophie doing in the drawing room?" Chad asked.

"No, the library. That's where she said she was going."

"The library?" Foreboding sank to the pit of his stomach. "What was she doing in there?"

"I . . . I don't know. She wouldn't say, exactly. She—"

"Never mind." He left her and strode into the north wing. The library door stood open, but he saw no sign of Sophie. As he returned to the hall, a moving shadow on the terrace seized his attention.

Readying his pistol, he eased across the floor to the dining hall threshold. He peered inside to discover the terrace door swinging gently on its hinges. Just beyond, a shoe and a dark trouser leg lay at an awkward angle across the paving stones.

Chad dashed outside to find the vicar sprawled on his back. Blood caked his hair and right temple. For a split second disbelief held Chad immobile. If the vicar lay here, unconscious, who had Sophie?

Then he crouched and tapped the man's shoulder several times. "Tobias. Wake up."

The vicar's eyes opened and then scrunched closed. Hall rubbed them with one hand, flinching when his fingers strayed to the wound on his brow. He ran his other hand over the paving stones beside him. "My spectacles . . ."

Seeing a flash of reflected cloud from beneath a holly bush, Chad retrieved the glasses and set them on the vicar's nose. "What happened?"

"The blighter hit me with the butt of my own pistol," Tobias said through chattering teeth as Chad helped him sit up.

"Who did? And where's Sophie?"

"Your damned groundskeeper, that's who. At least, I think he did. He took my pistol . . . the rest is a blur. I can't tell you what became of Miss St. Clair."

Chad sat back on his heels. "Nathaniel hit you?"

"I came outside because I thought I heard voices." The man frowned in concentration. "They may have been drifting from an open window upstairs, now that I think of it. I'm . . . no longer certain . . . but Nathaniel stepped out behind me. I thought little of his sudden appearance—he does work here after all, so I didn't take a defensive stance. The next thing I knew he overpowered me and took my gun. Then I felt the most dreadful pain." Wincing, he touched the side of his head. "Hurts like the dickens."

"This doesn't make any sense." Nathaniel, turned violent? Chad couldn't help but remember how the childlike servant had cowered when Chad had first discovered him in the kitchen.

Had someone else commanded Nathaniel to attack the vicar? Chad had been so certain about the vicar's guilt. The herbs. The poison. How else to explain his malady? "That tea you gave me yesterday. What was in it?"

"Why on earth should that matter at a time like this, my lord? What of Miss Gordon?"

"She received a bump on the head, though not as badly as you. Answer my question."

Tobias held up an empty palm. "Gingerroot, yarrow, feverfew. A bit of lemon rind."

"Do you swear?"

"Yes, as a cleric of the Church of England, I swear. What is this about?"

Chad hadn't imagined his symptoms last night or this morning. Something had made him ill in a way he'd never experienced before. If not the tea, then . . .

The brandy. But no, Kellyn had brought it. . . .

And she had left it behind specifically for him, according to Rachel. He tried to shake the thought away. To what end would Kellyn have poisoned him? Ellie Rose, her own daughter, claimed Kellyn needed his protection. It made no sense, then, that she might be capable of such an act.

Besides, had the brandy contained poison, the others would have felt the effects . . . unless the deadly ingredient had been placed in his cup only. Anyone could have slipped it in—Reese, even Gordon. For all he knew the two men had been walking him into a trap earlier with their scheme to overtake the scoundrels on the moor.

A host of possibilities filled his mind, leaving him confused, drowning in suspicion. He could trust no one: not the vicar, not Nathaniel, not even Kellyn.

Blood rushing in his ears, he pushed to his feet. "Reese," he called through the open door. When the man appeared, Chad's hand curled around the butt of the pistol tucked into his waistband. "The vicar's been attacked," he said. "Get him inside and clean the wound."

"So much for your theory, milord." As the barkeep stepped onto the terrace, Chad watched him for signs of sudden betrayal, but Reese only stooped to help the vicar up.

Chad preceded them into the dining hall and grabbed a candle in a pewter holder from the sideboard. Circling the table, he snatched the flint and tinderbox from the mantelpiece. "You and Gordon stay here," he said as Reese and the vicar made their way inside. "Tend to Tobias and Rachel."

"Where are you going?"

Chad paused in the outer doorway. "I've a notion where I might find Miss St. Clair."

But with whom would he find her? The brigands from the moorland farm? With Grady . . . or Kellyn? With no way of knowing, he bounded across the terrace, descended the steps two at a time and sped off toward the hothouse.

In her dream Sophie felt the ocean pitching beneath her, tossing her about like a piece of driftwood. A sharp wind sent needles across her face. Her stomach roiled with the rhythm of the swell, while the bitterness of brine coated her nose and mouth. The back of her head throbbed.

Knowing it was a dream didn't help. With each cresting wave her panic escalated. Would she be dragged out to sea? Sucked down by the Devil's Twirl? Dashed against the rocks? Chad should have been here by now. Should have kissed her awake, taken her in his arms and whispered reassurances in his smooth, rich voice. A voice that spoke directly to her heart, her soul.

Any moment now he would gently wake her and they would make love, bury their fears in shared ecstasy. With the joining of their bodies and hearts they would thrust away mistakes and lies and danger. Any moment now . . .

She struggled to conjure him. To fill her dream with his essence and his strength. But she remained alone, all alone in the great, heaving sea. Oh, it was her own fault. She had pushed him away. Called him a liar.

But hadn't she also lied after a fashion, insisting she could never trust him, never love him again?

Sophie. Open your eyes.

For an instant her heart leaped. But no. Though eerily similar to Chad's, the voice belonged to his father's
restless spirit. In the library Lord Wycliffe had tried to
convey a vital message: a mere fire hadn't killed him.

She struggled to open her eyes, but her lids felt as
though they were weighted with lead sinkers. The ache
in her head intensified.

Fight, Sophie!

Using all of her strength, the whole of her will, she
achieved narrow slits. Brooding clouds billowed above
her. The white bellies of gulls flashed and darted in
dizzying circles. To her left a wall of granite edged
her vision. Her hands groped for purchase on a rough
wooden surface. A splinter jammed her middle finger
and sent pain shooting up her hand.

This was no dream.

Murmuring voices competed with the waves and the
cries of the gulls. Voices she knew. Trusted. Or had.
She tried turning her head from side to side, wincing
at the pressure against a tender spot beneath her hair.
Curved wooden planking framed the sky above her
and a single mast swung in and out of her vision. She
was lying at the bottom of a small sailboat.

A series of images flashed in her mind. The rapier.
A harried march across the gardens. A dark and winding tunnel. Then a burst of light. Clouds. Waves. A
sunburned face framed in wild auburn hair. The Irish
mariner. Then she'd experienced a burst of pain, and
blackness. Had she dreamed it all? Had the message
Lord Wycliffe tried to communicate in the library
proved true, or had her imagination conjured it all?

The boat dipped, and a figure filled her view. A
figure draped in gold-and-crimson silk, looking down
on her in triumph.

Sophie forced a word past her lips, little more than
a croak. "Meg."

Chad groped his way through the tunnel, the flickering candle sending grotesque shadows dancing at

the corners of his vision. At times he thought he glimpsed the ragged little form he'd come to know so well, and thought he heard the whisper of her small feet against the ground behind him. But he knew now that it wasn't ghosts he needed to fear. The true danger resided in the hands of the living.

Pale light seeped from ahead. His lungs burning, he blew out the candle, set it down and pulled his pistol from his waistband. Then he crept toward the mouth of the cave, ready to shoot if necessary.

The opening in the cliff face formed a jagged frame around a scene that froze the blood in his veins, for all that he had anticipated it. Grady's sailboat was no longer chained to the breakwater. Though its sail remained tightly furled, the little vessel heaved up and down in the waves, fighting seaward against the incoming tide.

The Irishman stood at the center of his small craft, using an oar to guide it past the rocks just off the beach. Far out across the water, barely discernible on the hazy horizon, a ship waited. High on its main mast a red and black topsail nudged the sky. His pulse racing, Chad went still, arrested by the sight and trying to make sense of the situation. Once Grady reached open water and unfurled his sail, he would reach the ship in a matter of minutes.

The mariner leaned low for a moment, and Chad spotted Kellyn—who had claimed not to know where Grady was. She was sitting at the bow. But where was Sophie?

The boat dipped into the hollow of a wave, and he detected a scrap of russet on the deck. What had Sophie been wearing this morning? A carriage dress. Yes, a russet broadcloth carriage dress.

He waited another moment, willing Kellyn to disprove his suspicions by grabbing the second oar from the deck and using it to topple Grady into the waves. But she didn't. She sat still, hands braced on the seat on either side of her as the boat pitched and swayed, tugged by the devilishly swirling tides. Chad caught more brief views of Sophie. For every few yards the boat progressed, the forceful waves pushed it back again toward the beach. If he hurried he might be able to wade out to them before they reached open water.

He cocked his pistol, took aim and stepped from the mouth of the cave. "Grady!"

The ruddy face turned in his direction at the same time a blow struck between Chad's shoulder blades. The force sent him to his knees. At a shout from the dinghy a boot swung into Chad's vision and kicked the pistol from his hand. His fingertips exploded in pain. The weapon flipped end over end until it clattered onto the rocks of the curving breakwater. A second shouted order sent a worn pair of trousers streaking past. Chad blinked and discovered his own pistol pointing at his chest.

"Nathaniel, no."

The servant said nothing as he made his way back from the foot of the breakwater. He merely aimed the pistol and stared into Chad's eyes with his own faded brown ones.

Infinitely worse, however, was that the voice commanding Nathaniel didn't belong to Grady. It belonged to Kellyn.

His friend. His father's friend. This proof of her treachery pierced Chad through.

"He means to hurt us, Nathaniel," she shouted. "You must fire the pistol to stop him!"

"You don't want to do that, Nathaniel," Chad countered in as calm a voice as he could muster. "Kellyn is mistaken. I am your friend. I make certain you're home before dark, don't I? Would I do that if I wished to harm anyone?"

"Only by day." The man stopped at point-blank range a few feet away.

"That's right, Nathaniel. I'll see to it you are home by nightfall." He held out his hand. "Why don't you give me that thing so you don't hurt yourself."

"Shoot him, Nathaniel!"

"Don't like pulling the trigger." An expression of pained reluctance crept across Nathaniel's face. "Hurts my ears. Didn't want you to pull the trigger. Might have hurt the lady."

Chad wanted to blurt that Kellyn deserved to be hurt, but a softening in Nathaniel's face led to quite a different notion. "You mean Sophie? You were afraid I might hurt Sophie if I fired, weren't you? That's why you hit me."

"Mustn't hurt the lady."

"Did you attack the vicar?"

Nathaniel shook his head and pointed to the boat. "I took the gun. *He* hit the vicar." His voice plummeted to a whisper. "He's a bad man."

"Damn it, Nathaniel, shoot!" Kellyn gestured into the air with a lengthy object that reflected the pewter gleam of the clouds.

The rapier he had found beneath the house? Chad pondered the revelation for the briefest instant. Holding his breath, he stared into the end of his own pistol. From the corner of his eye he saw the sailboat change direction.

"She's coming." The servant's gnarled fingers tightened around the butt of the weapon. "She's angry."

"Quick, Nathaniel, hand me the pistol. I can protect you from her."

The hull scraped the rocky humps protruding from the water. Kellyn's red hair fluttered like flames around her shoulders as she stood up. The rapier dangled from her right hand. With her left she lifted her skirts and prepared to climb out of the boat.

"She's coming!" Nathaniel's body spasmed and the gun went off. The report echoed against the cliffs. The shuddering blast knocked Chad off his feet.

He landed on his back on the beach's pebbled surface. The fall stunned him, and a second or two passed before he determined that he hadn't been hit. That Nathaniel could have missed him at such close range

seemed a miracle, one he hadn't time to ponder. He
rolled to his feet . . .

. . . and saw what had thrown Nathaniel's aim so
wide of the mark—what continued to hold him spell-
bound. At the mouth of the cave pallid light and ashen
shadow mingled and swarmed, gathering in an image
so translucent it might have been no more than the
water's reflection, except that Chad recognized the
size and shape of the figure it formed.

Nathaniel stood immobile but for the quivering
smile forming on his lips. His hand went slack and the
pistol dropped. Chad wasted no time. Scrambling to
get his feet under him, he launched himself at the
weapon. He skidded headlong across the wet rocks,
seized the gun in both hands and sprang to his feet.

Nathaniel regarded him only briefly, exhibiting not
the slightest concern about the fate of the weapon.
"Roses. Little roses."

"My God," Chad whispered past his astonishment.
"You know her."

An explosion shook the deck beneath Sophie, and
the tender spot at the back of her head seemed to
split into a thousand piercing shards. The voices fell
silent, leaving only the wind and surf and the creaking
of the boat. A crushing dread threatened to choke her.

Chad. His voice had been among the others. Now
there was nothing but the menacing echo of what must
have been a gunshot. Dear God, had he been hit?

Despair spread through her at the thought of never
again beholding his face, or putting her arms around
him and beginning the process of forgiveness and healing. Of living the rest of her life burdened by the guilt
of an unspoken truth: that no matter what he had
done she simply but wholeheartedly loved him.

It was a burden she could not bear. With teeth
clamped and perspiration dripping down her face, she
fought past the physical pain and paralyzing fear. Sliding across the deck until she could reach up and clutch

the gunwale, she pulled herself to a sitting position and peered over the side.

The beach spanning the rocky inlet stretched only yards away. She could almost have reached out and scooped pebbles from the shoreline. Boulders dotted the water, some thrusting above the waves, others like crouching beasts just beneath the surface. Kellyn was making her way from the boat to the shore, using the rocks as stepping-stones. The rapier swung back and forth in her hand. Her silk skirts billowed like wind-filled sails, blocking a portion of Sophie's view. Where was Chad?

At a scraping behind her, she twisted around. The Irishman straddled the deck, propping an oar against a rock to stabilize the boat.

She clenched her fists. "What do you want? Why are you doing this?"

"Because you and the earl wouldn't be put off, not even when I said I'd go to Mullion to alert the authorities." Malice flashed in Grady's blue eyes. "This is your own fault for meddling in matters that were none of yer business. Our secret's out now and we need to get away. The authorities won't dare fire on our ship, not with Cornelius St. Clair's granddaughter on board."

"What ship?" Sophie glanced at the horizon, where the sight of a waiting clipper made her stomach lurch. "You're both mad."

Grady jerked the oar as if to strike her with it, before returning his attention to holding the boat steady. The utter change in his countenance raised a chill in her. The seemingly compassionate man she had met outside the Stormy Gull had vanished, leaving behind someone unrecognizable, inhuman, beyond reason.

Someone evil, like Kellyn.

Sophie's gaze shot toward the beach. Kellyn leaped into the shallows, soaking her boots and hems as she waded to shore. Suddenly Chad moved into Sophie's line of sight, and she felt a burst of elation. He was alive, standing next to Nathanial near the mouth of the cave. Their backs were to the water. Kellyn strode up onto the beach, the *espada ropera* extended before her like a petrified serpent.

"Chad!" Sophie screamed in warning.

He whirled. Even before he seemed to see Kellyn, his gaze locked with Sophie's. Across the distance she felt herself drowning in the emotion she saw blazing in his amber eyes, in the fierceness of the promise conveyed by his determined features: he would die before letting harm come to her.

"No. Oh, please, no." A second warning rose inside her, but before she uttered it his attention shifted. His arm swung up in front of him, hand curled around a pistol. The sight of it brought Kellyn to an abrupt halt several yards shy of him. She threw back her head and let go a bark of laughter.

"It's been you all along," Sophie heard Chad say. "You and Grady. The smuggling, the murders . . ."

Kellyn raised the sword and dipped a curtsy. "Surprised? Never imagined your orders could be coming from a woman, did you?"

"I believe there are more descriptive words for the likes of you." The arm holding the pistol stiffened to full length. Chad braced his feet as if preparing to shoot.

Kellyn tossed her vivid hair. "You won't do it."

"Care to wager on it?"

"You have one chance, my friend." Kellyn raised her arms out to her sides. "At such close range you can't help but hit me, unless of course that knight-errant conscience of yours sends the bullet astray. Mustn't hurt a woman, after all."

"Try me."

"And when you miss, you'll have to stop and reload. During which time I'll run you through. So then . . . is it a wager? Winner takes all. Your beloved Sophie against my favorite sword."

"*Your* sword?" Sophie heard the click as Chad cocked

the pistol. She waited for the report, but it didn't come.

Her stomach gave a sickening twist as she realized the truth of Kellyn's words. In all likelihood Chad wouldn't pull the trigger, would not be able to kill in cold blood, no matter how deserving of death Kellyn might be.

He was simply not that sort of man. And because of that there was a good chance he would not survive. His father's spirit had tried to explain this to her. Had tried to make her understand that without her to fight for, Chad might give in too easily and be killed.

She had to get to shore.

Looking behind her she spotted the second oar lying across the deck. She inched toward it. . . .

"No, you don't." Grady swung the oar in his hands out of the water. Dripping, it arced toward her. Instinct sent her hands up in front of her, but instead of merely deflecting the blow, by some miracle her fingers closed around the oak shaft. Using all her weight and strength, she gave a yank that thrust Grady off balance.

The boat listed, and a wave poured over the gunwale. Grady's feet slid out from under him. As he tried to break his fall with his hands, he lost his grip on the oar. Sophie wasted no time in turning it, lifting it in the air and bringing the flat of the paddle down on the mariner's head. He keeled over onto the deck with a thud.

"Oh . . . dear God," she whispered, regarding Grady's limp form and comprehending Chad's reluctance to fire his pistol. "I hope I haven't killed you." She studied him long enough to see that he was breathing, that no blood stained the deck beneath his head. A realization struck her: surely she could not have overpowered the man on her own; help must have come from beyond, from a source she hadn't believed existed until today. "Thank you, Lord Wycliffe," she whispered.

The sea now commanded the dinghy, propelling it into a languid spin. The waves thrust it landward, then tugged it seaward as the water receded. The hull shook as the boat struck the rocks. Looking over the side, she judged the water to be over her head, the waves certainly so. Her brocade traveling outfit would weigh her down if she attempted to swim.

She contemplated reaching for the other oar, slipping both into their brackets and attempting to row, but each instant she hesitated sent her farther from the beach. Besides, she had never rowed a boat before. In a snap decision she drove the paddle she held into the water and wedged it into a gap between the boulders. She held on tight, struggling to anchor the dinghy against the tide.

She peered to the shore. Chad and Kellyn faced each other, locked in a battle of taunts. Having moved down off the rocks and onto the beach, they circled each other slowly, feet alternately crunching over the pebbles and splashing in the wavelets.

"I thought we were friends, you and I," Chad said, his voice raised above the roar of the surf. He sidestepped out of the water. "Could you slice into me so easily?"

"As though you were butter." Leaning, Kellyn extended the tip of her sword and swiped playfully at Chad's shirtfront. "I wonder, though. Would you die? I put enough nightshade into your brandy yesterday to bring down an ox. First into your cup, and then into the bottle once I realized no one else was likely to drink from it. Didn't see the point of killing off everyone at once."

"Then the Gordons' barn should be falling over dead any moment." The sword point drifted closer again, and he tapped it aside with the barrel of his pistol. "I'm afraid I smashed your bottle against the wall in a fit of frustration."

"Such a fiery temper, darling. You must learn to master it."

"So I must." Despite the lighthearted nature of the exchange, as Chad circled to face Sophie she saw his pinched nostrils, the working of his jaw. "Did you use nightshade on my father as well?"

They circled again. A satisfied smile brought sinister beauty to Kellyn's face. "Like a good boy he drank all his down."

"You deceived him into trusting you." Cold fury blazed in his eyes. He gestured with the gun at the gown Kellyn wore. "You kept a wardrobe at Edgecombe. Were you and he lovers? Did you murder your lover, Kellyn?"

"Lover?" Again that biting, humorless laugh. "Never. All Franklin ever did was mourn that glacial paragon you called a mother. And bemoan the absence of his beloved son."

Sophie's breath caught at the abrupt change that came over Chad. As his mouth fell open in silent dismay, a look of anguish stole the light from his eyes and the defiance from his shoulders. In horror Sophie saw the pistol sag in his hand.

Her own shoulders burned with the strain of fighting the current. Her hands cramped around the oar. Fear burgeoned that she would soon lose her battle with the sea.

But one battle she refused to see lost, not as long as she had a breath left in her body. "Chad, you mustn't listen to her," she shouted. "She's half-insane. She believes she's Meg Keating reborn. And like Meg she won't balk at killing you. Or me. Do you hear me, Chad? Remember the legends, the atrocities Meg committed—and know that Kellyn will not hesitate to do the same."

Chapter 25

*S*ophie!

Chad's back was to her again due to this infuriating waltz he danced with Kellyn, but he had caught a quick glimpse of her pale face and shaking arms. He yearned to go to her, carry her to safety, but he knew that the moment he turned his back on Kellyn she would make good on her threat of running him through.

And then what would happen to Sophie?

He could end the confrontation with a squeeze of the trigger. By God, shoot Kellyn? Kill a woman? Even now, knowing that she had murdered his father along with countless others, he groped for what might have driven her to such lengths. Against all the evidence he still wanted to believe that no one could be entirely evil, and that somewhere inside Kellyn there still existed the good-natured woman he had met at the Stormy Gull.

Then, as he caught another glimpse of Ellie Rose's form, comprehension filled him in a torrent. *The evil is killing her. Killing her soul. You must help her.*

This was the task his little ghost had set him—a way to make amends for his own crimes. Kellyn's life must not end, at least not until he awakened whatever remained of her soul. Only then, perhaps, could he spare her from the eternal torment she faced.

"You're not Meg Keating," he said. "You are Kellyn Quincy, a woman who once had a little girl who died."

The mocking grin slipped from her countenance. With no other warning she lunged and thrust the rapier—not the one he had found in the tunnel, he realized, but the missing one from the drawing room. The one that had belonged to Meg. Sophie was right: Kellyn was insane.

His quick reflexes sent him springing back, but the tip of the rapier slashed his shirtfront and nicked his bottom rib. The skin split, stinging as blood blossomed on his shirt.

Behind him Sophie screamed. He wanted to reassure her, but he didn't dare take his eyes off Kellyn. Perhaps she did deserve to die without absolution. Seething, he thrust out his jaw, extended the pistol and took two strides toward her. At this range the bullet would neatly puncture her heart.

She held her ground. "Go ahead and shoot. If you can."

Mama.

Kellyn gasped. Her face snapped to one side and then the other. Near the mouth of the cave the child's faint outline hovered, even paler and more indistinct than at the chapel. Her ability to materialize in the corporeal world seemed to be coming to an end.

"Little roses." Nathaniel stood pressed against the cliff face, his eyes pinned on the ghost, his expression one of infinite fondness. "Sweet little roses."

Kellyn seemed frozen where she stood, eyes unfocused, head tilted as if she were listening.

"Ellie Rose, your mother needs you." Chad held his breath during an eternal moment in which the little ghost lingered uncertainly. Then she glided into the open. In the daylight more of her features became discernible—the hollow eyes, the gashed forehead, the streaming hair and ragged clothes.

With a pang Chad realized he no longer found the child's image repulsive. He saw her now for what she was: a little girl draped in tragedy, but no longer fearsome.

"Oh, my!" Sophie's cry of astonishment skittered across the water. Astonishment went through Chad that she too could see the child.

He gazed past Kellyn to the beleaguered sailboat. Sophie's eyes were huge with fear. Her knuckles glowed white around the oar as she held strong against the currents.

"I'm coming, Sophie," he shouted.

"I know. I'll be waiting for you. First do what you must."

Her conviction buoyed him with the faith it conveyed. Her undaunted courage filled him with the confidence that, for her, he would prevail. He loved Sophie, and if Ellie Rose's appearance proved anything, it was that love's spirit never died, never stopped fighting.

To Kellyn he said, "Your daughter is determined to save you from the evil of your own actions. You heard her calling out to you. Can you not see her?"

"My daughter is dead. There is nothing to see."

"Are you certain? I see her. Look at Nathaniel— he sees her too. Sophie as well. Only you have shut your eyes to her. On the outside she is scarred and frightening. But to my eyes she is beautiful, while you've become a dark and shriveled monster."

Kellyn laughed, a sound cut short as the glimmer that was Ellie Rose grazed her side. Kellyn recoiled. The rapier's length angled toward the ground.

Chad started toward her, halting when she swung the sword into place again. "Kellyn, Ellie Rose is here," he said, "and she's desperate to help you. The love she bears you will not allow her to rest peacefully, and her time is running short. She needs you to hear her. To see her and believe in her. To be her mother again."

"Don't be a fool," Kellyn sneered. "There is nothing here but air."

"If you look with the whole of your heart you'll see your daughter. Don't you want that? One more chance to see Ellie Rose? I can only imagine how much you loved her. How much you mourn her. Her love for you reaches beyond all boundaries. No matter what you have done, she loves you still."

"How touching. Why, I—"

Mama? With her transparent hand Ellie Rose reached out. Her skeletal fingers passed through Kellyn's crimson skirt as if the fabric were no more substantial than a cloud. Kellyn's body shuddered as if someone had grabbed her shoulders and shaken her. A guttural sound escaped her.

Mama, I've missed you so, the little ghost whispered.

"Do you hear her, Kellyn?" Lowering his pistol, Chad stepped closer.

She raised the sword to the level of his chest. Defiance thinned her mouth. "I hear nothing."

"I think you do. I see the pain in your eyes."

Mama. I've a message for you. One you must heed.

Kellyn gasped again and sliced the rapier through the air, whipping through Ellie Rose's form. Chad jumped back, raising a splash at the water's edge. Kellyn slashed frantically. "There's nothing . . . nothing. . . ."

Ellie Rose merely hovered, undisturbed by the blade.

"There is, Kellyn," Chad said. "There is your child's love, and your own need to be her mother."

With a howl dredged as if from the darkest of crypts, Kellyn swung the sword over her head and pounced at him. Chad ducked to the side but the tip caught his shoulder, piercing the skin and sinking into flesh. An inferno raged down his arm, across his chest, into his back. He staggered knee deep into the waves as searing pain stole the strength from his fingers. His grip opened and the pistol splashed into the water. With nightmare clarity he saw his only defense disappear beneath the surface.

Her face contorting, Kellyn tugged the blade free. Fresh agony cascaded from the wound. In a ghastly blur he watched her turn the sword this way and that, admiring the smear of his blood on the steel. She stretched her lips in a savage grin and prepared to thrust again.

Sophie's cry echoed against the cliffs and reverberated inside him. As the blade shot toward him, he could think only of her, see only her. "I'm sorry, Sophie. So sorry."

In his despair he fell to his knees. The sword came at him, but the sudden shifting of her target set Kellyn off balance. Her aim swerving awry, she stumbled in the waves.

A burst of hope filled him. Tucking pain into a corner of his mind, he worked his feet beneath him and pushed off the seabed. He surged through the water, threw his arms about Kellyn's waist and used the momentum of the surf to topple her onto her back.

His attack clearly stunned her, but her bewilderment didn't last long. Gripping her sword in both hands, she attempted to swing it down onto him. He pinned her with the weight of his body, reached up and caught her arms. In the struggle for possession the rapier undulated wildly above their heads, causing the air to shiver, Chad's arms to tremble. The waves broke over them as they tussled, enveloping them in a confusion of foam and spray, arms and legs. Water filled his nose and mouth. He coughed it out. Kellyn sputtered, choked, gagged for breath.

He felt the strength draining from her arms. *Ellie Rose, speak to her. You must get through to her.*

"Hold it right there, both of you."

Above the breeze and surf Chad heard a click above his head. He looked up into the barrel of a pistol, then higher, to glimpse a hawkish nose and a pair of cunning, close-set eyes glaring down at him from beneath the brim of a tweed cap. It was the stranger from the Stormy Gull who dressed like a fisherman but carried himself with a far more sophisticated air, a man Kellyn had professed not to know.

"You." Chad swore. His already pounding heart gave

a violent wrench, and his throat closed around a new sense of hopelessness. Why hadn't he foreseen that Kellyn would have help other than Grady?

A second pistol moved into his view, and then another, held by two men who flanked the first. Chad almost wished they would fire and save him the agony of watching Sophie meet a similar fate.

"Release the sword," the one in the cap said, "and sit up slowly, Lord Wycliffe. Very slowly."

He eased off Kellyn and sat up. He expected her to do the same, and to turn her mocking grin on him. When she remained on her back, the waves lapping at her boots and skirts, another contradiction registered in his brain. The man's pistol remained trained on Kellyn's head, while one of the other men took the rapier from her hands.

Whatever it all meant, Chad didn't take the time to comprehend. Scrambling to his feet he dashed into the waves. Perhaps they'd shoot him in the back, but he was going for Sophie.

Panic exploded. No longer wedged between the rocks, the boat had drifted out beyond the breakwater, with no sign of Sophie aboard. Frantically he searched the heaving waters. Between the rocks a bloom of russet eddied with the currents. Recognition launched his heart against his ribs. Sophie's russet carriage jacket. The terror of his dream roared through him: Sophie drowning, dying in his arms.

Bellowing her name, he dove beneath the surface.

"Sophie!"
Like a tortured wail ripped from the earth, the sound of her name tore across the waves.
Chad.
Before she had shed her carriage jacket and clambered over the gunwale, she had watched Kellyn thrust the rapier. Chad had gone down onto his knees in the water. Sophie had gone in too, determined to reach him.

Now, as she heard him shout her name, her chest swelled with exhilaration. He was alive. Alive and coming for her.

She tried to call out. A breaker rolled over her head and reduced her voice to a sputtering gulp. Her lips were stiff from cold; she shivered uncontrollably as the sea hauled her back and forth as though she were the rope in a tug-of-war. The foaming surf crashed over her, blinding her and distorting all sense of direction.

He shouted her name again. She couldn't see him, couldn't see anything but the swirling waters and the menacing rocks.

"Sophie? Where are you? Oh, God, answer me."

"Here! Chad, I'm here!" Water poured into her mouth. Gagging and spitting, she flailed her arms, groping for purchase. Wave after wave twisted her in a tangle of sea and sky.

From behind powerful arms encircled her, turned her, then pressed her to the rocky hardness of a chest and shoulders and to the strong column of a neck that felt like home against her cheek. Relief gusted through her in consuming gales, echoed by a fierce rumbling beneath her ear and the gruff sob that broke against her brow.

"Sophie . . . Sophie . . ." He spoke her name over and over. The water crested around them. Chad tried to lift her in his arms, but she felt the sudden give of his wounded shoulder. Pain contorted his features.

She flung an arm around his waist. Kicking until she found the seabed, she braced her feet, stretched to her full height and tipped her chin upward to steal breaths of air each time the waves dipped. Chad's good arm tightened around her. Borrowing from each other's remaining strength, they fought the undertow, struggling through the waves until they broke free of the water and collapsed together on dry land.

Then she was in his arms again, held so tight his desperate words vibrated through her. "I thought I'd lost you. I thought . . . Oh, God, it was like the nightmare. Rushing to reach you . . . fearing I'd never arrive in time . . ."

His words dissolved as he sought out her shivering lips with his mouth. His own lips were cold and tasted of salt, yet from their first touch a fire blazed, howling through her with the knowledge of all that had nearly been lost, while thrumming with the promise of forever.

He drew back, yet his lips touched hers as he spoke. "Are you all right?"

She managed a tremulous smile and slid her hand from around his nape to his shoulder. He winced. Blood trickled in threads down his soaking shirtfront. "You're hurt badly."

"It's only blood. A bit of flesh." Releasing a sound that was half sigh and half groan, he smiled with his eyes. "A small enough price."

"One you've been all too willing to pay for my sake." Her heart broke anew at how mistaken she had been about him, at how little faith she had put in this man who had proven himself to her time after time. Yes, he had made mistakes, serious ones, but to her he had never been anything but noble. "I was wrong to judge you so harshly, to treat you so ill. Wrong not to believe you about the ghosts."

His soft laugh traveled inside her, curling into a ball of warmth at her core. "None of that matters."

She wrapped herself around him and held on. He held her with equal fervor, and they lingered just beyond the water's edge until their trembling began to subside.

Lightly she placed her fingertips near the ragged flesh inside his torn shirt. "However did you manage to overcome Kellyn?"

"I had help." Turning, he pointed to three men who surrounded Kellyn some dozen yards away.

Sophie clutched Chad's shirt and pulled back against him. "Who are they?"

He stood and helped her to her feet, then thrust a possessive arm around her waist. "We'd best go find out. But I don't think they mean us harm."

"Lord Wycliffe," called the one who wore a tweed cap, and whose probing eyes made Sophie fight the urge to shrink, "I'm Inspector John Haversham of Truro." Boots splashing in the waves, he walked along the waterline and extended a hand.

Chad hesitated, his astonishment palpable. Then he shook the proffered hand. The inspector darted a glance at Sophie and touched a finger to the brim of his cap.

"Miss St. Clair."

It was her turn to experience a shock of surprise. "You know who I am?"

"You are Cornelius St. Clair's granddaughter, and you're here staying with your relatives, the Gordons. Two of whom are in a fair amount of trouble, especially if they choose not to cooperate."

"They'll cooperate," she said quickly. "I'm quite certain they will."

"I'm very sorry you became caught up in all of this, Miss St. Clair." Haversham tipped a respectful nod. "That was something we didn't anticipate. If we had, we'd have taken pains to see to your safety."

Haversham's associates pointed their guns at Kellyn as she came to her feet. One man held the rapier in his free hand. The other official stepped behind Kellyn and lashed her wrists together. When he had finished the task, they gestured toward the breakwater. All three started toward it.

Sophie gathered her dripping hair over one shoulder and squeezed the water out of it. "Inspector, what on earth is going on?"

"Yes, explanations are in order. I must admit, Lord Wycliffe, I thought you were onto me the other day, the way you stared up at me in my room at the Gull."

"I knew there was something not right about you.

You're no fisherman. It shows in the way you move, and in those shrewd looks of yours."

"I'll bear that in mind the next time I conduct a covert investigation."

"Investigation? You mean . . ."

"Yes, ma'am. My men and I have had our eyes on Lord Wycliffe for weeks now." The inspector's gaze drifted back to Chad. "We've been following you and anticipating your actions."

"On more than one occasion I sensed that I was being watched." When Haversham raised an eyebrow, Chad's arm tightened about Sophie's waist. "But I've already testified. I told the authorities everything I knew."

"Quite true, my lord, but it was what you didn't know that most interested us. We quickly established that the men you helped us apprehend were no more than lackeys, as were you yourself."

Chad stiffened, the edge of his profile sharpening. Sophie gave him a discreet nudge, and he blew out a breath. "I suppose you're right."

"Indeed, and that is why I sent you here," the inspector said in a somber murmur.

The crash of the waves against the shore marked the passing of the seconds that followed. Chad's face became an unreadable mask. His chest heaved. His fingers dug into Sophie's waist, though she doubted he realized it.

The tension pulsing through the air prompted her to break the silence. "I don't understand. What does that mean, you sent him here? Chad?"

"The message from Giles Watling." His eyes fell closed, and the heel of his boot ground against the pebbles. Then he met the inspector's gaze. "It was from you."

Haversham nodded. "Watling couldn't or wouldn't tell me what I needed to know. It seemed almost as if he feared retribution in the afterlife for betraying his leader."

"Perhaps he did, Inspector." Sophie pressed tighter to Chad's side. "Kellyn did much to perpetuate the notion that Meg Keating's ghost had returned. She half believed it herself, and I don't doubt some of her people came to fear Meg's curse."

"An interesting theory, Miss St. Clair. You may be right." Mr. Haversham tugged at his tweed cap. "However, Watling *was* willing to deliver my message to Lord Wycliffe in exchange for my pledge that his family wouldn't starve in his . . . er . . . absence."

"Good God," Chad said with a shake of his head. "All this time I thought whoever summoned me here meant either to force me back into smuggling or to kill me."

Sophie pressed her fingers to her mouth to stifle a gasp.

"I'm sorry, Lord Wycliffe. But yes, I perpetrated a hoax against you. We were fairly certain the ringleader operated out of Penhollow, but the individual managed to elude us. I gambled that bringing you here would force that person to play his hand and with any luck make a mistake. It appears I was right, and we're greatly indebted to you, my lord." Haversham cast a glance at Kellyn, sitting on the rocks of the breakwater under the close guard of the other two inspectors. "I understand now why we were so fooled. We never dreamed it could be a woman."

Sophie pushed out of Chad's hold. Hands on her hips, she took a stride closer to the inspector. "How could you have been so irresponsible? He might have been killed. It's unconscionable, what you did. . . ."

From behind Chad's hands closed over her shoulders. "Sophie, it's all right."

"No, it is not all right." She spun to face him. "Kellyn almost killed you. I watched from the boat. . . . She . . . Oh, your shoulder!" Fingers trembling, heart wrenching, she touched his bloodstained shirt. "It isn't all right. . . ."

"Shh. It is." His arms went around her, holding her close while she sobbed against his drenched shirtfront.

Clearing his throat, the inspector shuffled away.

Chad raised her face and caressed her lips with kisses that fired a raging tenderness inside her. The tears fell faster. He wiped them away first with the backs of his fingers, then with warm sweeps of his mouth across her cheeks. "Please don't cry, Sophie. It was all worth it, every moment."

She pressed her face to his sodden collar. "How could it be?"

"Because I have you back in my arms, and . . . dare I believe that you are beginning, perhaps, to trust me again? And to forgive me?"

Through her sobs, through the lingering horror of how close they had both come to losing their lives, she tightened her arms around his neck and smiled against his lips. "I do forgive you, and I more than trust you."

Chapter 26

Sophie's quiet avowal traveled inside Chad. He wished only to go on holding her, kissing her, reveling in her willingness to let him. Yet part of him feared to believe the evidence of his own ears; he hesitated also to read too much into her words: *I more than trust you.*

Did that mean her feelings for him ran deeper? Or was she merely overwhelmed by the day's events? She had been kidnapped. They had just dragged each other from the water, had narrowly avoided drowning. Either of them might have been killed by Kellyn or Grady. Of course Sophie felt grateful, immensely relieved that they were now safe. But once time passed, what would prevent her disappointment in him from roaring back?

His questions must wait. First he must get her off this blustery beach and into dry clothes, and begin putting this nightmare behind them.

Out in the open water a schooner rounded the breakwater. Even from the distance Ian's sandy hair and sturdy frame stood out against the clouds and surf behind him. Positioned at the ship's helm, he maneuvered the fishing vessel alongside Grady's drifting sailboat. A deckhand lowered a rope ladder. Two men climbed down while, from above, several others held weapons at the ready. Then Ian relinquished the wheel to a shipmate and climbed down as well.

Sophie held a hand above her eyes to shield them from the glare. "I doubt Grady's capable of giving them much trouble, even if he has regained consciousness." Her chattering teeth gave a guilty nibble at her bottom lip. "I hit him rather hard with the oar."

"Grady deserved it." Grabbing her close again, Chad pressed his lips to her forehead. His intrepid Sophie.

"The schooner reminds me . . . There was another ship waiting on the horizon." Gazing over her head, he squinted farther out to sea. "Damn. It's gone now."

Had Kellyn or Grady signaled the waiting vessel away? More likely the arrival of the schooner had frightened off the crew.

"It was where Kellyn and Grady were taking me," Sophie said. "Grady said that with me aboard the authorities wouldn't dare fire upon the ship, and they'd have a chance to escape." Her hand closed tightly over his forearm. "Chad, the topsail. Did you see it?"

He turned his gaze from the sea and cupped a hand to her cheek, his fingertips shaking as the full realization of what they had faced today hit him. "Black upon red."

"Do you think . . . ?"

"Yes. It's sheer lunacy, but it fits the legend." The Keatings' clipper had supposedly flown just such a topsail from its mainmast—a red background emblazoned with a black rose, a standard of blood and death. The mere sight was said to have struck despair into the hearts of sailors, who would surrender with barely a fight. "My God, to think that Kellyn emulated Meg Keating to the point of creating a modern-day version of the *Ebony Rose*."

"You called her daughter Ellie Rose." When he nodded, Sophie went on. "Ellie Rose. *Ebony Rose*. The lives of Kellyn and Meg are twisted into an impossible knot, a deadly one. And I wonder . . ."

"Yes?"

"Could Kellyn's actions have anything to do with

the sword she stole from the drawing room? You remember the strange energy we felt in its mate. If those swords *did* belong to Meg and Jack, perhaps . . ."

Chad shook his head. "No, Sophie. While the swords may carry an energy, or an echo from the past, I don't believe they possess the power to make an individual act contrary to his or her nature. You and I both held Jack's sword. We each felt the vibration, but neither of us felt compelled to perform wicked deeds of any sort."

"Then what *did* prompt Kellyn to commit such atrocities?"

"Perhaps it's time we found out."

On the rocks of the breakwater Kellyn sat hunched, head down, hands tied behind her back. Her bright hair streamed around her face and shoulders. As he and Sophie approached, they heard Inspector Haversham questioning her.

"Where is your ship hiding?"

"At sea." She scowled up at him. "You'll never find it."

"Of course we will. How many are aboard?"

"A dozen. All well-armed and fearless."

The inspector's eyebrows went up. "Perhaps they'll find something to fear when they learn their leader has been apprehended."

Kellyn shrugged and returned her brooding stare to the ground. She seemed shrunken and pallid, a shadow of the vigorous woman Chad had known, or thought he had known.

"I almost feel sorry for her," Sophie said in his ear.

He understood. Even now he had trouble reconciling the notion of a cold-blooded killer with the woman he had met at the Stormy Gull.

They stopped in front of her, and he dragged a hand through his hair. "Why, Kellyn?"

She squinted up at him, her pale eyes devoid of emotion. "He took her to France. I didn't want her to go—I knew the dangers—but they both insisted. It was to be special. Father and daughter. What could a mother do? I relented, and she went."

"It was for her birthday," Chad murmured.

Kellyn flinched. "How could you know that?"

"Ellie Rose told me. What happened next?"

An agony of pain twisted her features. "On the return trip they were to put in at Penhollow to drop off cargo. It was part of the usual run. To the French coast for goods, then stops at Penhollow, Mullion and then home to Porthleven. This time, as they reached the coast, a storm kicked up. The ship was dragged into the headland, smashed by the surf against the rocks over and over again. They fired their distress flares—" With a wrenching groan, she broke off.

Sophie sank to her knees in front of her. "Help arrived too late, didn't it?"

"Too late?" Kellyn's head snapped up. Her sudden vehemence sent Sophie to her feet and prompted the inspectors to raise their pistols. "The people of Penhollow rowed out to Rob's sinking ship. But instead of saving the crew and passengers, they filled their boats with whatever cargo they managed to haul from the waves. Only when they'd satisfied their greed did they turn their efforts to rescuing those who hadn't yet drowned. By then Rob was dead."

The icy malice in her features convinced Chad she would have lashed out were it not for the bonds holding her. "Rob Quincy lived a smuggler's life and knew the risks. Knew his devil's luck would someday run dry." The hostility suddenly melted from her features, trickling in tears down her cheeks. "But Ellie Rose . . . my innocent Ellie Rose . . . If only I hadn't let her go . . ."

She faltered, shutting her eyes. "A week later a surviving deckhand brought her body home to me. He told me what had happened, how he heard her screams through the shattered hull and tried to reach her. How he found her broken body washed up on the rocks the next day. And how, God rot them, the people here turned away as he carried her through their accursed village."

Her jaw working, she glared out at the schooner and at the little sailboat being guided by Ian back to the inlet. "That deckhand was an Irishman."

"Grady." Fresh tears glistened on Sophie's cheeks. She backed into Chad's arms, pressing her face to his uninjured shoulder. He wrapped his arms around her, held on and buried his nose in her hair, seeking a haven from the horror Kellyn had described.

"I put my baby in the ground," Kellyn continued, her voice tight, swollen with sorrow. "I buried her with roses, and then I swore revenge."

Mama. A shimmer illuminated the air beside Kellyn. Ellie Rose's intangible outlines took shape.

Gasping, Kellyn raised her head and searched the space around her. "Who's there?"

"It's Ellie Rose," Chad said. "That's what I've been trying to tell you. Not even the violence of her death could fully part her from you."

While the inspectors watched in bewilderment, Kellyn's eyes sharpened into focus, then blurred behind tears. "Ellie Rose? Oh, God . . . I . . . I *can* see you." Wrenching her shoulders, straining her neck, she struggled against the cords binding her wrists.

"Untie her," Chad said to the inspector.

"I don't think that's a good idea."

"Please, Mr. Haversham," Sophie urged. "What harm can she do now?"

Clearly puzzled, the man pulled out a pocketknife and slashed through Kellyn's bonds. She reached out with both hands, a sob tearing from deep within as her fingertips passed through Ellie Rose's form. "My child. Come to me. I wish to hold you. Just once. To feel you against me one more time and smell your sweet, precious hair . . . Oh, for that I'd give my life."

Haversham traded astonished glances with his men. "She's lost her mind, though it won't likely save her from the noose."

That last word sent a shiver across Chad's nape as he considered how close his own neck had come to meeting the same fatal embrace. "Why don't we back away," he said, "and allow her a moment to reconcile herself to what has happened."

When Haversham looked about to protest, Chad held up his hand. "A few minutes, Inspector, I beg you. Afterward I believe you'll find her willing to go along with you without a fuss, and perhaps to cooperate in helping you track down her ship, as well."

With a shrug Haversham signaled for his men to move away. Chad and Sophie followed them toward the mouth of the cave. He gestured to the rapier still held by one of the officers. "Do you feel it giving off an odd energy?"

The man regarded the weapon and wrinkled his brow. "It's wet. A bit cold."

"Nothing else?" When the officer shrugged, Chad said no to Haversham, "If I were you, Inspector, when I no longer needed that rapier for evidence I'd dispose of it where no one will ever find it." He looked to Sophie for confirmation. She nodded and he continued, "Kellyn stole it from Edgecombe, but I sure as hell don't want it back."

"Or its mate, either," Sophie added with a shudder. "We have another, almost identical sword up at the house, Inspector, and we believe the weapons once belonged to Meg and Jack Keating."

"You don't say." Haversham rubbed the back of his hand across his chin. "Given the bizarre circumstances of this case, Lord Wycliffe, we may need both swords for evidence. But the law is the law. Once we've finished prosecuting, both weapons will be returned to you."

"At which time," Chad said, "I'll either toss them into the sea or . . ."

"Or seal them both in the tunnel beneath Edgecombe," Sophie finished for him. She reached out, combing her fingers through his hair and caressing the curve of his ear. "If only Meg had found Jack before he died, she might not have gone on her rampage."

The revelation resounded through him. "And Kellyn would not have had Meg's example to follow. Good God, how many lives might have been saved, both then and now . . . ?"

"We'll never know," she whispered, and huddled against him as shivers traveled through her.

He tried to warm her, to absorb her trembling into his own body. "Inspector, are we free to go?"

"Indeed you are, my lord. But don't stray far. We'll need you and Miss St. Clair for questioning. And those relatives of yours as well, miss."

"And what about this fellow?" The man holding the rapier angled his chin at Nathaniel. "Shall we take him into custody?"

Chad had all but forgotten his groundskeeper, still standing on the rocky ledge outside the cave, gazing with a bemused expression at the soft glow surrounding Kellyn. "Mr. Haversham, arresting Nathaniel would be a mistake. He hasn't done anything wrong, for all Kellyn tried to use him against us."

"No, indeed, sir," Sophie said. "He's like a child, and doesn't understand any of this."

"Ah, but he does." Chad swept her damp hair from her face. "It's true that he didn't understand quite a lot of what happened, but in the end he recognized the evil of Kellyn's and Grady's actions and summoned the courage to defy them for our sakes. We owe him a debt."

Sophie's face lit up with a brilliance that stole his breath. "Thank you, Nathaniel," she whispered. She turned back to Haversham. "May we take Nathaniel up to the house with us?"

The inspector nodded and gestured to the cave. "You'll find our torches and means for lighting them just inside. Take one with you. And find some dry clothes as soon as possible, both of you."

After stepping up into the tunnel, Chad reached a hand down to Sophie to help her climb up. Once beside him, she stood for a moment with her arms around his waist, her body pressed to his, infusing him with hope for the future—a future with her.

"Take me away from this place," she said.

"Gladly."

As he set about lighting a torch, Sophie called to the servant, who lingered outside the mouth of the cave. "Come, Nathaniel, it's time to go home."

The torch flared to life as she said the word *home*. And Chad wondered, would Edgecombe ever feel like home to him, now that the danger was past and he was free to begin rebuilding his life? Or would the estate remain a place of abandonment and tragedy, with the memories of his mistakes always present to haunt him?

Nathaniel stepped up into the cave, then turned and raised a gnarled hand in a gesture of farewell. "Rest now, little roses."

A harsh and continual cry—*ker-rik, ker-rik!*—wrested Sophie from the warm pleasure of a dream. With reluctance she opened her eyes to see flashes of a black head and a gray wing as a tern took flight from the window ledge.

A moment later the bird's white underbelly soared into view, but farther away now, little more than a speck against a patch of blue sky. Sophie watched it disappear again as disappointment gripped her. In her dream she had returned to Edgecombe to find the house no longer abandoned or filled with menacing shadows. Sunlight had streamed through every window, while laughter and the beginnings of new, happier memories echoed through the rooms. Best of all, a grinning Chad had met her at the door, wrapped her in his strong arms and welcomed her home.

All too tempted to drift back into the beauty of that

dream, she let her eyes fall closed, but the tern doubled back and let out a squawk as it swooped past
her window.

With a gasp Sophie came fully awake. Her gaze
darted to the window with its emerald damask curtains, then up at the carved medallion in the center
of the ceiling. Where was she? This was not the room
she shared with Rachel at Aunt Louisa's house.

She pushed against the mattress, struggling to disentangle her limbs from the sheets—sheets far too fine
to have graced any bed in a farmer's house. It hadn't
been a dream after all, not entirely. She *was* at
Edgecombe . . . lying in the very bed where Chad had
first introduced her to passion.

But where was he? And how had she gotten here?

Memories tumbled back: Kellyn and Grady; the desperate struggle on the beach, the pain etched on Chad's
face as Kellyn drove her sword into his shoulder. . . .

"Chad?" Sheets and all, she swung her legs over
the side of the bed. She wore a chemise, nothing more.
But she didn't care—she had to find him, had to know
if he was all right. "Chad, where are—"

"Sophie, dear, you're awake."

She gaped as Aunt Louisa came through the doorway. The woman gently closed her hands over Sophie's shoulders and eased her back onto the pillows.
"There, there, now. You mustn't jump up so quickly.
We can't have you swooning again."

As Aunt Louisa straightened the bedclothes around
her, Sophie pressed a hand to her forehead. "I fainted?"

"Well, more like dropped from exhaustion. You'd
just gotten up from the dining table, and your legs
simply gave way beneath you. You might have fallen
and hit your head if the earl hadn't caught you. Then
Barnaby carried you upstairs. Don't you remember?"

"Oh, I . . . suppose . . ."

Vague at first, the details formed in her mind. After
leaving the beach, she, Chad and Nathaniel had returned to the house to meet with the anxious concerns

of the others—Rachel, Mr. Hall, Reese and Uncle Barnaby. Questions had been answered and lingering apprehensions put to rest over a meal prepared by Nathaniel. Mr. Hall had treated Chad's shoulder and had seemed confident that with proper attention the wound would not fester. Ian had joined them briefly before going back to the farm to fetch Aunt Louisa, and the inspectors, meanwhile, had conveyed their prisoners back to the village to await transport to Truro.

All that Sophie remembered. But as to what happened afterward . . .

"How long have I slept?"

"Oh, you've been out since yesterday afternoon. Sleep seems to have done you a world of good." Aunt Louisa pressed a palm to Sophie's cheek. "Your color is back, thank goodness. Your young man will be happy to see it."

"My young man?"

"Why, yes, the earl. He was terribly worried about you. Tried to carry you upstairs himself, but of course he couldn't quite manage it, not with that stab wound. Nasty business, all of it." Aunt Louisa reached for a pitcher, poured a cup of water and handed it to Sophie. "Drink this, dear, but not too fast."

Sophie sipped the cool water, but found difficulty swallowing around a sudden tightness in her throat. "You know, Aunt Louisa, he isn't *my* young man."

No, at least not beyond the boundaries of her dream. Yesterday, on their way back through the tunnel, Chad had held her hand but nonetheless led the way in pensive silence. A distance seemed to have opened up between them. Once back at the house Sophie had hoped he might devise a way for them to steal off together for a private word—there remained so much left unsaid between them—but he had shown no intention of doing so. She hadn't understood; she still didn't. She thought she had made her feelings quite clear down on the beach, and . . . she had believed he shared those feelings.

Thinking back on his embraces, his kisses, the urgent relief shredding his voice as he had helped her from the water . . . how could she but conclude that he cared for her deeply?

Then why hadn't he spoken?

Oh, but perhaps she *hadn't* made her feelings clear, or not clear enough. She had told him she trusted him—more than trusted him—but she hadn't said she loved him. Of course, there had been others looking on—the inspectors, Kellyn, Nathaniel. It hadn't seemed the right place or time.

Could Chad believe she still harbored resentment against him? Why hadn't she simply told him what she felt for him?

With a smile softening the lines around her mouth, Aunt Louisa sat at the edge of the bed and took Sophie's hand. "He isn't yours? Are you sure of that?"

With a sinking feeling, Sophie sighed. "I don't see how he could be."

"Odd thing, then, that he sat in that very chair for hours on end yesterday, just watching you." She pointed to the overstuffed chair near the window. "I finally had to order him off to bed—the vicar did say he needed to rest that shoulder as much as he can. Yet the earl was back again this morning as soon as the sun rose, sitting in that chair, keeping vigilant watch. The only reason he isn't here now, Sophie, is because I shooed him downstairs for some breakfast. He left but a few minutes ago."

Sophie's heart pressed against her breastbone. "He was here all that time?"

"Indeed he was."

She sat upright and pushed the covers away. "I need some clothes. . . ."

"I brought you a dress from home, but—"

"I'm fine, Aunt Louisa, I promise. Just help me dress, and quickly."

Downstairs Sophie hurried into the dining hall. A plate of untouched food sat at the head of the table before an unoccupied chair. Only a half-empty cup of coffee gave any indication that Chad had been here. She opened the terrace door and stepped out. A gentle breeze sifted through the dogwoods and fruit trees. The cries of seagulls out over the water clashed with the chirps of wrens and sparrows and the ceaseless *ker-rik* of the lone tern. But there was no one on the terrace or in the gardens below.

With a rising sense of urgency not to let another moment pass without speaking to him, she strode back inside and into the hall.

"Sophie."

She pulled up with a start. He stood just inside the drawing room doorway in breeches and boots, linen shirtsleeves pushed to his elbows, his collar and top buttons open to accommodate the bandages around his shoulder. He was freshly shaven, and a fringe of gleaming golden hair spilled across his brow to conceal the healing scrapes. To her he looked . . . magnificent; the sight of him stole her breath and held her immobile until he spoke her name again.

The quiet caress of his voice sparked immediate tears and sent her rushing into his arms. In deference to his injury, she stopped just short of jolting into him; instead she slipped her arms around his neck and pressed her cheek to his as he gently enfolded her.

All the things she had wanted to say abandoned her on a sob, absorbed into the heat of his skin and the smooth weave of his shirtfront. They held each other for some moments, his head bent over hers, their cheeks pressing, their heartbeats thudding in rhythm through their clothing.

Finally his head came up and he flashed a smile that lit his eyes with the full glow of a moorland sunrise and filled her with overwhelming joy. Then his head dipped again and his lips found hers. He kissed her deeply, thoroughly, as though he'd never have enough of her; he went on kissing her until the strength drained from her limbs and a fiery heat surged through her; until she knew, in the deepest part of her heart, that she could never let herself be kissed by another man.

He drew back again, still smiling. "That, my Sophie, is only a beginning . . . if you'll let it be."

Her breath quivering in her throat, she trembled against him. "We said so little to each other yesterday once we returned from the beach. I was afraid that perhaps you didn't . . ."

"Didn't what?" A shadow of his former sternness returned. His voice turned gruff. "Didn't want to be with you?"

Hesitating, she nodded and whispered, "Yes."

"How could you think such a thing?" He sounded angry. His arms closed around her with fierce insistence. "Never think that, Sophie. Never." His hands swept into her hair, and he tipped her face up to his. "I came to Penhollow wanting to redeem myself for the things I'd done, doubting whether that redemption would ever come. I'm not certain when it happened, but along the way everything I did, everything I risked, became for you. To be the man you deserved, one you could be proud of. Do you understand?"

"Oh, yes. And I am proud of you. So proud."

His hold on her gentled. "I didn't speak of these matters yesterday because I had a good deal of thinking to do. My future isn't clear, not by any means. My fortune is still in shambles and it will take me some time to restore it. But I will; I promise you that. As I sat watching you sleep last night and this morning I began making plans."

His arm around her shoulders, he walked her further into the drawing room. "I'm going to lease my London town house and Grandview, the Wycliffe family seat. Edgecombe will be my home for the next several years."

He became more animated as he spoke, his gaze darting around the room as if seeing Edgecombe not as it was, but as it would someday be. "I'm going make this estate profitable. I thought perhaps I'd approach your uncle about utilizing our lands together and expanding his herds, both the cattle and the sheep. Perhaps do more breeding. And with the profits from that I could invest in some of Penhollow's fishing ventures, and then perhaps . . ."

His enthusiasm became infectious. She swung about to face him and grasped both of his hands. "Your plans sound wonderful, but . . . rather complicated. Are you certain you can accomplish it all on your own?"

She hadn't even tried to mask her meaning, and now her smile faded as she waited, breathless, for his reply.

His expression turned solemn. "No, Sophie, I'm quite certain I can't. That is something I wished to speak to you about. . . ."

Her heart fluttered. "Yes?"

He didn't answer, and she realized his gaze had suddenly wandered beyond her shoulder into the adjoining game room. His eyes widened, and the color drained from his face. One of his hands slipped from hers and rose in an unsteady gesture. "The library door. It wasn't open a moment ago."

She spun around. The library door indeed stood open, and the shadow of a man fell across the threshold. "Lord Wycliffe."

"Father?"

"Yes, Chad, it is." Sophie reached an arm around his waist. "I know now that it was your father I saw that first day I came to Edgecombe, when I believed I saw you looking out from the library window. Your father brought me back to Edgecombe yesterday. He said you needed me."

"He was right." Gaze pinned on the doorway, he put an arm around her shoulders and walked with her through the rooms until they came to the library threshold. "My God."

The interior appeared as it had to Sophie the first

time she ventured to Edgecombe—filled with furniture and books, and illuminated by the light of a deep bay window. Within the recess the wavering figure of a man hovered, his face nearly as familiar as the one beside her, but older, etched with fine lines—Chad in twenty years.

She felt a catch in Chad's chest as his breath hitched. His mouth opened, but no words came out. He stared, eyes burning with emotion.

A sudden smile dissolved the years from Lord Wycliffe's face until he might have been Chad's brother. *You've done well.*

Sophie felt the tremor that passed through Chad. "Thank you, Father."

Be happy now.

Chad's throat convulsed; he gave a nod. "I'll try."

Love her.

"By God, I do." He pressed a fervent kiss to Sophie's hair.

Marry her. Laughter undulated through the words, fanning the air and sending a warm current across Sophie's face. Chad felt it too, for he raised the tips of his fingers to his cheek before grasping her chin with the same hand and turning her to face him.

"That would be entirely up to her," he said. "She has a mind of her own, Father, a strong one, and she has proven to be a woman of singular stubbornness when she wants to be."

"I beg your pardon?" Through feigned indignation, she couldn't help grinning. But her heart stood still, waiting.

Hands closing over her shoulders, he leaned closer, filling her view with his broad shoulders, strong neck and handsome features, and bringing his musky scent to tantalize her senses. "Are you willing to take the biggest risk of all, Sophie? Can you love a rogue? Love him as he loves you—completely and without a single doubt?"

A laugh escaped her as a tear spilled over. "I'm

afraid I've loved that rogue for some time now. Because, you see, to me you've always been a hero."

He kissed her soundly. Then, laughter dancing in his eyes and on his lips, he looked toward the window. "Do you hear that, Father? This angel thinks I'm a hero."

His smile waned. Where Lord Wycliffe had stood in the curve of the bay window, flush and empty casements reflected the sky outside. The furnishings and books had vanished, leaving a vacant room around them.

Without relinquishing his hold on Sophie, Chad took a stride forward, then stopped short. "Father?"

Sophie pressed tight to his side. "It's all right. He knows all will be well now. Like little Ellie Rose he can rest in peace. They both have you to thank for that."

With a growl that startled her, he grabbed her and crushed her to his chest, then froze. His features went taut with pain.

Sophie pulled back. "Your shoulder."

"It's nothing."

"You've made it bleed again."

He glanced down at the trickle of blood on his shirt and winced. "Yes. I'm afraid it might need further attention. A lifetime's worth. What do you say?"

"You're in luck." Her heart brimming, she nipped his lips, once, twice. "It so happens that I've a lifetime to give."

More carefully he put his arms around her. As his kisses ignited a blaze at her core, she knew with the entirety of her being that no matter what the future might hold, he would always love her, would always be there to protect and support her.

A hero could do no less.

If you enjoyed
Dark Temptation,
don't miss

Dark Obsession

A NOVEL OF BLACKHEATH MOOR

by Allison Chase

They wed in haste—Nora Thorngoode to save her ruined reputation, and Grayson Lowell to rescue his estate from foreclosure for unpaid debts. Each resents the necessity to exchange vows that will bind them for all time, and yet from the first, passion flames between them . . . quickly engulfing them in a sensual obsession.

Turn the page for an excerpt from the book, which begins just as Nora and Gray exchange wedding vows. . . .

The voices came at her as if from across a snow-smothered valley. *I will* echoed twice, first in a subdued rumble, his, then higher and softer, hers. Different yet equally uncertain. Unsteady. Both, one might even say, apologetic.

While the blood pounded in her ears in counter-rhythm to the flailing of her heart, her knees wobbled beneath a crashing conviction that she shouldn't be here. Shouldn't be doing this.

But the vows had been spoken. It did not matter whether the words were sincere, or that they had seemed to come from some source beyond herself. Indeed, perhaps they had.

Last night she'd slept fitfully, tossing, turning, slapping her pillows. Eventually she had dozed, dreaming of a fair-haired woman standing by her bed. In her dream Nora had sat up, frightened and trembling, clutching the bedclothes to her chin. *What do you want?* she'd demanded. The woman smiled, and for some inexplicable reason Nora's fears dissolved.

You needn't be afraid. Marry him. He'll never hurt you.

"Who are you?" But the woman had vanished, and Nora had awakened to find herself sitting up in bed, the linens balled in her fists.

Now she had given her consent, made her pledge,

because some nameless woman in a dream—a figment of her own wistful hopes—had said she should.

"I pronounce you man and wife. . . ."

She belonged to him now, for better or worse, for always.

Her veil came away from her face, swept back between Grayson Lowell's long, straight fingers. For an instant Nora marveled at the difference between those hands and her father's, once worn to bleeding on a regular basis in the effort to survive.

Vastly different from her own hands too. Sturdier, stronger. Hers were small and delicate but often paint stained, the nails and cuticles suffering from contact with powders and oils. And yet with her frail female hands she created, sifted life's singular moments through her fingers and set them to canvas. At least, she did so as best she could and with an open heart.

Could Sir Grayson make a similar claim? Had he ever created anything with those fine gentleman's hands?

His face came into focus and filled her vision, became the whole of her world while masculine scents settled over her. Lifting her veil did little to brighten the prospect before her, for the dusty church forbade entrance to all but the slenderest fingers of sunlight. Even close up her new husband seemed drawn from a midnight landscape, his startling blue eyes the only brilliance in his shuttered expression.

His lips were cool and smooth, just moist enough to leave a trace of dew across her own. She resisted the urge to flick her tongue across the spot while the rector concluded the ceremony. Resisted but could not quell the temptation to compare this kiss with the other one they'd shared.

She had bitten him. The memory nearly raised a grin. He'd deserved it, cad that he'd been. Though she must admit it hadn't been so much the kiss but the insults flanking it that had provoked her temper.

But . . . she'd made a shocking discovery that night,

a little secret he must never learn. It lived inside her, a quivery predicament with the power to trip her heart, hitch her breath, send her better sense for a tumble.

The organist struck up the exit march, discordant notes that blared through the building and rattled inside her. With a hand at her elbow, Sir Grayson, her husband, turned her about and nudged her toward the back of the church.

What a sad affair their wedding was. Between her and Sir Grayson they'd mustered all of a handful of guests—the Earl of Wycliffe, the Stockwells, the odd assortment of elderly aunts and uncles, all of whom appeared just the tiniest bit confused.

Mama had insisted on the church, at the same time bluntly refusing to allow any of Nora's artist friends to attend. Somehow she saw Nora's downfall as their fault, even though not one of them had been involved in Alessio's deceit. Mama needed someone to blame, and in Alessio's absence her anger settled on anyone even remotely connected to the art world.

At the open doors of the vestibule, the morning sun hit Nora full in the face. She blinked and wished Sir Grayson would release her elbow. Did he believe her incapable of remaining upright on her own? A new, gleaming black phaeton pulled by a pair of matching bays—a gift from her parents—awaited them on the windy street. They ducked beneath a shower of rose petals and well-wishes and made their way to the vehicle's open door.

"After you, my dear." Again he nudged her elbow as if she were unable or unwilling to proceed on her own.

Feeling cross, she gathered her skirts and climbed inside, then experienced a heated sense of panic when he clambered in after her, filling the empty space with a bulk of shoulders, arms and legs.

The door closed, sealing them in dusky solitude, she and this stranger. He was all muscle and rambling limbs, with no particular regard for her own need for space. His knee tapped hers as the coach rocked forward. His coat sleeve brushed her bare forearm while his shoulder knocked solidly against hers. Even as she attempted to negotiate an inch or two between them, that little secret whispered to her pulse points, murmured its quivering message to the deepest places inside her.

Her fingertips traveled to her lips, pressing ever so gently. . . .

"Thank heavens that's over."

Snapped from her musings, she scowled up at him. "Can you never refrain from insulting me?"

He regarded her blankly. Then his eyebrows gathered. "I did no such thing. You can't mean you enjoyed that?"

Her breath caught. Had he read her mind, somehow guessed . . . But then she realized which "that" he meant. The ceremony, not the kiss. A laugh of relief escaped her as she relaxed against the squabs. "Goodness no. It was torture."

"Deuced right." He paused. "Wait. You're not insulting *me* now, are you?"

Her gaze traced the strong lines of his face and she wished, for the briefest instant, that those vows they'd repeated hadn't rung with such hypocrisy. She merely faced forward again and shrugged.

"I suppose I'd deserve it."

She smoothed the layers of her lace and satin skirts. "Indeed you would."

From the corner of her eye she saw him studying her. She couldn't be certain, but she believed she detected the beginnings of a smile. With a tremor of anticipation she wondered what he was thinking, what he might be planning. As she'd learned at Wycliffe House, Grayson Lowell was nothing if not unpredictable.

When she braved a glance, however, the smile had vanished.

"I wish to apologize for my behavior that night at

Chad's," he said, uncannily following her thoughts again. "I don't usually say or do those kinds of things."

"Oh?" She pulled the lace mitts from her hands and tossed them into her lap. The ring he'd placed on her finger only minutes before glimmered with indifference. "So you save that privilege specifically for me?"

"Not exactly." He released a breath. "I was angry but not at you. None of this is your fault."

"Meaning?"

"I had to marry. If not you, then someone else."

"Someone with a generous dowry."

He nodded.

"I suppose your options were limited."

Another nod, accompanied by a shrug.

She glanced at his profile, itself a fascinating world of jutting angles and rough planes, as inhospitable as any barren landscape. Several days ago she had begun a painting of him from memory. Now she realized she could never hope to capture a spirit as volatile as Grayson Lowell's.

She sighed. She had been his last resort, just as he had been hers. No one else would accept either of them. No wonder he was angry. She was angry too. But did he have to say it? Rub it in? Wouldn't a gentleman at least preserve the illusion of this day, make a gift of it rather than handing her an empty plate of reality and bidding her chew it well?

"Supposing you could have it without me, then? The money, I mean. What would you give in return?"

He shifted to peer down at her, one arm sliding across the squabs above her shoulders so that if she leaned her head back, it would rest in the crook of his elbow. He drew closer, searching her face until she pulled back. And then there she was, caught between his arm and his piercing regard. "Explain."

"I—I'll insist Papa give you full control over my dowry, in exchange for my being able to spend my time as and where I wish." Her breath trembled despite her effort to appear calm. "I had one hope for this marriage. One. And you dashed it that night at your friend's house."

"I have no idea what you're talking about."

"Your Cornwall estate."

"Ah, that again." A hard look entered his eyes, like a wall that could not be scaled. "Blackheath Grange."

"Yes. I'd hoped . . . you see . . . I've been to Cornwall. The light there is extraordinary, the scenery unmatched. I'd give anything . . . But you refused to allow it. Still, surely there must be another of your nephew's estates where I might bring fellow artists in the summer months. . . ."

She stopped, biting down and swallowing a sudden and mortifying urge to cry. How could this man understand how important this was to her?

An artists' retreat. For women only, of course. A place to study and experiment unhindered by society's eye, or by the disapproval of parents and husbands who considered a woman's constitution too delicate, too corruptible for any but the most trifling exploration of the art world. To have such freedom . . . oh, it would constitute a boon of immeasurable worth.

"It isn't possible." The words were decisive, his expression implacable.

"But why not . . . ?"

"Because there aren't any others. Estates, that is." His voice grated; his jaw turned stony. "Surely your father explained. Two have already been sold off. A third is being leased in the hope of saving it from the auction block. Blackheath is all that's left and . . ."

"And you won't allow us to corrupt the mind of a child." Oh, *blast* him for passing judgment. He didn't know her, didn't know her colleagues, yet he was determined to believe the worst. Did that mean she too should fall prey to rumor and condemn him whether innocent or no?

He'll never hurt you. . . .

He grasped her chin. "You must understand. Jonathan is the best of what is left of the Clarington name. He embodies our future—the whole of it. I won't take chances with his welfare. I will not risk him. Not for anyone. Therefore I must be certain—"

Tears pricking the backs of her eyes, she shoved his hand away. "If you believe I could ever harm a child in any way . . . then there is nothing more to discuss."

"Perhaps not," he replied softly. His hand engulfed her shoulder, his fingers clamping with an insistence that startled her. "Perhaps I simply don't like the terms of your bargain, Lady Lowell."

The term jarred her, for she'd not heard it spoken aloud before, nor had she once considered that it belonged to her. As her mind thrashed in confusion, he grasped her other shoulder and held her firmly against the squabs, then leaned in and set his mouth to hers.

The only points of contact between them were his hands on her shoulders and his open lips on hers, yet his touch kindled a fiery presence between her legs. Her thighs burned, turned to heated butter. Her bones dissolved and her breasts strained painfully against her bodice, seeking something unnameable, heretofore unthinkable.

As if he understood their mute cries for attention, his hands slid from her shoulders and covered her breasts, thumbs finding her nipples through all that satin, lace and linen. He rubbed them in rough, urgent circles that had her moaning into his mouth, squirming beneath him, had her pressing for more even as he deepened the kiss and explored the entirety of her mouth with his tongue.

Nothing existed beyond those kisses, beyond the desire that left her scorching, throbbing. And greatly fearing he *had* discovered her secret and planned to use it to his advantage.

For the truth was, she had enjoyed that kiss on Lord Wycliffe's terrace . . . and this one as well. More than enjoyed; she delighted in the sensation of his hands upon her, savored the taste and heat of him in her mouth and all through her.

He lifted his mouth from hers, so tenderly she again felt the inexplicable sting of tears. He propped a hand beside her head. The other cradled her cheek, effectively trapping her within his gaze, within the breadth of his arms.

"What I had been about to say before you so rudely interrupted me is that I must be certain of rendering the right decision. I may have been hasty that night. I shall think more about your request, and I shall take my time thinking about it, so do not ask again. You'll know when I've reached my decision."

He brushed his lips against hers, and the graze of his tongue raised shivers that left her weak and feverish. He pulled back again and his eyes, blazing in the dimness, held her immobile but for her trembling fingertips. "Never put words into my mouth, my dear. Your tongue, your lips, your sighs of pleasure, yes. But never words. I will not stand for it."

For the first time she felt afraid of him, truly afraid, and not because of anything anyone might have said about him. He didn't need rumors to make him fearsome. He need only kiss her and look at her like that.

ALLISON CHASE

DARK OBSESSION
A Novel of Blackheath Moor

They wed in haste—Nora Thorngoode, to save her
ruined reputation, and Grayson Lowell, to rescue his
estate from foreclosure for unpaid debts. Each resents the
necessity to exchange vows that will bind them for all
time, and yet from the first moments, passion flames
between them—quickly engulfing them in a
sensual obsession.

But soon the lover that Nora married becomes a dark
stranger to her, a man torn apart by guilt over his
brother's recent, mysterious death—and driven half-mad
by ghostly specters who demand that Grayson expose the
truth. Has Nora married a murderer whose wicked deeds
blacken everything around them? Or, together, in the
secret passageways of Blackheath Grange and along
Cornwall's remote coastline, can Grayson and Nora
discover what really happened that terrible night—and in
setting free the troubled ghosts, free themselves as well?

"Anyone who loves...a well-written
historical romance will relish this tale."
—*New York Times* bestselling author Heather Graham

Available wherever books are sold or at penguin.com

KIM LENOX

NIGHT FALLS DARKLY

A Novel of the Shadow Guard

Ever since an accident took away her memory, Miss
Elena Whitney can't recall the secrets of her own past.
All she knows is that with her mysterious benefactor
Archer, Lord Black, returning to London at the behest of
Queen Victoria, she should seize the chance to get
some answers.

A member of the immortal Shadow Guard, Archer has
been summoned to London to eliminate the soul of an
evil demon—Jack the Ripper. Archer feels bound to
protect not only the women of the night, but also his
beautiful young ward, Elena, whom he spared from death
two years before. But with a wave of panic spreading
across London, Archer fears that Elena is his weakness—
a distraction he can't afford, especially since she's likely
to become the Ripper's next target...

"Lush, dangerous, and darkly sensuous...
The Immortals have arrived!"
—*New York Times* bestselling author Kerrelyn Sparks

Available wherever books are sold or at
penguin.com